FREE MEN *and* DREAMERS
DARK SKY AT DAWN

OTHER BOOKS AND AUDIO BOOKS
BY THIS AUTHOR:

Unspoken

FREE MEN *and* DREAMERS

DARK SKY AT DAWN

L. C. LEWIS

Covenant Communications, Inc.

Covenant
Communications, Inc.

Cover design copyrighted 2007 by Covenant Communications, Inc.

Published by Covenant Communications, Inc.
American Fork, Utah

Printed in the United States of America
First Printing: February 2007

13 12 11 10 09 08 07   10 9 8 7 6 5 4 3 2 1

ISBN 978-1-59811-258-0

ACKNOWLEDGEMENTS

The greatest thanks for this project must, of course, go to the people who lived and shaped the events depicted in the series. Though not without flaw, they were without precedent for their vision and accomplishments, having established and defended a nation whose Constitution remains the world's benchmark of codified law. Their colleagues and constituents—and the political crucible in which they lived—still awe and inspire, reminding us that heritage is a gift, while citizenship is its accompanying duty and privilege.

On a personal note, my appreciation for my own ancestors, some of whom arrived in Maryland in the seventeenth century, has greatly increased in scope and measure. Their simple, bucolic lives were fashioned by the events surrounding the founding and defense of this nation, just as their children's and grandchildren's lives were similarly affected by the War of 1812, the second war of independence, which was fought on the farms and towns where they lived. Writing this book has made me more mindful of the debt I owe them.

Research can be both exhilarating and frustrating. To those who made it a delight, either by assisting in collecting information or by being a patient listener as I rattled on about my findings, I offer my deepest thanks.

My dear husband Tom offered both forms of support. He arranged trips to historic locations, served as an able navigator in getting us places, and was my patient research companion. He trudged through forts, cities, and museums with me. Most importantly, hardly a day passed that he didn't ask how things were going, knowing that the very question might well set me off on a long tale or complaint. That support was invaluable. Thank you, honey.

My love and thanks also go to my children and their spouses—Tom, Krista, Amanda, Nick, Adam, and Josh—who kept Lewis family life flowing smoothly when Mom was sidetracked and preoccupied. Spending hours at a computer does have some advantages, though. My grandchildren and I became great buddies via webcams this year. Grandma loves you, Tommy and Keira!

Thanks go to Paul and Stephanie Mortenson, dear Idaho friends, who made the trip to study historic Philadelphia a memorable delight. Roland Wilhelm and Marc Smith and their inspiring talks provided me with invaluable tidbits of history that influenced sections of this book. My appreciation also goes to longtime friend Kay Curtiss, an icon in the LDS booksellers' world, for reviewing the book and advising me on the marketplace.

I express special thanks to Edward Lawler Jr., the Independence Hall Association Historian, for answering innumerable questions and for guiding my Philadelphia research over the course of the past two years. Despite his involvement in the "President's House Project" in colonial Philadelphia, he generously took the time to edit this book, and he added additional insights at the eleventh hour to assure its historical accuracy. After all the emails we have exchanged, I now consider him not only a resource but also a friend.

Heartfelt appreciation also goes to Scott Sheads, a curator and historian specializing in the War of 1812 and Baltimore history, who is himself an accomplished author. I primarily intended to tap his knowledge for book two, but during last-minute edits on *Dark Sky At Dawn,* he made time to answer many questions and to check my Baltimore research for accuracy. I appreciate his help immensely and hope our association will continue as the battle scenes unfold.

Lastly, my sincere appreciation goes to Angela Eschler, my editor, and to the entire Covenant family, for investing in this project. They made it a far better novel than it would have been without their assistance. Equally important to me has been the way they have lent their support to me and my family over the duration of our association.

I also thank you, reader, for sharing this glimpse of history with me.

To Tom,
my partner in making Lewis family history

PROLOGUE

Calvert County, Maryland
Along the Patuxent River
November 1781

A dank fog hovered over the shores of Maryland's Patuxent River as Jonathan Edward Pearson stepped from the wagon, awaiting the approach of the two men who would help him see to the painful task ahead. He stepped upon the shipping dock, the grand prize of his entrepreneurial cunning, and shivered as he imagined the frigid bite of the icy water. He wondered how long it had been before her muscles had cramped, before her once-warm soul had become a frozen weight, drawn deep until her last watery gasp denied her a reprieve. He shook his head to remove her pale, blue image from his mind and peered back through the grayness at his home, one of the finest in the infant nation. None of it meant anything to him now.

He had fought in the Seven Years' War and the Great Revolution, seen patriots die while traitors prospered, burrowing invisibly into the craw of the new nation only to raise their foul heads some other day. None of that seemed as unjust or as agonizing to him as the news that awaited him upon his return from Yorktown the previous day. Charles Kittamaqund, oldest son of his good friend Chief Four Eagles, had come to his home and delivered the news.

"Nagadaan ikwe!" Charles Kittamaqund had stated earnestly as he pulled Jonathan all the way from the house to the dock. "Nagadaan ikwe!"

Jonathan took a moment to translate the Algonquian words. "Leaving woman?"

Charles had nodded vigorously, thumping Jonathan on the chest. "You leaving woman."

It took several seconds for Jonathan to register Charles's meaning. "My leaving woman?"

Again, Charles's head bobbed vigorously. "I find. I bring."

She'd been wrapped in a Piscataway blanket and laid in the tall grass by the thicket. Jonathan froze in his tracks, unable to believe the sight that set his body quivering. He knelt beside the body of the debutante whom he'd blamed for stealing his heart and tossing it back when he was still an indentured schoolteacher. Her once-lovely face was river swollen and as pale as parchment. She wore a blue dress, the same shade as the one she had worn that far-off day when she'd irreparably broken his heart. "She's cursing me," he remembered muttering under his breath as he'd scooped her small, stiffened form into his arms.

The rustle of grass brought Jonathan back to the present. He turned and saw his black-haired friend emerge, dressed in buckskin. "Thank you, Charles," Jonathan sighed with a weak smile. "Is the reverend coming?"

Charles shook his head somberly. "I no see."

Jonathan hung his head. "I didn't really expect he would," he admitted soberly.

The Indian and the British-born American unloaded a small walnut coffin with the initials *SBM* and the date, *1781 A.D.,* inscribed into its lid. "Let's dig here, near the dock where she left her note," Jonathan instructed. Before they laid the coffin in the hole, Jonathan opened the lid and stared down at the still face. "I've dressed you in blue. It is how I remembered you in anger. Now it is how I will remember you in grief." He lifted a locket from his vest pocket and gingerly touched the engraving, *SABM.* The *M,* added later, was slightly different from the other letters, and one sad laugh escaped Jonathan. "You made your point with style, dearest," he said, slipping the locket back into his pocket. Then he closed and buried the coffin.

"You know our story, Charles. What would your shaman say if we were Piscataway?"

"Strong lodges make strong tribes. To weaken a lodge is an attack on a nation."

"And what would the shaman do to someone who was a threat to your tribe?"

"Send bad magic."

Jonathan grew quiet. "I've caused bad magic to fall upon our lodges, magic I cannot undo. Will you watch over them when I'm gone and help bring peace to our lodges again?"

Charles's people were moving north, to the Delaware, and to honor this promise he would need to remain behind alone. The Indian looked back at the anguished face of his father's friend, a man who had brought peace between the white men and the Piscataway. He was now needed to bring peace to two lodges. *A full circle* . . . He lifted his face to his friend's and nodded.

CHAPTER 1

Coolfont Estate, Baltimore County, Maryland
Late June 1804

Hannah was missing! Selma wrung her hands with worry about her master's ten-year-old raven-haired daughter. Before Hannah, caring for the sullen Stansbury daughters had been a miserable chore whose only reward was that it spared the slave woman from the grueling labor of fieldwork. But the smiling, green-eyed baby's unplanned birth had brought Selma great joy.

She glanced nervously out the window at the master and missus of Coolfont Manor, Bernard and Susannah Stansbury. Dressed in their finery, they stood outside their opulent Baltimore country home, greeting the stream of buggies and carriages ferrying guests to their annual barbeque. Such homes were more lifestyles than abodes, replete with social conventions as rigid as the lines of the brick manor house. To Selma it seemed tragic that a creative, visionary child like Hannah was born, unwanted, into this particular world where her non-conformity was as welcome as a weed in the manor's immaculate lawn.

Hannah questioned everything. She was forever running out to the slaves' quarters or following one of them around to see how her clothes were made or to lend a willing hand in the garden or kitchen. Day after day, Hannah's mother placed another item on the list of things Hannah was forbidden to do, or worse yet, for which she would receive another punishment. It was so today. She had engaged in the behavior that seemed to draw the greatest rancor from her mother. Hannah had heard the singing from the worship services held in the slaves' quarters, and her spiritual curiosity had lured her outside to enjoy the music for a few moments. As Hannah returned to the house and made her way back inside, her mother heard her singing one of the Negro spirituals. She dragged Hannah upstairs, shaking her at every step while forbidding her to associate with the slaves or participate in their "ungodly" music.

Each protest brought a slap until the crying child melted at her mother's feet in utter submission. When Susannah Stansbury's small frame finally exited the room, her green eyes still flared and her graying auburn hair was mussed from the encounter with her child. While Selma scooped Hannah into her padded arms to calm and bathe her, Susannah and her two elder daughters dressed in their gowns, ready to take their places with their guests.

Myrna, a dowdy twenty-year-old with light brown hair, scowled so frequently that her face seemed permanently pinched. Beatrice, two years older, was a mousy brunette with sad, gentle eyes. As Selma watched them living out their dreams, all she could think was that theirs were probably the only dreams coming true on the country estate. And she knew it didn't matter if you were white or black. Miss Hannah was proof of that.

It was likely a hunger to live out her own dreams that had sent the ten-year-old off on a second escapade that day, and Selma shook with fear at what would befall her if the missus found Hannah before Selma did. Before she could clearly see the face, she knew the bouncing figure coming up from the creek was Hannah. However, there was something strange about the child's appearance that made certain identification difficult. As Selma strained to understand the dark shadows that obscured the child's features, another form, a boy considerably taller and more mature than Hannah, jumped from the most-recently arrived carriage and ran in her direction, drawing the adults' attention.

Selma recognized the expensive European carriage; it belonged to Jonathan Edward Pearson II, one of the well-connected but infamous Pearson clan. The beaming young man running in Hannah's direction was his only son, Jed. He was brilliant, charming, and handsome, possessing a wide-eyed face with full lips and high cheekbones. Selma knew the affinity the young man held for her master's precocious girl.

It had begun at the barbeque of 1794, the summer she was born. Only four then, the boy was confined to a chair while recovering from a broken leg, and he spent the entire day inside with Selma, holding the wriggling infant. At that moment an attachment began that had continued ever since. Though they saw one another only a few times a year, the handsome, brown-haired lad had become as dear to Hannah as a brother. Nonetheless, Selma now cringed, knowing that Jed's attention to the child would also draw her mother's interest at a time when Hannah's appearance clearly testified of where and with whom she had been.

Clutching a bouquet of wildflowers in her hands as she ran to greet Jed, she was a study in disarray. Her previously curled hair was now braided, and two dark streaks of red and blue were smeared diagonally across her face. Selma tore from the kitchen with the hopeless notion of snatching the child before her mother noticed the Indian markings. But the younger, faster Jed had reached Hannah first and was regarding her appearance with appreciative wonder that obviously delighted the girl.

"Hannah!" He touched her chubby, painted cheeks. "Are you an Indian princess today?"

"Jed!" she squealed in delight. "You're only fourteen, yet you're as tall as Papa!" Her green eyes sparkled with pleasure. "Had I known you were here I would have greeted your rig."

He pouted and rapidly blinked his brown eyes to stave off pretend tears. "Are you saying that you didn't dress up as an Indian princess for me? Was this for someone else?"

"Indian princesses do not wear blue frocks, Jed, but Charles Kittamaqund painted my face. He gave me a real Algonquian name, too. *Kizis Ikwe.* It means Sun Woman."

Her last word ended in a gasp as an angry hand clenched painfully around her arm, twisting her small frame to face the fury of her mother's countenance. Hannah's smile vanished, replaced by a plea for mercy as Susannah Stansbury's voice hurled accusations.

"Why 'Sun Woman'? Because you are an idol-worshiping and ungodly child?" she spat.

Hannah's eyes shot from her mother to Jed and back again. "N . . . n . . . no," she stammered.

"Of course it is! What else could he mean by such a name?"

Hannah cowered and stood silently.

"Answer me!" Susannah Stansbury demanded as she shook her daughter. "Answer me!"

"H . . . H . . . He said it was because the Great Spirit watches over me. He said He shines down on me," she muttered as each word faded into further silence.

Susannah shook the child until the flowers fell from her hands onto the ground. "Indeed, trollop! Do you purposely go seeking the company of sinners? This morning it was the slaves, then it is a savage . . . and now . . ." She shot a disapproving glance at Jed Pearson, and his inclusion was not lost on him. "Have I not forbidden you to see that filthy red man ever again?"

Hannah was crying now. She glanced down and saw her mother's feet treading upon her floral offering. "I went to pick you a bouquet . . . to apologize for this morning," she cried.

Jed could bear it no longer. The privileged boy stepped in and placed his hands upon Hannah's shuddering shoulders. By intruding between the mother and her child, the lad knew he was risking more of the irreverent talk that was frequently spread about his family. Nonetheless, he could not stand by idly without at least attempting to abate the woman's rage.

"Mrs. Stansbury, did you not purposely arrange this frivolity for your guests? My parents commented that your Hannah reminds them very much of our dear Frannie. I imagine once news travels of Hannah's unique greeting, you will be the toast of hostesses this summer."

Susannah Stansbury was quite sure she was being artfully mollified by the Pearsons' pup, but with the entire company of guests now focused intently on the scene, she temporarily bridled her anger. Without relaxing her grip on Hannah, she forced a strained smile and knelt before her daughter. In a voice intended to chill Hannah's very soul, she whispered to the frightened girl, "This is the last time you will ever embarrass me. Do you understand, child?"

Hannah stood wide-eyed and as still as death. Then, feeling her mother's grip tighten again, she finally nodded a fearful acknowledgment.

Susannah raised her voice for her company's benefit. "Hurry and clean up, Hannah dear. Then come and join us so I can introduce our little Indian princess to the rest of our guests." She shot a warning glance in Selma's direction before spinning on her heels and departing.

Selma rushed over to the child, who slumped into the woman's arms for the second time that day. She lifted Hannah and carried her toward the house with Jed following close behind. Before they reached the door, Selma turned, cast him a look of warning, and shooed him away.

"I know you're fond of this little one, but you'd best join your family for now, Master Pearson," she said as she stared at the mistress's back. Then, wrapping her arms more tightly around the child, she nodded at Jed and left with the terrified ten-year-old.

It took only a few minutes to clean and dress Hannah, but it took nearly an hour to coax her back out of the house. For the remainder of the afternoon she sat as still as a porcelain doll. Jed watched protectively from afar as he joined the other young men in games of sport until later in the afternoon, when the men headed off to an adjacent pasture to joust, a medieval sport enjoying great popularity among Maryland's gentry. As the crowd hurried to the arena, Jed offered his arm to Hannah to escort her. She remained stoic as they walked, despite his best efforts to engage her in conversation.

"What's the matter, Hannah? All is well enough now. No need to worry, pet."

Hannah's eyes brimmed with tears. "As soon as everyone leaves, Mother will beat me."

"What do you mean she will beat you?" he asked as he spun her around to face him.

Hannah knew she had confessed something, the telling of which could only serve to get her in more trouble, so she raced away to stand warily by her father.

Susannah's accusatory eyes followed the child, regarding it as an additional act of betrayal when Bernard Stansbury absently laid a gentle hand on his daughter's head. The child was his shadow the remainder of the day, nearly tripping him with her constant nearness, a fact that further agitated Susannah. However, she carefully concealed her fury, wary that as conscious as she was of Hannah's movements, her own were being scrutinized by the heir to the Winding Willows estate, young Jed Pearson.

Jed Pearson was no ordinary lad. His notorious grandfather virtually snubbed his privileged family, naming his infant grandson the heir to the bulk of his powerful estate mere hours before he died. Interestingly enough, his grandfather's choice proved to be a shrewd one. Time bore evidence that Jonathan Edward Pearson III, called Jed, had inherited the best of his ancestor's business acumen along with his wealth. He had an instinctive understanding of the scope of his good fortune as well as an understanding of the responsibility it carried. From childhood, while other boys his age were reading *The Juvenile Magazine* or stories about Indians, Jed read farm journals, until, by age fourteen, he was influencing decisions regarding the Willows, the largest estate in the area. Thus, self-interest prompted Maryland's prudent elite to crack their snobbish doors to the notorious Pearson clan as they counted the days to the boy's coming of age and the moment when his wealth could affect their own fate.

In this one area Susannah Stansbury initially chose to disagree with her gentry neighbors. She had personal reasons for her reluctance to capitulate to the Pearsons. Though her reasons were not founded in solid facts, they were supported by powerful, negative impressions of the occasions when the elder Pearson had driven his fine carriage past her childhood home and into town. Still, lacking actual proof for her stand made her appear imprudent in the eyes of polite society, and she'd gradually yielded, considering it shrewder to know the family of her foe and to keep her opinions guarded.

But Susannah noticed something more in the boy this day—the same cocky arrogance his grandfather had possessed. She saw the way the lad hovered between her and her daughter, while alternately flashing a mixture of scorn and fury whenever his eyes met hers. She wanted to walk up to the boy and slap his face, but all she could do was charge Jed's cockiness against Hannah. It was yet one more act of defiance and betrayal that she would address with her insolent child later. So the young irritant, the grandson of her enemy, became her foe this day as well.

Jed had sensed the shift in his own social import as well. He was already more man than boy. His stature and carriage befitted a young man years beyond his age, and, as if in preparation for what would come, he had also been given a will of steel, tempered by an innate sense of right and wrong. Therein began his personal quest to understand the particular rancor the gentry aimed at the Pearson clan. Even as a small child he had understood the prattle that circulated whenever the fine people gathered, making sport of smiling to someone's face before discreetly eviscerating him behind his back. Jed heard his own parents engage in the snobbish sport, but sensed something more derisive about the way Maryland's upper class tittered about his own family in their private circles. It was particularly so with the dame of Coolfont, whose animosity seemed acridly and personally aimed at him. Though he didn't understand the reason for it, he was well aware of the measure of it, and that it was cast as disparagingly at Susannah's own daughter as it was at himself.

This social haggling for position angered Jed, giving him one more reason to adore his younger sister, Frannie, a free spirit with little tolerance for the affectations of the gentry. But his parents were a different story. He was infuriated over their posturing for the favor of the elite, seeing little disparity between their blind deference to achieve social standing and Hannah's pitiable overtures to win some measure of parental love. He also saw similarities between himself and the Stansbury's dark-eyed child. Hannah bore the weight of the world upon her shoulders because no one of significance in her life regarded her as valuable. Jed bore it because the family honor and name rested so heavily there. Understanding early on that he would eventually have the power to rise above the social fray, he had vowed to wield it—to carry his sister and Hannah beyond it as well. Hannah's revelation today, however, had opened Jed's eyes to the immediacy of her plight. He pledged that moment to be her self-appointed advocate and to protect her from her mother.

As the Pearsons prepared to leave for the inn where they would spend the night, Jed and Frannie followed along behind their parents, adding their own parting words to the Stansburys'. Jed bowed politely to Myrna and Beatrice and then stopped directly in front of Mrs. Stansbury.

"It was a lovely day," he began as his eyes bored into hers. "Thank you for inviting us."

Susannah Stansbury's only acknowledgment of the boy was a wary nod of her head.

"Francis and I would very much like to write to Hannah." He strongly emphasized the point to Mrs. Stansbury before shifting to a friendlier tone when addressing her husband. "That is, of course, if you approve, sir, though we would be heartbroken if you were to deny us this."

Bernard Stansbury bent close to Hannah and whispered excitedly, "You'd like that, wouldn't you, Hannah? It would be good practice for your penmanship, too, now wouldn't it?"

Hannah stared wide-eyed and cautious, but the delicious offer was too enticing to be squelched by hesitation. "Oh, yes. And I'll write fine letters too!"

"I'm sure you will," beamed Jed as he shook her hand and entered the carriage. He watched her mother's glare until the carriage slipped beyond a bend in the lane and out of sight.

"I can't believe her mother beats her," cried Frannie as soon as they had turned from view. "How can your letters help her?"

"At the very least she'll know she has a friend. In time, I intend to find a way to do more."

* * *

Guests or no guests, Susannah was unwilling to allow Hannah's crimes to go unpunished. She ordered Bernard to see to the task. His stomach tightened as he recalled the all too frequent occasions when he had heard his daughter's pleas for mercy and the crying that followed their denial, but never before had he been assigned the heinous task. Holding the strap in his hands forced him to face his silent complicity in the child's mistreatment, and he was ashamed.

Still, while it was true that Hannah had been born long after Susannah had lost her nurturing qualities, Beatrice and Myrna had somehow adapted to their mother's dwindling affections, choosing to be obedient to Susannah's rules, though they seemed as tedious as the Mosaic Law. Submissively, they had accepted as gospel every word that proceeded from their mother's lips. Hannah, on the other hand, though not an unruly child, had her own ideas about things. Her curious mind could not accept a notion without having first tested it for herself. Then, if her pondering proved the idea to be unacceptable, only coercion could force her to comply.

Though religion and salvation were of little consequence to Bernard, they had become the ultimate battleground between mother and daughter. Susannah was the daughter of an Episcopalian minister, and she had tried to instill the same fear of God's wrath in Hannah that had kept Myrna and Beatrice at their evening bedsides pleading for mercy. Hannah would have none of it. She prayed happy little prayers about heaven and Jesus' love, gleaned from Selma's songs, assuring Susannah that the child was not only demon-possessed, but bound for hell as well.

As Bernard climbed the stairs, he remembered the sweet, protective feelings that were stirred within him when Hannah tucked herself beside him during the joust. Ironically, his tall frame now sagged under his guilt-ridden burden as he searched for a way to satisfy his wife's demand for discipline and his daughter's right to mercy. He opened the door to Hannah's room and was surprised at the sight. The child already lay across her bed, apparently awaiting the fall of her mother's strap. Expecting her mother's rebuke, she appeared startled when she instead heard the shuddering of her father's breath as he struggled for control. When she felt the weight of his body slump beside her, although surprised to see him sitting there, she did not move. She realized that he had been sent in her mother's stead.

Bernard reached his arm under her and hoisted her onto his lap. He wrapped his arms tightly around her, and she clung to him.

"I love you, Hannah," he began, as if offering an apology.

"I know, Papa," she whispered with a sniffle. Her father's love was a strange and vacillating thing, warm and expressive when they were alone, but cool and distant when her mother was hovering nearby. Still, aside from Selma's, it was the surest love she knew. "Mama sent you, didn't she?"

A shallow gasp escaped him. "Yes, dearest. I heard you were bad today."

She looked into his eyes with truth shining from hers. "Mama says the things I do are bad, but my heart doesn't think they are. I guess my heart and Mama's heart are different."

Bernard knew they were the truest words ever spoken. "I think you are right, angel."

"Mama said that Charles Kittamaqund is a filthy savage. Isn't he your friend, Papa?"

Bernard searched for an answer that would satisfy his astute daughter. "Charles isn't Christian, Hannah. Mother doesn't want you associating with people who don't love Jesus."

He rocked her for a few minutes more until Hannah's head shot up again. "But he uses the Christian name the minister gave him. And this morning, Mama called the slaves' music ungodly even though they have all been baptized and they sing about Jesus more than anyone I know."

Bernard realized reason would not satisfy this child. "Hannah, religion is about more than simply how or whom we worship. It also defines the society with whom we associate. I have no doubt that Selma and the other slaves sing tunes about Jesus, but if you continue to associate with the slaves you will forfeit the society of our good Christian neighbors. Do you understand?"

Hannah's face indicated that she clearly did not. "But Jesus said . . ."

"Hannah!" Bernard's voice was sharp, quickly silencing the child. "I know perfectly well what Jesus said." He closed his eyes and regained his composure. "We do not live in the days of the Apostles. The sooner you learn that, the better it will be for everyone. Did you know that your mother ordered James whipped for taking you into the barn to show you how he makes your shoes? Now you don't want to cause James or any of the other slaves to be beaten, do you?"

The horror of the news made tears well in Hannah's eyes, and she shook her head numbly.

"And if you see Charles again, she will insist that he be driven away. Do you want that?"

In panic, Hannah grabbed her father's jacket lapels. "He is a guardian, Papa. The last of his tribe left here. He made promises. Please don't let Mama make him leave."

"It's up to you, Hannah. Can you promise to stay away from Charles and the slaves?"

Her voice broke as a new fear filled her. "Can I still spend time with Selma?"

Bernard sensed the terror that losing Selma raised in Hannah. "Of course, dearest," he said as he pulled her close. "Selma is different. She's your nanny. You can always have Selma."

His face contorted with sorrow. Someday she would discover the even greater social complexities of their genteel world, but she would never understand them. *He* barely understood them. In many ways life had been simpler before wealth came to them. In those days his titled ancestry and impeccable upbringing were enough to keep them on the fringe of polite society, one step up from the rustics, where custom allowed free association amongst neighbors in either class. Wealth brought more than the privileges of the fine home and household accoutrements. Families lifted by both wealth and heritage carried the burdens of entitlement. Not only were they expected to accept the social affectations of their stations, but they were also duty bound to define them. This was the duty Susannah relished and for which she had planned.

Hannah's head fell back against her father's chest again. Bernard checked the clock on the nightstand. He knew Susannah would be nearby . . . listening . . . and again his assignment presented itself. Hannah felt him stiffen, and she raised her head and looked into his lean, lined face. His dark eyes were moist, and his moustache trembled over his tightly pursed lips. She reached a hand up to touch his thick, black eyebrows and noticed something for the first time.

"We look the same, Papa . . . green eyes, dark hair. We have the same eyebrows, too."

"Yes, dearest. You are the spitting image of Papa."

"Who do Myrna and Beatrice look like? They don't look like you or Mama."

"They look like Mama once did, when she was young."

"I can't remember when Mama was young."

"Mama was very different then. You would have liked the way she was."

"Did she smile when she was young, Papa? I can hardly remember Mama's smile."

"Sometimes, dearest . . ."

He still remembered fondly the day he'd met Susannah. It was 1772, the year his father's greed and poor investments had left him humiliated and penniless, forever altering Bernard's privileged destiny.

An uncle had arranged for Bernard to be indentured to a furniture maker in the city, and at age seventeen, he departed his home in Calvert County for a new life in Baltimore. An Episcopalian minister, the Reverend McClintock, noticed him hunched in the back pew of his church. The reverend and his wife, Sarah, were kind enough to invite the young man to supper, and among their four children was one daughter, a blue-eyed waif named Susannah.

Hannah's voice pulled Bernard from his reverie. "Tell me about Mama, Papa."

"She was always a quiet girl, but yes, she smiled and laughed when she was happy."

"What happened to her smile, Papa?"

Bernard was thoughtful as he considered how to answer the child's question. "I was apprenticed for ten years before Mama and I could marry. During those years Mama's mother became very, very sick, and one day she . . . she died. That's when Mama lost her smile."

Hannah's face became more sober. "Is Mama sick, Papa . . . like her mother was?"

Bernard hugged Hannah protectively. "No, Hannah!" he whispered nervously. "She has . . . headaches, but Mama is not sick like her mother. She is not going to leave us."

Hannah stared up at her father, trying to reconcile the difference between his reassuring words and the worry in his face and voice. "What will we do if Mama does get sick like her mother?"

Bernard closed his eyes and sighed deeply. "Did you know that if it weren't for Mama, we would still be living in a tiny apartment above my little furniture shop in Baltimore? Mama was the one who encouraged Papa to hire and teach other people how to build furniture from my plans. Now Papa's furniture is in all the finest houses in the state. Even the governor and his wife have some of my pieces." He sighed again and rocked his daughter numbly. "Yes, we owe everything we have to Mama. No matter what happens . . . we will take care of her."

"Papa, I would live in a tiny apartment if only I could see Mama's smile."

Bernard held her tight as a sound from the other side of the door made them both jump.

"Bernard?" The stern voice was Susannah's.

"I'm here, Susannah." Defeat tinged his voice.

"Then attend to the task," she insisted. "You're neglecting your guests."

His teary eyes looked into those of the child. There was no sound of retreating feet beyond the door, and father and child knew the moment had come.

"I'm sorry, Hannah." He hung his head and shook it as the child, sensing no reprieve, climbed from his lap and back onto the bed. He took her shoulders and looked deeply into her eyes. "Someday, Hannah, I promise you, you will have the life you want. You will be free to choose who will be your neighbors and to worship the God you know. But for now, remember what I have said."

She nodded and wrapped her arms around his neck before turning and lying across the bed. Before he raised the strap, Bernard uttered a prayer for forgiveness to the loving God in whom his daughter believed, and then he let the strap fall.

CHAPTER 2

London, England
January 1805

Juan Arroyo Corvas walked nervously along the dark, lamp-lit streets of the snow-laden city. The frigid air added to his suffering over the assignment. How he hated England, longing instead for his beautiful Cadiz, Spain, for the blue sea view from his home by the sparkling Atlantic, and for the warm Mediterranean. He missed being with his friends, enjoying the music and smells of the lavish carnival his countrymen were celebrating before the beginning of Lent.

Lent . . . The word ran through his young, tortured mind . . . *A time to rededicate oneself to the Christ.* He closed his eyes and bowed his head in grief. He looked at his olive-colored hands. They looked the same to him, but he knew they were filthy. Oh, how he hated this dirty business.

He thought of his angelic, deceased mother and made the sign of the cross. Then his thoughts turned to his father, a hardened ship captain who had left his son a beautiful home, an old ship, and a hideous debt. His father had agreed to a gruesome arrangement to procure his ship and a real home for Juan's mother. In effect, he had sold his soul to his creditor, becoming a slave of sorts, doing the onerous bidding of an anonymous devil, and upon his death, settlement fell to his son. Juan offered to forfeit the ship that had been tainted by his father's evil errands, but he begged the creditor's messenger to allow him to keep his home, the place of his mother's sanctuary, and pay the rest of the debt over time, but the man with the ram's head umbrella had become infuriated at Juan's attempt to negotiate with the creditor. Juan quickly relented, agreeing to forfeit all, including the house, but his capitulation had come too late. "Favors for favors" were the terms, and death for default. Thus Juan found himself involved in deeds so heinous that he could not drag himself to confession until he could finally be free from his sin.

Why had the messenger demanded that the meeting take place in St. Paul's Cathedral? Juan didn't want to enter God's house while entrenched in sin. He was a believer. *A sinner, yes, but still a believer.*

As he walked up Ludgate Hill, he saw the dome of St. Paul's and the twin towers that guarded the two-story stone façade. Juan's eyes rose upward, following the façade's columns to the pediment where, within the triangular frame, the scene of St. Paul's conversion was sculpted. He shivered, feeling unworthy even to behold the image of the Apostle.

He reached the Great West Door, removed his cap, and straightened his errant black hair, then brushed the snow from his coat and rubbed the top of each boot against the back of his pant legs. Drawing a deep breath, he cracked the door. The haunting sound of a baroque chant washed over him, adding to his melancholy. His slim frame slipped through the narrow opening, and he bowed his head low as he entered the nave. Each footstep echoed upon the black-and-white checkerboard floor, seemingly announcing the arrival of the wicked Juan Arroyo Corvas.

As a child he had found peace and comfort in the Cathedral of Cadiz. After his mother died, he had returned often, knowing it to have been her place of refuge. The smells of St. Paul's old wood were comforting, the ornate woodwork and stonework familiar. He felt drawn to the High Altar, far away at the eastern end of the quire, but he knew his business lay elsewhere. He pulled a slip of paper from his pocket and read, *The Morning Chapel, left of nave entrance.*

Crumpling the paper, Juan turned left into the chapel, where rich wood walls met stone panels, forming elaborately carved Roman-style stone arches. A well-dressed man, fair haired and in his late thirties, sat nervously on a bench near the west wall. He disregarded Juan, though his eyes continuously scanned the doorway. Juan knew that look. He had seen it before on the faces of the creditor's other victims as they awaited the arrival of the expected messenger foretold in his menacing blackmail letters.

The young Spaniard sat gingerly on the same bench and offered the oft-rehearsed phrase in memorized English: "A man with a keen eye will find that the cathedrals of Great Britain rival those of Spain and Portugal."

The man glared at him. "What did you say?" he asked in an agitated British accent.

Juan repeated the rehearsed phrase slowly, "A man with a keen eye will find that the cathedrals of Great Britain rival those of Spain and Portugal."

The man continued to glare at Juan, but Juan persisted, fearful of angering his creditor. "A man with . . ."

The British man pinned him against the wall. "You?" he snapped furiously. "You are the one who summoned me? Do you take me for a fool?"

"Por favor, señor!" Juan cried out. "No hablo Inglés. La respuesta . . . por favor."

The man swore and spat out the expected response. "The best things testify of God."

Juan nodded, pulled a letter from his jacket, and watched as the man broke the seal and silently read the words Juan knew so well. Satisfied that he had fulfilled this assignment, Juan again made the sign of the cross before turning to leave the creditor's latest prey in solitude.

After a ten-minute wait, the Brit followed the instructions in the letter. He turned left and headed east to the Great Circle under the magnificent dome where the axis of the nave and quire met the axis of the transepts. He nervously made his way on to the west end of the north transept to the large marble font. On a bench nearby sat a dark-haired fellow with gray showing at the temples. He was polishing the ram's head figure that formed the handle of his umbrella.

The British man recognized him and was emboldened as he approached, shaking the letter. "Ramsey? *You* work for these people?"

"Some are blessed by birth, Mitchell. Some get lucky. The rest must make our own luck."

"Why all this intrigue?" Mitchell grumbled. "Why didn't you simply call for me? You know perfectly well where I live."

Ramsey stared Mitchell down, delaying his response. "My employer saw no reason to disclose the nature of my employ unless you showed interest in the offer. It is only because of our childhood friendship that I petitioned to detail the creditor's plan myself."

Mitchell grunted. "I am *not* interested. Tell your people my vote cannot be bought!"

Ramsey smiled smugly at Mitchell. "It's a curious thing . . . to whom you Mitchells bestow your favors. You financed a traitor yet refuse to use your influence to benefit our poor."

"What are you talking about?" Mitchell barked.

"Your maid . . . isn't she the third generation of Pearsons you Mitchells have employed?"

Mitchell strained to remember. "What is your point?"

"Your grandfather paid for Jonathan Pearson's education as a favor to his mother. Imagine, out of all the hungry dock rats of Liverpool, my own pitiful father included, your family bestowed the prize upon a traitor."

Mitchell shifted uneasily. "Is this the great revelation your people are threatening to use to discredit me? Even if it were true, which I doubt, who would care after all these years?"

"Lord Ensor would, for one. He hired Pearson to tutor his children and arranged later for his passage to America by indenturing him to his cousins in the colonies. Ironically, the earl's own grandson was killed in the Revolution in a battle where Pearson was commanding troops."

Mitchell's jaw tightened as he moaned, "He betrayed the very people who helped him?"

"Yes . . ." Ramsey murmured. "Imagine what my father or one of his mates could have done with such opportunities. Instead, this traitor's posterity lives like American royalty while loyal Brits wring their hands worrying how they'll feed their babies when the slave ships no longer launch from Liverpool. It's the gravest injustice, but . . . my employers have a plan that will help your constituents and provide you an opportunity for redemption . . . and remuneration."

Mitchell's jaw tightened and Ramsey knew the Parliamentarian was taking the bait.

"Lord Liverpool's clan has controlled the local seat in the House of Lords for generations, amassing power and influence," Ramsey taunted, adding snidely, "You Mitchells have served in the House of Commons for over fifty years, yet your service has afforded you little financial reward."

Mitchell studied his boyhood friend's face. "It has always been reward enough to enjoy the trust of the people we have represented," he argued weakly.

Ramsey had carefully planned his response. "Of course, but lately, high taxes and talk of antislavery legislation have bitten deeply into the revenues of your constituents. They are heavily invested in the slave markets with ships, supplies, and manpower. Now, rumors are circulating that the wealthy British plantation owners in the Caribbean will be sweetly reimbursed for their losses when slavery is abolished, and Liverpool's poor citizens are even angrier. Whether or not you agree with the practice of slavery, you must understand the dilemma of those you represent."

Deftly working on Mitchell's vulnerabilities, Ramsey recognized a vacuum of equity on this issue, and he would capitalize on it. "They are looking to you for help in their hour of need."

Mitchell knew what Ramsey was saying was true. The European governments had encouraged the establishment of sugar-cane plantations in the islands, whose profits were enhanced by the use of slave labor. When calls for abolition made slavery unpalatable, the British Parliament offered compensation to the plantation owners to ease their burdens, but no such plan had been offered for the others whose livelihoods were equally affected. Mitchell's constituents had been beleaguering him for relief, but he had been powerless to help them. Where handshakes and waves had once heralded him, angry fingers now pointed at him.

He tried to remain nonchalant. "And what is this plan?"

"Vote to stall all legislation that hinders slavery while the Consortium uses these final months to heavily work the American markets. Should anyone in Parliament question your shift on this matter, simply explain that you are advocating for your constituents. You can calm your voters' fears by assuring them that there are anonymous sympathizers in the area ready to compensate them when this legislation eventually passes, as it surely will. The Consortium will provide you with a generous fund from the profits earned during this period. Keep some for your troubles and distribute the rest, making sure that its path is untraceable. This additional financial security should make it easier for your people to diversify their cargo from slaves to mercantile goods in the future, and you will be restored as the hero of Liverpool."

Mitchell felt his heart race as he struggled to rationalize the plan. "My reward is not my primary concern, of course. I am worried about my constituents. Now tell me how all this will clear my family of this Pearson mess."

"It is no secret that losing the colonies has greatly unnerved King George. He will try to reclaim America. A strong economy will help fund the war, and when it's won, traitorous families like Pearson's, who supported the rebellion, will find themselves penniless—or worse—and you will have played a part in that."

Mitchell bit his lip, then nodded his agreement to the plan. "How do I reach you?"

"You do not!" Ramsey instructed sternly. "If my employer needs to reach you, he will send the courier again."

CHAPTER 3

The Willows Plantation, Calvert County, Maryland
August 1806

"Jed! Jed! Wait for me!" fourteen-year-old Frannie wailed as she bolted across the field in his direction, her auburn hair flying wildly behind her. "Why didn't you tell me? How cruel a thing for me to discover today that you are leaving for school next week."

Jed couldn't face her. "I was trying to avoid this very scene. Besides, it wasn't my choice to be shuttled off to the University of Pennsylvania! I begged Father to enroll me in Georgetown's academy, but he refused and is sending me off to Philadelphia. I'm a thorn in his side. He just wants to be rid of me."

Frannie grabbed Jed's shoulder and turned him so he faced her. His shining eyes and iron-set jaw testified to how hard he was fighting to check his emotions. "That's not true, Jed," she said softly. "The university is Father's alma mater. Besides, Georgetown is a Jesuit school, and Father is an agnostic. I'm sure he just wants you to find your own way in matters of faith."

Jed considered that possibility before replying. "I wish it were that simple. You've seen how cold he has become with me . . . as if he cannot bear to speak to me."

"You've been cold to him as well, Jed—tit for tat."

Jed dipped his head and kicked at the ground. "Only because he seems to have pulled away from me."

"Did you ever consider that perhaps he seems withdrawn because he'll miss you?"

"Ha!" Jed scoffed loudly. "Him miss me? We are nothing alike. He knows I love the Willows. He only lets me make decisions regarding her in the hope that I'll fail and be forced to sell her!"

"I don't think you're being very fair, Jed. It's not his fault Grandmother raised him to prefer the city. He loves the bustle of Baltimore, yet he brought us here regularly and did his best to keep the place afloat. When you turned fourteen, he started allowing you to make your own decisions about the Willows. How many other fathers would have acted as their son's agent and executed their plans? He didn't have to. The Willows isn't legally yours until you turn eighteen."

Jed hated it when Frannie took any side other than his, particularly when she was right.

"Why didn't you take his pocket watch when he offered it to you? I think you injured him by refusing his gift."

Jed hung his head and collapsed in the grass. "The truth?" he muttered. "I didn't want to break down. I wanted that old watch so badly. But it's been so long since we've really spoken that I feared if I so much as touched his hand my reserves would crumble. I'm trying to be a man."

Frannie flopped backward and stared at the August sky, then tucked her dress in around her legs without regard to decorum. She imagined the gasps from her genteel mother if she saw her fourteen-year-old daughter so arrayed. "I'm glad I'm not a man."

Jed chuckled as he threw a handful of grass at her. "I wish you could forever remain exactly as you are, Frannie."

"And what is that, Jed?"

"My very best friend."

"Of course I will always be your very best friend," she replied nonchalantly. "We'll always like the same things . . . hunting, fishing, riding horses, swimming in the river . . . diving from the old dock. Nothing will change that."

"I liked it best before Frederick Stringham started spending so much time with us. When we set out to ride I want to ride, not stop under a tree and listen to Frederick spout off on some poem he's read or tell some dazzling anecdote. And you," he said, pointing accusingly in her direction, "you who are arguably one of the finest horsewomen and hunters I know, worry more about your hair than your horse when Frederick's around. Frankly, I wonder what will await me when I get home after you and Frederick spend an entire fall primping and reciting together."

Frannie rose to her feet abruptly, sputtering. "He's our neighbor and has always been your friend. I am only being polite." Her voice became sullen. "Besides, you needn't worry about Frederick. His father put him in a coach this morning, headed for Boston. So, as you can see, I am completely abandoned. Does that make you feel better?"

"I'm sorry, Frannie. He's a fine enough chap. I shouldn't have spouted off so. It's just that . . . I hate change, and yet it seems as though everything is about to. And what of Hannah?"

"You'll write to her as always. We can't stop growing, Jed. I wish I could keep you here on the Willows forever, but you are going to be the master of one of the finest estates in Maryland . . . perhaps along the entire Atlantic Coast. Such a man needs to be educated."

"Yes," he admitted soberly. "Like Grandfather was."

"And like Father is," she emphasized.

"I know," he surrendered. "Watch over Bitty and Jack for me?"

"You know I will. Bitty is as dear to me as Mother."

Jed nodded his assent. "And the others . . . Sooky and his family? I want them to always be happy here. If a man buys slaves, he must assure them some measure of happiness."

Frannie touched his head softly. "You are going to be a great man someday, Jed. You have a kind heart. You should exercise it by mending things with Father."

Jed cast his eyes down and blushed. "I'll try, but not just yet. I'd like to lie here, like we did when we were children, and pretend that nothing is going to change for just a little while longer. Remember how Bitty used to sing to us when we were small? Would you sing to me, Frannie . . . one of those sweet little songs?"

Frannie smiled, pleased to be able to offer her beloved brother some comfort. "How about 'O'er the Crossing'?" she asked as she returned to her stump.

He nodded and lay back under the boughs of the old Wye oak as she began singing a song that Bitty, their slave-born surrogate mother, learned at her own mother's knee.

CHAPTER 4

London, England
Winter 1809

Time had toughened Juan Arroyo Corvas, who once again found himself at St. Paul's to meet the same fair-haired man. "I am to recite a statement and get answers to three questions."

As Juan noted the man's nervousness, his own concern abated. "This is the statement: 'Eighteen hundred and nine is a new world and you have failed. The wind has shifted. Warmer waters head south, leaving a loud wind to whistle your name through Westminster.'"

Juan noted the nervous twitching in the man's face and pushed on. "The three questions are, 'What? How? and When?' Deliver your sealed response to me at this address by tomorrow evening." Juan handed him a slip of paper.

Mitchell stared at the address and nodded, saying nothing as Juan slipped away. He waited ten minutes, and in a panic, hurried to Ramsey's house, ignoring the man's previous instruction. The butler showed him into the opulent study, where Ramsey stood with his back to the door. When Ramsey turned around, though his voice resonated anger, Mitchell thought he caught a smirk on the man's face.

"What are you doing here?" he demanded.

"I'm sorry . . . but you've ignored all my previous messages over these past months, and today, the courier sent for me again! The Consortium is pressing. I have been found in disfavor."

"You have?" Ramsey asked with feigned concern. "What did the courier say?"

"Something about eighteen hundred and nine being a new world. They implied that because I have not exercised my influence suffi- ciently, they may take their business south and expose us!" Mitchell's voice was nearing hysteria as he wrung his hands and paced in circles.

Ramsey played his hand carefully. "Calm yourself and tell me how you replied."

"I didn't! We have until tomorrow evening to answer their concerns."

Ramsey tilted his head, disappointed in Mitchell's inability to grasp his failure. "They paid for your influence. You were to improve their Spanish dealers' ability to transport slaves to the States. Unfortunately for you, the war with the French has caused an increase in antislavery patrols, and now America has passed her own trade ban."

"The reference to eighteen hundred and nine being a new year . . ." Mitchell slumped and then raised his head in frustration. "How can they hold me responsible for the effects of the war with France? That began long before my help was requested."

Ramsey cleared his throat with deliberateness. "My employers only see the bottom line. They are now forced to look at the legal markets in Brazil and Venezuela. Trade still runs fairly unfettered in the Indies as well, but their American markets, the markets you were to ensure, are almost worthless now. Your failure may cost the investors a fortune in lost American revenue."

Edward Mitchell covered his head and moaned. "And now they want to ruin me. What did they expect? I am but one voice in the House of Commons. I do not control the entire vote!"

Ramsey tapped the ram's head on Mitchell's shoulder. "You should have thought about that before you accepted the investors' payment."

Mitchell looked visibly shaken. "I simply tried to help my constituents by occasionally throwing a cog in the wheel of legisla- tion—I was just trying to buy them time to make suitable economic adjustments."

Ramsey's blue eyes narrowed in scrutiny below thick, dark brows. "But you took payment for services you did not render, and that reflects badly on me . . . a thing I cannot afford. We must now make ourselves appear indispensable." He leaned in close and asked menacingly, "How real does the threat of war with America appear?"

"British invasions of American ships are increasing, as are tensions, though our blockades preventing trade with America will likely be the match that ignites this fire."

Ramsey snickered and Mitchell felt a chill course through him.

"Then that is our answer."

"You want me to support the outbreak of a war with America? What good purpose will that serve?"

Ramsey raised one eyebrow ominously. "Don't you believe we could crush them?"

Mitchell grew increasingly wary. "Of course . . . but . . . that was not our agreement. How would that help my constituents? What are your people really planning, Ramsey?"

Ramsey sighed. "The war is practically inevitable. You've said so yourself. It simply affords us a new way to achieve our goals in light of the complications we've encountered. If America wins she will need slaves to rebuild, and that will cause the markets to reopen. If Britain wins there will be rich land to exploit. The maintenance of trust is our main goal. Parliament would not understand our efforts, so you must maintain a low profile to avoid their suspicions while I pacify our associates. Use your vote and influence to escalate the timetable of the war . . . and I'll use mine to make sure the sword cuts deep into America's flesh."

* * *

Three days had passed since Juan handed the letter over to another courier who was designated to deliver it to the creditor. Before leaving, the courier instructed Juan to remain at the inn in the London suburbs until he returned with a response. Knowing that the next letter would determine the next turn in his future, Juan waited anxiously, barely leaving his room except to buy a morsel or two of food. Finally, when he thought he would go mad from the waiting, the courier arrived.

Though the knock on the door was soft, it nearly caused Juan's heart to explode from his chest. He cracked the door and peered out to see the face of the young courier, who quickly slipped the letter through the opening and then hurried away.

As Juan held the letter in his hands, he dared again to hope that this would be the message that would finally declare his debt paid and himself free. His hands shook nervously as he opened the envelope and read:

> When weather permits, sail into Paynes Bay on Barbados's western coast—to the Holetown Port. Deliver the letter to a woman named Carlita at the Cantina de la Mer. You must arrive by April 20th. Cargo and instructions will be waiting. Upon the successful completion of this errand, your debt will be satisfied.

He made the sign of the cross and uttered a prayer to the Almighty.

* * *

An unusually temperate February had encouraged Juan to set sail for Barbados. He now stood at the helm of his ship, the *Ynez,* barking orders to the crew that had served his father and was now his own. Though he worried about this assignment, the taste of fear grew stale in his mouth while anger became an increasingly more familiar taste.

Juan knew what the cargo would be, since slavers saw the port as a perfect midpoint between Africa and their customers. He had sworn he would never desecrate the ship christened with his sainted mother's name . . . yet he was so close to fulfilling his debt and being free.

He pondered the paradoxical situation—the price of his own freedom might require his participation in the enslavement of others. Shaking his head to clear his mind, he turned the ship into Paynes Bay.

One of Juan's crewmen knew the Holetown Port well, testifying to the fact that the *Ynez* had sailed here before. The same sailor knew the cantina and pointed out Carlita when the time came.

The woman eyed Juan suspiciously and questioned him before she led him to a back room. An interesting-looking man, dressed all in white, sat at a table playing cards, while a dark-skinned woman trimmed his black, curly hair. He looked to be only a few years older than Juan, but the gold and jewels that hung around his neck formed a chasm that separated the two by a far greater distance than age alone could have. Additionally, the man had a strange complexion that Juan assumed to be typical of the island. But it was the eye-shaped tattoo at the base of the man's throat and his equally disconcerting sneer that riveted the Spaniard. It was as if the man could see into his soul, finding immense pleasure in his guest's discomfort.

The man offered him no greeting, then no seat or beverage, though both were available in abundance. Instead, as if to mock Juan Corvas, he leaned back and stretched his feet out on the empty chair closest to Juan and loudly guzzled a large tankard of ale. He dabbed at his mouth with the skirt of the woman's dress, and Juan marveled that she smiled as if flattered by the crude attention.

As the man read the documents, his jaw tightened and his eyes narrowed. "So it begins," he muttered, then called for Carlita to bring him a quill and an inkwell. He scratched a note on the paper in a finely penned hand, and Carlita held it near a small wood stove to set the ink. The man then folded the document neatly, tapped it against his chest, and turned to Juan. His bravado had dimmed. "Would you rather sail to America, Spaniard, or carry this letter back to London?"

Juan tightened his jaw, struggling not to lose his temper at the man with the cultured voice. "London is nearer my home port," he responded coldly, "but what of my cargo?"

"I am the cargo. I've been summoned to return to America." His voice had a tired tone. "But if I must leave paradise, I'd prefer to arrange for more comfortable passage. I therefore release you to return to London to deliver this letter instead."

Juan had paid too high a price to be tricked by this cocky exotic. "To satisfy my debt I must deliver my cargo. Will delivering this letter likewise set me free?"

"Free . . . ?" the man mused. "No man is free, Spaniard. We are each proof of that. Whether to God, the devil, or man, we are all in debt to someone." He added a note to the letter and then sealed it with candle wax before holding it out in Juan's direction. "But if you speak of meeting your obligation, then yes, delivering the letter will free you," he said, slumping heavily into his chair and closing his eyes in thought. "Now leave me."

CHAPTER 5

Baltimore, Maryland
Early June 1810

On Jed's final day at the university, his professor began a debate over whether or not America had ever actually won her independence, since the years following the signing of the peace agreement had been strewn with breaches of the treaty. At first, Jed had found the question to be ridiculous, but as he considered how those violations impacted life, liberty, and the citizenry's ability to pursue happiness, he found that the question had some merit. Britain's most egregious crime, the impressing of American citizens, stemmed from her difficulty in maintaining her world-dominating fleet. Many of her seamen had deserted and fled to America, where higher wages and a better life awaited them. In retaliation, by 1810, British ships had seized nearly five thousand sailors as deserters or citizens of the monarchy, with no regard to their claims of American citizenship or their desires to renounce their British loyalties.

Baltimore's rage over trade interferences was the topic this day as Jed Pearson exited the carriage at the Baltimore station. France and England were determined to prevent one another from engaging in maritime trade, even with other neutral nations. As a result, American merchants found their ships and goods seized and Europe's ports closed by blockades, both literally and legally. Imports and exports of goods—including exports of tobacco, the cash crop of the region—were severely decreased, wreaking havoc on the economy. Some men were yelling for their elected representatives in the State House and in

Washington City to act swiftly, while others begged for restraint, fearful of another round with the British military behemoth.

As passions flared all around Jed, he vowed to keep his wits about him and wait and listen. His grandfather's own legacy taught him that decisions made during such times could make or erase fortunes. Jed was mentally grappling with all the political enigmas when he saw Frannie. Suddenly, thoughts of political gossip and intrigue faded as his face broke into a smile at the sight of his sister standing on the far side of the platform and waving wildly in his direction.

"I've planned a busy summer now that you've graduated," she ventured as they embraced.

"It's so good to see you," Jed replied with pleasure. He pulled back from her, observing the changes that had occurred since he had seen her at Christmas. At eighteen, she wore her beautiful auburn hair swept up in a stylish hat, and her womanly figure was dressed in a sporty traveling suit and riding boots. Though she looked wonderful, as he touched her freckled cheek and looked into her brown eyes, he saw only glimpses of the sister he knew, and he was saddened. She had grown up, and he had been home so infrequently he had missed the turn.

Frannie saw the cloud pass over his face. "Don't fret. I can still best you," she teased.

Jed drew his arm around her as he scanned the rest of the platform, then asked, "Where are Mother and Father?"

"Mother swore she would die of heat stroke if she didn't have a breeze to cool her, so Father is circling the carriage around the block to fan her. That's why they didn't travel to commencement."

"It's just as well. It was hardly the type of social gathering Mother and Father prefer. My professors and I debated politics until the hour of my departure. Father would have been bored and Mother would have fretted, wondering if her ensemble was suitable for Philadelphia."

The pair looked at one another and chuckled. Fortunately for Frannie, Julianne Ensor Pearson, a frail product of genteel society, had allowed her daughter to be raised with a freer hand, where conformity was requested but not required. For example, Frannie had once agreed to don a waist-whittling corset under her Christmas gown, but she'd tossed it out after being nearly asphyxiated. She'd suggested to her mother that perhaps corsets were the reason Julianne herself was always so weak. Her mother considered the notion ridiculous, but merely tittered softly, owing to the fact that she barely had enough oxygen in her lungs to offer anything more. Frannie often questioned whether corsets were designed for that very purpose—to keep women weak and complacent. That day she'd determined that she'd be strong and thick before fashionable and frail for any man.

"Are we heading straightway to the country for the Stansburys' barbeque?" Jed asked.

"In quite a hurry, aren't you?" Frannie teased as she reached for his bags. Despite Jed's protests, she gave his hands a loving smack and carried off his two smaller bags as he hefted a large trunk and followed along after her. "Don't tell me you've forgotten that your sister is your equal, brother," she added, lifting the bags a little higher.

Jed grunted good-naturedly, but as Frannie waddled under the load of baggage, he no longer approved of her bravado, instead worrying for her well-being. He had also noticed the curious attention being directed both at his sister's spectacle and at his churlish participation in it.

"Honestly, Frannie," he uttered under his breath, waving to a bellman. "You've proven your point. Now, would it be too condescending of me to simply pay a man to move our bags?"

Frannie scanned the disapproving assembly. She dropped the bags to the ground and tossed a laugh over her shoulder. "Has life at the University of Pennsylvania made you soft, Jed? I'd hate to think that at the pitiable age of twenty your best days are already behind you."

Frannie's humor melted his resolve. "When I first saw you, I was delighted to see the reincarnation of the sister I remembered, not that fragile wisp you attempted to be at Christmastime. But now I am inclined to wish that a little of that femininity had remained."

"You've become stuffy," she laughed. "Mother always said that hunting with you and Father would ruin me." She shook her head woefully. "She is always threatening to send me off to one of those Philadelphia finishing schools to make a lady out of me. I swear I shall die if she does."

"Your death will be guaranteed if Mother hears you swear. Besides, you could finally get some vocal lessons and improve that squeaky voice of yours," he teased.

Frannie teased back as the bellman followed her to the rendezvous point, pulling the loaded flat wagon behind him.

"I don't see them," Jed muttered in frustration. "We probably missed them during your little performance back there. Now we'll have to wait until Father circles around again."

"You used to laugh at my rebellion. What about our plans to return the Willows to her glory and spend our days together hunting and riding?" She tugged at the lapel of his coat and wrinkled her nose. "You seem more inclined to hold a business meeting than to go on a hunt."

"Running an estate *is* business, Frannie, and hard work. That's why Father and his brothers dislike it so. It will require more than fox hunts and play if we are to buy back the rest of Grandfather's squandered land and restore the Willows. Sometimes the thought staggers me."

"You're right," she conceded, suddenly contrite. "Everyone else has sold their interests in the Willows, and Father visits it only to make a cursory check on your interests. Truly, Providence must have guided Grandfather." She tightened her hold on Jed's arm. "It still riles the family that he changed his will on the spot simply because your birthmark matched his own."

Jed's thoughts drifted to the point of her humor, his apocryphal good fortune, which still left him humbled and overwhelmed with responsibility. His grandfather dubbed him "Jed" on the day he was born, then died hours later, as if he had refused to give up the ghost until he had a worthy heir. Upon seeing Jed's heart-shaped birthmark, he was said to have received his sign.

Jed knew the mighty Pearson name had a clouded history, to be sure, with as many versions as a garbled fairy tale. His parents refused to acknowledge the rumors, though the most prevalent implied that his grandfather had amassed his great wealth as much by artifice as good fortune.

In 1712, the first Jonathan Edward Pearson had been born in poverty in Liverpool, England, to a young woman who served in the home of a Member of Parliament—the Honorable Mr. Mitchell. Nature provided more than ample compensation for Jonathan's poverty, blessing him with stature and good looks as well as a keen mind, a dazzling wit, and a bit of luck.

His mother's employer paid for his education, which he parlayed into a twelve-year indenture in the colonies. Jonathan contracted to tutor the Ensor family children in all subject areas, including music and dance lessons, elocution, and voice. In exchange, he received his passage to America, a small cabin, and fifteen acres of waterfront land along the Patuxent River that flowed into the mighty Chesapeake Bay, plus one side each of pork and beef each winter, a chicken a week, fifty pounds of flour, and two dollars a month. Additionally, he soon offered to exercise his talents in arts and letters to serve as the family's legal counselor in drawing up wills and formal deeds as such transactions were needed. It was here that the legend of Jonathan Pearson began to vary.

Most rumors held that so amusing was the bright and strikingly handsome Mr. Pearson that within weeks he was a welcomed dinner guest at homes all along the river. Others remembered him as a destitute interloper who charmed his way to massive land holdings and then used his newly acquired wealth to shove his way into Maryland society. In either case, eyebrows were raised when many of his hosts asked him to witness their wills. Even more curiosities were aroused when Pearson's name began appearing as executor of their estates and later as a minor heir. Though the bequests were generally small—a few granted acres here, a horse and cow there—by the end of his indenture, Pearson's estate constituted grants to over one hundred fifty acres of well-stocked, prime waterfront property.

At that time, Jed recalled, the governor, Lord Baltimore, was outlawing private docks and controlling the placement of others to spur the formation of towns. Realizing that proximity to a dock would affect profits, Jonathan devised a plan to bring the dock to him. He made a wager with Lord Baltimore that he could construct a new public wharf on a corner of the Willows property, requiring absolutely no outlay of government cash. If he failed, he would enlist in another indenture to pay for the building of this failed dock and another wharf elsewhere. But if he succeeded, he would hold a hundred-year lease on the docks for public use, which would then be deeded back to his estate. The governor agreed immediately, only to curse later when Pearson's gamble paid off. The shrewd negotiator sold lottery tickets for one piece of eight each until he accumulated enough of the silver Spanish coins to pay the winner's purse, fund the construction, and make a hefty profit as well, which he quickly invested in seeds and slaves.

The dock not only reduced the effort and cost of shipping Pearson's goods, but it also afforded him an advantage with the ships' captains who moved his goods and with the buyers who marketed them. Within ten years he became one of the wealthiest men in the region. His estate had tripled, with land grants adjacent to, and separate from, his primary residence. Within twenty years he had acquired rights to all the land in between his tracts of property. This excess of land allowed him the luxury of rotating his crops and resting his fields so that ultimately the Willows produced some of the highest-quality tobacco in all the colonies. Indeed, his nearly two thousand acres of prime, deeded land became one of the most desirable estates in three counties.

When the Revolution broke out, tobacco exports ground to a near halt, and enemy raids targeted the rich Patuxent wharves and homes. A militia was raised, and the sixty-four-year-old Pearson and his sons rallied to the call. In return for their valiant service, they were given the opportunity to immediately purchase their deeded land. Jonathan stripped his estate of valuables to raise the funds that would secure permanent ownership of the Winding Willows as well as numerous deeds to properties in Baltimore City. His estate was soon worth a fortune in cash and investments.

Jed found his grandfather's story fascinating, and wondered at who the man really was. It was believed that equal to Jonathan Pearson's passion for wealth was his passion for family. Some painted him a dashing man who could pick and choose his affections, while others regarded him as a rake who wooed multiple ladies during his seventy-eight years, marrying and burying four choice wives who came from influential families and who bore him eleven children. All Jed knew was that his grandfather's bloodline was intermingled with every powerful name in the state, a fact that provided little comfort to Jed, since Pearson's spoiled heirs had acted precisely as his grandfather had feared. Though the monetary bequests to each of his children had been generous, they stripped the glorious Willows estate and sold everything not directly deeded to Jed or his father to finance the city life they preferred. Jed had been left the old manor house, the water-front and docks, and eight hundred of the most fertile tobacco-growing acres in the state.

Frannie nudged Jed and laughed. "Breathe, brother. We have a lifetime to rebuild her."

Jed looked lovingly at his sister, whose passion for life, for the land, and for the outdoors equaled his own. He placed a kiss on her head as he spied their parents' carriage winding toward them through the crowd of buggies. "You know the Willows will always be as much your home as mine," he assured gently.

She leaned into Jed, acknowledging his promise, and then his voice erupted into laughter.

"Do I see two horses tied to the rig?"

Frannie smiled broadly and nodded. "I knew you'd prefer riding Tildie to another carriage ride."

Jed looked admiringly at his sister. "You do know me as no one else does."

After exchanging hugs and handshakes with his parents, Jed made certain the baggage was loaded into the rig, and he and Frannie mounted the horses. As always, the siblings rode side by side, while their parents went ahead in the carriage.

"Will you be completely engulfed by Willows business this summer?" asked Frannie.

"I won't know until I see her. Markus's crop reports sound favorable, but from what I can decipher from Bitty's notes, my foreman has done little to keep up the fences and buildings."

Frannie chuckled at the thought of Bitty's enduring love for the two of them. Bitty had jumped the broom in marriage to a man named Josiah, but he'd died of pneumonia three winters later. Widowed and childless at twenty, it was only her love for Jed and Frannie that had kept her going during the lonely months that followed. Eventually, she had become content with her situation, and though barely five feet tall, she was the queen of the house, second only to Mrs. Pearson, and as Mrs. Pearson preferred city life, Bitty had a fairly free hand to direct life at the Winding Willows.

"Bitty has the house looking as fine as possible under the circumstances, but all the buildings need a great deal of repair. I'm pleased to hear she wrote to you, though. We practiced for hours this spring. Her penmanship is lovely but her spelling is . . . interesting."

Jed laughed. "Everything at the Willows is 'interesting.' Markus is arguably the worst foreman in the state. He can't get the workers to accomplish half the work I assign, but we haven't had any runaways since he was hired, and he does ignore things that could cause us a great deal of trouble—" he paused to scowl at Frannie "—like teaching Bitty to read and write." He looked somberly at her. "It's a punishable offense, you know." He closed his eyes and took a deep breath. "The slave issue makes me more uncomfortable every day. We now have preliminary laws prohibiting slave trading, so laws that would abolish slavery altogether cannot be far off."

"But British ships still unload slaves in the Patuxent docks."

"I know. The laws may have been passed, but few obey them. The debate stirs me."

"Is it debated in Philadelphia?"

Jed laughed. "Everything is debated in Philadelphia, but oddly, it is Hannah Stansbury who continually raises my sensibilities on the issue."

"Little Hannah Stansbury? What could she know of such things? She is barely sixteen."

"Don't disregard her because of her youth. Everyone dismisses her, but she has character and a keen mind. It is because of her age that her comments burn my conscience so." Jed stalled awkwardly. "She is a treasure, Frannie. I don't know how she has survived having such an odd relationship with her parents. Things are better with her sisters now, but only because she has completely capitulated to her mother's every whim. Her world is so small." Jed winced in sorrow. "Yet she writes to me, trying to 'elevate' my thinking. She assures me that once she is grown she will live in a cave before consenting to owning slaves. I tried to explain the financial difficulty of estate life without slavery, but as her arguments reverberate in my mind and heart, I have come to agree that there simply has to be a better way."

Frannie squeezed his arm gently. "After four years of city life at the university, life at the Willows will be a difficult transition for you, won't it?"

Jed nodded thoughtfully. "It's one thing to own the Willows on paper. All my life that place has been my diversion, but I cannot afford to see it that way any longer. I need it to be profitable, and I need to make sure it is a good home. Markus and I are making additional changes."

"I had no idea how greatly Hannah's opinion matters to you."

Jed noted the hurt in Frannie's voice. "No more than yours," he replied quickly. "I worry about her. It is only with Selma, and through my letters, that she feels fully loved and whole."

"Well, that explains your hurry to get to the barbeque."

"What are you implying?" Jed queried defensively.

"Hmm, some might misinterpret your interest as having a more . . . romantic element."

"That's preposterous," he argued—far too fiercely from Fannie's viewpoint.

"So you do have personal feelings for her."

Defeat clouded Jed's face. "We've corresponded all these years, and I have treasured each opportunity to see her. But, Frannie, over the course of time, my feelings began to change from a brotherly, protective love to those of a more tender nature. I told myself this recent affection was a natural extension of our friendship that deepened as she matured. Now, I have become uncomfortable—even embarrassed—with these changes, yet I am unable to dismiss her from my mind. I fear I am destined to simply remain her tortured friend forever."

"You must tell her, Jed. Perhaps she loves you in return."

"I cannot. No . . . she knows too little of life. Though she may be sixteen in years, she has had few of life's opportunities. All her reading and pondering cannot fully compensate for her lack of experience— something that will give her the strength to assert her own will. I will not risk the chance that she would obligate herself to me out of fear of losing my friendship."

Silence overtook them for the next few miles, then Frannie smiled a melancholy smile. "You have a lot to mull over. You know I'll help you in whatever way I can." Her voice was soft and tinged with understanding. "And you do not need to worry about entertaining me. Frederick is already home and desires my company."

Jed registered her comment and replied sarcastically, "So, how is my old friend?"

"Perfectly well," goaded Frannie. "He arrived home from Boston nearly a month ago, and we've been nearly inseparable."

Jed knew she was purposely baiting him, but there was something about the thought of her being entangled with the Stringhams that made him apprehensive. He also understood that any attempt on his part to push Frannie one way would likely cause her to move in the opposite. He decided to bridle his worries and playfully investigate.

"So how have you two filled the past month?"

"Oh, with this and that," she answered vaguely.

"Was it more of this . . . or would you say it was more of that?" Jed probed jokingly. He knew he would have to tread carefully where Frederick was concerned, particularly now that he had graduated from college. Despite Frederick's diploma, his life was not without worries. Still, as Stringham's only child, Frederick was the sole heir of White Oak, so his prospects were bright enough to consider marriage, and it made Jed nervous to think that he was setting his attentions on Frannie again.

"You don't visit him at White Oak, do you?" Jed questioned sharply.

"No, Jed. Frederick calls for me at the Willows. You needn't worry."

Oh, don't I? he thought. "It's rumored that Mr. Stringham suffered severe losses on his past two tobacco crops, forcing him to sell off some of his slaves to meet his debts. I've seen the barbaric way he handles his people in good times. I surely don't want you near White Oak now."

* * *

It was dusk when the Pearsons drew within two miles of Coolfont. Jed was desperate to get to the Stansbury home to see Hannah, but his parents refused to go on, choosing to take rooms at a nearby inn instead. As they rode down Coolfont's lane the next morning, certain changes caught Jed's eye. The windows now had iron grates in them, giving the stately home a medieval look, and though the flowerbeds and shrubs were perfect, the overall appearance of the manor seemed dreary. That realization prompted Jed to worry about the Willows' haggard state.

Susannah and Bernard Stansbury stood at the edge of the carriage circle, greeting each family as they arrived. Mrs. Stansbury was dressed beautifully, but it took no more than a swift glance to notice her wild eyes and to assess that she had applied far too much rouge and lip tint. She prattled on incessantly, barking repetitious commands while wringing her hands or playing with her skirt. Mr. Stansbury already looked weary. Though he smiled and kept an affectionate hand on his wife at all times, it was evident he wished the day were over.

"Can you tell me where Hannah is?" Jed asked as nonchalantly as he could muster.

Susannah Stansbury's brow furrowed, but Bernard tightened his arm around her shoulders and replied, "She's on the side of the house, Jed, organizing games for the children."

Jed grabbed Frannie's hand and hurried off. As soon as he turned the corner, he felt the same familiar mixture of euphoria and worry return. He was overjoyed to see Hannah, but it took him a moment to process the changes in her. She still wore a mid-calf dress, the style of which a young woman her age normally should have abandoned years earlier, and her hair was still long and loosely curled like a child's. But nothing else about her was childlike. She had grown several inches taller, and even the generous fabric of her dress could not conceal that her body had matured in other ways as well. Her bearing was straight and strong with flowing movement that no longer reminded him of a skittish baby goat, and her voice was deeper as she instructed the children—but it was her face that marked the greatest changes in her.

Jed was captivated. Hannah's once chubby cheeks were gone, leaving high cheekbones, a lean face, and a slightly pointed chin in their place. She was flushed from running, and her green eyes shone against the frame of her dark hair and thick brows. But Jed's heart nearly broke when he noticed how their momentary flashes of sparkle quickly faded to soberness in the quiet moments.

"Did you press us along every mile so you could stare at her from behind a tree?"

"Shhh, Frannie," he coaxed. "I just want to look at her for a moment. Once she sees me she'll plaster on a smile and pretend that life is grand, and I'll never know how she really is."

Every few moments Hannah would turn her attentions from the games and scan the yard as if searching for something or someone.

Frannie shook her head in frustration. "She's looking for you. Why play these games?"

Again he shushed her. Finally, in aggravation, she said, "Do as you please, but I did not travel this far to stand behind a tree." Then she left to join a small group of eligible young men.

Jed remained mesmerized by the way Hannah interacted with the children, drawing out even the shyest imp with her unfeigned interest. He noticed her eyes again. They were still childlike, but instead of gleaming with innocent wonder, they were fearful and nervous, like a deer on the lawn, anticipating danger at every turn. It pained him to consider what abuses she must have endured to have such wariness planted in her otherwise innocent heart.

It was at this moment that Hannah turned, catching sight of him. She squinted against the bright sun, trying to be certain it was Jed standing tall and broad against the backdrop of the old swing and tree. He stood serenely, with his head cocked slightly as the breeze ruffled through his dark hair. It wasn't until he smiled at her that she was absolutely certain.

She beamed happily, coming toward him with the slow, measured gait of a lady. But once he raised his arms in her direction, she ran to him and leapt into them, snuggling her head deep in the sweet-scented crook of his tanned neck. He spun around with her in his arms, pleased to be in a corner away from the scrutiny of her mother's eyes.

"Oh, I've missed you," she repeated over and over in his ear.

"I hardly recognized you," he said breathlessly. "Let me take a good look at you." He placed her on her toes, and she straightened her dress and wriggled comically before speaking.

"All right. And how do I measure up?" she inquired with mock seriousness.

His voice was wistful. "You've grown so much since I last saw you . . . and you're more beautiful than ever." He laid his arm playfully across her shoulders and drew her near to kiss the top of her head as his heart pounded. "I brought you a gift."

Hannah beamed with wonder. "But why?"

"Why?" he stammered as he struggled for a suitable response. "Just—just because." He withdrew the package from his pocket, jutting it in Hannah's direction.

She held it gingerly in her hands, marveling over the kindness. She gasped softly at the stack of fine writing paper, the bundle of envelopes, and the metal stamp with the initials *HMS* embossed into it. "My initials," she whispered. "How did you know my middle name?"

"I don't actually." Jed blushed. "I saw it embroidered on one of your handkerchiefs."

She gazed admiringly at him. "I'm flattered that you remembered something so trivial."

Jed felt himself falling into the green of her eyes. "There's nothing trivial about a person's name. It's who we are and who our children will be. What does the *M* stand for?"

"McClintock. It was my mother's maiden name."

"McClintock . . ." mused Jed. "It's a strong name. A good name to pass to a child."

Hannah cocked her head to one side, raising one eyebrow curiously.

Jed hurried on again. "Now show me this dragon of a horse your parents bought for you."

Hannah took his arm tightly, jabbering all the way to the stables and on to a door marked *Druid,* behind which a muscular, jet-black stallion stood stomping and snorting. Jed was taken aback by the massiveness of the horse, a beast more befitting an armor-clad knight than a wisp like Hannah. "Your father bought you this horse?" he asked worriedly.

"No. Mother actually picked him out. I couldn't believe it at first. It's so uncharacteristic of her. One day she was severely vexed with me, and the next day she gave me Druid. It was such a loving gesture." The wonder was apparent in her voice. "I'm just afraid to ride him."

Jed remained jaded about the gift. "Has he been ridden yet . . . by anyone?"

"Mother had Mobey, the stableman, take him out once to prove to me that he's a safe mount, but I've never been brave enough to get near him without a door or fence between us."

Jed felt the muscles in his jaw tighten. "Let me take him out."

"Are you sure?" Hannah's voice was filled with apprehension. "What if he throws you?"

"Hannah, I've no interest in dying young. I'm sure if old Mobey can handle him, I can as well. I'll give you an honest appraisal of whether or not I think you're safe in riding him."

A few minutes later, Jed carefully gauged the horse's reaction as he placed the blanket and saddle on his back and tightened the cinch. Druid snorted as he took the bit, but overall Jed was pleasantly surprised at how he responded to being saddled. He mounted and felt Druid tense with anticipation, but the animal neither bolted nor bucked. As soon as heel met side, Druid leaped forward like a shot, giving Jed one of the most exhilarating rides of his memory. The animal responded quickly to every command in fluid, even strides. He jumped a downed log and moved through a wooded patch like a thread through the eye of a needle. They turned and rode back toward the stables with Jed constantly expecting the horse to show some threat or streak of orneriness that would confirm his suspicion that crazy Susannah Stansbury's gift bore malicious intent. The longer he rode, though, the more those fears subsided until he began to wonder if he had falsely judged the woman. Susannah had, in actuality, given her daughter a truly magnificent gift.

As they approached the stables, Jed reined the horse in. Druid responded with a snort, immediately halting. "Go change, Hannah," Jed said with a smile. "He's a fine horse."

"I can't do it, Jed. Please don't ask me to ride him yet. Not today."

He framed her face in his large hands and smiled protectively down at her. "Do you trust me, Hannah? Do you think I would ever ask you to do anything that would harm you?"

Hannah's concession was complete and immediate. "All right. I'll just be a few minutes."

A few minutes later, Beatrice and Myrna Stansbury entered the barn, accompanied by a thirtyish man in an artillery officer's uniform. Beatrice smiled warmly, hurrying her guest in Jed's direction while Myrna hung back, showing the same disdain for Jed so apparent in her mother. "Mr. Jonathan Pearson, allow me to introduce Lieutenant Dudley Snowden," Beatrice stated with pleasure.

Jed immediately liked the man with the quiet face and sturdy handshake. "Lieutenant," he said with a nod. Then turning to offer the women a greeting, he bowed and said, "Ladies."

"Lieutenant Snowden is stationed in Baltimore, serving under my father's great-uncle, Tobias."

"I see. You soldiers have quite a presence in the city," noted Jed.

Lieutenant Snowden grimaced slightly. "We must carefully guard states like Maryland that are vulnerable to attack by water. Britain and France are intimidating adversaries."

"France?"

"Yes, even France," replied the lieutenant. "Both countries are harassing our ships. I'm sure you've heard the calls for war."

Jed found the soldier's candor interesting. "I would enjoy discussing this with you later."

"Yes, I doubt these ladies would relish such subjects. Today my plan is to enjoy their company as they give me the grand tour of Coolfont."

"Of course." Jed smiled as Beatrice beamed with delight.

"Jed, Hannah should be down soon," Beatrice called over her shoulder as she and the others departed. "She asked me to have you saddle the gray so you could ride together."

Jed thanked her and hurried on to the task, finishing just as Hannah reappeared in the doorway. She was dressed in a smart riding habit, a brown split skirt with matching jacket and polished brown boots. She tapped the crop against her boot comically to draw Jed's attention, but no effort was required to obtain and hold his notice.

"New outfit?" Jed choked out, trying to remember that the vision standing before him, however lovely and sophisticated in appearance, was still barely sixteen, and the daughter of Susannah Stansbury.

"It's Beatrice's. She let me borrow it. Isn't it wonderful?" she exclaimed as she twirled.

"Very wonderful," he muttered under his breath as he turned back to tighten an already tight cinch, bringing a wince from the dapple gray horse.

"Mount up," he instructed, barely looking at Hannah.

"Where's my sidesaddle?"

"I think you'll be more secure with this saddle at first."

"Mother will become apoplectic if she sees me."

"More apoplectic than if you slide off the sidesaddle and break your neck?"

She just stared at him, allowing him to draw his own conclusions.

"Fine," he sighed impatiently. "Then we'll ride where she won't see you." He backed down and added softly, "Let's get you comfortable with Druid first before we worry about style, agreed?"

Hannah nodded, but stood several feet away from Druid, simply staring at the horse.

"Now what?" asked Jed, who longed to ride and clear his head.

"Aren't you going to help me?" she asked, pointing to the stirrup dangling near her hip.

Jed moved close to her and cupped his hands, keeping his eyes fixed on the ground. She placed her left foot in his hands, grabbed the pommel, and leaned into Druid, allowing the horse to adjust to her weight. Then she stalled nervously. "He's twitching, Jed. I don't think I want to do this."

"You're fine, Hannah, and I'm right here. Just mount up."

She turned, bringing her face within inches of his. "You won't let go of him, will you?"

"No, Hannah," Jed chided her softly as he watched her face for a response. He could feel her trembling down through her boots and into the palms of his hands, and he knew at that moment there was more at stake than just the opportunity for a ride. "You've got to learn to trust in someone, someday. Trust me, Hannah. I won't let you down. I promise you."

She tightened her jaw and lifted her right leg over the saddle. Her posture stiff and tentative, she was prepared to react if the beast did indeed carry her away beyond Jed's reach. Offering her the reins, Jed smiled proudly at her, but she shook her head.

"You hold them until you're mounted as well. I'm not taking any chances that Druid might gallop away with me unless you are in a position to immediately come to my rescue."

Jed knew he had asked as much from her as he could, so he mounted Granite, the dapple gray, and led out gently. After the horses had walked a few yards, Jed handed Hannah Druid's reins. They continued on at a steady walk until they reached the edge of the paddock. Jed noted Hannah's wary smile as he nodded encouragingly to her, while urging Granite on to a slow trot, which Hannah and Druid followed. Hannah did her best to appear willing, and after a quarter of an hour her body relaxed as she matched the horse's rhythm. A while later, Jed smiled at her and she eased Druid into a rhythmic cantor. When Jed sensed that she had again become comfortable with her horse's pace, he nodded encouragingly and asked, "Ready?"

She took a deep breath and nodded as she dug her heels into Druid's sides and yelled, "Ha!" The horse bolted and as Jed watched panic wash over her, he knew she had only prepared herself for an easy gallop, not the heart-pounding race Druid was running. Jed urged Granite alongside and noticed that as soon as she felt the horse responding to her commands, pleasure replaced her fear.

Jed dropped back a few strides to keep an eye on her, allowing her to choose a course with which she was familiar and comfortable. She rode well for her age, though he couldn't help compare her novice skills to those of Frannie, who rode a horse as if cradled there from infancy. Still, the freedom of the ride brought an expression of sincere joy to her face, and they rode on for miles, reaching the northern fence line of the Coolfont boundary and turning west.

Once the open fields had given way to a stand of trees, Hannah slowed her horse to navigate the more treacherous terrain. Her confidence grew as they broke back into open, higher ground. Before she realized it the horse came upon the six-foot-wide brook and leaped across, easily clearing the hazard but leaving his unprepared rider struggling to remain seated. Jed knew she was in trouble and urged Granite forward, matching Druid stride for stride. He leaned out across his own horse to grab Druid's bridle and eventually slowed the horse to a stop.

Hannah slid from the saddle onto quaking legs too weak and unstable to bear her weight. She toddled about for a few steps, and when Jed jumped from Granite's back and rushed to her side, she fell against him and into his arms. He carried her to a tree and set her against it, checking to be sure she was not injured. As soon as the shock from the scare wore off, silent tears fell from her dark lashes. She sat speechless, resting one hand on her head and the other against her stomach.

When Jed was sure she was all right, the shock hit him as well, and suddenly his knees felt as weak as Hannah's had seemed. He fell down on the grass and stared up at the sky, grateful she couldn't see the fear in his own eyes. "You are crazy, Hannah. One minute you are afraid to touch the horse, and the next you're jumping water hazards!"

"Oh, please don't call me crazy, Jed," she pled between gasps of breath. "Call me a fool . . . call me irresponsible or childish, but please don't call me crazy. It hits too close to home."

Jed sat up, propping one hand behind him. "Your mother?"

She leaned forward as if she were going to vomit. Jed rushed beside her, bundling up her hair and placing a comforting hand on her back. She breathed deeply for a few seconds until the nausea abated and then leaned back against the tree and took Jed's hand. "We all fear Mother is going insane. That's what has bound my sisters and me these past few years. For so long I was the outcast because Mother made it appear I was always bad or unruly, but recently, her rage has turned on my sisters as well. No one is exempt, and they realize it wasn't me that stirred her up."

"And what about your father?"

Hannah stared blankly into the meadow. "He's a victim too, I suppose. I think he truly wants to love us, but Mother seems jealous of any attention he pays to any of us. So, he avoids angering her by moving about the house most days as if we weren't there. Sometimes, when Mother falls asleep early, or when she's sick and confined to her room, he plays chess with us or reads with us. In those hours I gain some sense of what life could have been like, but sometimes a glimpse of the unattainable is more painful than being blinded to the possibility."

"We've shared everything, but never once have you mentioned this," Jed declared solemnly. "I am supposed to be your protector, your one and true confidant."

"It seemed disloyal to air our dirty laundry. Besides, what could you have done?"

Jed wished he could tell her how desperately he longed to carry her away. "Sometimes it helps just to talk . . . just to know someone understands."

"You are my dearest love, Jed. What if I didn't have you and Selma? Now I have my sisters as well, but this lieutenant may take Beatrice away from me." Her head fell back against the tree again. "First it was Charles, then my slave friends, and now Beatrice may leave me."

"What of Charles Kittamaqund, Hannah? Do you see him anymore?"

"Funny you should ask. Remember the year I met you with my face painted and braids in my hair?" she chuckled. "Mother nearly shook me to death that day."

Jed marveled that she could look back on that day with a smile.

"That was the last time I ever spoke to Charles, but someone spots him in the brush every year on the day of the barbeque, as if he purposely comes just to take a look at us. Mother is sure he's planning to scalp us all," she laughed. "He was a good friend to me."

"I'm sorry you lost Charles, but I'm glad you still have Selma. You love her the way I love Bitty," said Jed. "She's as dear to me as my own mother."

"I'm not afraid to say that Selma is *more dear* to me than my own mother," explained Hannah. "I wish I were the master of my home like you are, so I could set her and all our slaves free. Someday I'll find a way. I don't know how, but if it takes everything I own I will do it."

Jed always shrank when this topic arose with Hannah. "Is there any part of you that could accept that retaining slaves, under the kindest of conditions, mind you, might be more compassionate than throwing them—poor and uneducated—to the wolves? At the Willows we restricted the number of hours worked per day, and every slave gets at least one day's rest per week. Their cabins are solid, water-tight and spacious, and no families are ever broken up. Isn't that better than the risk of being without a roof or means?"

Hannah looked at him in utter disbelief. "You don't really believe that, do you?"

Jed hedged, wishing he had never let the thought escape his mouth. "No, of course not."

"It doesn't matter how kind or unkind a master is when you are inventoried as a man's property. Consider the insecurity of bearing a child with no power to protect or even retain her. Would anyone choose enslavement over self-determination, even if the price were poverty?"

Her compassion and courage awed Jed, and it was reflected in his face.

"What does that expression mean?" she asked.

Jed blushed, knowing he had been caught revealing a part of his heart he had vowed to conceal. "What expression?" He feigned nonchalance.

"I'm not sure. Your eyes looked all sleepy and mysterious as if you were hiding a secret."

"I think you bumped your head too hard against that tree."

"Tell me, Jed, today of all days. I trusted you with my life. Trust me with your secret."

Jed wondered if the time had come to make his intentions known. *But she is too vulnerable to make such a decision,* he told himself. Instead he said, "I marvel at you, that's all."

Hannah seemed pleased by the comment. "What do you mean, you marvel at me?"

"You're wondrous, Hannah. You have cause to be so angry and yet you are not. You could justify being melancholy, but you choose happiness, despite your situation. Someday, Hannah, a worthy and fortunate man will come along and you will be his treasure."

She leaned forward, anxious to hear more. "Why will a man treasure me, Jed?"

Jed fought to keep his feelings less transparent as he answered, "Because you are the kind of woman who will take a cottage and make it a castle, filled with beauty and learning and laughter. No place will make your husband feel as loved or as important as the door that leads back to you." Hannah began to giggle as Jed rose to his feet, dramatically embellishing his points. "He will know he has won the heart of the most devoted woman in the land, one who will rear his children to be strong and independent people who will leave their marks upon the world." He leaned close to her. "And do you know why they will be able to do these things, Hannah?"

She stared into his eyes, soaking in the portrait he had painted for her. "Why, Jed?"

His voice was soft. "Because you have a vision of a better world . . . of a world most of us don't even dare to dream of anymore. You believe it belongs to everyone, and you help them see it, too. Moreover, they begin to believe that it's obtainable and worth fighting for."

Her eyes began to glisten. "Do you really see me that way?"

Jed smiled admiringly at her. "You are truly the finest person I know."

A chill swept through her at such a compliment, because it came from the person whose opinion of her mattered most. "I hope that whoever I marry someday will see me the way you do, Jed."

Jed stood abruptly and turned away from her to hide his emotions. "Don't marry anyone who doesn't, Hannah. Never settle for someone who'll simply make a pet of you." He turned to her. "Before you get swept away by love, come to me. I'll judge if you've chosen the right man."

She brushed the grass from her skirt. "I doubt I'll ever find such a man, Jed, because you are already my dearest love. Who will I ever find to measure up to you?" She laughed and placed a kiss on his cheek. "After all, you just saved my life. How can anyone ever surpass that?"

As they laughed together, the two never heard the footfalls of the man whose long silver hair now marked the years he'd waited and watched. "Kiizis Ikwe and Pearson," he whispered, linking his fingers before him. "Peace come." With a hopeful heart, Charles Kittamaqund watched them walk slowly back to their mounts.

* * *

"Will you recite the Beatitudes to me, Selma?" Hannah pleaded a few days after the barbeque. "I love to hear all the 'blesseds.' You sound as if you were there listening to Jesus when He taught them."

"That's 'zactly how it is when I hear words from the Good Book. It's like I'm lis'nin' to Jesus. You do the same. Some people read it like a newspaper, but you hear His words. That's why your faith is so strong. More'n that, you listen to what He promises and you believe. Why ain't you goin' to Sunday school now?"

"Well, the reverend said doubt is of the devil, but when I told him I didn't doubt Jesus' words, just the reverend's interpretation of them, he threatened to hit me. But when he calmed himself he had me write 'Doubt is of the devil' a hundred times. I asked Father if I could study at home now. I read and understand better than anyone else in my school, so I can manage the texts, and I can always ask Jed to help me."

"Jed." Selma almost spat out the name. "You spent the entire day with that young man last Saturday, tyin' up his 'tentions. He'll soon need to start courtin', Hannah. He can't spend all his time worryin' over you. You're old enough to stand on your own two feet now."

"It's not like that, Selma. We can hardly find enough time to cover all the subjects we want to discuss. I know he'll marry someday, but he said managing the Willows consumes all his time right now. And when his situation changes, he promises to tell me."

"Well, I just don't want you gettin' any strange notions in your head. That's all I'm sayin'. You've been hurt enough in this life. I don't want a Pearson to be the cause of more, and you best stay clear of your mama today. She had more of her nightmares last night. She was runnin' around the house hollerin' in the wee hours. She finished off the medicine the doctor left, and your father spent hours holdin' her so she wouldn't run outside and do herself in."

Hannah sighed. "Her condition is getting worse. I wish there was something I could do to help her, but the very sight of me stirs her up. And yet she bought me Druid. It's the strangest thing, Selma. Lately she's been aiming for anyone in her sights. Poor Myrna brought her a cup of tea, and Mother took a single sip of it and flung it at her, spinning off in a tirade because Myrna failed to sweeten it to her liking. The poor dear was so browbeaten by the experience that she spent an hour on her knees begging God to forgive her for being a thoughtless and selfish daughter. And, oh! I forgot to tell you—Uncle Tobias brought along that lieutenant, Dudley Snowden, to dinner again. Now Beatrice thinks she's in love with him. How can she love him, Selma? He's twelve years her senior and he reminds me of an old opossum with his pointy nose and small black eyes."

Hannah shivered comically. "I can't imagine her being the wife of a soldier. I think she is simply anxious to get out of the house and away from Mama's tirades. I wouldn't be surprised if Myrna agreed to the first offer she gets as well."

Selma shook her head. "I ain't always had charity for those sisters of yours, but the tide's done turned in this house, and ain't no one spared from your mama's wrath no more. That bein' the case, I s'pose you're lucky to have your letters from Mr. Pearson to cheer you after all."

"You do like Jed, don't you, Selma? Mama seems to hate him and I can't understand it."

"That hate goes way back, child, to the days when I worked for the good Reverend McClintock."

"Mama's father? But he died before I was born. How could Jed be involved?"

"'Twere his grandfather. He done somethin' powerful bad to your mama's family. It's what done set your mama off and her mama afore her."

"But . . ."

Selma shook her head firmly. "I done said all I'm sayin'. Most of the Pearsons just ain't respectable folk is all. They go their own way. Now Jed's different than the rest, but even so, there's nothin' but trouble ahead if you mix with the Pearsons. But, seein' as you have so little happiness, I can understand if you feel to follow where kindness is offered."

"And you, Selma. I would die without you."

Selma sighed. "I prob'ly die without you too, child. Now, let's talk 'bout the Lord again. That's somethin' I can do without worryin' 'bout other ears."

CHAPTER 6

The Willows
June 1810

After his visit to the Stansburys, Jed opted to sail from the Baltimore harbor down the Chesapeake, up the Patuxent, and home, in order to assess the effects of the trade blockade evident along the river. Hogsheads of tobacco sat unclaimed on docks, and ships that would normally be transporting inventory up and down the river sat idle and in disrepair. Fortunately, despite the overgrown, untilled fields and the shabby outward condition of the house and outbuildings, things at the Willows were no worse than he had expected. The large, white frame house built by his grandfather had once been the grandest of such homes, and had sat proudly amid a smattering of log cabins and roughly constructed shanties, but many seasons had passed since paint had last touched its façade, and some of its glory had faded. The few accoutrements left on its exterior—the wide-paneled shutters, the hand-carved cornices over the doors and windows, and the cupola and weathervane on the roof—hung slightly off square and were in sore need of the caress of a paintbrush.

Because the European markets were essentially closed, only a few acres of Pearson land were being tilled for tobacco. Fortunately, since the northern buyers preferred the mild leaves produced by the sweet Willows soil, some revenue was generated there when little could be sold by their neighbors.

Jed realized that diversifying was his only hope of keeping the estate solvent. He needed to shift some attention away from tobacco and into the growing of grains, eventually moving more heavily into livestock. He knew the senators and congressmen were fond of the horse races in Georgetown, some thirty miles away, and he considered dallying in the breeding of good horses—an expensive area in which he had little or no training. Regardless of how he chose to diversify, one thing seemed inevitable: expansion would require more laborers, and that meant the unpleasant task of buying additional slaves.

Of the thirteen slaves currently living at the Willows, only Bitty and her older brother Jack had lived their entire lives on the estate. The other Pearson heirs had sold every other slave that wasn't specifically deeded to Jed's father, who'd gifted Jack and Bitty to Jed on his fifteenth birthday. As repugnant as the idea sounded, Jed convinced himself that doing so kept Bitty and Jack together and, more importantly, kept them on the Willows. Even more repugnant to him was the fact that he had personally purchased the estate's other eleven slaves at a slave auction the summer of his sixteenth year when a neighboring farm went bankrupt. Jed had hated the wretched errand, but his former farm manager had convinced the teenaged, novice landowner that buying more slaves was good business. Wanting to appear wise, he had agreed to make the purchase.

He had vowed only to purchase slaves from other farms and to keep families intact where possible. Then the United States sealed his decision legally by following the European precedent of banning trans-Atlantic slave trade. He had always appeased his guilt by telling himself that he had not directly lent support to actual slavers, due to his decision, but that defense was about to end. The United States' decision created a black market for ship owners who found the slave trade lucrative enough to risk imprisonment. Some American ship owners continued to unlawfully transport slaves to various ports, while Spanish, Venezuelan, and Portuguese ships were still legally able to move slaves through the Caribbean and South American ports of their countries. Jed had heard rumors that such a ship departed out of Brazil for the coast of Florida, where the slaves were then being transported northward through the States by wagons and the riverways. He could no longer be sure that he wasn't contributing to new markets.

Even though life on the Willows was gentler and more humane than life on any other estate he knew, there was a sweeter life yet—a life of freedom. And though he had the power to grant such a life for his own slaves, something made him unwilling to offer it, and for that he was ashamed.

That truth tore at him as he prepared to head back to the woodsy town of Calverton, where the rumored slave transport was expected. He was glad Hannah was far away, but he knew eventually the whole sordid affair would come up. She would be disappointed in him, perhaps even disgusted by his choices, but he would find a way to regain her faith in him. All he knew was that the future of everyone he cared about depended on the rebuilding of the Willows, and he felt instinctively that it had to begin today.

He rose long before his parents or Frannie began to stir, but he could hear Bitty in the kitchen mixing eggs and batter for hotcakes. As he smelled the woodsmoke, his stomach began to growl with pleasure. He stood in the doorway and glanced at the woman who was as much a mother to him as his own, despite that fact that she was only twelve years his senior. She was dressed in a blue muslin dress, covered from neck to ankles by a white pinafore apron that tied in back. Her head was wrapped in matching blue fabric, completely concealing her hair except for a tuft of cottony black that peeked out in front. She was a lovely sight, more precious than beautiful, with large, round eyes that could stare a lie right out of an impish boy, and a thick, upturned smile ready to restore security in a moment. She darted about like a tiny ballerina, as if meal preparations were being scored on grace.

"Morning, Bitty," Jed called out cheerfully. "I barely got to see you last night."

She smiled and crossed the room in his direction, simultaneously wiping her hands on her apron and sizing him up as she made her way. "One of Mercy's little ones was stung real bad, so I made some poultices to take the fire out of her hand. But now, don't you look just fine," she commented favorably as she hugged his waist. "A little peaked," she added as she reached up to pat his cheek, "but Bitty'll take care of that soon enough."

"I didn't think I was hungry when I woke up, but I believe I've changed my mind. I have errands to run in Calverton this morning though . . ." His voice trailed off and he turned away, but Bitty followed after him, pulling a dangling thread from his white button-up shirt.

"You're goin' to lose that button if I don't tighten it up. It seems the first few weeks you come home all I do is mend your clothes. Don't you have tailors in that big city of yours?"

"I don't even notice a loose button or a tear until someone points it out to me."

She shook her head and picked up her bowl. "Take it off whilst I put this batter on the griddle. My sewin' box is there on the shelf." She pointed abruptly and strode out the door.

Despite her caring tone, Jed knew she was upset and he knew why. He had asked Markus and Jack to accompany him on the day's errand. Jack had likely told Bitty. As much as she loved him, and as close as they were, it was asking too much of her to expect that she would be agreeable to his purchase of more slaves. He understood that—as much as it pained him to disappoint her, he understood.

Minutes later she came in with a plate filled with hotcakes, ham and eggs, and a little dish of strawberries and cream. "Do you want to eat this in the dinin' room?" she asked despite the fact that she had already put the plate down and set the silverware in place.

"No, no," he chuckled to himself. "I'd rather eat right here."

"That's what I expected you'd say," she answered, barely looking at him. "Now give me the shirt and get to eatin'. I know you plan to leave soon." She crossed the room and called out the door until an adolescent girl appeared. "Jenny, keep makin' those hotcakes and eggs and don't let the ham burn, hear?"

Jed handed her his shirt and sat nude to the waist, completely unashamed as she scrutinized his torso and glanced at the birthmark. "You're filling out nicely, not all gangly like your father was said to have been at your age. No, you're more like your grandfather. He was broad shouldered and taut 'til the day he died." She smiled at the memory. "When I was a child, I'd look up at him, all tall and hand-some with a head of thick, wavy hair and muscles bulgin' as big as any of the workers . . . but dressed real nice . . . and I thought he must have been as close to what God looks like as a man can be." She bit the thread off and sat back.

Jed tapped his fork on the table, drawing Bitty's attention. "And I remind you of him . . . hmm," he paused playfully. "Are you saying that you see God in me, Bitty?"

Bitty fought the smile tugging at her lips and raised one eyebrow, preparing for her retort. "Some say that the devil was a handsome man too. You, child, are definitely a little devil." She tossed him his shirt and left to check on Jenny.

Markus O'Malley passed through the doorway with a full plate and a smile. He was a short, thick, fair-skinned young man from Virginia, a few years older than Jed, with a Southern drawl tinged with the Irish lilt. His father had been a successful tobacco buyer with a keen eye for quality which he'd passed along to his only son. Three summers before, Markus's father had died from a British bullet when a few of Her Majesty's less noble sailors broke ranks and went a-pirating.

Markus had been a buyer's apprentice when Jed first met him two summers previous, coming off a flatboat to check the Willows' crop. The result seemed heaven-sent. Markus knew tobacco instinctively, and Jed offered him a home and a future. Like Jed, Markus had accepted the necessity of the institution of slavery, though neither relished it. Except for his knowledge of tobacco, this gentle bear was likely the least qualified person to be a foreman, but the two had become instant friends with a similar vision for the Willows.

Markus had already wolfed down most of his food when Bitty's brother, Jack, ambled in. Jack was Bitty's alter ego, slow where she was fast, tall and round where she was short and slim. His manner was mellow, whereas Bitty was feisty with a constant checklist of chores to be accomplished. Nonetheless, each was fiercely loyal to Jed, and he, in turn, trusted them both with all that he had.

"So," Markus hedged as he twisted his hat, "I don't suppose Frannie is comin' with us."

"No," chuckled Jed as he winked at Jack, drawing a crimson blush from Markus. "Did you eat, Jack?" Jed asked.

"First thing," Jack replied in the lazy drawl of fieldspeak. "The wagons are hitched."

"Are the new cottages ready?"

"They are, Jed," chimed in Markus, "but Bitty had us move Mercy and her family into one and Sam and the other single fellas into the other, freeing up two of the older ones."

Jed dropped his head and shook it humorously, then looked up. "Why?"

"Bitty said so," explained Jack, his hands raised for emphasis. "She said Mama told her that when they first came over from Africa they didn't want beds and the like. So Bitty and the girls swept the dirt as soft as cotton and set a layer of straw and mats along the walls in ways more suitable for Africans. There's loaves of fresh bread and bowls of rice and berries waitin', and Royal made two new buckets so they can draw their own water from the well."

Jed nodded. "I'll be sure to thank Bitty."

The morning sun was already bright and hot for early June, and Jed squinted as he exited the back of the house and approached the wagons. As Jack and Markus filled the bench in the first wagon, Jed headed for the second, but he found Bitty already seated on top.

"Bitty?" Jed exclaimed.

"I've got errands to run too," she replied, facing the front of the wagon.

"B . . . Bitty, this isn't a good day for you to come to Calverton."

"I know you're goin' to buy Africans. My goin' or stayin' won't change that, but my sister Priscilla is shoppin' for White Oak today, so it'll give me a little time to spend with her."

As usual, the slave network was an efficient communications system. Jed admitted that much of what he knew about the neighboring estates was acquired through the snippets of gossip passed from slave to slave over fences, or as wagons passed along the roads, or when errands were run from property to property. He also knew a few things that Bitty had failed to share with him.

"Thank you for making the preparations for the new arrivals."

Bitty kept her folded hands in her lap and nodded slightly. "You can't do things the same for the Africans. They'll be frightened. They'll need time."

Jed had never felt so distant from her.

"I know you're upset with me, Bitty, and I'm sorry. We need more help. You know that."

She grunted and turned to stare off through the trees to the moving water to her left.

"Bitty, I wouldn't do this if there was any other way," Jed said mournfully. "What would you prefer I do?"

"You're breakin' your promise." Her disappointment was evident. "You vowed you'd never buy from a slaver. I took a lot of pride in knowin' that your name didn't appear on any slaver's receipt." She turned to face him. "I took a lot of pride in thinkin' it never would."

Jed grunted in frustration and slapped the reins down hard on the horses, urging them to hurry along and make his misery as brief as possible.

The wooded river road soon opened to the clearing where the town of Calverton sat. Bitty caught sight of her sister straightaway and motioned for Jed to stop so she could jump down and dash past the White Oak entourage to join her. After Jack and Markus secured the teams, the Willows' men headed in the direction of the dock where the "secret" auction would be held, first passing the mill and the White Oak wagons. Jack noticed Abel, Stewart Stringham's tall, brawny miller, loading lumber and supplies into a wagon. Each time the miller bent to lift another load, his shirt shifted, revealing the long, ridged scars of whip-torn flesh—a testament to the treatment of slaves on Stringham's estate. Jack sauntered over to him and placed a friendly hand on his back.

"Mornin', Abel. I'm glad I'm not one of your horses," Jack joked. "That's quite a load, even for four good pullers."

Abel glanced warily at the two white men behind Jack, arched an eyebrow in silent agreement, and kept loading the order.

Markus's curiosity was piqued and he asked, "So, what's Mr. Stringham building now?"

Abel dipped his head in deference to the white man and answered cautiously, "This here order is for the younger Master Stringham, sir. For his new house." He bent to pick up another burlap sack of cement and tossed it into the wagon bed with ease.

Now Jed's curiosity was raised. "I'm sorry . . . Abel, is it? Abel, did you say that the *younger* Mr. Stringham is building a house?"

"Yes'm," the slave answered tentatively as he bent for another sack. As he came up, Markus noted the increasingly wary look in his eyes and tried using humor to put the larger, more defensive man at ease. "What happened, Abel? Did Mr. Stringham throw his son out?"

Markus laughed heartily, but Abel's stony face never broke for even the tiniest smile. He stood motionless, suspending a fifty-pound sack of cement in his arms while his eyes darted warily back and forth from man to man, studying their faces.

Suddenly Jack realized how thoughtless his behavior and that of his companions had been. Thirty years of life on the Willows had left him naive about the life most slaves endured. He frequently forgot that most Negroes shared little conversation with whites beyond the passing of instructions, or the casual banter of strangers, whose attentions were usually intended as sport. Jack smiled warmly and now placed a comforting hand on Abel's tense, bulging arm.

"He's just joshin' with you, Abel. He's all right. Don't worry," Jack offered, but the big man remained tense and immovable.

Like a hummingbird in flight, Bitty darted over, placing herself between Abel and the other men. She rose to her scant five feet and spoke calmly to Abel, then turned so her fiery eyes bored into the Willows' men, shaming them for their thoughtlessness. "Don't you pay them any mind, Abel. They forget that some men work for their living. Shame on them for that."

She shot them a final glance that made them want to disappear. Then her healing hands gently went to the front of Abel's sweat-soaked shirt with a calming power that was visible and immediate. Jed retreated from the scene contritely, with Jack and Markus close behind.

Bitty lingered protectively near Abel for a few minutes until the pair began drawing attention and Abel became nervous. She read his face and knew their brief encounter had ended. As she walked away, she felt Abel's eyes on her and warmed at the thought. But at the same time, across the street she noticed another pair of eyes scrutinizing her until the normally self-assured woman shivered. The young mulatto man was posed against a porch column, obviously aware of how his dark blue ferryman's uniform hugged the lines of his muscled body. His face was exquisite and his complexion as fair as milk-laced coffee—the physical gift that qualified mulattoes and other light-skinned Negroes for the special privileges scorned by those of a darker tone. Some mulattoes saw their lighter color as an additional burden that separated them from their darker brothers and sisters, but others flaunted their good fortune. There were none such at the Willows, but Bitty knew immediately what manner of man this character was.

He whistled and catcalled to her, and though Bitty ignored his advances, she feared his persistence would set Abel off and unleash trouble aplenty. She glanced at Abel and nodded her intentions before she crossed the street to a shop near the man's position. He immediately approached her with a snigger of lust just before she spun on her heel and shot him a look of repulsion. "Why are you doin' this?" she spat.

"Doing what?" he teased in a voice like none Bitty had ever heard before.

"Usin' me to taunt that man." She nodded in Abel's direction.

"I capitalize on my opportunities. You'd do well to do the same. One such opportunity is coming your way right now," he taunted, inching closer. "Besides, that man means nothing to me," he stated in perfect, calculated diction. "Neither must he to you, or you wouldn't be here, now, would you?"

"I crossed over to ask you politely to leave me alone."

"Really?" He leaned closer. "You could have just ignored me . . . but here you are." He allowed his final three words to carry an overt insinuation also reflected in his stare.

No one had ever pressed himself upon Bitty before, or made her tremble in fear. She had heard horror stories of men who treated women like concubines, but she'd had no such experience. This man made her wish she weren't a woman.

As she nervously turned to make her exit, she cursed herself for weakly letting the scoundrel intimidate her. She thought about the impetuous and confident Frannie. *I bet no man could back her down . . .* But Frannie was different—she was a princess who commanded the power of the Pearson name and fortune. She had Jed to guard her and, if need be, to fight for her. Jed loved Frannie . . . *but Jed loves me too, differently to be sure, but deeply and truly.* She became emboldened and faced the man again.

"You're right. Comin' over here was my mistake. You see, I thought I might find a gentleman in that mix o' colors you're obviously so proud of, but I was wrong. Good day, sir."

His anger flared and he caught her arm and held it fast. "The name is Duprée—Sebastian Duprée—and you, Bitty, are a lucky woman. I like you, and there's much I can offer you."

"You don't know me!" Bitty shot back as she tried to free her arm.

"Oh, yes . . . yes I do," he insisted in a voice that matched his leer. "I am a free man, Bitty, the son of a plantation owner and his slave woman. A man like me, not truly Negro or white, can still feel imprisoned. Mister McRainey and I have recently bought the ferry

Elizabeth, and I'm looking for a suitable . . . traveling companion. You, madam, have caught my eye."

Bitty stood dumbfounded by the man's arrogance.

"I've watched you come into town the last few weeks or so to shop, strutting around town as if you were free and white," he snickered. "Some men don't fancy uppity women, but I like a lady who knows who she is. And you, madam, are a woman who knows she is someone special." He tightened the hold on her arm, and Bitty drew her head away from him. As she did, he touched his index finger to the hollow of her throat and began to stroke her neck upward.

Prepared to slap Duprée, Bitty caught a glimpse of an increasingly anxious Abel and refrained. She gritted her teeth and played her trump card, snarling under her breath, "Do you know whose household I represent? I run the home of Mr. Jonathan Edward Pearson III, one of the most powerful men in the county. If you ever speak to me or harass me again, you'll have him to answer to, and I promise he will see that you and your ferry are banished from here."

The man never flinched. Instead, he let out a cackle that made the hair stand up on the back of her neck. "Oh, I've been studying Mr. Pearson and the Willows for quite some time. In fact, I know that most nights you sleep in the manor house, but you also have a little cottage with blue and white curtains in the windows." He savored the fear his words elicited in the woman's eyes as his voice dropped to a low growl. "Be careful who you threaten. You may run the Willows' household, but at the end of the day you're just property . . . just like him." He pointed in Abel's direction. "You have no idea who you're dealing with. You do not want to make an enemy of me." He cast a long sneer at Abel, then straightened slowly before turning and walking away.

Bitty shook so hard that she dared not try to cross the street, so she turned back toward the store window and stared blankly at the displays of hardware and household goods while struggling to calm herself. *Breathe, Bitty . . . breathe.* Abel was now at the edge of the street, standing on the balls of his feet like a cat ready to pounce. Tears filled her eyes as she cursed herself for her pride. Who was she to toss Jed's name about, as if she had the authority to command him? As Duprée had said, Jed was her master and she was his property.

Even as she thought the words, she knew the legalities didn't make it so. She loved Jed like a son and knew he loved her as well. At the end of the day, that was what mattered. Suddenly, she felt physically ill with worry that her insolence had also made Jed a target of Sebastian Duprée's wrath. Then she noticed Duprée's image reflected in the glass, standing behind her, staring Abel down, and she worried that Abel too would pay a price for her audacity.

* * *

"It's hard to see a man like Abel cowering like that," said Jed incredulously as the men made their way back to the dock.

"Did you see the scars on his back? Some men treat their oxen better," Markus growled.

As they walked on, Jed couldn't dismiss the look in Abel's eyes. Before the men even arrived at the docks he heard the crack of the whip, and a vaguely familiar nausea cramped his stomach. Plodding on mechanically, he considered Markus's words as Abel's face continued to haunt him. The crowd of gawkers far exceeded the few buyers present, and as the young Pearson heir drew closer, they parted like the Red Sea, giving Jed a view of the swaggering Portuguese slaver. He circled around the platform distributing handbills describing his remaining slave "inventory," while a terrified black man no older than Jed stood on the platform wearing a more exaggerated version of the look in Abel's eyes. And then Jed caught sight of the rail-thin form of Stewart Stringham, with his son, Frederick, standing close by.

Stewart Stringham ran a hand through his perfectly groomed gray hair. He wore black pants with a black vest over a white dress shirt, looking imperial among the simply clad farmers and townsfolk. He held a black derby in his hand with which he regularly fanned his angular face and which he now raised condescendingly in Jed's direction. Reedy-looking Frederick, also dressed as one manor-born, followed his father's gaze until he saw the casually attired Jed. As he saw his old friend, his arm came up in an enthusiastic wave, drawing immediate censure from his father in the form of a sharp jab to the side and an audible reproof. Publicly humiliated, and now the subject of the crowd's snickers, Frederick quickly withdrew his greeting and cowered penitently behind Stewart, with eyes that also reminded Jed of Abel.

The slaver stepped upon the platform while two of his men shoved the shackled African man forward. He was barely more than a skeleton, his ribs showing through his malnourished flesh. A soiled cloth was haphazardly wrapped around his loins, from which thin legs trembled on bare, shackled feet. His elbows were pressed behind him and locked in the painful position by a bar shoved through the gap formed between back and elbows. The tortuous arrangement was further aggravated by shackles that bit into the flesh of his bony wrists and ankles, and by a chain that linked shackle to shackle.

When the slaver called out an opening bid of one hundred dollars, Stewart Stringham brought his derby up. The slaver noted the bid and raised the amount, but no second bid sounded.

"Stir heem up!" the slaver growled. His men responded with a cruel blow to the captive's elbow, eliciting a pained scream and rapid recoil, both of which thrilled the brutal crowd.

Jed wanted to scream out a ridiculous bid to end the auction and send all the slaves to the Willows where he could offer them a peaceful home with a reasonable workload. Then the old argument returned to his mind. Each shipload of new slaves sold encouraged the enslavement of others. In utter discouragement, Jed turned his back on the whole affair and strode away.

"I feel soiled," he groaned to his companions, who walked sullenly behind him. Adding to his consternation, the face waiting for him at the head of the crowd was Bitty's. But he no longer saw disappointment there. The worry and love that had always characterized her affection for him had fully returned.

Jed slumped against the wagon as his chin fell to his chest. "I'm truly sorry, Bitty. I don't know what to do. I am at odds with myself. I need the workers but . . . I cannot be a party to this."

She touched his cheek. "It's because you've got more than a good head for business. You have a good heart. Nature marked you to remind you." Bitty searched the face of the boy she had guided into manhood as she prayed the silent prayer that entered her mind every day.

Jed looked into her eyes, knowing the words she hungered to hear. "I can't, Bitty," he sighed. "Not now. I would lose the Willows, and it would be suicide for you as well. How would you live? I hope there'll come a day when I can afford to free everyone properly and ensure their future as well as my own, but that day is not here, not yet."

Bitty's eyes glistened. The answer stung, but it was not unexpected. It was the sincerity of his explanation that inspired her tears. Her immediate worries had not been erased, but someday he would do the right thing. For now her mind raced to search for another remedy to the looming threat of Sebastian Duprée.

"I am sorry about making Abel uncomfortable." Jed shook his head in wonder. "What sword does Stewart Stringham wield over that giant's head to make him cower so?"

"He has a family. His wife died bearin' their fourth. He's been alone now three years. His father was Mr. Stringham's miller until an accident left him broken and weak. Stringham threatens to sell his family off, so Abel bows and crawls to protect his kin."

Jed placed a hand on her shoulder and smiled. "Now I understand."

"What do you understand?" Bitty asked defensively, reading more into his tone.

"I heard you were sweet on Abel. How did that come about?"

Bitty blushed and cast her eyes to the ground. "Small ways mostly. We started out just talkin' over the fence when we'd see one another. I think Priscilla egged him on after that, 'cause once he noticed that I do the marketin' on Tuesday mornings in Calverton, he started findin' reasons to be workin' near the road. That went on for a while, then he started givin' me little things. He whittled me a new thimble, and a hair comb . . . and when Missus Stringham tossed out the satin cuttings from one of her new dresses, Abel saved them for me . . . had his mother, Sarah, patch them together into a pin cushion for my sewin' . . ." She touched her flushed cheek. "Probably all sounds silly to you since I don't want for anythin'."

"No . . . no it doesn't at all," Jed offered warmly. "It sounds lovely. And I'm guessing Abel has been treated to some of your good cooking?" he teased.

"Can't fault the man for likin' my cherry pie." Bitty smiled and her eyes misted.

Jed pulled her close, whispering, "White Oak has claim on people we each care about."

Duprée's threat echoed through Bitty's troubled mind, sending a cold chill that made her shiver. *And now I've gone and put the two men I love most in harm's way.*

"Did you know that Frederick is building a house of his own? I'm afraid he will ask for Frannie's hand." Jed's voice betrayed his fatigue. "I don't feel good about her moving to White Oak, Bitty . . . Bitty? Did you hear me?"

Bitty was lost in her own worries. She considered telling Jed about Duprée, but she knew he would never understand the threat the mulatto posed. Abel understood, but at White Oak he was powerless to protect anyone. The one who believed was without means and beyond her reach, while the one with the means would dismiss her concerns. How could she protect both the men she loved? Suddenly, the glorious solution flashed through her mind.

"Jed, do you really want to buy your new workers from standin' farms?"

"Of course, Bitty. Do you know someone who has workers to sell?"

Her eyebrows arched as if she knew a secret. "Every man will sell at the right price . . ."

Jed looked skeptically at the tiny woman, unable to follow her train of thought.

"You mentioned that you wanted to start growin' grains to have a broader crop, right? Well, I know where you could come by a miller for the right price."

Now Jed understood. He grimaced and replied sympathetically, "Stringham would never let Abel go, Bitty."

"But for the right price . . ." She smiled, almost singing her point. "Just think about it. He's biddin' on new workers. We already know he's sold slaves before because he couldn't meet his debts. Imagine if he had a chance to make enough money to replace Abel and his old parents and babies—two for one—with adult workers. Don't you think he'd jump at the chance?"

Jed raised a worried eyebrow. "Do you know what that would cost me, Bitty?"

"You'd be savin' a family . . . and maybe I'd finally have a family of my own."

"Oh, Bitty . . . I want that for you, but I'm not sure I can raise that much cash on the spot."

"I've never asked you for a thing, and I'll never ask you for anything else, Jed."

Her plea tore at his loyalties. He could not give her freedom, but he could give her this. "You know we'd be sending those Africans to White Oak and lining the slavers' pockets."

Bitty's head dipped, but when her eyes met Jed's again, her resolve was set. "I know. I've already thought about that. That's how terribly important this is to me."

Jed remained silent, staring into her eyes until he understood what it had cost her to make such a request. "And what of Priscilla, Bitty? You would take Abel and his family and leave your sister and her family at White Oak?"

Shame clouded Bitty's face, and she reminded herself that Priscilla was the head maid and her husband was the Stringhams' butler. "They're safe, leastwise safer than Abel."

Jed could only imagine the agony of her situation, choosing between family and love. He acknowledged her choice with a nod that was imperceptible at first, but which grew stronger as he confirmed her decision. "If you're certain, Bitty, then Markus and I will try to make the deal."

CHAPTER 7

Calverton, Maryland
June 1810

The message invited Stewart Stringham to meet Jed at the Cattail Inn at four o'clock, shortly after Stringham would be finished buying new slaves. By three thirty, Jed and Markus had secured the back table, but it was a quarter after four on the Williamsburg clock before the Stringhams showed. Stewart opened the door and stooped, exaggerating the effort required to fit his tall, thin frame through the hundred-year-old doorway. Jed rolled his eyes at the man's theatrics, finding it particularly amusing that he, who was at least two inches taller and thirty pounds heavier, had managed to enter with far less effort.

"You requested to see me?" Stewart asked as Frederick, still somewhat sheepish since his father's earlier rebuke, offered Jed a subdued smile.

Jed rose, indicating the two empty chairs. "Please, Stewart . . . Frederick . . . sit and have a drink before we begin. I'm buying."

"I'd like to know the purpose of our business before I decide whether or not I'll stay."

Jed tensed and nodded. "Very well. I'd like to offer a bid on your miller and his family."

Stewart raised an eyebrow and sighed as he and Frederick sat. His face contorted as he muttered calculations. Most men behaving thus would have appeared foolish, but not Stewart Stringham. Dressed in his finery, downing and refilling his glass at Jed's expense, he exuded an authoritative air. He knew he fascinated the locals sitting nearby, inciting him to even higher drama. Frederick, however, sat mute, his eyes glued to the table.

Jed pitied his old friend, who, when away from his father, was never at a loss for humorous anecdotes or poetic recitations. He realized he knew a side of Frederick that the young man's father never would. It dawned on him that Frannie could probably say even more of the same, that Frederick was perhaps a giant of a man in her presence compared to the fellow that even Jed knew, making it even more pitiful to see the shriveled person to which his father had reduced him.

Jed's frustrations about his own father's lack of involvement in the Willows paled in the face of Frederick's situation, where his father maintained a python-like grip on the family estate. He could understand why Frederick had asked to help Jed build fences at the Willows and work with the livestock, even though Frederick had herds of animals and hundreds of acres of his own land to work. Stewart Stringham had likely never allowed his heir to do a day's worth of manual labor or see a decision through. He was clearly equally unwilling to involve Frederick in today's negotiations.

Jed shifted in his seat. "I'd appreciate hearing a price, Mr. Stringham."

Stringham poured another shot of whiskey and sat back, dramatically crossing one thin leg over the other while laying his hands on his knee. He punctuated the clearing of his throat by raising a hand to massage his neck.

Jed noticed with annoyance that several of the inn's other customers were riveted. He began rapping his fingers rhythmically on the table, making clear his irritation at the delay. At long last Stringham leaned in, wrinkled his brow, and opened the dialogue. "I have some figures to present to you, but first I would like to know why having Abel is so important to you."

Jed sat stoically. "It's very simple. I need a miller. You have a miller and an apprentice."

"Then why don't you take my apprentice? You see, Abel is far more to me than simply my miller. Surrendering him would require a great sacrifice. One I doubt I could consider."

Jed heard the word *doubt*. "I need a stableman and another maid in the house. I think his parents will also make fine additions to the Willows, and I prefer to keep families intact."

Stringham raised his eyebrows and smiled deliciously, emphasizing his words. "Losing Jerome and Sarah would be a hardship as well, not to mention the dear children . . ."

Jed's patience was wearing thin. He knew that, as in poker, the more rounds they went the higher the stakes would become. "A price . . . please, Mr. Stringham."

The onlookers in the room carried their mugs of ale and drew nearer to witness the scene, knowing the outcome would make good telling for days to come. Less scrupulous customers began placing wagers on what the agreed price would be.

Stewart Stringham knew that money was not the most important issue at stake. Reputation and respect were, and a public negotiation such as this would send ripples up and down the Patuxent River, where standing and status spoke louder than wealth. Luck could bring even an idiot wealth, but respect brought power—power that translated into political and social clout. The Pearsons had inherited some of each from their predecessor, but Stewart Stringham had used their past complacency to his advantage while the locals noted the Willows' decline. Many now expected Jed to become the preeminent influence in the region, a distasteful assumption Stewart Stringham wanted to end by besting the young heir today. He knew Jed assumed the asking price would be dear. How dear would be determined by how long Stewart could prolong the game, and he did not believe he had yet played his best hand.

"If it is a maid and stableman you need, then Abel's apprentice and *his* parents will work nicely for you at a more reasonable price."

Jed no longer bothered to conceal his irritation. He leaned forward and spoke with a brusque and low growl. "A price, Mr. Stringham. For Abel . . . his parents . . . and his children."

Stringham cracked his neck to hide his intimidation, then stared Jed down for what seemed like minutes before responding. Then he smirked and finally stated the scandalous figure.

"Three thousand dollars."

Frederick closed his eyes and turned his head to hide his shock, while the crowd retreated amidst gasps of awe. Jed's reaction was physical and immediate. His face flushed red as he bolted out of his seat. "You must be mad!" he shouted before breaking into an incredulous laugh. "Such a price would be a fair amount for ten able-bodied, fully grown men."

Stringham leaned back in his chair. "It's yours to refuse, but I won't accept less than two thousand dollars for Abel, and one hundred fifty dollars each for his parents and children."

"Two thousand dollars for one man? You know there has never been such a price paid! Abel's parents are nearly crippled and his four children are under eight years old!"

Stewart folded his hands neatly in his lap and smiled confidently. "As you know, the domestic market is thin and the risk of buying elsewhere is high. As I said, it's yours to refuse."

While Jed seethed, Markus waited calmly and did some calculations of his own. "That adds up to only two thousand nine hundred, I believe."

Stringham smiled admiringly. "Wardrobe allowance," he replied. "The inconvenience required to dress seven new bodies is well worth that, I believe."

Bitty or no Bitty, Jed refused to be hornswoggled. As he tensed to rise from his chair, Markus nudged him, encouraging him to stall a moment.

"Mr. Stringham's earlier point does have merit," began the Irishman with a twinkle in his eye. "We haven't even begun to build the mill yet, nor have we planted a single acre of grain. We'll have plenty of time to train the apprentice and muscle him up before we're ready to mill. And one set of parents will serve just as well as another in the stables and kitchen."

Jed knew Markus was a notorious gambler with a reputation for winning a hand of cards with nothing but a wink and a frown. "Good point," he agreed, then turned to Stringham, who had not yet flinched. "Name your price for the apprentice and his parents."

Stringham sat mute, meeting Jed's stare, knowing full well that the pair was bluffing, and knowing equally well that they were at a standoff where the next man who spoke would lose the advantage. Seconds passed while the eyes of the curious assembly of locals began to bear down again on the four men. Frederick could no longer endure the scrutiny, and he began blinking rapidly, looking for some point in the room where he could escape the crush of eyes. He began wringing his hands under the table, desperate for one of the principles to break the standoff. Finally, when his frazzled nerves could bear it no longer, he involuntarily tapped on the table, naively breaking the barrier of stillness. He followed with a timorous question. "What do you think, Father?" Frederick's intrusion fell upon his own head like an ax.

Stewart shot Frederick a murderous look, and his son's pathetic reaction caused the crowd to titter. Jed nearly agreed to Stewart's original demand just to spare his friend, but Markus eyed his employer, signaling him to withhold. Markus knew the bargaining power had somehow shifted, and the foreman's delight was apparent. "We'll entertain your offer on the apprentice's family now," he declared glibly.

Defeated and humiliated, Stewart Stringham knew he had lost the contest of wills, knew he would have to settle for less than the hefty profit he had nearly commanded. "Let's be honest with ourselves, gentlemen," he uttered through tightly pursed lips. "You want Abel, and I want fair compensation. What is your offer?"

Jed looked at Frederick's diminished form, rose from his seat, and smacked his hand upon the table with a loud thud. "Let's be done with this. We offer two thousand five hundred for the family. I want no further dickering over the worth of a man." Jed stood and extended his hand to seal the contract. "That's my offer, and as you have so eloquently said, it's yours to refuse."

Stewart shook his hand, clearly pleased to have received an amount far above what he expected after his son's humiliating outburst.

* * *

The *Elizabeth* had returned from a run across the river when the jubilant crowd began pouring out of the Cattail Inn, anxious to recount the tale of the negotiation. Sebastian Duprée was a more-than-willing audience.

"What happened in there?" he asked an older man with swill on his breath.

"Stringham and Pearson just bargained on a slave sale. Highest price ever paid."

Duprée raised a brow. "Who was selling and who was buying?"

"Pearson bought Stringham's miller and his family. Paid twenty-five hundred dollars!"

"Is that a fact?" Duprée muttered under his breath as he looked to where the slave had been standing earlier. He was still there, tending to the horses, apparently unaware of the recent change in his fate. Duprée also found Bitty and another woman nervously tending to three new Africans in the back of a White Oak wagon. Her eyes conspicuously darted from the door of the inn to the miller and back again, and Duprée knew she'd had a hand in the day's events.

"So, Miss Bitty," he whispered under his breath. "I underestimated you."

* * *

It had been Abel's duty to load and guard the Africans while Bitty helped Priscilla do her best to make them comfortable. They fetched water and some bread, which the three men downed ravenously, but there was little else the women could do to relieve the suffering caused by the slaves' shackles. Abel heard the commotion as a crowd of tipsy Cattail revelers poured into the streets, but he paid them little mind until the men made it a point to gawk at him as they passed.

"So, he and his fetched twenty-five hundred dollars!" they jeered.

Abel didn't understand the talk, but every time Mr. Stringham bought new slaves, he was reminded that he was nothing more than property in most men's eyes. He had been reminded of that by the ferry captain, and he could see it in the faces of the men from the Cattail Inn.

Walking over to one of the Africans, Abel studied the man. "You hate me as much as you hate the whites, don't you, brother? I wonder which would be worse . . . to be wrenched from a life you loved, or to have never known the life you were intended to live." The African seem calmed by the gentle tone of Abel's voice, and though Abel knew the man couldn't understand a word he was saying, he relished a moment to free his educated tongue.

"Do you have people weeping for you in Africa?" Abel moaned sadly. "Of course you do! My father should weep for me and my children. But he has accepted our fate as God's will."

A poor, white farmer walked by, and Abel quickly hushed his voice and dropped his eyes. When the man passed by, Abel straightened his posture and resumed his clear dialogue.

"My father was also shanghaied into slavery, but he was a scholar beforehand. He was not meant for this. I was not meant for this . . ." Abel looked into the man's desperate, ebony eyes. "Neither were you, my brother. Perhaps that's why my father views his enslavement as some divine calling. He believes he was sent here to succor God's captive children. I'm sorry . . . I cannot accept that this is God's will for me . . . especially when I look at my children."

He turned away briefly to fight the encroaching bitterness. When he turned back around he asked softly, "Did you have family, too?" Abel's heart swelled with compassion. They had nothing, while he, at least, had his family. "My father leads our community. He will do all he can to temper your captivity, and he will teach you some of the things he taught me.

"And we will show you that you are not alone. Tonight, he will ring the prayer bell, and everyone will gather. From this day forward, such as we are . . . we will be your people."

He thought of something his father often said. "Like Joseph of Egypt, God has a plan for everyone, and in time we will see it. Do you even know of God, brother? My father will tell you stories, teach you about Jesus, the Christian God. When you are ready, he will ask God for permission to baptize you." He reached a hand out to touch the slave's shoulder. "You will know hope again . . . I promise you."

* * *

Bitty noticed Abel standing aloof and quiet. She worried that her plan had been a foolish one—to protect a man she loved without knowing if her feelings were matched or just politely received. Then, with each groan from the Africans, her guilt and grief doubled. Twice she tried to approach Abel, and both times he had retreated, busying himself with the horses and repacking the load. His detachment had stung her like the flip of a whip against her heart, and she eventually returned to the Willows' teams where Jack napped in the wagon bed.

"Jack," she called out, lifting the hat that covered his face. "Have you heard any word?"

"Shh," he warned. "Don't go makin' a ruckus. Jed struck the deal but it cost him dear."

Bitty's joy was swallowed up in her worry over Abel's detachment. "Does Abel know?"

"I just found out myself. Besides, I've been busy. There's a fella across the way, dressed in a uniform. He's been appearin' and disappearin' all day. I think he's scoutin' our wagons."

A familiar knot formed in Bitty's stomach. "You say he's wearin' a uniform?"

"Dark blue . . . not military, though."

"Is he there now?" she asked, her voice trembling.

Jack noticed the fear in her voice. "No. He's disappeared again. You know him?"

"I've got to go."

Jack sat up and reached for her hand. "How do you know this man, Bitty?"

"I've got to find Abel," she insisted as she fled down the street.

The streets were filled with lingering people, making passage difficult. Bitty decided to take the alley and cut up to the mill where the White Oak wagons sat. She was just about to turn the corner and head back onto the main street when Sebastian Duprée appeared in her path.

She shrieked and began to run in the opposite direction. But before she had gone far, the bullish young man grabbed her wrist and held her in place. "It's all right, it's all right, Bitty," he said soothingly. "I'm not going to hurt you. I'll let you go if you promise to just let me speak. Agreed?"

Bitty's eyes were wide and cautious as she nodded her agreement, though she remained poised to run at the slightest provocation. Duprée slowly relaxed his grip and stepped back.

"I just wanted to apologize for this morning," he began. "I'm not accustomed to being turned down by women, and that, I fear, has made a rogue of me. It's clear you are accustomed to being treated as a lady, Miss Bitty, and deservedly so. I said I was looking for a woman that was suitable for me? Well you, madam, are clearly my equal. Again, I hope you will forgive me."

Duprée bowed low, meeting Bitty's wary eyes on the way up. "I heard what you did for the miller today. You truly must be a treasure to have such influence over a man as respected as Mr. Jed Pearson. A woman who commands that type of respect could go far."

Bitty felt the knot return. She moved to the right but Duprée matched her step.

"You said you run Mr. Pearson's household. Well, I believe you now. That means you must have access to his office and personal papers, perhaps to his strongbox and valuables."

"I want to pass . . ." she repeated defiantly. "I'll scream if you don't let me pass."

Duprée's chilling sneer returned. "I'll just say you asked me to meet you back here."

Bitty tried once more to pass but Duprée blocked her again. "The *Elizabeth* passes by the Willows' dock twice a month. I'll get word to you about what I want you to do."

Fire flew from Bitty's eyes. "I'm not gonna do a thing to help you."

"Oh, yes you will, Bitty," Duprée threatened. "Like you, I'm used to getting what I want."

"You call yourself a free man, yet you prey on your own people."

"I have no people, though I'd take you along and show you how to truly live."

Bitty stared at the man in utter disbelief. "You can't offer what you don't understand." She took a step forward, daring him to block her way. He held fast in place, but this time she was not deterred, and eventually Duprée snickered and stepped aside.

"I'll be in touch," he yelled as she turned the corner and ran until she reached the street.

She didn't realize how ferociously her heart was racing until she felt the burn in her chest. Elated to catch sight of Abel, whole and well, she let out a loud sigh. Abel spun at the sound behind him, concern showing immediately on his face as he caught her.

"You're out of breath. Jest sit yourself down," he encouraged.

"I bumped into our friend from this morning," she said between hungry draws of air.

"Did he lay his hands on you?" Abel glared in the direction from which Bitty had come.

She shook her head to deflect his concern. "No, Abel. I'm fine, just a little startled is all."

He knew she was protecting him, another reminder of his neutered ability to respond as a man. As he turned back to harnessing the teams, he felt as if he were one animal hitching up another.

Bitty saw the defeat in his eyes. She had been unsure what to say to him about the changes she had set in motion. Seeing him there, burdened with despair, she felt moved to forewarn him. "I've done somethin', Abel. I hope you'll be pleased with it."

Abel barely turned his head, continuing to attach the leather straps.

"Jed came to buy some new workers today. I asked him to buy you and your family."

Abel froze with his back to Bitty. Obviously distracted by her words, he unconsciously let the straps slip through his fingers and fall to the ground.

"Y'all are comin' to the Willows . . . your parents, the children . . . your whole family."

Abel stared at Bitty, checking to be sure he had heard correctly. "Master Pearson bought my fam'ly from White Oak? Even my babies?" he asked with a shaky voice.

"Yes, Abel," Bitty replied through shining eyes. "Every member of your family."

"And . . . and you're sure my master agreed to this?"

"Yes, Abel. And life will get better now that you're all comin' to the Willows to live."

Bitty thought she saw tears in his eyes before he stooped to pick up the straps with trembling hands. "Thank you. Thank you," he muttered as he returned to his work.

CHAPTER 8

The Willows
June 1810

The next day, Jed drew up a personal note to cover the balance due to Stringham for Abel's family, recalling the argument that ensued when he'd confessed the amount to his father. He knew it made no business sense, but he felt right about it as he stared at his grandfather's portrait, painted ten years before he'd died. He sat on his horse, with his last wife and several grandchildren playing in front of the house in the background. Dressed in riding gear, the first Jonathan Edward Pearson had a musket across his legs and a woman's locket dangling from his fingers. To Jed the portrait symbolized everything the man loved in life—the women he had married, his posterity, and the Willows. That painting offered Jed proof that a successful life was measured in terms not definable on a balance sheet or a bank statement. He knew he had made the right decision, and aside from Bitty, he had Hannah to thank for it.

Markus came to the door. "We're heading to White Oak to fetch Abel's family." His smile became inane and Jed knew he had caught a glimpse of Frannie bounding down the stairs.

"Talk to her, Markus," encouraged Jed. "It's obvious you're mooneyed over her."

He shook his head and pled for Jed's silence. "Her eye is set elsewhere," he whispered.

"Well, you two are alert for having had so little sleep," teased Frannie as she entered. "I heard your discussion with Father last night, Jed." She grimaced. "Feeling better?"

"Much . . . wonderful as a matter of fact." He smiled, placing his feet on his desk.

"Was that partly because a letter from a certain young lady arrived?" she prodded mercilessly.

Markus's interest was piqued. "A letter? From a lady? Well, I'm impressed," he swooned.

"It was just a letter from Hannah, thanking me for taking her riding."

"Oh, I see," Markus corrected, "It wasn't actually from a *woman*. It was a note from a friend."

Jed blushed but came back with a wink, "As if either of us has had time for courting! Frannie, we're both pitiful. Perhaps you could give us each some womanly advice."

Markus sputtered into a near panic. "Don't listen to him, Frannie! Why, I . . . I . . . oh," groaned the Irishman. "Fine, then. Jack and I'll just be off on our business now!"

As soon as Jed's laughter slowed, Frannie sat on the edge of his desk and pressed him for answers. "So, you haven't even told Markus about Hannah. What does the letter say?"

"It is exactly what I said, simply a thank-you note for taking her riding."

"A thank-you note does not require so many pages, brother, but if it is too personal to share with your dearest confidant . . ." she taunted.

"Here," he acquiesced, pushing the lavender-colored letter in her direction. "It's just gossip and her opinions on politics and the like. She is so hungry to learn." His laugh was soft and sad. "She is increasingly interested in spiritual matters. She has asked me to study the Bible with her."

Frannie chuckled at that notion. "You . . . read the Bible? So you don't ascribe to Father's belief that religion is insurance for marriage and death—assuring that someone official will preside over the ceremony?" She smiled exaggeratedly. "How are you planning to answer her?"

Jed's expression became thoughtful. "I think I will agree to it. If I care about her, I should care about the things that interest her, shouldn't I? Besides," he joked, "I may need the help of the Almighty if I am to survive these next months."

"Does she have any inkling at all that your feelings exceed friendship?"

Jed's reply was forceful. "None. I am as an adored brother, and that is what I will remain until I am convinced that she is mature enough to make her own choices based on love and not on obligation or convenience. I owe her that. At least someone on this earth owes her that."

The angry stomp of Markus's boots resounded down the hall, drawing Jed and Frannie to the doorway while bringing Jed's father from the parlor. All looked at him expectantly.

Markus always felt odd in these situations, not knowing to whom to direct his reply—father or son. He chose neither, directing his comments to a spot on the floor between the two men's feet. "That Stringham. He's trying to pull the wool over us, he is!"

Jonathan Pearson II stomped his own foot and pointed an accusing finger in his son's direction. "I knew it, I knew it. Didn't I tell you, Jed? That man is a dishonorable cuss! Now what?"

Frannie stifled a laugh at her father's display, seeing a slim trace of the impetuous rascal he was rumored to have been in his youth. He was tall and still well built for a man in his sixties, sport and adventure having kept him alert and muscled. According to the gentry, he was rumored to have been a scoundrel with the women. There may have been some truth to that prattle, for it wasn't until his fortieth year, when he met Julianne Ensor, that he thought of settling down. The delicate, artistic twenty-year-old was completely unimpressed with his bravado and ego, which ultimately made her the most attractive woman he had ever met.

While Frannie was amused with her father, Jed leaned against the doorway, preparing for another round of debate with him. "Tell us, Markus. What's the problem?"

"Stringham just sent Abel with a note saying he'll send the children over as a show of good faith, but he'll not release Abel, Jerome, or Sarah until he's purchased their replacements."

Jonathan pointed at Jed and grunted while his son downplayed the problem. "He's received payment enough to release Sarah and Jerome as well. What is he asking now?"

"He says he needs them until he has replaced them. He claims he'll need Abel to haul the new slaves back, but the Portuguese's barge won't return to Calverton for two weeks."

"What do you think?" Jed asked the fuming Irishman, but it was his father who piped in.

"I don't like it," raged Jonathan Pearson. "By now everyone in the state has heard that he negotiated the highest price ever paid for a single slave, and he wants to make the exchange as public as possible so he can thump his chest. I don't think you should give him the honor."

Jed raised his eyebrow appreciatively at his father. "Good point." His father was not suited for the rigors of running an estate, but he was undeniably an astute businessman.

"I agree with him," chimed Markus. "You owe him nothing, Jed. I say you threaten to send the sheriff after him if he doesn't release your rightful property."

Jed winced at the term as he fell into his chair. "There's more to be considered here."

"What more?" Jonathan and Markus asked simultaneously.

Jed shot Markus a knowing look. "There's a reason why Stewart is thumping his chest."

Slow to understand, when Markus finally did his eyes slipped involuntarily in Frannie's direction. "Aye. You're right," he muttered under his breath.

"Right about what?" she demanded. "Why are you two being so secretive?"

Markus blushed crimson at his indiscretion while Jed tried again to hedge his answer. "It's Frederick. We're concerned about Frederick."

"What has that boy done now?" muttered Jonathan with sudden disinterest as he turned and strode back to his wife and their card game.

"Why are you concerned about Frederick?" asked Frannie worriedly.

"Frederick fell apart during the negotiations and caused Stewart considerable embarrassment. I could have gotten Abel and his family for half the price because Frederick folded under the pressure, but I offered twenty-five hundred dollars to deflect some of Stewart's anger away from his son."

Frannie leaned against the door. "Stewart Stringham is a beast. He will never know what Frederick is capable of because he browbeats him into submission. I can't stand the man."

"Frederick is little freer than the slaves at White Oak," Jed concurred.

"Speaking of which . . ." Markus groused softly as he thrust an envelope at Frannie. "This is for you . . . from Frederick." He tipped his head apologetically as he strode out.

"So, we each have a secret letter," remarked Jed dryly. "And what does our friend say?"

After reading the note, Frannie responded guardedly. "It's as you said. Frederick's father is furious over his blunder yesterday. He asked me to meet him later."

Jed rose from his chair and challenged her. "What is happening between you two?"

"What business is it of yours?" she demanded angrily before seeing the worry on her brother's face and calming herself. "We're *friends,* Jed. Like you and Hannah. Surely you of all people can understand that."

Jed noted her sarcasm as he returned to his chair, spying Hannah's letter as Frannie left the room. Perhaps it was his frustration over his hopeless situation with Hannah that made his heart ache, but the feeling of being utterly alone swept over him again. He thought about making more of an attempt at courting, but immediately thought of Hannah again. He wondered if his investment of time would someday find him watching her pledge herself to another man whose love touched her in a nonbrotherly way. Until then, he knew his heart was irretrievably hers.

He began reading her letter for at least the fifth time:

Monday, June 18, 1810

Dear Jed,

I hope this letter finds you well. I went to the stables and decided that I shall not ride Druid again until you return. I do believe he has grown even larger and more ferocious since that day. In truth, riding without you could never compare to the pleasure we shared racing through the meadows. Thank you for our chat. I shall try to live equal to what you see in me.

It was the loveliest afternoon of my life. I told Selma so, and she scolded me fiercely, saying I monopolized your time, thus preventing you from socializing with other young ladies. I told her we are the dearest of friends and that you would tell me if and when you were to tire of my company. You must ever promise me that you will. I would think myself horrid if I selfishly prevented you from finding a full measure of the happiness you bring to my world.

Selma would chasten me for moping so. Her latest advice to me comes from Proverbs 10:28. Are you familiar with it? You may find it amusing, considering my sullen mood.

He skipped down a few paragraphs . . .

By the way, I have decided to read the entire Bible. It seems to me that one can hardly consider oneself educated if she studies the great works without including the Bible, which, if the story of Adam and Eve is true, is the basis from which all the others have root. Do you believe the Bible stories are fact, Jed? The Reverend Wilcox says they are like parables, intended to teach us a broader truth. But then how would one know where miracles end and fables begin? Selma tells me the Holy Spirit will guide me. Would you care to study with me, dear scholar?

I dread closing. Sharing these letters makes me feel my dearest friend is nigh at hand. Don't worry about this morose little girl. I am fine enough though the entire household has suffered another dreadful night of Mother's distress. Poor Father looks ghastly, but his is as true a love as ever man possessed. Wish the same for me someday.

Love,

Hannah

Each time he read the letter, Jed felt torn between smiling at her dramatics and wanting to weep for her. He had looked up the scripture in Proverbs last evening. *The hope of the righteous shall be gladness,* it read. He wondered why some children were raised in loving security while others were born into such distress that they had to be reminded of the existence of things like hope and gladness. Jed's thoughts returned to Abel, who was still outside awaiting the decision regarding his future. As sad as Jed was for Hannah, he knew others' fates were even more distressing.

He had to deal with that matter first, but decided to wait until Frannie had left the house before wording his reply to Stringham. When she left, he and Markus composed it.

June 23, 1810

Dear Mr. Stringham,

Owing to the fact that you have already received more than sufficient funds to cover the sale of the four children and the two parents of the slave you call Abel, I am requesting their immediate transfer from White Oak to the Winding Willows. However, understanding that the timing of our arrangement has placed some degree of hardship upon your available workers, I consent to allow Abel to remain at White Oak to assist in the transfer of new workers, so long as said transfer is completed within two weeks hence, at which time we shall settle the remaining financial matters and move Abel permanently to the Winding Willows.

I will consider any inability to comply with these terms reason for nullification of our entire agreement and forfeiture of all previously paid monies.

Sincerely,

Jonathan Edward Pearson III

Jed melted wax over the flap and pressed his seal, a flamboyant *JED,* into the center.

Markus grunted. "Let's back that up in two weeks by showing up on the docks when that barge ties up. We'll personally make sure Abel gets here without any more complications."

* * *

Frannie was still distressed by Jed and her father's displeasure with the Stringhams and their management of White Oak. She knew their irritation had more to do with the father than it did with the son, but she could easily separate Frederick's character from his father's, whereas Jed clearly could not. By three o'clock she was at the west gate that marked one of the original boundary lines between the two estates. She tied her horse to the ancient oak and sang to amuse herself as she waited for Frederick. Within minutes she saw him astride his bay, racing toward her. He was not a particularly handsome man. His hair was dark and straight, and his brown, widely set eyes were small. Neither were his narrow nose nor thin lips of particular note, but no man looked more striking than Frederick upon a horse. His slim frame virtually hugged a mount seamlessly, allowing the pair to move in breathtaking unison that reflected a confidence he exhibited nowhere else.

Frederick barely allowed his horse to halt before he was on the ground sweeping Frannie into his arms. He buried his face in her neck and held her, more from need of comfort than of passion. "Thank you for coming . . ." he uttered. "I feared you wouldn't, so thank you."

"Of course I would come, Frederick. What would make you think otherwise?"

"I was afraid that Jed and your father might be of the same mind as my father, who believes I am unworthy to ever run White Oak. I feared you'd no longer consent to marry me."

Frannie bit her tongue about the day's earlier conversation. "Nothing could change that. Jed has been concerned about you, but he cares for you. Though I think it's safe to say there's no love lost between him and your father at the moment." She framed his face with her hands and continued softly, "But you are nothing like your father."

Frederick took her hands and placed kisses in each palm. "And what of *your* father, Frannie? When I finally make my formal request for your hand, what do you think he will say?"

Again she stalled, choosing her words carefully. "That whom I marry is my decision."

"Look at me, Frannie. As long as my father lives, all I can offer you will be a small house on White Oak with me genuflecting to him until he takes his last breath. I can barely stand the thought of it. Will you still be able to see me as a man under those circumstances?"

"If things are too uncomfortable, we will simply build a home on Willows property."

"He would cut me off completely were I to cause him another embarrassment. Could you be happy the rest of your days merely living off a few acres gifted to you by Jed?"

"It wouldn't be that way," she assured him. "Jed feels the Willows is as much mine as his. I'm sure he would feel the same way after we are married. Besides, my grandfather left me an inheritance and a dowry. We'll have a good start with or without a bequest from your father."

Frederick's mind began to race. "The financial freedom your grandfather established for you is more than I enjoy myself at this time. People deride your father for being so liberal with you, but it offers me hope. Do you love me that much?"

Frannie stared at his face before answering. "Of course I love you, Frederick. You're my dear friend. I would do anything for you, just as I know you would do anything for me."

Disappointment swept over Frederick's face and he turned from her. "I had hoped you felt . . . more for me . . . but if it is enough for you, then it is enough for me as well."

"It's a perfect pairing. We're compatible. That's more than many people find in a lifetime. You'll see. Dear friendship is a solid start. And our love will grow, but best of all, things will remain as they have always been between us . . . comfortable and established. We will ride and hunt together and someday raise our children beside Jed's. It will be a perfect life. You'll see."

"I hope you won't mind if I plan to love you quite more than that, Frannie." He took her hands in his. "I didn't realize until yesterday that I have never loved anyone or anything as much as I love you. That's why I had to see you today, to be sure you still loved me, even though it may be as your dear friend. If you marry me, I promise I will make you love me completely someday."

Frannie had not counted on such storybook emotion from the young man who had previously been so reserved in his affections. The feelings he stirred in her were both thrilling and unsettling. Though logic had convinced her to pursue the choice that would keep her currently idyllic life on course, her nature was driven to investigate what kindled her senses. Impetuously, she rose on her toes and pressed her lips to Frederick's in the first kiss either of them had experienced. The sensations the kiss stirred in Frederick left him breathless and hungering for more. His eyes narrowed as he grabbed her shoulders and pulled her back to him. Startled to the edge of fear, Frannie pushed him away. As she did, an unfamiliar darkness filled his eyes as if, for a moment, a stranger had replaced her dear friend.

"I . . . I'm sorry, Frannie," he cried out as she backed away from him. As his finger traced the kiss that still burned upon his lips he tried to excuse himself. "I was overcome by your offer of affection, but I never should have pressed myself upon you."

Frannie turned away, needing a semblance of privacy as she sorted through an array of emotions. "We were both momentarily overcome, Frederick." She moved to her horse and began to mount, muttering as she went, "I should never have . . . I'm sorry, I . . . I must go . . ."

Frederick clutched at her to hold her there, calling her name and pleading for her to remain, but she kicked her mare and sped away to the safety and peace of the Willows.

* * *

Jed wished he could consult Frannie on how to respond to Hannah's letter, but he was too humiliated to ask. He drafted five notes before finally penning a suitably casual note that would maintain their correspondence and offer Hannah his continued support.

June 23, 1810

Dear Hannah,

I looked up your verse in Proverbs. Commend Selma for her selection, as hope and gladness are the greatest of virtues. As to your question regarding Adam and Eve, I apply the following logic. As you pointed out, biblical text has formed the basis for modern law and ethics and has been quoted by men of great wisdom, including our own Founding Fathers. I have also given considerable thought to the miracles of Moses. Your reverend views these experiences as metaphorical hyperbole, but I do not believe that centuries of the world's greatest minds would have based civilization's laws upon God's commandments if the only witness was a man known for philosophical exaggeration. In short, I believe they trusted the biblical account to be true, and I tend to follow great minds. Let us make good use of this Holy Spirit that Selma attests to and study this for ourselves. Where shall we begin?

In response to your worries regarding my romantic pursuits, please assure Selma that your letters are a welcomed diversion, as is your charming company. If and when I should choose to pursue a courtship, I shall be sure to inform you first, affording you the same privilege you have promised to me. And yes, Hannah, of all the things in this world, you can be sure my greatest and daily wish is that you find someone who will treasure you as you deserve. I pledge myself to do all that is within my power to make this so.

Your most devoted,

Jed

* * *

Next to the side table where Jed's letter lay awaiting the courier, Frannie found another unsettling note from Frederick. It seemed the only thing she and Jed did anymore was read or write letters. Frederick had sent her one each day since their encounter at the gate. Each one professed greater love than the first, accompanied by a confession of some malady such as his inability to breathe or his lack of interest in food or drink. Frannie found the letters somewhat disturbing, though she assumed this unsettling phase would pass in time, as her father loved her mother and was still able to breathe, drink, and eat with normalcy.

It was all becoming so complicated. Her parents were her only real example of married life, and though their union was seemingly a satisfying one, she could never bear the societal expectations under which her mother had been raised. Likewise, Frannie could not understand the politics of marriage. It seemed to her that when the union was entered into with the wrong sort of man, it bore a striking similarity to slavery, taking an independent human being and suddenly making her a man's property. She had other plans about how her own home and family would be run. She remembered her mother's kisses and storytelling, but there was no playing. Frannie decided that perhaps it was due to her under-oxygenated constitution, or perhaps it was the result of societal expectations. In either case, Frannie vowed to be a different type of mother, one who would ride and hunt and fish with her children. To be able to do that, she needed a husband who would value her for those qualities and not just for those of a more intimate nature. This was the very reason she had encouraged Frederick's advances. He was known, he was gentle, and he loved her as she was, and despite her brother or father's objections, she would accept his marriage proposal.

CHAPTER 9

Shire of Whittington, England
Late June 1810

The creak of the heavy oak door awakened the boy, who stretched and wriggled under a down comforter. He opened his eyes and smiled at the sight of his papa, His Honor, the Earl of Whittington, who lovingly watched over him.

The aroma of lavender drifted into Whittington Castle, turning the earl's thoughts momentarily from his son to the boy's mother—his beloved Sevrina. Her father, a Scottish earl, had heard the mysterious name on a venture in the Far East and placed it upon his first daughter. When she was fifteen, the earl had arranged a meeting between Lady Sevrina and the young Viscount, heir to Whittington Castle. On her sixteenth birthday, when the future earl was still under twenty years, Sevrina and Whit, as he was called by his family, were wed.

Whit now stood over his own son, recalling the events leading up to the boy's birth and his dear mother's demise. They'd lived a fairy-tale life, living and loving in Whittington Castle for three years, enjoying the privileges of nobility while the primary burden of it was borne by the Viscount's father. Their idyllic life lasted until Lord Whittington was killed in a hunting accident and Whit, at twenty-two years old, was placed in his father's seat in the House of Lords at Parliament. The political ceremony was nothing in comparison to the celebration that heralded the birth of the young couple's first child, a daughter named Lily. Music played and banners were hung. Then they were put away with reverent solemnity when it was announced that the child had died a few hours later. Three more children were born and lost to them. In 1802, however, a son named Daniel was born—and lived. Sevrina never let the child leave her arms, barely sleeping herself until he was past his first winter and as fat as a spring piglet. Then she passed away, leaving her adored Whit widowed at thirty-three.

While Lady Whittington lay in state, the young earl found the burden of nobility too onerous to bear. Then, beyond the walls of the castle, came the townspeople in throngs to pay their respects. They sang and prayed, laying wreaths and bouquets of flowers at his doorway and her grave. Whit's understanding of duty and his love for the people melded in his heart at that time, filling him with a sense of responsibility as a watchman over his own people, and over England as a whole. And despite England's current concerns, he vowed to honor his post until Daniel was ready for the post, or until his own death.

"Good morning, Papa," yawned Daniel as he crawled into his father's arms, bringing the man out of his thoughts.

"You're getting so big, Daniel. Soon Papa won't be able to hold you this way."

Daniel giggled at the very same phrase his father had greeted him with every morning for as long as he could remember. "Are we returning to London today?"

"Yes, son. I'm afraid we must. I have business I must attend to in the city."

"For the king?"

"Yes, Daniel. For the king." He kissed his adored son's brow. "I'm sorry we cannot stay here and play together longer, but His Majesty has been ill and has summoned me. The Earl of Whittington must always obey the call of the king. You are my only heir, Daniel, as I was my father's only heir. Someday the same will be expected of you. Do you remember why?"

The boy smiled and nodded. He never tired of hearing the story.

"In 1518 our ancestor, Lord John Whittington, answered the king's invitation to sit in the House of Lords and keep watch over the actions of Parliament. That duty was passed along to his son after him, and his after him, and so on and so on for nearly three hundred years, down to me and then someday to you, Daniel. It is at times a heavy load we bear, but the peerage for the House of Whittington rests with us, son, with you and me. You understand that, don't you?"

Daniel's eyes sparkled with pride as he nodded modestly.

"These are worrisome times for England, Daniel. Napoleon and this war have cost us dearly, and now it appears the king may attempt to reclaim the colonies. We need America's resources to rebuild our economy and reunite our people."

"Is that why you look so sad, Papa?"

Lord Whittington kissed his son's head as he wrestled with what to tell the boy. In moments like this, his heart grasped onto simpler times—times when loving his wife and playing with Daniel were his chief concerns. But now duty pressed upon him, as it would his son. He believed it would be better for Daniel to learn this lesson early than to be affronted with it as he had. "There is trouble in Parliament, Daniel. While the king has been ill and the government has been distracted by Napoleon, some of Parliament's Members have wavered in their loyalties.

"England's resolve is being sorely tested now. The king and the good people of England are depending on us to keep our government strong and noble, and to protect our citizens. We are blessed to have been called to this great work. I will prepare you and teach you all you must know to fulfill the post when your time comes. We Whittingtons must always fulfill our charge."

Ten hours later, when their carriage rolled into London, Lord Whittington asked the driver to continue past St. Stephen's Chapel, the debating chamber for the House of Commons. He gently moved his sleeping son from his lap to the opposite seat and called for the carriage to stop. As he stood on the stone steps of the entryway, he vowed to root out the traitors and clean Britain's House.

CHAPTER 10

Calverton, Maryland
Late June 1810

"Even I can't abide the atmosphere in Calverton when the auction is held. I certainly don't want you there, Frannie. Choose any other time for this talk you want to have, please."

"Why can't I ride along, Jed? You don't have any business at the auction, do you?"

Jed stalled his answer. "I'm not . . . *buying*, Frannie," he squirmed, "but I do have business there. Besides, Father doesn't want you there any more than I do." His frustration over the situation left him tired and irritable.

"You're going to make sure Stewart replaces Abel and his family so he'll release them."

"Yes. And if he doesn't honor our agreement it could get unpleasant."

"I have no qualms about you quarreling with Stewart Stringham, as long as you don't hold a grudge against Frederick." Jed was unmoved and she continued. "I feel more strongly than ever that I should be there, Jed. If Stewart is harsh with him, he might need me, but I won't go near the harbor. Tell Father I'll stay near the apothecary and the mercantile. All right?"

Jed reluctantly agreed, and Frannie was ready and in the kitchen with Bitty early the next morning. "Are you certain you don't want to go with us?" Frannie queried excitedly. "You know we're bringing Abel home today."

"No, no," declined Bitty. "Thank you all the same, though," she came back appreciatively. "I've got things to ready here, Frannie darlin', but you go on and enjoy your day."

"I wish I hadn't promised Jed and Father that I wouldn't go near the harbor. It's already sweltering. A ride on the ferry would be lovely today."

Bitty rushed to her with terror in her eyes. "Promise me you won't go near the ferry!"

"Why on earth are you so worried about me taking a ferry ride, Bitty?"

"Call it a bad omen. Just promise me you'll stay away from the water altogether, hear?"

Knowing not to argue with Bitty, Frannie nodded and headed out. Jack already sat on the wagon, and Markus beamed from the carriage box as Jed stood with a picnic basket in tow.

Frannie clapped her hands together and gushed, "What a lovely surprise, Jed! Thank you for convincing Father to let me come. And all this! You didn't have to make such a fuss for me."

He bowed low and swept his hand, inviting her to enter the carriage. "I'm still holding you to your promise to stay away from the harbor," he reminded firmly as he helped her climb into the vehicle. Once she was settled, he joined her inside and signaled for Markus to set off.

Jed took her hand. "I sense changes looming in our futures, Frannie. That being the case, I don't want to miss opportunities to let you know how wonderful and how loved you are. You deserve the best of life . . . the very best. I always want you to remember that."

Frannie took his arm and gave it a loving squeeze. She felt certain that carefully couched in his affectionate words was his concern about her relationship with Frederick. "There's no one on this earth I trust or care about more than you, Jed, but I do love Frederick," she confessed. "I hope you and Hannah are as happy as Frederick and I."

Jed nodded solemnly, then reached into his shirt pocket and pulled an envelope from inside. "Perhaps we shall be. This was waiting on the credenza for me this morning."

"Another letter? She couldn't have received your reply yet. She must miss you terribly."

"Or it could be bad news," he sighed as he unfolded the pages. "I haven't read it yet. Her situation is not good." He silently began reading the letter.

Wednesday, June 27, 1810

Dear Jonathan,

Note the change in mode of address. My sisters claim that I am no longer a child and insist that I no longer address a man of your station by so familiar a term as Jed. I am hereupon planning to address all future correspondence to you by your good Christian name, Jonathan.

I am further writing to share the saddest of news. Father feels Mother's health is too precarious, so we are declining all invitations this season. I suppose we shall not have occasion to see one another until Christmas, and only then if you are able to spare a little time during the holidays to make your way to whichever house we will be in at that time.

I still think fondly on our ride earlier this month. I had hoped we would share others before summer's end, but it doesn't appear that that is to be so. You should find my horsemanship quite improved by spring, however. At Mother's insistence, Father hired a handsome young man to serve as my riding instructor, citing it a necessity for all young debutantes to have such skills at their disposal. I am speechless (and somewhat guarded) over her sudden generosity and interest in me. Nonetheless, riding Druid has become a sweet diversion, and my instructor is patient.

Oh, Jed, I am so dreadfully sad about the summer! Myrna and Beatrice are at this moment crying upon their beds. Will you continue to write? I have not received a response from my previous letter. I know I am being impatient, but Father's news has left me disconsolate. Please consider my invitation to study the Bible with me. Hope of that other world is all I have at times. I am like a lump of clay. Help me become the woman you believe I am destined to be.

Until then, I am forever

Your dearest Hannah

Frannie offered him a supportive smile as he finished. "I take it the news is not all good."

Jed smiled wistfully, shaking his head as he placed the letter back in his pocket.

"Don't lose hope, Jed. Perhaps I am more of a romantic than I dared believe, but I do believe that love will triumph . . . even when crazed family members stand in our way."

Jed leaned back and squeezed her hand. "And so, this topic you so badly wanted to discuss with me. Does it involve Frederick?"

She closed her eyes and smiled. "It can wait."

They passed the time chatting about days past, both knowing that change would come. As they neared Calverton, wagons loaded with merchant goods and building materials rolled by their carriage. Two wagons provided proof of the slave auction—terrified brown bodies shackled to the rails or led behind like livestock. For this reason Jed had decided to bring the carriage with its window shades. He had spent the previous evening wrestling with the inevitable changes that loomed on the horizon. Like it or not, he realized that the very spirit that made his sister so unique and wonderful also made her of a mind to choose her own destiny. He could not love that characteristic one moment and then attempt to bridle it the next. Whatever . . . whomever she chose would be her decision, and likewise the life it afforded her. In the meantime, however—and in whatever way the future allowed him—he would protect and shelter her.

Markus maneuvered the carriage near the mercantile and set the brake. Jed looked out and noticed a crowd assembled down the street, their mood apparently surly. He saw Jack step cautiously from the wagon and stare nervously at the swirling controversy near the harbor. As Jed exited the carriage, the hair on the back of his neck immediately rose, and he threw a worried look in Frannie's direction, cautioning her to remain inside. "Stay with her, Jack," he instructed as he and Markus set off toward the ruckus.

Jack stood trembling with uneasiness as the two men headed into the throng. His heart raced and beads of sweat formed across his brow with each whoop from the crowd or churlish look from a passerby. As another wagon rolled by, he caught the pleading gaze of the human cargo tied to the side rails. In many ways Jack felt completely different from the pitiable young man in the wagon. He was trained with an inventory of skills most whites couldn't boast, including a knowledge of the world far beyond his own experiences, gleaned from the books from which Miss Frannie taught him. Yet he knew that, stripped of his clothes, he and that slave were very much the same to most people, and that to others they were no different at all.

Ownership meant everything, and luck was at the crux of that. Who bought you—and what kind of people they were—decided your destiny, even your identity. He thought of Abel, who would surely be pleased to shed all reminders of White Oak when he moved to the Willows. Therein lay the source of Jack's worry—he knew he was among the most blessed of slaves, but he also knew that circumstance could change in an instant. Watching his master walk into the storm frightened him, reminding him ever more clearly how fragile his fortunes were, and that they were tied to the disappearing form of Jed Pearson.

* * *

As soon as Markus and Jed passed through the fringe of people, the source of the hullabaloo became evident. Stewart Stringham was recounting the tale of his shrewd negotiations to a crowd he was filling with free ale. Markus shot Jed an indignant *I told you so* glance and started to leave when the two men caught sight of Abel. Stewart had him standing on the bed of his wagon like a trophy, shackled between three loin-wrapped black males and three equally under-clothed females. Fitchins, Stringham's barbaric overseer, strutted about cracking his whip, terrifying the Africans and taunting Abel for the enjoyment of the inebriated crowd of drunken idiots who stood below, screaming for filth or sport.

Jed's face turned crimson and his heart beat thunderously as he plunged through the crowd in the direction of the wagon, Markus close on his heels. One swaggering man fell against Jed, and with a single toss Jed cleared the drunk from his path. When Stewart Stringham caught sight of Jed's approach, he shuddered, calling to Fitchins for protection. But the cries of the Africans mingling with the jeers of the bystanders drowned out his pleas.

As Jed fought his way through the crowd, people laughed and jeered, grabbing at his shirt and blocking his way. With every step his blood boiled hotter until he longed to reach across the crowd and put his hands around the throats of Stewart Stringham and the cretin he employed.

Jed kept an eye on Markus, whose outrage seemed equally provoked by the entire crowd—by every hand that pressed upon them and every tongue that wagged. With his short, stocky frame, he didn't bother searching for a clear path to Stringham. Instead, he barreled through or over anybody that stood in his way, landing stray punches in every direction with such rapid delivery that each man looked to his neighbor for blame. Now that Markus had incited the crowd to riot among themselves, Jed moved easily on toward Stringham, now a mere stride away.

With one forward thrust Jed flew onto the platform and straight into Fitchins's torso, doubling the bulky man over. Placing all his anger into one powerful uppercut, he knocked the man out cold and dropped him onto the cheering crowd below. Next, he turned to Stringham and clenched his thin arms with a manacle-like grip. "The key," he barked mercilessly. "Give it to me or I'll snap your arms in two." Stringham trembled so fiercely that his response was incoherent, so Jed's hands slipped down his arms to his wrists, wrenching them upwards and away from his jacket. "Which pocket? Tell me which pocket or I swear I'll shred your clothes looking for it."

"The . . . the breast pocket," he stammered as his wide eyes scanned the crowd for help.

As soon as Markus arrived, he flung Stringham's jacket open, fishing for the key while Jed held him in place. "I've got it," Markus sneered as his blazing eyes bored into Stringham's.

"Unlock Abel and let's leave," directed Jed under the cacophony of the brawling crowd. He watched Stringham searching the throng and knew he'd spotted his son.

"Frederick!" Stewart Stringham cried out.

Jed twisted and saw Frederick, far off across the perimeter of the storm, looking ashamedly at the macabre drama his father had set in motion. Frederick's eyes shifted nervously from his father to the man he hoped would soon be his brother-in-law, and Jed knew he wrestled with the conundrum of where to place his loyalties. Jed's own dilemma was equally onerous, and he groaned at the complications young Stringham's involvement in the situation could create between himself and Frannie. "Hurry, Markus, before Frederick finds his nerve and gets involved!"

"It's the wrong key!" Markus yelled as he dug through each of Stewart's pockets.

* * *

Across the street, Sebastian Duprée was tying up the *Elizabeth*. As he drew near the inflamed crowd, he immediately recognized the men struggling on the wagon bed. Curious as to who else had accompanied Pearson into town, he meandered behind the throng, searching for the Willows' wagons and teams. He noticed Jack, whose face he remembered from the previous week. Then he saw the attractive, chestnut-haired woman peering through the carriage window and smiled at his good fortune. Duprée slipped behind a wagon and summoned a barefoot boy from the street. He handed him a penny and whispered in his ear, sending the lad off at a run towards Jack.

"Are y-y-y-you from the Willows estate?" stammered the lad when he reached the carriage. "Jed Pearson needs you!"

Frannie gasped and began to exit the carriage, but Jack pressed his body against the door.

"Wait, Miss Frannie," Jack warned as he turned to the boy. "Who sent you to find me?"

The nervous boy's eyes grew large in fear. "He said he was a friend of Mr. Pearson."

"What was his name?" called Jack to the boy as he ran off. "What did he look like?"

"Maybe it was Markus," worried Frannie. "Jed could be in danger. He needs our help!"

Jack paced nervously as he considered the dilemma. "I promised Jed to keep you safe."

"Will you go, Jack?" begged Frannie, aware of what she was asking of the man. Jack would be in a position where his Willows privileges would be of no help to him. Once he entered the mob, he would be just another slave, a being without rights or voice.

Jack was terrified, but his life was inseparably connected to Jed's. "Stay inside the carriage, Miss Frannie. No matter what, stay inside," he warned.

Duprée waited a few minutes to be sure Jack was gone before he moved from his hiding spot. He checked up and down the street for signs of anyone from the Willows, and then, assured that the young heiress had been left completely alone, he began to move across the street.

* * *

By the time Markus found the ring with the three keys, the fracas in the crowd had begun to play itself out and attentions were again focusing on the wagon. The crowd resumed its jeers, and Jed knew they were running out of time before Fitchins would awaken. Even if by some chance that failed to occur immediately, some intoxicated rowdy could easily leap aboard the wagon and further incite the slaves. The captives were already straining against their tethers with such ferocity that blood flowed freely from the shackle cuts on their ankles and wrists. Jed also saw utter rage in Abel's face and he knew instinctively that if he wasn't released soon, his fury would not be contained. And right or wrong, with cause or without, there was no justification sufficient to spare the life of a slave who rose up against a white man.

As Markus tried the first key, Abel struggled against the restraints, increasing the difficulty of the task. "Easy, Abel . . ." he said to the large man as he turned the key without success.

While Markus began to work the second key, Jed continued to hold Stringham firmly in place, while keeping his eye on Stringham's overseer, who began to stir. He gestured to Frederick, assuring him that his father was not in any danger. It was evident, however, that Frederick had begun to calculate the price he would pay for his reluctance, and he slowly began to move forward.

"We're running out of time, Markus," muttered Jed under his breath.

Markus tried the second key and the lock released. Abel roared ferociously and threw his free arm high in the air, sending the seven Africans into a wild frenzy. The frightened whites below began to cry out. Markus quickly released Abel's other hand and bound the line of males and females to one another. As he then began to unlock the shackles from Abel's feet, fury shot from the big man's eyes. Stringham shrank from his glare, crying out loudly, "If you release them they'll kill me! Look at him. He'll kill me!"

Before the last shackle fell, Jed released Stringham and turned his attentions to Abel. "Abel, we can't have any more trouble. When Markus releases this shackle we need to leave immediately. We'll go straightway to the Willows, but no trouble, do you understand?"

Abel's mighty chest heaved in anger before he nodded his understanding. In return, Jed nodded for Markus to open the final lock.

Attempting to inflame tensions once again and whip the crowd into a frenzy, Stewart Stringham waved his arms hysterically, shouting, "Do you see what he is doing? Jed Pearson is putting you all at risk by unleashing these crazed slaves! I fear for my safety . . . I fear for all our safety!"

As Abel's last shackle fell, a remorseful Markus locked the Africans' chains to a bar on the wagon, sealing their fate. Jed was poised for an incendiary response from the crowd, but Abel stood serene and calm. Unexpectedly, the onlookers' voices dropped to mere prattle and then to a hush as Jed stepped down into the crowd. He came face-to-face with Frederick, and a momentary stalemate occurred as a thousand unsaid words passed between the two strained friends. Abel followed Jed with a wary Markus close behind, leaving Stringham standing humiliated and alone on the wagon, gazing down on Frederick and the crumpled form of his mighty overseer.

* * *

Sebastian Duprée's plan was simple—lure the young heiress away from the carriage and hold her for a hefty ransom, which her doting brother would gladly pay. He took another look at the auburn-haired woman he was about to approach and smiled at his thoughts. *What transpires until the payment of the ransom is yet to be seen . . .*

"Miss Pearson?" his voice dripped with feigned worry. "Did my warning reach you in time?"

"You sent the boy?" Frannie asked. The man seemed a soldier of sorts.

Her apparent intrigue empowered Duprée. "Sebastian Duprée at your service, ma'am," he said as he bowed low and long. "I would have come myself, but I thought it best to keep watch over the situation in the event your man was unable to arrive in time to assist."

Frannie nodded her understanding. "It was very good of you, sir, but I haven't heard any word yet. Do you have further news? Is the trouble resolved?"

"I believe it is. I would be happy to escort you . . . for your safety, of course."

Frannie contemplated the offer. "Would you give me a moment to collect myself?"

"Of course," he replied with another courtly bow as the woman pulled the shade.

Frannie felt her pulse race with each thought of the man standing beside her carriage. Not only was he among the most handsome men she had been privileged to meet, he was also the most mysterious person she had ever seen. His name and vocal inflections hinted at some French ancestry. Furthermore, his manners and elocution seemed so courtly that she dared fantasize that he was a prince of some exotic island country. Nevertheless, the current situation prompted caution in her, and she was grateful she'd had the good sense to ask for a moment alone, beyond the gaze of his black eyes.

Duprée could scarcely contain his pleasure. His plan was working flawlessly, and he would have the young debutante miles downriver before anyone even noticed her absence. Then he would ask for a ransom large enough to get him beyond the sight of his creditors. Perhaps he would head west to the Missouri or Nebraska Territories . . . or perhaps to the Antilles, farther beyond the reach of American law. Perhaps he could strike two victories with one stone. Perhaps, if the woman were truly as taken with him as he imagined, he could exact the ransom and persuade her to come along with him. *Persuade? Convince? Coerce? What would it matter?*

He nearly salivated with anticipation when the carriage door opened and Frannie stepped out. Duprée offered his hand to steady her, but once her feet were on the ground she began heading off in the direction she had seen all the men take.

"Not that way!" His voice was sharp and intimidating. Recognizing his mistake, he immediately calmed his temper, speaking softly and politely. "It would be safer to go the back way and avoid the crowds. Tensions were still high when I left the scene."

Duprée directed her to the right and down the only other street that ran to the docks. She was beginning to doubt herself, and she began making small talk to settle her nerves.

"Forgive me for asking such a personal question, Mr. Duprée, but your uh . . . accent . . . it's very unfamiliar to me. I was wondering where you are from."

Duprée smiled. He had rehearsed his story many times in the past few months since arriving in the States. "Louisiana, ma'am, more specifically, Baton Rouge."

Mesmerized by the voice, Frannie queried, "Are you French then, Mr. Duprée?"

He smiled approvingly. "My father's father was a French colonist. His mother's people were Spaniards. They met and married and settled in the same area their parents founded."

"Your voice sounds neither perfectly French or Spanish. How is that?"

Duprée laughed convincingly. "My father arranged for me to be educated by various European tutors. Their instruction has altered my accent somewhat."

"No, it's not that," she said, staring curiously at him, trying to sort out his strange coloring. "There is an exotic air about you, sir." She blushed. "I mean . . . it's very unique . . ."

"Perhaps you've heard of the term *Creole?*"

"You are a Creole?" Frannie answered with wonder. "I have heard of them but I have never met one, nor do I truly understand the term."

Frannie began to turn back toward the town's center where the dispersing crowd had been assembled. Duprée quickly took her arm and guided her back toward the harbor, never breaking conversation. "It has many meanings. The original use of the term referred to the French and Spanish families that settled the area where I am from, but now it includes many peoples."

Frannie's instincts told her they were heading away from Jed, and the voice of caution spoke loudly enough to overcome her intrigue. "I think we should turn here, Mr. Duprée. This direction leads to the docks."

"Trust me, Miss Pearson. You'll soon see I know exactly where I am guiding you." He forcefully took her arm and pushed her in the direction of the harbor.

"You're hurting me, Mr. Duprée." She wrenched her arm free and began running toward the center of Calverton. With a few quick steps, Duprée caught her by her hair and wrenched her back against him. She kicked and fought against his hold while he clamped his hand over her mouth, pressing her forward to the end of a dock where a sloop was tied. He spun her around and brought her face close to his own. "You are a very beautiful woman, Miss Pearson, and beauty deserves to be appreciated. How long has it been since you were told how lovely you are?"

Frannie tried to bolt, but her retreat was countered by Duprée's advances. He gripped her shoulders, covering her mouth again with his hand, and walked her back to the edge of the dock. "You're trembling. Are you frightened by me, or is this the closest you have ever been to a man?" He turned her to face the boat and shoved her forward. With her back to him, Frannie reached into her handbag, grasping an object within. Duprée sneered at her. "Get in the boat, Miss Pearson. You will make me a fine traveling companion."

She spun around instinctively and struck him with the object from her bag. The surprise of the blow startled him, giving Frannie a moment to flee, but Duprée caught up to her at the edge of the grass and the two struggled again. He laughed at her, withholding his far greater strength to enjoy the game, toying with her as her fury increased, until he noticed the small revolver clutched in her hand, the one she had snatched from the carriage and tucked into her bag. As his eyes caught sight of it, Frannie remembered it as well, and she fired.

* * *

Jed, Markus, and Abel headed for the gunsmith's shop as soon as they left the wagon. Jed smiled with relief when he saw the man's pale, round face peering from around the corner of the back room. "Matthew, do you mind if we wait here until the crowd thins?" Jed asked.

"Crazy out there, ain't it?" the small, balding man noted as he shook the hand of his friend's grandson. "Fellers been askin' to borry my guns. Ever' time that barge pulls up there's trouble. Most of 'em is good people 'til someone gits 'em all likkered up and riled."

"I'd just as soon avoid trouble if I can," replied Jed, posting Abel near the window.

"We ought to be fightin' them British instead o' fightin' amongst ourselves. The gov'ner's gonna have a hard time raisin' an army out of folks that can't git along."

"What's this talk about raisin' an army?" asked Markus.

"It's jest talk right now, but some folks is jest plain sick of them redcoats. Some are pressin' the gov'ner to go directly to the pres'dent. If he don't take a stand, they're gonna take matters into their own hands. That's why the shop's in such a state. I'm tryin' to make as many guns as I can. I feel like I'm back in the Ohio Territory again." He laughed heartily.

Markus slapped his hand to his thigh. "I'd like a piece of that fight when it comes."

Jed frowned. "I'm not sure if we'll be ready for it, or if it's a prudent move, but I have no doubt it will come."

"You sound like old Light-Horse Harry," chuckled Matthew.

"Who is Light-Horse Harry?" Markus wondered.

Matthew looked to Jed. "Surely you know him, Jed. He soldiered a spell beside your grandfather. Named Henry Lee, from Virginia."

"Light-Horse Harry . . ." Jed pondered. "Do you mean General Henry Lee? My father spoke about him. He gave the eulogy at George Washington's funeral, didn't he?"

"'First in war, first in peace, and first in the hearts of his countrymen . . .' That was his greatest honor. But he was a rascal in the big war. Got hisself such a reputation for raids on British supply wagons that they started callin' him Light-Horse. He served in the Continental Congress and was gov'ner of Virginny three times, but he's fallen on hard times since."

"And why do my worries remind you of Mr. Lee's?" Jed asked.

"Well, he's not one to shy away from a fight, but he's a genius when it comes to fightin' them Brits. That's why he was so successful at attackin' 'em . . . 'cause he was always able to keep one step ahead. He don't think we're ready for this fight. No sir. Harry says we can't begin to compete on the water and we ain't got an army yit that kin keep up with 'em on the land either."

A random sound from outside drew everyone's attention. "How's it look out there, Abel?" Jed questioned.

"It's thinned out some, sir. Seems quiet enough now," the broad-shouldered man answered as he met the face of his new owner for the first time in a moment of peace. "Thank you, sir, for what you did back there."

Jed clenched his teeth again and shook his head. "I'm so sorry for that, Abel. I'm just glad it's over. Soon you'll be reunited with your parents and children. They've made a good adjustment since they've come to the Willows."

Abel closed his eyes and nodded his head slowly. "We'll make you pleased you brought us over, Master Pearson. I promise."

"I have no doubt, Abel. I promise you, life on the Willows will be better. All right?"

The quiet giant nodded silently and returned to watching at the window.

"Well, Matthew, we'll take our leave now." Jed stood and offered Matthew his hand. "I'd appreciate any information you can pass my way. I'd be especially interested in chatting with your Mr. Lee. Send a runner around with the news and I'll be glad to pay you for your troubles."

"I'll do it, Jed. If I hear from ol' Light-Horse again, I'll git you word. It was yer grandfather what spotted me fer this shop after I was wounded in the war. If a little heads-up will help the Pearsons, then I'll be sure to git you notice."

The three men left the shop and headed for the Willows' carriage and wagon. As they neared the location, they saw a frantic Jack running their way. "Jed! Jed!" He was running so hard he could barely breathe, let alone speak. "Is . . . Miss . . . Frannie . . . with . . . you?"

"With me? You were told to stay with her and to keep her safe! Why aren't you with her?" Jed demanded as he grabbed Jack by the shoulders.

Jack slumped in his owner's grasp until he caught his breath. "A boy came runnin' to me with a message. Said it was from a friend. Said you were callin' for me to come help. I told her not to leave the carriage. She said she wouldn't, Jed!"

Jed clenched and unclenched his jaw. He trusted Jack's story, and his heart went out to the man standing before him. "Perhaps she's in one of the shops. Did you . . . ?"

"I already checked every one, Jed. She's nowhere to be found!"

Jed's mind was reeling. "Markus, you take Jack and head up the street. Abel and I will head back toward the docks. Fire a shot in the air if you find anything, agreed?"

* * *

Duprée clamped his hand over his ear and fell backward to the ground. Blood trickled between his fingers from where the bullet had grazed him. He removed his tie and pressed it against the wound, the unbuttoned collar of his shirt revealing a disarming tattoo at the base of his throat. Frannie stood quaking, but the instincts of the experienced hunter finally took over. She raised the gun again, taking aim at the man's chest.

"I have the right to kill you, right here, and it would bring me great pleasure to do so."

"That's what you'll have to do, you know. I'll die before I'll submit to prison. It's another form of the slavery from which I was freed." He suddenly snickered. "Prison," he spat. "There'll be no prison. I assaulted a white woman. For that I'll hang."

Frannie's mind staggered from the implication of his words. "What do you mean about the slavery you were freed from?"

Duprée smiled sarcastically. "I'm part Negro, Miss Pearson—a mulatto man. Would it offend your lily-white sensibilities to admit that you were attracted to a man of color?"

"But . . ." she stammered weakly, ". . . you said . . . you said you were Creole."

"A man will say anything when he wants something." He rose up on one elbow. "And even more when he believes he is wanted in return." He watched her face flush deep red and knew he had a card left to play. "The man who made you shiver a few minutes ago is black Creole, Miss Pearson, otherwise known as a *gens de couleur libre*, a free person of color. What part of that statement upsets you more, the fact that I am part Negro . . . or that I made you shiver?"

Frannie's hand dropped as Duprée's words hit their mark, and he saw his chance. He swept his foot across her stance, tripping her backward. The gun slipped from her hand, and as she and Duprée scrambled for the weapon they heard voices and footsteps approaching. Duprée hurried to his feet and disappeared into the foliage before Frannie could note his direction.

"Frannie!" The frantic voice was Jed's.

"Jed!" she cried out. "Jed!"

When he and Abel reached her, her posture and appearance turned Jed's face ashen. Her hair was disheveled, and dirt and leaves clung to her wrinkled skirt and blouse as she lay upon the ground. It was all Frannie could do to convince him that he had arrived in time, but as he cradled her in his arms and rocked her, she soaked his shirt with her tears. Jed pressed his trembling lips to her head, closed his eyes, and murmured, "Thank God we heard the shot."

Minutes passed before Frannie could relay any credible information about her assailant. Jack and Markus had arrived as well and were prepared to track down the dog and rip him apart.

"Can you tell us anything . . . what he looked like or what he was wearing?" Jed probed.

"His name is Duprée," she relayed between shuddering breaths. "He is a mulatto man . . . from Louisiana. He wore blue breeches, a uniform of sorts, and he has the tattoo of an eye on his throat. Oh Jed!" she began sobbing again. "He told me he would take me to you. He said he sent Jack to help you, and he told me that he would escort me to you."

Jed held her close as his fury-filled eyes searched the faces of his three companions. "Have any of you seen such a man as this?"

Markus seethed silently, but Jack stepped up. "I saw a man like that last week," he offered regretfully. "Miss Frannie, could his breeches have been part of a ferryman's uniform?"

Frannie's eyes grew wide as she considered the suggestion. "I suppose so."

Jack shot Jed a look of resignation. "I saw him, Jed. He was sizin' up our teams from 'cross the street. He musta known I'd recognize him so he used the boy to get me away from Miss Frannie." He looked at Frannie and hung his head in failure. "I'm truly sorry."

"You couldn't have known, Jack," Jed said softly. "Given the same set of circumstances, I may have done the same thing." He noticed Abel's quiet, thoughtful form standing nearby and knew something was on his mind. "Have you seen this man, Abel?"

He answered reluctantly, still wary of his new owners. "Yes, sir. I saw him."

"When?" snapped Markus as he ground his fist into his other palm. "Was it today?"

"Same day as Jack . . . the day you bought me, Master Pearson."

Jed grimaced. "What was he doing? Did he seem interested in our wagons?"

Abel looked at Jack and shook his head.

"Speak up, Abel. It's all right," Jack encouraged. "Just tell Jed what you saw."

As Abel's gaze fell upon Frannie, his face softened and his eyes darted away. "He was bothering Bitty. Laid his hands on her," he muttered angrily. "Had her scared out of her wits."

"Why didn't she tell someone?" Jack asked. "Why didn't she at least tell me?"

Frannie clung ever more tightly to her brother. She understood why, and as Jed felt her tremble in his arms, he knew why as well. He looked at Markus with anger in his eyes. "I'm going to pay a visit to the ferry captain and see what he knows about this Duprée."

Markus stepped close to Jed and forced himself to speak softly. "Frannie needs you most now, Jed. Send me." Jed saw the vengeance in the smitten man's eyes. "You know I'll get answers from him if there are any to be had."

Jed looked down upon his sister's rattled form. He had never, in all his life, seen anyone break her spirit in this way. As desperately as he wanted the head of the man who had done this to her, he knew Markus was right, and he knew the infatuated Irishman would search as fiercely as he would. He nodded and growled under his breath, "Markus, find out everything you can about this Duprée character . . . where he came from, where he might find refuge . . . everything. Then tell that ferryboat captain that if he gets any word about this man and doesn't come to me immediately, he will be finished on this river. Do that for me, Markus."

"With pleasure," Markus assured him. The foreman reached a tentative hand of comfort toward Frannie, but when she recoiled at the unexpected touch, he paled and left quickly.

A shout sounded from the square again, and Jed lifted Frannie into his arms and led his men in the direction of their rigs. The small group moved down the back street and past the square, hoping to miss the ruckus and cross the main street to the apothecary where their teams and vehicles waited. All Jed wanted was to see the gates at the corner of the Willows property, where safety and peace awaited them.

* * *

Stewart Stringham stood on the wagon bench, still dirisively berating Frederick. Fortunately for Frederick, most of the day's crowd had departed Calverton, and most of the town's residents appeared to have already had their fill of Stringham family drama. Father and son had been alone for the past hour except for the seven tense slaves huddled together and a few shopkeepers passing time on their porches.

"Coward!" Stewart spat at Frederick as a look of utter revulsion passed across his face.

For one quiet moment, Frederick considered the words, then found himself surprised as anger, not fear, whipped through him.

"No!" Frederick shot back, pointing a daring finger in his father's direction. "I am not a coward. You sold Abel, Father. I couldn't condone your tampering with another man's property."

Stewart grabbed his son's lapel and glared at him. "Reputation is everything, idiot! This week Abel became the prize of the Patuxent—a slave who commanded the highest purse ever paid. Now look at what happened. With Jed Pearson's characteristic luck, a purchase that should have made him a laughing stock unforeseeably elevated his bargaining status along this river. I could not relinquish Abel to Pearson without first reminding our neighbors that he is simply another slave and Pearson just another master . . . nothing more. And that, Frederick, is why I 'tampered' with another man's property."

Frederick lowered his head in defeat. "I'm sorry, Father, it's just that . . ."

"This isn't about propriety or the law, is it? I know exactly what this is about, Frederick. You were reluctant to support your father today because the adversary was named Pearson. You're fond of Francis Pearson, aren't you? Don't think I've had my eyes closed my whole life. You made your loyalties quite clear today."

Frederick heard the threat underscoring his father's words as Stringham went on. "You've disappointed me lately, Frederick. The future of White Oak requires the respect of our neighbors and most assuredly the respect and fear of the Negroes. I can't turn my life's work over to someone whose stomach turns easily when the hard choices must be made."

"I can make the hard choices, Father," Frederick groveled, almost near tears in his frustration.

"Can you, son? Then prove it! Can you prove your competence and readiness to run White Oak?" goaded Stewart Stringham.

"Yes, sir," muttered Frederick, barely lifting his chin from his chest.

Stewart looked away, disgusted with his son's pathetic form. Then he caught something of interest from the corner of his eye. Sitting several yards away was a wagon and a carriage—Jed Pearson's fancy European coach. Suddenly his mood brightened. There would be only one reason Pearson would have bothered to drive the coach into town, and that reason was somewhere nearby.

"This is your time, Frederick," Stewart encouraged with a smile.

Frederick sat dumbfounded, staring at his father as if he were mad. "What are you up to?"

"You have purchases to load and seven slaves to do the work," his father answered.

"Yes, seven slaves who don't understand a word of English and who are likely to revolt if unchained in the town square," Frederick retorted, incensed.

Stewart snatched Fitchins's whip from his hands and tossed it to his son. "You have a good teaching tool. Instruct them."

Frederick had never held a bullwhip in his hands. Throughout his life it had been disturbing enough just to see one, worse yet to see it used. But to hold the flesh-chewing lash in his own hands made Frederick sweat and the Africans cower. From the looks in their eyes to the welts and scars on their backs, it was apparent that they had each had contact with it, and watching it move from man to man made them wary again.

"This is why we hired Fitchins, to train the new slaves and keep order," argued Frederick.

"Well, now," began his father snidely, "Fitchins is somewhat inca-pacitated, isn't he? And by whose hand?" Frederick understood the implication clearly.

"But I have no experience in such matters," he cried to deaf ears.

Stewart looked over Frederick's shoulder and saw Jed Pearson heading their way. He carried Frannie in his arms, and Jack and Abel followed behind. He smiled inwardly at their fortuitous arrival, then barked at his son through gritted teeth. "Now is the time to get the experience. Prove yourself, or I will find someone to do it who is worthy of White Oak."

Frederick fingered the leather wrapping of the whip's handle as he weighed his position. He had told Frannie he would consider living at the Willows and forfeiting his inheritance to avoid genuflecting to his father. But that was in a moment of passion, words he'd regretted as quickly as they'd flown from his lips. He felt almost confused by the anger and frustration raging within him. Did no one believe him worth anything? White Oak was his for the having, and he saw no reason why he shouldn't have both the woman he wanted and the land he was owed. He wondered what it was about the whip that turned his stomach. Was it the brutality it represented, or was it his fear that even the slaves would judge him weak—not obeying it when rooted in his hand?

Timing the little group's progress toward the carriage, Stewart calculated the optimum moment to play his hand and knew the time had come. He leaned closer to his son and snarled, "If you are not man enough for the task, then hand me the whip. But know this—once you have cowered in view of these slaves, they will never fear or respect you. Like a fever, that disrespect will spread, leaving me no choice but to look for someone who can restore what you have lost here today."

Frederick clamped his jaw and moved the whip, getting the feel of it and the way it responded to his command. He began to notice the beauty of its motion, like the swish of a horse's tail. Pleasantly surprised, he found that in many ways the whip responded to him like a horse, becoming an extension of himself. He raised it above his head and snapped it decisively, smiling at his success in mastering its use so quickly. He raised the whip and cracked it over his head again, basking in the approbation his father showed him each time the whip cried out in midair.

"Now over their heads, Frederick. Get their attention," Stewart prodded.

Frederick turned uneasily in the direction of the slaves and made an exaggerated sweep overhead before calling the whip back with another eerie crack. The slaves huddled more closely, fear showing in their eyes. Frederick knew he now commanded their attention.

Stewart saw Jed's group drawing near the street and feared his moment would be lost. "Now get to it!" he shouted to Frederick in a voice intended to draw the Pearsons' attention.

Frederick pointed to the ground, indicating for the slaves to step from the wagon. When no movement occurred, he waved the whip above their heads and snapped it loudly. "Get down!" he shouted, repeating the motion until the first man inched to the edge of the wagon, his eyes riveted on the man with the whip for some sign of understanding. Frederick nodded approvingly and repeated the command and the snap of the whip until all seven stood on the ground. He grinned at his father, whose proud expression further boosted his confidence.

Although the poor people being directed by the snarling whip quickly began to comply with his requests to lift and load the supplies, Frederick continued to occasionally crack the lash overhead. He was still completely unaware that Frannie Pearson's attention was now drawn to the scene.

"Well done," said Stewart Stringham with a grin. "You may do fine as the master of White Oak. That is what you want, isn't it?"

"Of course it is," Frederick answered, somewhat curious about the question. "I've always assumed . . ."

"So did I until your feelings for Francis Pearson changed. I had begun to worry . . ."

"Worry about what?" Frederick asked as he focused his attention on his father's words.

"Whether the Pearsons were using your affections for Francis to get their hands on White Oak." He raised an eyebrow to emphasize his point. "After all, you are my only heir, and a marriage between you and Francis could put you in a—shall we say—compromised situation."

Frederick's eyes grew wary as he drew nearer to his father. "How so?"

"Well, their intentions have always been to expand the Winding Willows. What could be easier than to marry Francis off to the heir who stood to inherit an adjacent property?"

"But . . . Frannie loves me . . ." Frederick countered weakly.

"Of course she does," Stewart agreed sarcastically. "But she also loves the Willows. Do you believe she could ever love White Oak equally? She is a strong-willed woman, Frederick. I fear you are the Pearsons' fatted calf. Oh, she'll be the adoring wife for a time, but then she may rise up and begin exerting her influence over White Oak, little by little."

Frederick's jaw tightened and his hand worked nervously over the handle of the whip as he measured Frannie against his father's intimations.

"One day you could find yourself receiving orders from the Pearsons . . ."

Frederick considered such a possibility. "No," he muttered, shaking his head in denial.

". . . or their Irish overseer . . ."

"No," he said louder as his breathing grew more rapid.

". . . or a slave."

"Never!" growled Frederick, slapping the lash against the ground and gawking at his father in utter refusal.

Out of the corner of his eye, Stewart noticed that Frannie had asked Jed to put her down. As soon as her feet touched the ground, she began making her way toward Frederick. The elder Stringham had calculated his timing well. Now he needed to push things just a little further.

"The way they run things at the Willows, you could find your whip in Abel's hand one day. Abel, the Pearsons' slave, could be more in charge of your own land than you, unless . . ."

Venom shot from Frederick's eyes. "Unless what?"

"Unless you are the master, the absolute ruler of White Oak," he finished. "You must govern your world with complete authority, because only fear will keep them from rising up over you. It's a precarious balance, Frederick. Can you maintain it? Can you be the master White Oak requires?"

Frederick was tired of being measured and found wanting, and his mind was spinning from the poisonous scenarios his father had fed him. He wanted this wretched testing to end. Incensed, he raised the whip over his head and began to send its bite into the seven captives.

"No, Frederick! No! Please stop!" Frannie screamed.

His head snapped in her direction, and he cringed at the look of horror on her face. He turned back to face his father, and then he saw it again: derision. Why could he never satisfy his father? For a moment, he stood suspended in time, with the whip poised above his head. One moment it had been the emblem of his power, and now it was the token of his shame.

"So . . ." his father sneered, shaking his head, "I was right."

Frederick felt he was being ripped apart by the two people whose opinions of him mattered most in the world. One would offer no forgiveness, but one might. With a loud wail that split the evening's peace, he brought the lash down upon the startled group, whose cries mingled with his own. Again he lifted the whip.

"No, Frederick! This is not you!" Frannie screamed as she rushed to grasp the end of the leather thong. Jed sped after her to pull her away just as the lash came down, slashing through the fabric of her jacket and into the flesh of her arm. Only then did Frederick gather his wits about him enough to drop the whip.

Out of his mind with disgrace and regret, Frederick rushed to her. "Frannie, I'm sorry," he cried out.

But he had gone too far. Jed shoved Frederick violently, knocking him to the ground as he picked his sister up in his arms. Jed drove his pointed finger at Frederick's huddled form and in a merciless voice growled, "I'll kill you if you ever come near her again!"

Frederick scrambled to his knees, pleading for forgiveness. "It was an accident! I love her, Jed. You know I do. Frannie, tell him how much I love you."

Jed moved quickly away. As the distance between them increased, Frannie looked over Jed's shoulder, keeping her eyes fixed on Frederick in a hollow stare.

Stewart Stringham watched his son surrender his manhood as his heir dropped to the ground, the image of weakness. The father regretted overplaying his hand, but what he had said *was* true. He would burn White Oak before ever allowing a Pearson to get a hand on her. However, he had never really held that as a concern; in fact, he had dared fantasize that with a little good fortune and some enterprise the Willows could just as easily have fallen his way. But he had pushed his sniveling son too far, and instead of strengthening the Stringhams' standing, Frederick had again folded and failed. The question now was what card was left to play. Stewart paused thoughtfully, then settled his eyes on Frederick's precious Francis, and smiled. He had perhaps the best and most powerful card of all.

CHAPTER 11

The Willows
Early July 1810

Frannie had barely left her room since the devastating day in Calverton. Jed was beside himself, as was Markus, who vacillated between wanting to set fire to the *Elizabeth,* challenging Frederick to a duel, and proposing to Frannie himself. Instead, he settled for flooding her with daily kindnesses—leaving flowers, books, and sweets at the threshold of her door.

The Willows men wrote Frederick off as a loss worth losing and tackled the next item on the list. They headed to Calverton to visit the captain of the *Elizabeth,* George McRainey, to see if he had received any word from Duprée. Markus had left McRainey shaking with fright the day of Frannie's attack, though he soon felt confident that the Creole had also duped the ferry owner by convincing McRainey to take him on as a partner. Nevertheless, doubting that the cad would easily walk away from his investment, Jed and Markus felt chances were good he would try to get word to his colleague.

They were waiting on the dock when the *Elizabeth* arrived. The captain stood at the bow shaking an envelope in his hand. "I swear it just came yesterday!" he declared, handing the envelope to Jed. "My boy will verify that. Tell 'em, son. Tell 'em how I was gonna run it out to 'em this evenin', after our last run."

Jed read the brief note:

McRainey,

The Elizabeth *is not out of my mind. I will contact you shortly. Begin making arrangements to buy me out. Tell no one or neither of us will have any part of the old girl.*

D

"I told you I didn't know anything more. Now go away and leave me in peace."

"Think hard," Jed persisted.

"He showed up here with gold coins, so I didn't ask many questions. I already told him!" He pointed to Markus. "Duprée's mother was his daddy's slave. When his father died, he left him his freedom papers and a nice inheritance."

"Was there any place he spoke about, a place he might have gone?" Markus pressed.

"I told you he talked 'bout Barbados. Said disparagin' things 'bout the Chesapeake. Said she couldn't compare to the view of the Caribbean. He must've spent some time there."

Jed glanced curiously at Markus, who nodded. He offered McRainey his hand in a gesture of gratitude, but the ferryman cringed in fear. "We don't intend you any harm, Mr. McRainey."

McRainey stared at Markus again. "Seems I recall him meanin' me harm a while back."

Markus offered no apology as Jed tried to explain. "Your partner hurt someone very dear to us. We had to know if you were involved and if you could lead us to Duprée."

McRainey looked skeptical. "Then why do I think you two still ain't finished with me?"

"We still want Duprée," reiterated Jed, "and you are our best hope of finding him."

"You read his warning! If he finds out I told you anything, he'll sink my ferry."

Jed looked McRainey in the eye. "Do you have his share of the money? He said he's coming back. Do you want to spend the rest of your life looking over your shoulder for him?"

"Once he's got his investment back, I'll be rid of him," McRainey stated.

"I don't think so," Jed replied calmly. "Why did he come here in the first place? He was wealthy and free. He could have gone anywhere. He told you he hated the area, yet he not only came but invested in a business here. No, something brought him to the Patuxent, sir, something important, and it will bring him back."

"All the more reason for me to keep my mouth shut then," McRainey pointed out.

"Help us, and we'll make sure he never bothers anyone again," Markus promised.

The man stalled. "And if he ruins the *Elizabeth*?"

Jed reached into his pocket, pulled out several silver coins minted in Philadelphia, and placed them in McRainey's hand. "Then I'll compensate you for your cooperation."

* * *

Like Frannie, Jed felt lost and lonely after the debacle in Calverton. He pulled Hannah's last letter out again, but it offered little comfort. Although her melodrama amused him, he was no longer sure where her reality began. Was she such an innocent that she did not know what teasing about her "handsome riding instructor" would do to him? Or was she purposely baiting him? Deciding to think the best of her, after three attempts, he finally penned a suitable response.

July 10, 1810

My Dear Miss Stansbury,

A debutante now? I long for the person you were just weeks ago, when you were still my own dearest Hannah. Please remember that these rules about familiarity also apply to handsome riding instructors. In any case, Hannah, I am delighted that you are riding Druid. I regret that I cannot be by your side, and look forward to the day when we will ride together again.

I doubt I will show up on your doorstep this summer, especially in your mother's current state, and don't fret about missing the summer parties on my account. Pressing matters consume my attentions, leaving me no time for entertainment. Perhaps we'll share a Christmas reunion.

In the meantime it pleases me immeasurably that you now have the additional company of your sisters to add to Selma's loving attention. You are three times as blessed as you were just a short while ago. Go to your sisters and console them, Hannah. This is my first instruction for my little lump of clay. In the meantime, let's assume the best of your mother's intentions and try to find a measure of happiness in her nurturing as well.

Please give my best regards to your entire family. My pen is ever poised to write to you.

As always, I am yours,

Jonathan Pearson

CHAPTER 12

Coolfont Estate
August 3, 1810

Dear Jed,

*I am writing this letter under the most difficult of circumstances.
By now your family should have received the official news that
Beatrice and her lieutenant are engaged. We sent an invitation to
an engagement party being thrown in their honor on the twentieth of this month. However dearly I wish to see you, I fear I
should warn you of some unscrupulous prattle circulating among
the gentry that could influence your inclination to attend.*

*It is rumored that Mr. Frederick Stringham was secretly engaged
to your sister, Frannie, and while it is also rumored that he had
not as yet officially asked your father for her hand, innuendoes of
indiscretions with a mulatto man are being silently charged to
her as the reason for the breakup. Poor Frannie! Sympathies side
with the groom, who is rumored to have soothed his broken heart
by immediately asking for the hand of another young woman, a
distant cousin, from Virginia. The wedding is taking place
within the month, and opinions are running harshly against your
dear sister for causing the young man such scandal and distress.
So much so that my parents speak of discontinuing all ties with
your family, and they have forbidden me from corresponding
with you. Were they not so confident that your family will decline*

*the invitation due to the aforementioned circumstances, I feel
certain they would send word to revoke it.*

*Oh, Jed! What shall we do? If you say this is not true, I will believe
you without question and will champion Frannie's good name.
And if by some innocent error any portion of it is true, my love
and my loyalty to you and yours will forever remain unchanged.*

*Is our friendship as dear to you as it is to me? Dear enough to risk
intrigue to continue it? I would risk the punishment for
disobeying my mother, but I fear that no amount of courage
would enable me to slip our correspondence past her wary eyes.*

*Please give my love to Frannie and know that l shall spend the
entire evening of the twentieth watching to see if you pass through
the door. If you do not, it may be some time before I can find a
way to contact you again. Until then.*

I am, as always,

Your dearest Hannah

Jed's hands shook and Hannah's letter slipped from his fingers and
floated to the floor. Her note explained everything . . . the humiliating
treatment his mother received on her recent Baltimore trip, the whispers
and snickers that followed him as he last walked through Calverton, and
worst of all, the real cause for Frannie's sorrow. He had been so
consumed by the hunt for her attacker that he had foolishly discounted
the impact losing Frederick would have on her. He had tried to ignore
the seriousness of their relationship, but he could no longer deny how
great a sorrow a broken engagement posed. Worse yet, it now appeared
that either her intended or his nefarious father had purposely twisted the
facts to save face, and they had cruelly allowed people to speculate upon
the reason at the expense of Frannie's good name.

Jed headed upstairs to check on her. Three attempts to raise her
were required before he heard her stir. He thought how much he
missed the strong sound of her impulsive steps, now replaced by a weak

shuffle. When she opened the door, a mere shadow of her normal self appeared. She peered out and smiled halfheartedly, "Is it time?"

"Soon, Frannie. May I come in?"

She headed for a velvet-covered chair by the window, offering Jed the other one. She lifted a quilt and book of sonnets and sat, placing both in her lap.

"Good book?" Jed asked benignly.

"*Poems,* by William Drummond," she answered. "Frederick gave it to me a few weeks ago." She sounded listless and sullen. "It's a collection of poems written for his bride who . . ."

"I am familiar with the work," Jed interrupted carefully, attempting to remain silent on the incongruity of Frederick and his love. "Shall we ride along the river after Bitty and Abel's wedding?"

"Perhaps," she said wistfully as she stared blankly out the window.

Jed could see that he did her disservice by ignoring her trauma, and he steeled himself to face it. "I'm sorry about you and Frederick. I didn't realize you two were engaged."

"We hadn't told anyone because we feared your reaction and Father's. He planned to speak to Father soon. Interestingly enough, having your blessing mattered to him as well."

Jed felt the sting. "Were you truly in love? I only ask because I never felt a sense of intimacy between you."

Frannie spun around, her pain so evident it stifled his response. "There are many types of love, Jed. You say that you love Hannah. I don't try to analyze or measure it—I just respect it. Your lack of understanding and disapproval doesn't change what I shared with Frederick. Were it not for his father . . ." Her voice trailed off.

Jed knelt beside her, surrendering the need to make his point. "My heart breaks for you."

Frannie's eyes met Jed's and her voice became thin. "I was so sure about his loyalty. Now, here I am, feeling fragile and alone for the first time in my life. I realize now that my bravado was, in great measure, a result of having been so completely sheltered by Mother and Father. I have never truly been hurt, Jed . . . until now . . . and suddenly, life seems so . . . temporary."

Jed shuddered as he worried how the revelations in Hannah's letter would affect his sister. "Frannie . . ." he started nervously.

"Oh, Jed. Tell me I'll be happy again. Tell me this ache will go away."

He couldn't tell her about the note, not yet. "Frannie, this family dearly loves you."

She laid her hand on his head. "I can't explain it, but when I thought I was going to be married and start a family of my own, something changed in me, as if I had a sense of my real purpose. That's gone from me now, and the hollow left in my heart aches terribly, Jed."

Something in Frannie's words reminded Jed of Hannah's spiritual hunger. He wondered if it was naturally inherent in women and if men were equally disposed to such promptings. Or if that was at the crux of the relationship between man and woman, that perhaps it was a part of women's purpose to help men find it within themselves.

"I can understand why people seek to know if there is a God who cares for us." She chuckled wistfully. "Imagine . . . talk of God coming from us," she mused. "It's nice. Hannah's influence is spreading to you, and now to me. Have you two begun your study of the Bible?"

"Just barely," he answered dolefully, "though I find it both fascinating and frustrating. How can I reconcile an angry God who floods the world in Genesis with the merciful Lord on Calvary? Either He has a specific plan for us that He is determined to see fulfilled at every cost, or there is more to the story than is recorded in just the Old and New Testaments."

Frannie smiled. "You're beginning to sound like Jerome. Have you heard him preach?"

Jed nodded and grinned, pleased by his sister's brightening mood. "Do you think Abel and his family are really happy here? I want them to be truly happy on the Willows. I want all the slaves to feel that this is their home."

"Jed, don't worry. I think tonight is proof of that."

"I just don't know anymore. Our people have sturdy homes and good food, and although a lash has never touched their backs, I still have to ask myself if this sets me measurably apart from Stewart. I hold deeds to human beings. I own *people*. At times I think I am the worst type of hypocrite."

Frannie walked to the window. "I've been wrestling with similar concerns myself."

"You?"

"Yes," she replied somberly. "Duprée is a vile, evil man, but he made me face some ugliness within my own heart, and I haven't been able to find peace since. Please do not ask me to explain. I can't get the image of those poor Africans from my mind, either. What can we do, Jed? One-third of all the Negroes in Washington City and Georgetown are freemen now. Some are skilled and make a decent living, and yet many of them live in worse conditions than when they were slaves. Can we simply toss our people into this culture and expect them to prosper?"

Jed sighed. "The state legislature may soon make it illegal to free slaves above a certain age, for the very reasons you have stated." He slumped back into his chair. "While I want to give all of them their freedom papers and some remuneration for what they've *given* the Willows, the bitter truth is that I don't want it enough to risk *losing* the Willows. So it is my greed and my pride that drive my need for them to be happy in their current state. What kind of man does that make me?"

"Just a man, Jed, a man caught up in the plague of his day. The fact that the issue troubles you so is a measure of your character. Let's do the very best we can by them, until we find a way to do what we know is right." She smiled suddenly. "Let's start by celebrating Bitty and Abel's marriage. Shall we go?"

* * *

"Bitty?" Abel inquired through the door. "I need to speak with you. It's important."

"Can't it wait, Abel? I have things to tend to before the ceremony."

"No, it can't."

She knew by the urgency in his voice that it indeed could not. She begged him to wait a moment while she folded the dresses and carefully concealed them within a basket of linens. Then she smoothed her apron, adjusted the scarf in her hair, and opened the door with a nervous smile.

His burden showed on his handsome face, and though the towering man was four years her senior, his jittery hands made him appear childlike and vulnerable.

"What is it, Abel?" she fretted as she led him to the rocker in the corner. "Tell me quick. Your worryin' frightens me."

He refused the offer to sit, leading her to the rocker instead while he paced around the cabin floor. "There's things I need to square with you, Bitty, before we share vows today. It wouldn't be fair to you if I don't, 'specially knowin' how fond you are of the Pearsons."

The hair rose on the back of Bitty's neck. "What is it, Abel?" she questioned nervously.

"Bitty, do you know your family's story? How or when they came to America?"

"Yes," she replied curiously, wondering what importance this information could hold at such a moment. "My gran was brought to Virginia on a slave ship when she was fifteen. She moved north when her mistress married Master Jonathan. She met my pap right here on the Willows." She reached for his enormous hands and squeezed them reassuringly. "And now it's your home. Yours and your family's." She smiled shyly. "Our family's."

Abel knew that what he was about to say would crush Bitty, but it had to be said before she pledged herself to him. He drew himself up proudly and spoke in a strong voice with perfect diction. "I cannot tell you my family's story, Bitty, because my father refuses to tell it to me."

Bitty stared in shocked silence at the sharp diction and bearing he suddenly commanded. Nearly absent was the lazy drawl that had previously characterized his speech and manner.

"He speaks five languages, Bitty. Five! He knows the Bible inside and out, and he can recite the works of Plato and Socrates, and Shakespeare's poetry." Abel could see that Bitty had no concept of such things, nor of the magnitude of his father's accomplishments.

He pointed to the manor house. "Those fancy books in the Pearsons' library? My father has read most of them, Bitty. He was a free man, an educated man, but somehow he ended up on a slave ship bound for America. He won't tell me how it happened or where he came from."

Bitty stared at Abel as if he was suddenly foreign to her.

"Everything was taken from him, Bitty. Jerome is not his real name. It was Gerard, given to him by his real parents. He won't tell me his last name because it would cause me pain if I was ever sold and forced to surrender it. Can you imagine how it feels to know you have to ignore who you really are? Missus Stringham assigned my father the name Jerome because that's where she was in the alphabet at the time he was bought." The indignity of it still festered in Abel. "He accepted his fate, believing it was somehow God's will. Only within the safety of our shack did he allow his mind to be free to recite the beauty that slavery locked inside him. He taught my mother and me to speak correctly and to read and write, warning us to hide our talents, as he did, but to use them to further our understanding of the world and to remind us of who we are in God's eyes. Everywhere else he kowtows, slurring his eloquent tongue and telling Bible stories and Greek fables in jumbled slave talk to entertain the others.

"He was once tall and strong like I am, but Stringham sent him to work in the mill. One day he fell into the water and was nearly pounded to death by the giant wheel while I stood by, a helpless little child, and watched. I finally threw him a rope and he managed to jam the wheel and climb out, but he was busted up inside, Bitty. The overseer called him stupid and worthless. I stood there and watched my accomplished father be abused by a half-wit. He could not even defend himself because the overseer was white and free, and my father was a slave.

"Something inside me changed that day. I refused to believe that this is what God wanted, and I decided if I ever got my chance I would change my destiny." He leaned over her. "I have the tools, Bitty. I can read maps and signs, and I have skills to earn a living and build a home. I just needed the opportunity. Now the Willows has given me that."

Bitty felt as small as she had ever felt in her life, and she wondered what Abel thought of her. "What are you sayin'?" she asked warily, clutching the arms of the rocker.

"I'm saying that in time, when the opportunity presents itself, I plan to take my family and run north, over the Mason-Dixon. As my wife, I'll expect you to come as well."

Bitty shook her head slowly. "I begged Jed to bring you here. He paid a fortune to keep your family together, and this is how you'd repay him for all he's tried to do for you?"

"Life might be a little better here, but my family and I and everything we think we own are all Pearson property in the end. Here or at White Oak I am still not free! And neither are you."

Bitty started to cry. "You never did love me, did you, Abel? You just wanted me to get you off White Oak and away from the whip. You used me just like that man Duprée wanted to."

Abel's shoulders sagged and he slid to his knees before Bitty's quaking frame. "No, no," he soothed as his arms wrapped around her tiny torso. "I love you, Bitty. I didn't pretend that. I never thought I would love another woman after my wife died, but I do love you . . . I have loved you for a long time. Ask Priscilla. She knows."

Bitty lifted her head from Abel's chest and pushed him away. She went to her baskets and began unpacking her things. "It's the measure of the people that counts. I can't stand beside you anymore and feel proud now, Abel. You've made me feel small and stupid, and there's no one, white or colored, 'cept that man Duprée, who'd ever done that to me before this day."

Bitty's confession took Abel's breath away. "I'm sorry, Bitty. I wasn't trying to hurt you. Believe me. I don't think I'm better or smarter than you. It's about opportunity. There are no opportunities for slaves. I wanted to tell you about me, about my father, so you would know I can take care of you. You don't have to wait for Jed. I can make you free."

Abel moved to her side to speak to her eye to eye. "I know how smart you are with medicines and herbs. People call for you to fix them up before they ask for a doctor. I know Jed Pearson wouldn't trust you to run the house and order the goods if he didn't think you were capable." He took her hands and stilled them. "Do you think I would marry you and ask you to raise my children if I didn't think you had wonderful things to teach them?" He smiled and stared into her doe-like eyes until her expression softened. "Do you think I would ask you to grow old with me if I didn't look forward to what those years with you will be like?"

Her head dipped shyly. "You're a different man to me now. All fancy and learned. I don't think I'll ever be able to walk by your side, yoked equal now."

"Why did you want to marry me before?"

Her sad face stared up into his. "You made me feel safe and loved. I wasn't afraid of growin' old anymore because I would have you and the children." She teared up again.

"Nothin's changed, Bitty." His voice slid back into its familiar drawl as he stood. "You know the man I am inside. I just wanted you to know that when the opportunity comes, I can get us north and blend in. I just wanted you to know that."

Bitty stepped away from him and placed her hands on her hips. "Let's talk about opportunity for a minute. First of all, there are a few things you don't know about me. For example, I can read some and I can write, and you know how I learned? Miss Frannie teaches me. And Jed knows. Don't think anything goes on around here that he don't . . . doesn't know." She cringed at the error. "In fact, he wrote me letters and I wrote to him at the university. I can do the orderin' 'cause he's taught me about sums and such. So maybe you ought to ask yourself where else a Negro can get such chances as Jack or me have had. Before you start dreamin' about runnin' north maybe you ought to stay a while and see what develops for you here. Besides, I know my Jed. He's goin' to make things right, in time. You wait and see. He'll make things right."

A knock sounded on the door.

"Bitty?" It was old Jerome. "Iz Abel in there wid ya?"

"Yes." She looked sadly at Abel, who cringed at his father's slurred speech. "Yes, he is."

"We needs ta be startin' da weddin'. People's gatherin' an' you two ain't even ready."

"We need a minute, Pa," Abel answered. He looked into Bitty's eyes and took her hands. "It'd be a shame to let all that good food go to waste when people are hankerin' for a weddin'."

Bitty searched his face. "Do you love me, Abel? That's all I need to know. Here . . . now . . . while we are livin' on the Willows. Do you love me?"

He bent down and kissed her softly. "What does your heart tell you?"

Bitty wiped her hands across her eyes and tried to see past his angry heart to the soft place that shone in his eyes when he looked at her. She smiled as she pushed him toward the door. "Out with you," she said, half laughing, half crying. "The bride needs to get dressed."

Abel bent down and placed one soft kiss on Bitty's cheek. As he left the cabin he saw his father speaking with Jed, and he sidled alongside to check on the conversation.

"I know it ain't nothin' the law would honor," Jerome spoke softly, "but in the years ta come it would be good for rememberin'."

"Of course, Jerome," Jed agreed.

"It's a wonderful idea," said Frannie. "I have some parchment that would be perfect for a certificate." She started to head back into the house when concern crossed her features and she spun back around and whispered to Jerome, "What names should I use?"

A sad smile clouded Jerome's face. "Jes Abel and Bitty is all. That'll do jes fine."

"No surnames . . . last names?"

"No, ma'am," Jerome answered politely and smiled.

She looked to Jed for advice, then turned her attention to Abel. "Would you like me to use the name *Pearson* as your last name, Abel, since you don't have one of your own?"

Jerome quickly grabbed Abel's arm and tried to break the tension with wit. "Abel and Bitty will be fine, ma'am," he began as his voice became bolder and resonant. "As Shakespeare so beautifully penned, 'A rose by—'" The shocked faces of the Pearsons silenced his tongue.

"Jerome!" Frannie smiled in wonder. "You know Shakespeare?"

Jerome's voice slid back into fieldspeak. "You knows how that young Master Stringham did love ta recite. I s'pose a bit of that poetry done rubbed off on ol' Jerome."

The mention of Frederick sent Frannie off on her errand, leaving the men standing in awkward silence. Standing side by side, Jed noticed that Abel favored his father. Their features were similar except that Jerome's face looked as if it had been salted and dried, leaving sunken cheeks and deep lines around the eyes and mouth. On the other hand, Abel's cheeks were full and his face firm. Jerome's eyes were intriguing. He had learned to lower them in deference to whites, but when he met a man's gaze they were strong and wise, hinting that he had known laughter as well as sorrow. His short, tight hair was salted with gray as were his short beard and moustache that ran into similarly colored sideburns. All in all, Jed thought he could stare at the man indefinitely and never tire of his face.

"They is fine cabins, suh," Jerome remarked to break the silence.

"I'm glad you think so, Jerome. I hope your family will come to regard the Winding Willows as your home. Here, most of the hands call me Jed. I hope you will also."

Jerome masked his uneasiness with a smile, while Abel simply stared.

Searching for a topic, Jed finally announced, "Well, I don't know about anyone else, but the aromas coming from the refreshments make me hope the service is short."

He headed for the table, greeting the Willows' more tenured residents, shaking hands with the men and patting the heads of the children who tugged on his jacket, pulling him off to play. Jerome and Abel marveled at his ease with the Negroes. Even more marvelous, however, was the comfort the fieldhands demonstrated in his presence. Jerome closed his eyes and clasped his hands together. "Our deliverer!" he whispered excitedly. "Thank you, Lord!"

But Abel was still unconvinced.

Moments later, Frannie came down the hill in the direction of the meadow with a rolled document in her hands. She was headed straightway to see the bride and passed her brother on the way.

"Where are Mother and Father?" he asked.

Frannie rolled her eyes. "I couldn't find them. They must have changed their minds. They are squirreled away in their room discussing some deep, dark secret."

Jed's stomach tightened as Frannie hurried to Bitty's door.

The bride was dressed in a simple, white cotton dress her mother-in-law had embroidered at the neck and hem. She clutched her hands to steady them. "When Josiah and I were wed, Sooky just played the flute and we jumped over the broom, but Abel's father insists we have a Christian weddin' with vows and such. I declare I am as nervous as a young girl again."

Frannie towered over Bitty as the two women hugged. "I'm so happy for you, Bitty."

"You two will always be my babies . . . but a family of my own . . ." she mused, clapping her hands together. "Well, I stopped dreamin' it would come true."

"Are you ready? I think there is a groom waiting on the other side of that door."

Abel, dressed in a new white shirt Bitty had made for him, stood under an arbor made of willow branches woven through with lilies of the valley. His four children, Caleb, Eli, Grandy, and Helen, stood by their grandmother, Sarah, while Jerome stood beaming proudly in front. All the Willows' hands, plus Markus, Jed, and Frannie, watched Bitty's entrance to a tune played by the fieldhand named Sooky who had also played at Bitty's first wedding. Three steps before she reached the arbor, Abel took her hand, drawing her to him.

Frannie sang "Ah! How Sweet It Is to Love" in her rich alto voice. Then Jerome offered a beautiful prayer. After the amens sounded around the group, he began the ceremony.

"Lawd," he began in his awkward fieldspeak, "just like Thou did gave Eve unto Adam to be his helpuh, Abel comes here ta take Bitty as his helpmeet and wife . . ."

Bitty dropped Abel's hand and walked to Jerome. As she whispered in his ear, his eyes grew wide. He looked from her to Jed and back again, then swallowed hard and smiled as Bitty returned to Abel's side. Jerome continued, but this time his voice carried the resonance and meter of music. As he quoted from Genesis and Psalms, his words rolled off his tongue like poetry. Bitty looked into Abel's proud eyes and whispered, "It's a good opportunity, isn't it?"

He hesitated and then nodded, recognizing that it was, at the very least, something good.

When the time came for the vows to be spoken, Jerome led the couple through a recitation from the first chapter of the book of Ruth, verses sixteen and seventeen.

Intreat me not to leave thee, or to return from following after thee; for whither thou goest, I will go; and where thou lodgest, I will lodge: thy people shall be my people, and thy God my God.

Where thou diest, will I die, and there will I be buried: the Lord do so to me, and more also, if ought but death part thee and me.

Once the vows were spoken, Jed approached Jerome. He smiled as he extended his hand to the nervous man. "You didn't learn to read and speak like that on White Oak, did you?"

Jerome swallowed hard. "No, sir. Tonight was the first time in years I was able to speak freely, outside my own four walls. I'll never do it again, Master Pearson, if you wish me not to."

Jed breathed deeply as he prepared his reply. "There are some men who would arrest you and me for what happened here tonight. You do understand that don't you, Jerome?"

"I do," he answered nervously as Abel stood nearby, clasping and unclasping his hands.

Jed spread his arms to the perimeter of the meadow. "This is your home now. These are your new walls. You may speak and think freely here. You may even teach freely here, but the first thing you must teach is that what is learned here must remain here. Are we agreed? All our safety may rely upon that understanding."

Jerome's face shone with incredulity. "We are agreed, sir."

"Call me Jed," Jed reminded him with his hand outstretched.

"Jed," repeated Jerome almost reverently.

"And any other ideas or improvements you would like to make can be brought to me without worry. I cannot promise that every one will be approved, but I can promise that we will discuss them as men." He noted the new brightness in Jerome's eyes. "Now, what I want most of all are some of those little cakes and some strawberry lemonade."

As the crowd moved to the inviting spread of food on the table, Bitty and Abel enjoyed their first married moments alone. "Do you remember our vows?" she asked him softly.

"Yes," he replied. "I've heard my father recite those verses many times."

"'Thy people shall be my people . . .'" she repeated to him. "Jed and Frannie are my people, Abel, just like Caleb, Eli, Grandy, and Helen are yours. I'm takin' yours as my own. Will you do the same for me?"

"We'll give it some time," he promised, "but in the end, remember the other part of that vow. 'Whither thou goest, I will go.'"

She paused before closing her eyes and nodding. "I'll remember, Abel. I'll remember."

* * *

Dusk had settled over the meadow like smoke, adding to Jed's anxiety as he walked Frannie back to the manor. A worrisome scenario haunted him as he tried to remember where he had laid

Hannah's letter. As soon as they crossed the threshold, he saw his father holding it in his shaking hand. His mother stood behind him, pale and ethereal as if she were about to faint.

That night Jed had begun to see a glimmer of his beloved sister return, but as she now took the letter from her parents and read, so great was her anguish and anger that she let out an agonizing cry that dropped her mother to her knees. Jed held Frannie in his arms, regretting that he had not disclosed the news to her himself, as his father began outlining how her thorough retreat from Maryland society would transpire.

"Jenny, hurry and pack Miss Frannie's things," barked Jonathan Pearson to the maid as guttural *no's* spilled from Frannie's lips.

"How could he have betrayed me so?" she tearfully pleaded to everyone in the room.

"An engagement, Francis? Why were we never told any of this?" raged her father.

"Perhaps because we made our feelings about the Stringhams quite clear," Jed replied.

"Stewart Stringham . . ." muttered Jonathan. "I'd wager anything that he orchestrated this entire affair. He probably had Frederick's cousin selected in advance!"

"There was no *affair!* Frannie was being kidnapped!" Jed corrected fervently. "She shot her assailant and he ran off."

"Why didn't you come to us?" her father ranted. "You've left us with our guard down, completely vulnerable to all manner of scurrilous talk. If we only had known, perhaps then . . ."

"Please, Father!" Frannie begged between shudders. "I'll tell my side of the story. Oh, please don't send me away, Papa. Not like this."

Julianne Pearson drew her daughter's head to her bosom and cried. "This is what we think is best, Francis. Under the circumstance, there's simply no other way."

"She's right," Jonathan conceded with a groan. "There is old history you don't understand. The gentry feeds on scandal, is slow to forgive . . . and it never forgets."

"Then hang the gentry!" cried Jed. "Is their favor more important to you than Frannie?"

"It's not that simple. They will destroy her reputation if she remains. No decent man—"

"She's innocent!" shouted Jed. "She did nothing wrong!"

"The only truth that matters is the one people believe," moaned his mother. "You two fell under the gentry's scrutiny the minute you were born Pearsons. We debated what path to follow, whether we should be strict, as my parents were, or whether we should let your natures guide our actions. We chose the latter, and for the greater part, we were pleased with the outcome. We enjoyed good association with our neighbors and you two were thriving." She paused to settle the shuddering breaths that seized control of her speech. "But in attempting to ignore the scrutiny of the gentry we made a greater mistake. We became too liberal, especially with Frannie. People predicted that unfettered access to her inheritance and too much freedom would be her undoing. Now it appears they were right. Thus is my failure," she sobbed.

"No, it is both of ours," Jonathan corrected soberly.

Frannie watched her father's face slacken as he comforted his wife, and the totality of the situation finally hit her. She knew she had done nothing wrong, nothing to deserve the feelings of responsibility that weighed upon her, but guilt was suffocating everyone she loved. And while no one said as much—Jed even rallying to her defense—she understood that her departure would begin the healing.

She sighed and fought the urge to surrender a moment longer, praying another solution would present itself, then finally, when she could no longer bear another moment of the agonizing rift dividing her family, she uttered, "I'll go." The words fell from her lips like the final exhale of a dying woman.

"What?" Jed asked incredulously. "No! You'll not be exiled due to gossip generated by someone else's sin, be they a dead Pearson or a Stringham. The shame is not yours!"

Frannie rose heavily and began climbing the stairs to pack her bags. "It's all right, Jed," she declared, seeming suddenly resolved. "Just let me go. Please . . . just . . . just let me go."

CHAPTER 13

Baltimore, Maryland
Early April 1811

Beatrice Stansbury Snowden blossomed as the wife of a military officer. Not only was her husband, Captain Dudley Snowden, good to her, but her budget was ample and her freedom complete. A renewed love of life brought the plain woman a beauty she had never before possessed. And that, along with her husband's military station, placed the couple on the finest guest lists. They purchased a stylish brownstone along fashionable Calvert Street, where many of the gentry maintained city dwellings. Now that she lived in such comfort, however, she felt even greater worry for her sisters, who alone bore the brunt of their mother's ravings. She would never admit to it in public, but in her heart she knew her mother was going mad, nearly as crazy as Susannah's own mother—Beatrice's grandmother—was reported to have been when she died. *Died?* Beatrice cringed and shook her head. *Or so the story goes . . .*

Beatrice frequently evaluated her own mental state, fearing that every cross word, every angry thought might be the beginning of her own emotional plummet. She knew that if she didn't get her sisters away from their mother, the woman would surely drive them mad. Her poor Hannah had never known anything but her mother's tyranny. Oddly enough, however, it was Myrna who seemed the most damaged. Like Beatrice, she had enjoyed a normal early childhood, completely unaware of their poverty. But their mother's preoccupation with wealth increased proportionately with her failing mental stability. Beatrice had discerned Susannah's deteriorating mental state early on, distancing herself somewhat and adapting to her mother's mood swings, while poor Myrna became the proverbial frog in the pot. Each increase in Susannah's psychosis became as normal to her as not, until perfection and its accompanying guilt had beaten her badly. Hannah, on the other hand, had always sensed that something was awry in her mother and had maintained a semblance of self-worth. But Beatrice feared time would take its toll on Hannah as well. And now she finally had the means to help her sisters.

She decided to feign illness and send for Myrna and Hannah. When the pair arrived, their condition tore at Beatrice's heart. Hannah was seventeen and a woman in stature and form, but she still wore mid-calf frocks with ruffled hems and collars. Conversely, Myrna seemed old and worn as if, like a piece of jerky, the life had been salted out of her. Beatrice wondered if she herself had looked similar before her marriage. Her gratitude soared again for the somewhat dull but generous and kind Dudley Snowden, who had been her own salvation.

The women headed for Lexington Street at first light. The market had swelled greatly from its humble beginnings in 1793, a pastoral gathering point on General Howard's estate where farmers could congregate to sell their meats, produce, dairy products, and other assorted wares. Now wagons lumbered along all night to make the twenty-mile trek from Reisterstown and Towson to be ready to sell their goods with the sound of the opening bell at two in the morning each Tuesday, Friday, and Saturday. From then until the noon bell rang, the market was a sprawling shoppers' paradise. Standing side by side were sheds and stalls in which hams and chickens hung from the ceilings. Fish were laid out on mounds of ice or were salted and dried. Beef and veal, lamb and pork were available in abundance, as were eggs, butter, cheese, milk, bread, and assorted baked goods. Grains of every variety filled barrels, and seasonal produce poured in fresh from the fields. Merchants brought sundries to the market, and a lively barter and exchange program developed, adding homemade goods such as clothes, weavings, candles, and leather items to the mix.

The sisters filled the storage area of the carriage with food and miscellany, and then headed to the dress shops on Calvert Street.

They purchased gowns and other essentials until they could barely fit themselves and their purchases into the buggy. The mile-long trip back to the Snowdens' home offered them scant time to plan the additional adventures they hoped to enjoy before the Stansburys forced Hannah and Myrna back to Coolfont. Their first venture was a dinner party, planned for the upcoming Sunday, for which Dudley's help proved priceless.

"You're certain everyone is coming?" Beatrice asked Sunday evening as she rushed around dressing. "The whole evening will be a disaster if no suitable gentlemen attend tonight."

Dudley fastened the last button on his blue dress uniform and placed two calming hands on his wife's shoulders. "I'm more worried we'll have more single men than women and end up hosting a duel for your two sisters' attentions."

Beatrice smiled apologetically. "I'm ranting, aren't I? It distresses me when I do that."

He kissed the top of her head. "Not to worry. I believe it's every hostess's prerogative."

The butler announced the early arrival of the first guest, and the flustered pair hurried downstairs to welcome him. His name was Harvey Baumgardner, the precision-driven legal advisor to the city council. He was fortyish, balding, and short, with a stump of a nose and a nervous chuckle that quickly wore on one's nerves. Judging from the newness of his apparel, he took great interest in his appearance, though somehow the outfits he assembled mimicked theatrical costumes. Moreover, despite the fact that he was never at a loss for an amusing anecdote, he was among the loneliest of men. This made Dudley suspect that he was also among the most eligible.

"Mr. Baumgardner," greeted Beatrice with a curtsy. "I apologize that we were not here to greet you personally, but your punctuality has taken us by surprise."

Baumgardner handed her a small bouquet of flowers and pulled his watch from his vest pocket. "Let's see. Punctual but not early. It is precisely seven, and I am quite sure my invitation stated seven as the hour." He chuckled nervously. "But please forgive me if my timely arrival has upset your schedule. I could exit and walk the block until other guests arrive."

"No, no," Beatrice assured as she looked to Dudley for some relief. "Your arrival is perfect, and thank you for the flowers. They are lovely."

Dudley quickly took Baumgardner by the arm and led him to the library for a drink while Beatrice hurried back upstairs to check on her sisters. "The guests are arriving!" she whispered excitedly. "Myrna, Dudley was right. Mr. Baumgardner is the most socially dispossessed man, but he is thoughtful. If you find him interesting, I believe he would be a highly attentive suitor."

Myrna sighed audibly and walked into the center of the room, nervously fingering her blue velvet gown. "Oh, how I long for that to be true." A wave of guilt hit her and she added, "Of course, he would have to be someone very special to pry me from Coolfont and our parents."

"Of course, he must, Myrna. You'll marry for love and nothing less," Beatrice responded.

"Do I look presentable?"

"You look lovely," Beatrice answered as she smoothed a rebellious strand of dark hair against the others plastered to Myrna's head. "Mr. Baumgardner will be quite taken with you."

"I can't wait to become a woman so I can fall in love," Hannah said as she walked out from behind the dressing screen. Her two older sisters stared at the transformation that had changed the child into a woman in a few hours. Their awed expressions nearly frightened her, and when they spun her around to gaze into the mirror she barely recognized herself.

Beatrice had insisted she choose the green silk dress that made her eyes leap from the rose palette of her complexion. The gown was cut wide across her shoulders with a demure neckline, and it buttoned up the back like a second skin, emphasizing her tiny waist and slim hips. Myrna had loaned her a strand of pearls and earrings to match, and Beatrice had smoothed a film of mineral oil along her lips to make them glisten. Her long black hair was braided and then twisted into a bun and pinned at the nape of her neck, where a few curly strands had been coaxed to cling provocatively to her soft skin.

"You are a woman, Hannah," Beatrice marveled.

"It's the corset," she mumbled in wonder. "I was not shaped this way before I put it on."

Her sisters laughed at her innocence. Beatrice smiled and said, "A corset helps, Hannah, but I assure you, you were shaped like that all along. It was those childish dresses Mother insisted you wear that made you feel you were still a girl. You're seventeen now. You should have had your coming-out party already. It's time for you to begin courting."

Hannah stared silently at her image in the mirror.

"What are you thinking about?" Beatrice asked.

"Jed Pearson," she replied sadly. "If I really am a woman, and if women should marry for love and nothing else, then I wish Jed could see me tonight and fall in love with me."

Myrna glared at Beatrice and looked back at Hannah. "Even if your dream were to come true this very minute, you know Mother would forbid you from ever marrying into a scandal-ridden family like the Pearsons, Hannah," warned Myrna.

Beatrice shot Myrna a scalding look and wrapped her arms around her little sister, who now looked quite devastated. "Many men will love you, Hannah. Give it time. These things have a way of working themselves out."

Hannah pulled free of her sister's embrace and fell onto the bed as tears began. "It's all a fairy tale, Beatrice . . . a beautiful, fleeting dream that will end as soon as we return home to Mother. I will never have any say about my own destiny. Everything I wear and every person I love is controlled by her whims. Even my beautiful Druid. I dared to believe he was offered in love, but I soon discovered that once she knew I loved him, he became a pleasure to dangle in front of me like a carrot, one to deny me when I displeased her. It has been weeks since I was allowed to ride him. And now it's Jed. She won't even allow me to write to him anymore. We have been corresponding since I was ten, but now I am denied that last familiar pleasure. Beyond you two, I have no one but Selma," she cried. "And Beatrice, I owe you an apology. I was so terrified of losing you to Dudley that I was dreadfully horrid to him while you two were courting. I said despicable things about him to Selma. I just didn't want you to go."

Beatrice wrapped her arms around her sister. "I know, darling, I know." She had rarely seen Hannah cry, and was surprised at the depth of her sister's emotions.

"Can you forgive me?" Hannah begged.

"There's nothing to forgive. Both Dudley and I knew how hard my leaving would be on you both. We should be asking you to forgive us. We should have discussed things with you and told you that we would always be there for both of you."

"Oh, Beatrice, I wish it could be so, but I fear it is already too late. Mother is past ill. I think she is mad, and it terrifies me to think of what other deprivations she will mete out against us when we return home." She turned to Myrna, whose sorrowful expression registered complete agreement. Minutes passed as the sisters attempted to comfort each other until Hannah asked to be alone.

Hannah's words burned into Myrna's mind as she followed Beatrice out of the room, leaving a disconsolate Hannah to spend the night alone with her sorrows. But as soon as Myrna's foot touched the landing at the top of the stairs, the sounds of cheerful voices drifted to her ears, imbuing hope within her dreary soul. If Beatrice had escaped, there was hope for all of them. Myrna pinched her cheeks to brighten them, threw her shoulders back, artfully arranged a smile on her face, and descended the steps, determined to find a new world this night.

As Myrna came into the room, Beatrice noted that all but one guest, a young lieutenant named Andrew Robertson who served under Dudley, had arrived. She sought out Mr. Harvey Baumgardner, but her husband was one step ahead of her, guiding the loquacious man to his sister-in-law.

"Mr. Harvey Baumgardner, may I present my sister-in-law, Miss Myrna Stansbury."

Myrna curtsied and greeted him with a pleasant smile. Mr. Baumgardner offered her his arm and the two strolled into the parlor.

A few minutes later, the butler rang a bell announcing dinner as a knock sounded on the door. He hurried to give entrance to the final guest, Lieutenant Robertson. The lieutenant wore the ornate uniform of the highest-ranking enlisted officer—a gold-trimmed, dark blue coat that extended to the waist in the front and sported tails and false turnbacks on the back. On his shoulders were gold epaulets and fringed shoulder boards bearing the single stripe that indicated the office of a lieutenant. In his arms he carried his tall, black shako hat. As impressive as his uniform was, the lieutenant's personal attributes were of equal note, and as soon as Beatrice laid eyes upon the man, she believed he was the answer to her prayers.

He was tall, nearly six feet, and he looked to be in his twenties. Golden curls covered his head like a fleece cap, and his large, cobalt blue eyes looked out beneath long lashes. He had a generally fair complexion, except for his cheeks, which flushed with color so bright that he nearly looked feverish. His mouth was narrow and full as if he had just bitten into a green apple, his jawline taut and angular.

"Andrew!" Dudley cheered as he thumped him on the back. "We had nearly given up on you, old man. How good of you to come!"

"I apologize for my tardiness," he started, bowing low. "Evidently, one Miss Stowe accepted a young man's proposal of marriage tonight. As a result, all of his heartbroken rivals rushed into my office this evening, anxious to enlist. I just recently finished processing paperwork for a dozen recruits. Please, do forgive me."

Dudley smiled dubiously at his comrade in arms, then placed his hand on the small of his wife's back and guided her forward. "Lieutenant Robertson, my wife, Beatrice."

Beatrice offered her hand to the soldier. "Lieutenant Robertson, what a tale," she chuckled, taking his arm to make introductions to the other ten guests.

Robertson scanned the room and his face clouded. "Your sister Hannah? Dudley raves on and on about her. It was the pleasure of meeting her that drove me on at this late hour."

Beatrice looked to Dudley and replied, "I'm afraid she's under the weather, Lieutenant."

"Is she here? Is she still your houseguest?"

"Well . . . yes . . ." stammered Beatrice, surprised by the lieutenant's persistence.

"Oh, please. Do encourage her again. Tell her a lonely officer who has just recently returned from a desolate post would delight in simply sharing a few minutes of her company."

Dudley persuaded Beatrice to try again to encourage Hannah to join the party. As she mounted the stairs to Hannah's room, she wondered how much more awkward the evening could become.

She tapped on the door. "Oh, dear," sighed Beatrice, finding Hannah dressed in her nightclothes.

"What? What's the matter?" demanded Hannah.

"I need a favor, dearest. I need you to dress and come down to supper. Dudley has invited a handsome young lieutenant who is determined to meet you. If you don't come down, I will appear a thoughtless hostess and my party will be ruined."

Hannah turned away from her sister and sat on the edge of the bed. "I can't, Beatrice. As much as I would love to please you, I'm simply not good company tonight."

Beatrice knelt beside her and took her hands in hers. "Hannah, he's very handsome and well spoken. It would be good for you to laugh and have some conversation."

Hannah considered her sister's counsel, but the reality of the evening's earlier conversation still wore heavily on her. "I don't want the attentions of anyone but Jed, Beatrice." Her eyes began to shine as she continued sorrowfully. "And since you have all admitted that Mother will never allow me to have this one wish, than I cannot bear to feign interest in anyone else. It would only serve to remind me that I had settled for Mother's will over my own heart."

Beatrice laid her head in Hannah's lap, nearly teary-eyed herself. "My poor Hannah," she said softly. Her head slowly rose, and when her eyes met Hannah's, a sparkle was evident. "I have a bargain to offer you."

"What type of bargain?" Hannah asked cautiously.

"If you come downstairs and keep the lieutenant company, I'll help you get a letter off to Jed. What would you say to that?"

Hannah's eyes lit up instantly. "Do you promise, Beatrice?"

Beatrice nodded, overjoyed to see happiness return to her sister's face. "You can draft it in the morning and we'll deliver it to his parents' home. The address is just a few blocks from here. They can forward it on to him by courier if he is not soon expected. Agreed?"

"Agreed!" squealed Hannah as they hurried through the tedious task of redressing. With the letter as an inducement, it was little more than a quarter of an hour later when the two women descended the staircase. The guests were already into their second dinner course when Beatrice and Hannah appeared in the doorway. Dudley rose first, followed quickly by the other men, who turned to see the source of the extreme pleasure and pride evident on their host's face. He raised a glass to toast the women as he presented Hannah.

"Ladies and gentlemen, she is fashionably late but obviously no less lovely. May I present to everyone my youngest sister-in-law, Miss Hannah Stansbury."

Lieutenant Robertson was on his feet and making his own introduction to Hannah before the toast had even ended and the "here, here's" were sounding above the quiet buzz of affirming compliments. Beatrice wondered how her socially deprived sibling would handle the crush of attention pressing upon her, but Hannah seemed relatively unaffected by it all, prompting Beatrice to wonder if Hannah saw herself as merely a character in one of the many novels she had read, or if she truly didn't care about any of the interest being paid her.

Lieutenant Robertson led her to a seat he had reserved next to his and called for the steward to bring Hannah the previously served course, crab bisque.

"Thank you, Lieutenant," offered Hannah shyly as she tried to avoid his attentive gaze.

"Please, Miss Stansbury, I would be delighted if you would consent to call me Andrew."

Hannah nodded affirmatively and smiled. "All right. Andrew it is."

Pleasure washed over his face as he toyed with his food while she ate her soup, but as the steward cleared her bowl and brought the second course, Andrew turned to her and spoke. "I feel as though I know you already, as the captain—Dudley—has carried on so about you, and he is like a brother to me. What I am saying is . . . though we've just met, may I call you Hannah?"

Hannah considered what she would have said to Jed if he had left her such an opening for frivolity, and she responded likewise. "And what are my other choices?"

Robertson sat in momentary confusion, then nearly choked as he tried to suppress his laughter. As he grabbed for his napkin, Hannah patted his back. Once his spell ended he cast a sideways glance in her direction and whispered, "I believe I am now owed the privilege since I nearly lost my life securing it."

Hannah smiled appreciatively, and as their playful banter continued, her family members secretly prayed that it would not only persist, but flourish.

After dinner, Beatrice invited the guests to join her in the parlor for tea and dessert, but Dudley leaned across Hannah's seat to lay a hand on Andrew's arm, bidding him to remain a moment. Then he whispered a question to his young military attaché. "The true cause of your delay tonight . . . was it something of which I should be aware?"

Andrew shot a worried glance in Hannah's direction, but Dudley waved off his concern. "Don't worry about speaking in front of Hannah. She is already more knowledgeable about the current political situation than most men."

"I wouldn't want to upset her," Andrew cautioned.

Hannah shot him a scornful look.

"It's a man's duty to protect women, Hannah, a duty I take very seriously."

He seemed sincere, evidencing no bravado, so she softened, controlling her frustration. "How is it that men can believe they are protecting women by keeping them in ignorance?"

"By sparing you from some of the ugliness of this world." He sounded earnest. "Perhaps our motives are selfish. By keeping our loved ones innocent we hope to make our homes a place where our own souls can heal. At least I pray that such a thing is possible."

"And how do women heal once they are scarred? I believe that life affords us each but one safety net, Lieutenant . . . that having done all we can, the Lord will make up the difference."

Speechless, Andrew looked to Dudley, who sat mutely with raised eyebrows.

Unflustered, Hannah continued. "I doubt the world will ever be without conflict, and despite his most sincere efforts, no man can completely shelter his family from every pain. Women bring the children into this world, and I for one would like to know what manner of world that is so I can prepare them. I choose not to hide from it, but to meet it, fully prepared."

"Touché!" Andrew uttered admiringly.

Hannah folded her napkin and faced Andrew. "I don't mean to be rude, it's just that the world you describe reduces women to little more than walking, talking kaleidoscopes of pretty thoughts and frivolities. We're capable of being so much more than that."

"I didn't mean to offend," he stammered. "It's just that I cannot believe a young woman of seventeen has had time to ponder the purpose of life so deeply."

"One cannot measure life by time alone," Hannah retorted. "Some lives are filled with idle pleasure. Others have only thoughts and questions as companions." She turned to Dudley and smiled as she took his arm. "I am grateful life has afforded me a portion of each."

"As am I," Dudley agreed, placing a kiss on the top of her head. He began to escort her from the room when Andrew spoke up again. "Please, don't leave, Hannah. I would love to hear more of your opinions. It's a fascinating glimpse we single men rarely get." He laughed shyly. "Perhaps that's why we have these flawed romantic notions of being knights in shining armor when women actually long for something else. Teach me, Hannah. You'll find me a willing student."

Dudley gently lifted Hannah's hand from his arm and placed it on Andrew's. "The air is warm tonight. Why don't you two sit outside in the garden? I'll make your excuses."

A knowing smile passed between the men, and Hannah caught it. "Am I in the middle of a conspiracy?" she teased as Andrew placed her wrap around her shoulders and opened the door.

"My family is in New York. The captain knows how lonely Baltimore has been for me. He has teased me for weeks about your arrival, promising to make an introduction for me."

"You're a handsome man and an officer. I wouldn't think finding a suitable lady with whom to keep company would be an issue for you."

Andrew laughed loudly as they entered the garden. "Hannah, you are a treasure."

"What's so humorous?" she asked sincerely.

"Not many women . . . actually none that I currently know . . . would be so open with their compliments. Most of them try to keep the upper hand, making the man constantly aware that he is the lowly suitor who must prove his salt to be worthy of her. But I thank you, nonetheless."

Hannah lowered her head and blushed. "I don't have experience at such games, I'm afraid." She met his gaze and lifted her nose into the air. "But if you like, I'll try to make you feel as lowly as possible the rest of the evening . . . strictly as a favor to you, of course."

"No, no, no, thank you," he replied, waving his hands in protest. "I am honored to be the handsome junior officer who currently has your attention."

They strolled quietly past flower beds where jonquils and daffodils were enjoying their last days, even as tulips prepared to usurp their stage. The lamplight at the end of the walk projected onto the branches of budding forsythia, casting eerie shadows on the ground and fence. The lieutenant turned to face Hannah. "I'm glad you don't have experience playing idle games. It wouldn't suit you anyway. You are honest and genuine. Those are rare qualities these days."

Hannah blushed. "Whenever I get out of sorts, Jed puts me squarely in my place."

Andrew's attention piqued at the mention of a man's name. "This Jed, is he your brother?"

"No," she replied pensively, "though I've known him all my life."

"And these notions about love and the relationships between men and women . . . you've discussed these with Jed, have you?"

She laughed. "I discuss everything with Jed. He knows me better than anyone else in the world, better than I even know myself. He makes me feel I am remarkable when I can only see my flaws. Knowing my social opportunities are limited, he fears I will settle short of what will make me truly happy, so he is my guardian and protector as well. Sometimes it is only Jed that keeps my head above the swells. He is my dearest love." Her admission caught her off guard.

The lieutenant's heart sank. "You're very lucky to have such a friend as your Jed, Hannah. Does he have someone special? Someone he is courting?" he asked hopefully.

"No, though he's terribly handsome and tall." Her voice became thoughtful. "He jokes that because his attentions are diverted elsewhere, I will likely marry before him."

Andrew stopped walking and faced Hannah. "I hope in time, Hannah, that you will come to think as affectionately about me as you do your friend."

Hannah was speechless.

* * *

Dudley was beginning to think he would have to issue an order to secure Lieutenant Robertson's departure. It was only after Hannah accepted an invitation to join him for lunch that the young lieutenant finally left. Before Beatrice had a chance to evaluate the evening with her sisters, Hannah bolted upstairs to gather her wits before beginning her letter to Jed.

She gazed into the mirror to become familiar with the reflection staring back at her, the reflection that had captivated the young lieutenant all evening. She had never had a suitor before, but she had carefully chronicled Dudley's starry-eyed fawning over Beatrice, and she was not so naive not to have recognized a similar look on Andrew's face. It wasn't exactly the hungry gaze that had occupied Dudley while he was courting Beatrice; it was more a look of respect and wonder, the same look Jed consistently offered her. She began to speculate. If the lieutenant's affections could summon expressions similar to those Jed wore with her, could Jed's similar expressions be the result of affections for her that were akin to those of the lieutenant?

Even the possibility made Hannah shiver. She pulled several sheets of her lavender stationery from the drawer and wrote on and on, explaining the obstacles that had prevented her from writing sooner, and trying to catch him up on her news, past and present. Well into her third page, she finally paused to consider how much of her heart to expose in the closing paragraphs. Then she heard her sisters approaching and quickly covered the pages before turning away from the desk to greet them with a yawn and a smile.

"Sleepy, dearest?" Beatrice asked sweetly as she crossed to Hannah and placed a gentle hand on her shoulder. "The lieutenant has worn you out."

Myrna dropped dramatically into the rocker in the corner. "I doubt I'll close my eyes all night. Beatrice thinks Mr. Baumgardner was quite taken with me, don't you, Beatrice?"

"Yes, dear," Beatrice agreed. "I'd say an invitation to dinner and an offer to escort you to church shows great interest. And what of you, Hannah? What did you think of the lieutenant?"

"He was fine," she replied flatly. Her sisters' wrinkled brows assured her that a further evaluation was required, so she added, "He invited me to lunch tomorrow."

Myrna marched up to Hannah. "How could you be so blasé? He is handsome and attentive. He obviously adores you, or are you too young to recognize the affections of a suitor?"

"I recognized it, Myrna," Hannah rebutted sharply.

"Then what more could you possibly want?" Myrna retorted.

"He's a lovely man, but I spent the entire evening trying to explain myself to him."

"Most people find discovering things about one another to be one of the most exciting aspects of courtship, Hannah," remarked Beatrice softly.

"Maybe I'm not like other people. I'd treasure making discoveries with the person I love, discoveries about other things and people, not about me. I find that exhausting."

"How else can you expect to get to know a person you've just met unless . . ." Myrna stopped and her expression grew cross. "This is still about Jed Pearson, isn't it?"

With her eyes, Hannah shot a plea for support in Beatrice's direction, and Myrna picked up on it. "Surely you're not encouraging her in this fantasy. We already discussed this earlier in the day."

"I'm not encouraging her. I simply made a bargain with her to get her downstairs."

Myrna gasped and stomped her foot. "Of all the things . . ."

"A promise is a promise!" Hannah cried.

Beatrice knelt by her younger sister. "I felt so sure that once you met the lieutenant your interest in Jed Pearson would subside."

"But you promised me," Hannah muttered sadly.

"Yes, I did, dearest," Beatrice said with resignation as she glared at Myrna. "You write your letter and I'll see that it's delivered. One letter, agreed? But I am going to ask a promise from you. I want you to continue seeing the lieutenant and see if your feelings change, all right?"

Hannah's hands were so shaky she could barely write. She knew Beatrice loved her, but in Beatrice's mind, marriage to any decent man was preferable to going home to Coolfont. Neither of her sisters had previously known the camaraderie of a male friend, one who knew you as well as you knew yourself and who helped you discover all that you already were and who you could yet become. Beatrice had been lucky. Dudley was her first male attachment, and though he was plain, he was gentle and generous, and he provided well for her. Myrna would obviously be glad for any portion of her sister's good fortune. But Hannah was different. She would need something more satisfying than what she already shared with Jed to convince her to marry anyone else, and that was what she needed to tell him in closing.

> *You told me that before I get swept away by love, I should come to you. My affections have not been stirred, but my sisters are intent on pairing me off before Mother and Father carry me back to Coolfont. Beatrice and Dudley have hand selected a young lieutenant as my first suitor. He is a fine-looking man with a gentle bearing and solicitous heart where I am concerned, but he is not you. Why is it that the one man whose opinion matters most to me still sees me only as a child? Please call for me at Beatrice's home. Either define for me, clearly, what love you feel for me so I can stop measuring all men against you, or tell me I am right to love you as I do no other. Please do not delay, Jed.*

> *Your dearest Hannah*

She sealed the letter and knocked on Beatrice's door. As she placed the letter in her sister's hands, she looked into Beatrice's eyes. "I have your word that you'll send this to Jed?"

"Yes, Hannah. I think you are setting yourself up for pain . . . but I'll keep my promise." Hannah nodded and went back to her room.

As soon as Myrna heard Hannah's door click shut, she went to Beatrice. "Are you actually going to mail it?" she whispered in disbelief.

"Yes, Myrna," her sister replied. "I made a promise."

"You know Mother will ostracize her before sanctioning a marriage to a Pearson."

"I know . . . I know," Beatrice sighed, dropping into a chair. "But what am I to do? My plan went awry and I cannot lie to that child. I did make her a promise."

Myrna shook her head and then looked at her sister soberly. "I didn't. Give me the letter."

"No," Beatrice retorted, rising abruptly. "I couldn't. I promised to have it delivered."

"And so you shall."

"What are you saying? It must be delivered. She deserves to have her promise kept."

Myrna looked worriedly at her sister. "There's a bigger promise to be kept here, Beatrice. How many times have we each promised to protect her, to try to make up for a portion of the chill we inflicted upon her in the early years?" She took her sister's hand. "We both know this letter can only bring her sorrow. Nevertheless, it will be delivered in the morning. You needn't know the details of where or how, and your conscience will be able to sleep well on both accounts."

Beatrice trembled as Myrna drew the envelope from her hand. In silence, Beatrice knelt by her bed, praying for God to confirm her actions or to forgive her for them.

CHAPTER 14

London, England
Spring 1811

The Earl of Whittington felt ill as he exited Kensington Palace. He had just witnessed undeniable proof that King George was as mad as the rumors implied. The newspapers and Parliament had tried to look aside, honoring their beloved Queen Charlotte's request for compassion regarding the king's illness and the antics his mania ofttimes caused. But today's spectacle would not be quietly hushed away. Today, the Parliament's responsibility to inform the populace would win out. Some said the king's decline had resulted from his depression following the devastating loss of the colonies, and from the ensuing ridicule he had endured over the last thirty-five years. Others said his disturbing medical symptoms evidenced a disease of the body as well as of the mind. In either case, the wolves were already at his door.

The earl watched sadly as Lady Thornton scurried over to a crowd of friends—many acquainted with her novelist nephew, E. M. Frostier—and began loudly sharing her observations. "There he was, sitting on the throne with his king's crown on, his robes scarlet and ermine, and his speech written out for him—just what he had to say. But—oh dear—he strode up and made a bow and began, 'My Lords and Peacocks.' Those of us there who were not fond of him laughed. Those of us who did love him cried."

Lord Whittington eavesdropped on her final remarks, unsure by the timbre of her voice whether she was saddened by the fall of the monarch or simply amused.

One of her friends added sarcastically, "I don't see how he'll carry on after this. The prince regent will have to rule in his father's stead . . ."

The earl's feet seemed heavy as he descended to the street where the prince regent's own debacle was on public display, the newspapers clearly enumerating his scandals. Though the earl had sworn to defend the monarchy, the future of his precious England was about to rest in the hands of a man for whom he held little respect. He pressed his eyes shut against the sting of his disappointment. *It cycles this way sometimes,* he thought to himself. *Men may come and men may go, but the institution must survive.*

Prince George, the future King George IV, would now become the face of the monarchy. His infidelity-strewn marriage—a ludicrous term for his union to his first cousin, Princess Caroline of Brunswick—was being exposed in the papers, where he was ridiculed and lampooned far above his unfaithful wife. The marriage had always been a loveless sham. George had married the woman to absolve his debts, but he couldn't abide her lack of personal cleanliness, her coarse manner, or her lack of good sense. She found him equally unappealing. A wine-induced tryst produced a child, but George eventually had his crude wife banished to the Montague House in Blackheath until public uproar finally forced him to agree to separate apartments within Kensington Palace. The titillating tales of each of their romps with lovers flavored the dailies, making a laughing stock of the House of Hanover. Soon Caroline became another tool by which radicals decried the current monarchy.

A small newsboy pressed a copy of the *London Times* into the earl's hands for a one penny fee. Lord Whittington read the repugnant headline condemning the royal shenanigans, and he felt to retch that something else he held sacred, the holy order of marriage, was now being disgraced.

He scanned the parting throng of confused nobility and Members of Parliament. He knew there were rebels in the mix, but he had no idea who they were or how to rout them out. Britain was vulnerable. The loss of the colonies, the expense of the Napoleonic Wars, the king's illness, the prince's unpopularity . . . all had distanced the crown from the people and worsened the conditions among the commoners. Now there were rumblings for another war with the

States. Major political questions awaited decisions, and Lord Whittington felt desperately that England must stay on the moral high ground on issues such as slavery, which were being hotly debated in Parliament. *Whom to trust . . .* he pondered as he watched the carriages pull away. *Whom to trust, indeed . . .*

CHAPTER 15

The Willows
Late May 1811

Jed had never been as beset with misery as he had been since seeing Frannie in Philadelphia at Christmas. It was as if something had hardened the caring in her, leaving only a shell behind. Initially, he had fought for her. Then he had backed down, finally accepting his parents' wisdom not to "stir the pot" while he waited for the rumors to settle so he could bring his sister home. He knew she understood that her parents' sudden interest in a Philadelphia holiday had provided a convenient alibi for their absence at the annual parties to which no invitations had come this year. Jed could see that the family's presence in the city of her exile marked her like a scarlet letter, making her more miserable with every passing day. Finally, on the day scheduled for their departure, Jed offered to remain behind so they could spend some time alone, but Frannie had declined his offer and sent him on his way with their parents.

Jed's parents closed their Baltimore home and moved into the Willows, touting the pleasure of country life to their friends and family in the hopes of dispelling the rumors that they too had retreated from Baltimore. Absence had taken its toll on his father's business ventures, and he planned to send his wife and Frannie to Europe for the summer so he could focus on reviving his accounts without worrying about entertaining his distraught wife or protecting his daughter. That would also leave Jed free to move about without restriction or scrutiny.

It had been nine months since Jed had heard from Hannah, and nearly a year since he had last seen her. But despite how desperately he yearned to see her, he knew it was reckless to mention to his parents his plan to attend the Stansburys' upcoming summer barbeque. He had hoped that since his mother would be in Europe with Frannie, and since his father had plans to bury himself with work in the city, they would be so removed from societal prattle that they might consent to his testing of the social waters. He had been abysmally wrong.

"We've been extended no invitation except for your belief that Hannah will welcome you! Her last letter indicated that we were unwelcome in their home!" his mother reminded him between sniffs into her handkerchief. "It's been months since you've seen or heard from the girl. You can't even write to her! I've heard rumors that she is receiving suitors now. She turned seventeen this winter, you know."

"What? You've heard that she is receiving suitors?" The thought stung him more deeply than he could have imagined. He had clung to the hope that Hannah's failure to get word to him had been more about inability than unwillingness, but he was no longer sure.

His mother appeared alarmed by his reply. "Surely you didn't hope to secure the Stansburys' permission to court her yourself? Not after receiving Hannah's final letter."

Jed glared incredulously at his mother as he considered throwing caution to the wind and hurrying off to Coolfont to do exactly that. But the old arguments stilled his impulsiveness. He had always blamed his reticence on Hannah's age and her lack of opportunities. While those things did concern him, he knew there was more. He had never consciously admitted it, but always, in the back of his mind, a haunting little voice remained—the voice that had pricked at his self-worth since childhood. It was the voice that hovered over his parents' words when they spoke of the family's checkered past, and which seemed to validate the gentry's snide whispers. Worse yet, it was the voice that told him that Hannah deserved to be given to someone who did not bear the taint of a Pearson.

In Jed's pain, he lashed out at his mother. "Why would I think myself worthy of her, Mother? Everyone knows we Pearsons are all lepers!"

His mother moved toward him, and for a moment he thought she might slap him, but instead she slumped into a chair with a handkerchief pressed to her face.

His father rushed to her and glared at his son. "We each have only ourselves to blame for this. We allowed Frannie too much freedom. I don't believe the rumors any more than you do, but had she not been so headstrong, and had we each not been so quick to grant her every petition, none of this would have happened."

Of course, Jed did blame himself equally. Had he not capitulated to Frannie's pleas and asked his father to permit her to go, she would still be home with her reputation intact, and there would be one less mark against his own name. His only consolation was that his sister was not married to Frederick Stringham.

Jed's mother leaned heavily on her husband's arm. "The owner of the apothecary claims Frannie was seen being led to the waterfront in the company of the ferry operator . . . a mulatto man . . . and that later that day you carried her out, all mussed, with sticks and debris littering her clothes. You can imagine what they are saying." Her voice broke and she began to cry.

Jed felt sick. He had failed Frannie. He stood in the doorway and stared at his parents, no longer willing to be bridled by societal courtesy. "Does no one care that she was being kidnapped, Father, or that she was being assaulted by someone she followed in innocence? Is it of no consequence that Frederick Stringham was mercilessly whipping slaves, while Frannie showed compassion, or does it simply follow that the one who cries foul first and loudest is the innocent while society hangs the one who cries second?"

His parents now shared a look of disbelief at the audacity of their son, but Jed continued. "While we, who should have championed Frannie, have sat at home waiting for divine justice, she has suffered not only the ignominious prattle of our dear, loyal friends, but she has been left to question our loyalty as well. No one has ever spoken up formally in her defense. No one! Well, I am months too late, but my belly is bloated from eating crow, and I am through."

Jonathan leapt from his seat to chase his son down the hall, but he was no match for the younger man. Jed was quickly on his horse and headed for Philadelphia. When he arrived at the Murdock School midday on May seventeenth, he heard voices coming from beyond the five-foot hedge that surrounded one of the many gardens at the ladies' academy. He peeked through the boxwoods and saw a stout woman in a wide-brimmed hat standing at the head of a group of thirty or so younger women. The assertive matron was the indomitable but beloved Mrs. Murdock, who had enrolled Frannie in the fall. She began introducing the day's lecture on "pests of the garden."

Frannie's numb expression made Jed chuckle, and a mischievous spirit of play swept over him. He picked up several pebbles and began tossing them into her lap with considerable accuracy. The first few sent her looking skyward for the source of the assault. As the gravel began falling with greater rapidity, her annoyance changed to curiosity and then to humor.

"Jed?" she whispered softly. "Is that you?"

He replied by tossing a rhododendron bud into her lap, drawing a broad smile from her while also capturing the attention of a blonde student seated nearby.

"Who is it?" the attractive woman asked under her breath.

Frannie looked curiously at Catherine Peltier, the debutante daughter of the mayor of Wilmington, Delaware. The girl rarely conversed outside her tightly knit circle of Wilmington friends, and she had never previously initiated a conversation with Frannie.

"I think it's my brother, Jed," Frannie whispered, drawing a "shush" from one of the school's chaperones, a thin-lipped spinster named Miss Tipton.

Jed grinned as the black-clad crone scowled at his sister, rendering it difficult to continue the game without unleashing the woman's wrath on Frannie. He stopped his silly assault and watched her look left and right for some sign that he was still close by.

"Why is he here?" the blonde asked as the day's visual aid, an infested plant, reached her.

"I guess he came to see me," Frannie said with a shrug. "He graduated from the university last year. He might have business at the school."

"The university is hosting a grand ball tomorrow evening!" Catherine whispered. "Get your brother to take us to the ball, and I'll get you released from this lecture," she bargained.

Frannie looked dubiously at her companion. "How?"

"Are you agreed?" Catherine mouthed with a raised eyebrow.

A suspicious grin tugged at the corners of Frannie's mouth. "Agreed," she whispered.

Feigning great interest in aphids, Catherine tipped the plant until soil spilled onto her dress. She squawked when her efforts to brush the dirt off merely ground it into the fabric, necessitating a change of clothes that could only be accomplished with the aid of a friend. As soon as the girls exited the garden and turned the corner, Frannie saw Jed waiting by the gate. He swept her up and held her close, and her happiness nearly brought her to tears.

"After the way you dismissed me at Christmas, I wasn't sure if I'd be welcome."

Frannie looked up at her brother and sighed. "I wasn't opposed to seeing you. I was upset that the only place I *could* see you was here, as an exile in a petticoat prison," she laughed sadly.

"Oh, how I've missed you, Frannie, and how I needed a respite from Father and Mother, who, incidentally, have moved in with me, lock, stock, and barrel."

The sound of Catherine clearing her throat reminded Frannie that they were not alone. "Jed, this is Catherine Peltier of Wilmington. She helped me escape," Frannie chuckled.

Jed extended his hand. "Thank you, Catherine. I've waited a long time to see my favorite girl." He gave Frannie an affectionate squeeze and began pulling her away, but Catherine gave Frannie's skirt a tug and nodded to remind her of their arrangement.

"What brought you to Philadelphia, Jed?" asked Frannie. "Did you come for the ball? Catherine and I were just saying how desperately we want to attend tomorrow evening."

Jed looked curiously at Frannie. "I thought we . . ."

"You could take your sister for a turn around the dance floor," Frannie coaxed with a shrug.

Catherine sidled far too close and said, "I'll save you a spot on my dance card as well."

Jed bowed and then blushed at the brazen flirt. "I'll try to be as interesting as the aphid."

Frannie turned to Catherine, who still tittered over Jed's joke. "Please stall for thirty minutes or so, and then I'll meet you back in your room so we can return together." She took Jed's arm and led the way along a trail that meandered through the school's property. "What made you come now?"

"I needed to tell you how wrong we were to send you here. I fought for you initially, but I eventually accepted Mother's and Father's wisdom on the matter. I know you agreed to come here to spare the family from idle gossip, but I want you to come home to the Willows when you return from Europe, Frannie."

Frannie squeezed his arm and hugged him. "That's all I wanted to hear last Christmas. I was angry with you because, like Mother and Father, you appeared reconciled to my situation."

He frowned at the misery his delay had cost her. "I'll never forgive myself for accepting the notion that it was prudent to remove you from the line of fire. I'm no longer of that opinion."

"And what is your new opinion?"

"I say let's take the fight to them." He turned and faced her. "No more cowering or acting contrite. I never want you to back down from a fight again when you know you're right."

Frannie smiled at his zeal, but his passion failed to ignite hers. "Father and Mother have paid dearly too. It may not mean much to you or to me that their social life is so disrupted, but their friends, their parties—such are nearly everything to them. It was not so long ago that they were cast out of society because of family rumors, remember? I am not the only victim here."

"But they at least enjoy their own home and family associations."

"Do they?" she asked. "They're living at the Willows now, and isn't it true that Father's business has suffered substantially?" Jed offered no argument. "Let's not speak of it further." She took his arm and strolled back toward the school. "Mother will be here soon, and we'll head to New York and on to Europe. Most girls long for such a trip. In the fall I'll reexamine my options, but I've adjusted. Philadelphia is a fine city and I've made a few friends. And now I've made a brand new one. See? Catherine has barely spoken to me until today, and now she wants to be my dearest friend!"

Jed laughed softly. "That girl strikes me as one who is used to getting her way, Frannie."

"Be careful, brother. I believe she has set her sights on you."

At the gate he kissed her forehead and looked into her brown eyes, marveling at how brave and good she was. "When can I see you again?"

"You can come by tonight. We Murdock ladies are allowed gentleman callers to the parlor in the evening." Frannie giggled and fluttered her eyes teasingly, unable to miss an opportunity to taunt Jed. "Now, you must mind your manners if Catherine approaches you, as we are always chaperoned."

Jed chuckled, then walked away with a heavy heart. No amount of Frannie's humor could conceal the fact that she was miserable in this bridal college whose true purpose was to prepare young ladies from influential families to be the wives of future business titans and politicians. The girls Jed met that evening in the school's parlor were poised and lovely, but their range of conversation was limited. He cringed as he watched Frannie pretend to fit in, scarcely believing that this glove-handed, doily-tatting woman who now rode an English sidesaddle was the same woman who could ride, hunt, and fish better than most men. But Jed was determined to play out the charade with as brave a face as Frannie, so he charmed her friends and flattered her tutors, hoping in some small way to win his sister some measure of affiliation at Murdock if she was to remain there.

"Thank Markus for his letters, Jed," Frannie said later that night. "He has been the dearest and most loyal friend."

"Friend only? Surely you've realized that his interest has been too solicitous for friendship."

"Another testimony to my poor judgment, I suppose, that I could have encouraged a man like Frederick and been completely blind to someone as sweet as Markus."

"And now that your blinders are off? He's a good man, Frannie."

"I might be open to the company of a man, but I have no interest in the affections of one for now," she acquiesced, then changed the subject. "Have you heard from Hannah?"

Immediately tensing, Jed answered with as much matter-of-factness as he could muster. "No, not in months. Mother heard she is receiving suitors now."

"I'm so sorry my problems have prevented her from corresponding with you. That single day in Calverton altered your future as well as mine, but Jed, if she's courting, you must go and fight for her!" Frannie said with breathless urgency.

How many times had Jed given himself the same advice? He felt the weight of his forebearers' mistakes crushing his own prospects. Looking at Frannie, who had been denied justice because their predecessors' errors rendered her beyond the gentry's mercy, he knew he needed a way to avoid inflicting the same on Hannah.

"So, you think I should fight for her, do you? That's a bold statement from a woman who now shuns love herself."

"I still believe in love," Frannie countered.

Jed drew his sister close. "I agree that I've been too complacent. I need to remedy that."

Frannie noticed Catherine eyeing Jed hungrily from across the room. "I believe there is someone here who would gladly escort you out of your complacency."

Jed followed her gaze, noticing the sultry look Catherine offered him from across the room. "Promise me," he whispered comically to Frannie, "that you will not leave me alone with her."

* * *

Jed counted himself fortunate to find a shop with clothes appropriate for the ball. He purchased a black, double-breasted frock coat and black pants, along with a gold-trimmed vest and white silk shirt. Once dressed, he felt rather like a dandy, but he persuaded himself that he was, after all, in Philadelphia, a place where such dress was considered more stylish than ostentatious. Stopping by the barber for a fresh shave and a haircut, he allowed only a slight trim of his wavy brown hair. He preferred the longer cut, brushing his hair back to accentuate his sideburns and his tan face.

His face was leaner, his body as well, as was proven by the smaller sizes of his recent clothing purchases. He no longer constantly grazed from the kitchen as he'd done in happier times, and responsibility had chiseled changes in his face. It was a man's face now, he admitted contemplatively, still unlined but lean and defined by the worry in his brown eyes.

He headed down Arch Street and his spirit was touched. As contrary as he had been about attending the ball, he had to admit how good it felt to be dressed up and swept into the bustle of the city after so many months on the farm. He passed Christ Church, the mother church of Episcopalianism where George Washington, Betsy Ross, Benjamin Franklin, and their families had worshipped. How he loved this city! With every step along the Philadelphia streets, he felt the murmur of voices from the past . . . Washington, Franklin, Hamilton. All the great American fathers were gone now, or had their voices stilled by age or circumstance. Ironically, Jed passed a stand selling the *American Star* newspaper, which reported a furious congressional debate concerning the possibility of another war with England. He shook his head sadly. Even Jefferson, the mighty lion of liberty, barely voiced an opinion these days. The unpopularity of his failed presidential embargo act and his tremendous personal debt had quieted his voice.

Jed found the prospect of facing war an eerie one without the wisdom and courage of these inspired founders. He turned left on Sixth Street and saw the Georgian architecture of the State House where the Declaration of Independence had been written, where the Articles of Confederation were ratified, and where the Constitution was written and signed. He longed to hear the peal of the bell hanging in the building's upper tower, remembering how that distinctive ring had declared the death of great citizens, announced patriotic days, and called voters to their civic duty. He paused for a moment on the steps of the historic hall, wondering what the great patriots of the Second Continental Congress or the Constitutional Convention thought of the way his generation was caring for the infant nation that had been formed with blood and vision.

Jed turned right on Chestnut Street and arrived at the Murdock School, where the ladies anxiously awaited his arrival. Frannie wore a corset under a green satin gown that hugged her bodice and skimmed over her hooped petticoat. Her auburn hair was swept up, and a few curly tendrils dangled at the back of her neck at her hairline. A brooch, threaded through a green velvet ribbon, sat in the hollow of her throat. She was, quite simply, dazzling.

Catherine wore silk in a shade of pale yellow over layers of ruffled petticoats that rustled when she walked. The gown was cut low, both in front and back, with sleeves that descended almost from the cut of the neckline. Her long, blonde hair was pulled back and woven into dozens of connecting braids then twisted into a bun.

Jed called for a carriage and helped the two beautiful young ladies into the forward seat, then sat across from them. Although the building hosting the ball was only blocks away, the distance was sufficient for Frannie to note her brother's contemplative mood.

"A penny for your thoughts," she said with a worried smile.

Jed reached across and took her hand. "I'm fine. It's this city. It speaks to me somehow."

"It appears to be a sad message," commented Catherine, anxious to lend her assistance. Jed smiled awkwardly and leaned back against the seat to end any further discussion of his mood, but Catherine was determined to sally forth to his aid. She gathered her skirt and shifted around into Jed's seat. Placing a consoling hand on his knee, she offered the best of her seventeen years of wisdom. "A woman's ear is always open to a man's burdens."

Jed repeated his anemic smile, quickly squinting in Frannie's direction for salvation, but her grin offered him no rescue. He shifted nervously toward the door, and noticing that they were at Sixth and Market Street, he found a suitable diversion.

"I would love to share the history of this fine city with you ladies. Does either of you know what this lovely complex of red brick buildings once was?" He pointed to the main three-story dwelling. Thirteen windows faced the street, and several other rooflines extended the dwelling to the left and behind the house, where it appeared that more small buildings were arranged.

Catherine had not hidden her disappointment over Jed's rejection, nevertheless, his historical challenge pleased her. "This was the President's House when Philadelphia was the nation's capital," she answered. "George Washington and President Adams both lived here."

"That's right," Jed praised. As he stared at the home, his voice grew wistful. "Imagine who walked through those doors and what transpired within those walls. Just imagine . . ."

"My father came here to meet with President Washington in 1796," Catherine boasted. "Father was shocked to discover that he had slaves living on the property here in Philadelphia, and well after passage of the state's Gradual Abolition Act in 1780. One of the family's slaves, Oney Judge, escaped from this house a few nights previous to my father's visit, and the president was still vexed over it. Personally, I'm glad she escaped. I detest the practice of slavery."

Jed looked at Frannie, who discreetly shook her head, signaling that Catherine did not know the Pearsons owned slaves. Jed carefully moved away from the topic. "I respectfully yield my presidential narration to you, Miss Peltier."

Catherine blushed and bowed her head. "I sound like an awful bore. Please forgive me."

"Not at all," Jed replied. "Don't hide your knowledge to flatter my ego. I value a woman with a mind and spirit, as you can see in my sister." He patted Catherine's hand reassuringly, and, to his dismay, she placed her free hand on top, securing it with a tender squeeze.

"All right," she began softly. "I do know two other items of presidential trivia. Did you know that this was not the first presidential residence?"

"I did," Jed answered, wriggling his hand slightly in an attempt to free it. "Do you know where it was?"

"New York," she responded happily. "President Washington spent sixteen months there before moving to Philadelphia."

"Very good!" said Jed with an increasing appreciation of the young woman's knowledge.

"Here's another interesting piece of trivia," Catherine continued. "If you look at a map of Washington City and extend the path of New York Avenue, it crosses over Pennsylvania Avenue at what point?"

Jed admitted that he had no idea.

"The President's House," Catherine said with pride. "I don't know if it was a coincidence or not, but the two states that had previously served as Washington's presidential homes are also the names of the streets that overlap at the location of the current Presidential Palace."

Jed smiled admiringly, regretting that he had discounted the woman so quickly. He allowed his hand to rest on hers as he complimented her. "That's marvelous, Catherine. You've given me some useful parlor conversation."

He noticed that Frannie had become noticeably somber. "A penny for *your* thoughts?"

"The president's former home is now a rooming house with retail shops below. I would think President Madison would be sad to think so little regard has been paid to their home."

Jed wondered if homesickness prompted her melancholy. "If I recall, Mrs. Adams mourned leaving Pennsylvania, but plagues of yellow fever had passed through the city in the late 1700s, and some convinced the president that the air over the city was diseased. That was likely the end to Philadelphia as the capital. Pennsylvania tried to lure the president back, as you'll see by the building we're heading to. It was to be the president's home if he returned."

They continued on three more blocks to Ninth and Market Street where Jed declared, "This is our stop, ladies." The carriage stopped in front of a large, nearly square, four-story brick mansion with nineteen windows along the front wall. Each glass portal appeared afire with candlelight, and luminaries lined the walk. Two doormen dressed in colonial attire stood ready to greet each carriage as it arrived.

"Oh, Jed!" squealed Frannie with delight. "It's wondrous!"

"Can you imagine being offered such a home and turning it down to live in a barren city near a marshy bog? Well, that was Abigail Adams's dilemma, my dears. Pennsylvania built this grand home as part of a bid to persuade Congress to reconsider making Philadelphia the permanent capital of the nation. Obviously, their plan failed. So the university bought it at an auction and now uses it for teaching and lectures . . . and that concludes my tour of the city."

Jed stepped from the carriage and waited as the doormen helped the ladies down. He had barely crossed through the threshold when he heard his name called out across the floor.

"Jed Pearson, is that you?"

Jed craned his neck in the general direction of the sound and saw the jovial face of a schoolmate who was headed in his direction.

"Timothy Shepard!" Jed exclaimed with pleasure. "What brings you back, my friend?"

His lanky friend laughed sheepishly. "Banking was not to my liking, so I decided to return to attend some lectures required to enter the law. I'm headed to New York in the fall."

"The law?" Jed chuckled as he thumped his friend on the back. "Are you now planning on following in your father's footsteps and running for office as well?"

Shepard shook his head emphatically. "If my father does become Pennsylvania's next governor, he will more than satisfy our family's quota of politicians. And what about you, Jed? Things are obviously going well." He bowed dramatically, and as he rose he met Frannie's eyes.

Jed smirked at his friend's blatant appeal for an introduction, but finally offered it. "Mr. Timothy Shepard, may I introduce Miss Francis Pearson and Miss Catherine Peltier."

"No!" Shepard exclaimed in amazement. "Are you telling me that this feminine creature is the wild woman of the Willows, the girl who can outshoot, outride, and outwit most men? I would have expected to find her arriving in buckskins and boots. But I must confess, Miss Pearson," he took her offered hand and kissed it, "I am delighted to see that I was wrong."

Frannie smiled demurely at the young law student's attentions. He was shorter and leaner than Jed, with dark, curly hair that bounced when he moved, giving him a childlike quality that contrasted sharply with the seriousness of his dark eyes. Though Frannie found him intriguing, she would not allow herself to be easily swept away. Instead, she politely withdrew her hand and leaned closer to her brother as his arm wrapped protectively around her.

"Tell me, Timothy, what is the City of Brotherly Love saying about the escalating talk of war?"

Timothy Shepard's eyes grew wide and passionate at the mention of war. "It's already tearing at the fabric of our republic. Those who lived through the Revolution remind everyone of the price they paid, although—and this astounds me—there are some from that generation who maintain loyalties to Europe as if she were still nursing us like a suckling babe." He sighed with aggravation. "With the division amongst the elders in Congress and the Senate, perhaps it will be the young—who have only known liberty—that will bear sway."

"Henry Clay and John Calhoun?" Jed guessed.

"Yes. They and men of similar opinions. Kentucky and South Carolina have bred representatives who are intolerant of anything less than complete, unfettered sovereignty, and they do not see how we can call ourselves free when Britain all but rules our waterways."

"Maryland has been her target, and those of us along the waterfront feel particularly vulnerable. Are British ships impressing sailors this far north?" Jed asked.

"Delaware feels her breath upon its neck. It's a difficult situation. I cannot bear the way Britain challenges our sovereignty, but most of the northern states rely on foreign trade, and fettered or not, some is better than none. A nation is only as strong as her economy. Right now, our resources may be too meager to fund a war."

Catherine's disinterest was apparent, providing Timothy a more pleasurable topic.

"I want to hear everything you know about the Washington City gossip, but I am reminded that this is, after all, a ball, and we are allowing the two most beautiful women in the room to languish for lack of attention." He crooked his elbow and waited for Frannie to take it.

She was reluctant, but Jed nodded his approval, leaving himself in the care of the very eager Miss Catherine Peltier, who applauded his decision. "You know, however much you adore her, a woman does need the company of men other than her brothers. Perhaps Mr. Shepard can make Philadelphia more inviting for her. That would be a lovely thing, wouldn't it?"

"I suppose it would be," Jed muttered. He worried about Frannie, and yet he knew her friend was right. Still, his eyes continued to follow his sister around the dance floor until a coquettish hum at his side brought his attention back to Catherine, who was staring up at him.

"I see a few of my former schoolmates eyeing you from across the room. I could make some introductions," Jed suggested playfully.

Catherine placed her small gloved hand in the crook of his arm and stepped forward, apparently willing to accept his offer. It dampened his spirits slightly, but when they reached the perimeter of the dance floor, she stopped cold, nearly spinning Jed around to check on her.

"Is everything all right?" he wondered.

"It is now," she smiled.

Jed looked at other dancing couples then grinned at her. "I'm afraid I'm a little rusty."

"All the better," she replied, slipping her hand into his as a waltz began.

"You prefer a poor dance partner?" he questioned curiously.

"I prefer a man who hasn't had a woman in his arms of late."

Jed took the bait. "Perhaps I only hold my women off the dance floor."

Catherine nodded appreciatively at his playful comeback. "Then we shall see, won't we?"

Jed placed his hand on the small of her back and led out gracefully, drawing a raised eyebrow of surprised approval from his partner. As they moved about the floor, he occasionally glanced at Frannie, but as one dance blended into two, and then several, he barely thought to glance at his sister at all. It felt good to hold a young lady in his arms again—a delight he had not experienced since his graduation ball. That dance had been merely an amusement, and his partner nothing more than a friend. But Catherine?

For a second he allowed spite to motivate his pleasure, thinking that perhaps Hannah was thusly engaged at this very moment. Perhaps she was even falling in love. What purpose would his pining and suffering serve? He looked at Catherine's encouraging smile and searched his heart. She was lovely, and she made him the object of other men's jealousy, but even as he held her in his arms, and despite her dazzling attention, his mind drifted to another face, and his resolve to win Hannah was set.

Later, the orchestra laid their instruments aside for a rest. Catherine slipped away with Frannie to freshen up while the men gathered on the broad portico for a smoke and a chat. Timothy followed Frannie with his eyes.

"She's a wonderful woman, Jed," he stated. "It's no wonder you've guarded her so. Not only is she a beautiful dancer, but she can hold up her end of a conversation on any topic. Do you know how refreshing it is not to have to feign interest in female fancies? How hard it will be for you to find a woman her equal. I'd say she has ruined you forever."

"She's a treasure," Jed agreed.

"Catherine seems lovely enough. She's very beautiful."

"Yes. She is that."

"Guard your heart, friend. She's young—only seventeen—and spoiled, or so I've heard."

Jed looked at Timothy and laughed sadly. "That appears to be my lot."

"What? You? The fellow who spent his free time holed up with the philosophy professor or with his nose buried in some book?" Timothy noticed that his humor failed to comfort his sullen friend. "So tell me . . . the girl that broke your heart . . . which was she? Young or spoiled?"

"Is it so obvious?" Jed wondered, lowering his head to avoid his friend's gaze.

Timothy placed his hand on Jed's shoulder. "One broken heart is led to another like magnetic north, brother. I choose to believe that a heart once broken allows love to settle in more deeply the second time. Perhaps it is fate that has brought the four of us together. At the very least, we can all share some pleasant company for a time while we see if sparks exist."

"I'm afraid, as you so readily deduced, my heart has sparks for only one woman, and if anything, tonight has reaffirmed that to me."

Timothy worried that his friend might not have understood his hint. "But when are you heading back south? Are your plans set?"

"I had intended to leave at the beginning of the week. Why?" Jed inquired.

Timothy grinned playfully. "I'd hoped you could stay in Philadelphia a few more days and help me get to know your sister somewhat better. I am more than a little taken with her."

Jed fidgeted with the bottom of his vest. "I see no point in your beginning an attachment when she will be in Europe all summer and you will be leaving for New York in the fall."

"That's exactly why I want you to stay. If we go out as a company of four, I can get to know her in a casual, more natural way without all the pretense and pressure. Tell me you'll stay, at least for a few more days. Good company would be good for you as well."

"Perhaps you're right," replied Jed morosely as the women returned.

* * *

The next two weeks proved therapeutic for Jed and Frannie. Each afternoon the men met the ladies and ventured into the city for supper or for a row on the Schuylkill River and a picnic. They attended concerts at the university's Academy Building and spent lazy evenings around the piano at the Murdock School, where Frannie's musical talents earned rave reviews from Mrs. Murdock. Jed had seen Frannie eyeing a book of music, Andrew Adgate's *Philadelphia Harmony*, and he purchased a copy of it for her, never dreaming that the classically trained Mrs. Murdock might enjoy tunes from some of New England's own composers. Frannie's playful voice brought the songs to life, and Jed saw his sister come fully alive as well.

Although Catherine's company proved to be only a pleasant diversion, Jed could not deny that Timothy seemed smitten with Frannie. Therefore, Jed's favorite hours became those few during which he was able to draw his sibling away from the others. He cherished the times when they simply walked, where he shared with Frannie the places he had described to her in his letters and in their long chats by the fire at the Willows. It pleased him that she felt similarly awed by Philadelphia.

They strolled along Arch Street, turned left on Cherry, and then headed south on Fourth Street. Jed stopped in front of Zion Lutheran Church. "This is where the national funeral for George Washington was held. One of his dear friends—a fellow soldier and friend of Grandfather's, interestingly enough, a man named General Henry Lee—eulogized him with that great tribute, 'First in war, first in peace, first in the hearts of his countrymen.'"

Frannie was fascinated by the history and began grilling Jed with questions as they continued on past the yard surrounding Carpenter's Hall, where the First Continental Congress had met. Then they moved on to Library Hall.

"Library Hall was my refuge during school, Frannie. I love it because Benjamin Franklin established it so that books would be available to all citizens, not just to the wealthy."

Jed led her farther south for lunch in a tavern. Quaint brick and clapboard homes and shops stood along narrow cobblestone streets, and the siblings wandered there after lunch.

Shortly thereafter, they realized the hour was growing late, and they were soon to meet up with Timothy and Catherine for their last evening together before Jed returned to Maryland. With heavy hearts Jed and Frannie headed toward the Murdock School.

Most of the stops Frannie had shared with Jed that day were ones she had either seen from a carriage or visited on a tour, but the area she and Jed now approached, Southeast Square, originally laid out by William Penn, was a place she had been cautioned to avoid. She clutched her brother's arm tightly and noticed how his own mood grew measurably contemplative again as tidy, gracious homes gave way to hovels and huts. A lovely but lone commercial establishment stood amidst the area's decrepit buildings. Frannie wondered what had happened to the area that had once evidenced great enterprise.

"That's Lea and Febiger Publishing," Jed explained, pointing to the lonely structure. "They were established in 1785 . . . the first truly American publishing house."

"Then what happened to this square to cause its decline?" Frannie questioned.

"Soon after it was surveyed, it became a potters' field. This is where unknowns . . . the poor and the diseased . . . were buried—beyond the vicinity of the main city. They were wrapped in canvas and placed in a pit without benefit of a coffin or a marker."

The siblings were further sobered when Frannie pointed out a congregation of Negroes, some bearing flowers and some bearing food and bottles of drink, huddled over a fresh mound of dirt.

"Guineas, most likely," said Jed. "They often leave food and drink for their dead."

Frannie nodded quietly and watched until they had passed by. Several dark-skinned women, clothed in simple, tattered dresses, sat under trees or searched the area, appearing to examine each stone and tree.

At Frannie's curious expression, Jed explained, "They're searching for their loved ones' graves. They can't afford a proper marker so they place a stone nearby or count steps from a tree or a shrub."

Despair penetrated Frannie's heart. The disparity suddenly seemed obscene to her, that some people knew no want, while others were in want of something as elemental as knowing where their loved one was placed in death. Suddenly, her own troubles seemed trivial, and sympathy for these mourners filled her soul.

Jed's step increased as they moved toward the section of city he sought. A jail loomed on the southeast corner of Sixth and Walnut Streets, and Jed stopped on the uneven ground that lay before it. As Frannie looked up at the structure, Jed stated, "That's the Walnut Street Jail. It was a brutal prison for some, particularly during the Revolution, and a debtors' prison for others. Did you ever hear of Robert Morris? He was a wealthy Philadelphian who represented Pennsylvania at the Continental Congress. When the republic was in desperate financial straits and our military was suffering, Morris loaned ten thousand dollars to the government to procure needed provisions for Washington's soldiers. His generosity may have saved the nation."

"How so?" asked Frannie.

"Well, those troops went on to win the Battle of Trenton, which turned the tide of the war. But despite all that, he ended up here, in debtors' prison due to failed business speculations. It's funny—we're so quick to remember what's owed us and so slow to remember what's been given."

Jed focused his attention on the ground under his feet. "But this is why I come here, Frannie. This ground is sacred to me. When soldiers from Washington's army fell sick or dead, fighting for our liberty, they were brought to Philadelphia—to the hospital or to churches. Those that didn't survive were placed in plain wooden caskets that were piled box upon box in large pits—right here. When the British occupied the city, they placed our captured soldiers in that prison, where horrible conditions led to more deaths by disease."

He paused thoughtfully. "When I was at school, I came upon a letter written by John Adams that described what went on here. I read and reread it, committing it to memory so I would never forget the price of freedom. He described incredible suffering and said that it was 'enough to make the heart of stone to melt away.'"

Jed turned to look his sister in the eyes. "This is why I love this city, Frannie. It clears my thinking when I remember what it took to build our nation. Still, I don't think the Founding Fathers wanted us to stand on past victories, but to use them to expand their vision. It may take another war to do that."

"I don't want to think of such things," muttered Frannie. "Why must you, Jed?"

"Perhaps it's the wrestle I'm having over slavery, or perhaps it's Hannah's talk of God. I don't know, but I believe freedom is divinely inspired, and I cannot allow what has been gained to be lost. I don't want to be one who forgets the sacrifice of others. What I am saying is that . . . if something happens while you and Mother are abroad . . . if war should break out, Frannie, I will be going . . . and I'm willing everything I have to you in the event of my death."

Frannie buried her head against his shoulder. "Don't say such things," she begged.

"Don't fret, sweetness. I hope to enjoy a long life, but I wanted you to know that no matter what befalls us, you will be all right." He pulled her close. "I've made sure of that."

* * *

As the men prepared to depart, Timothy pulled Jed aside from where Frannie and Catherine stood. "I'm pleased that the timing of my invitation to clerk in Washington City allows us to travel together. I do hate leaving Frannie, though."

Jed looked his friend in the eye. "She needs a friend right now, Timothy. Please be that and nothing more until she returns from Europe."

Timothy frowned and then nodded. "My friend, Samuel Renfro, should be here shortly. He's a regular at Harvard Medical School, but quite politically connected. I shared our political discussions with him, and he knows a place in Gettysburg that will be of particular interest to us."

"I hope he's not burdening himself just to make introductions for us," Jed remarked.

"No. He was studying in Boston, but since he is from Baltimore and a medical school is opening there next year, Renfro wants to interview for a spot in the premier class. He also needs to perform an errand for his father, whose good friend—a Reverend Dobbins— passed away leaving a widow and nineteen children. He asked Samuel to check in on the family."

Jed nodded. "Another voice and set of stories would always be welcome."

"He'll introduce us at Getty's Tavern. The good Reverend Dobbins was evidently quite a political figure during the Revolution. He and James Getty, the son of the local tavern owner, laid out the city. Getty's Tavern is where the militia mustered with the Continental Army. It served as the local town hall as well, providing the citizenry a place to speak out against the British. Renfro says they meet similarly now to discuss Britain's latest incursions. We'll stop by and have a pint while we survey the local opinions."

"I'd like to hear from some Pennsylvanians whose purses are not tied to British trade."

As they spoke, Samuel Renfro, a gregarious, moon-faced young man with a ruddy complexion, rode in. "Timothy! I hope I'm not late, and you must be Jed Pearson." He turned to Jed, offering his hand and pumping Jed's arm. "Samuel Renfro . . . I'm so looking forward to traveling together!"

The company knew the hour of departure had arrived. "You'll write?" Catherine asked Jed as she smiled coyly. "Better yet, come for a visit. My parents would enjoy meeting the man who has so completely captured my attention."

Jed dreaded this moment. Although he had enjoyed their time together, neither Catherine's beauty nor her company had prevented his attentions from drifting elsewhere, and he had no desire to mislead her. "It may be weeks before I settle long enough to write," he indicated. "Don't squander the summer waiting on a nomad like me. Let my delay be another man's good fortune."

"Oh, no, Jed," she pledged. "If you come by, you'll find me there . . . waiting for you."

He looked at the ground to avoid the tearful flutter of her eyes as he reached for Frannie, who was likewise tearful. "Are you upset because Timothy is riding on with me?" he asked as he pulled Frannie away from the group.

"No. I'm glad for it. I'll prefer knowing you are in good company."

"He'll be back to see you in the fall before he leaves for New York."

Frannie nodded. "I am not crying over Timothy," she declared as tiny tears trickled down her cheeks, "although I do enjoy his company. He is so kind that I felt safe telling him everything about Frederick and Duprée, and he's been wonderful. But he knows I'm not of a mind to give my heart to anyone right now. Perhaps I'll feel differently in the fall." She tried to sound positive. "Tell me, how are you and Catherine leaving things?"

"I can't abide her fawning," he admitted quietly. "Such affections are as uncomfortable to me as a horsehair blanket."

Frannie smiled sadly. "They won't when the right person is doing the fawning."

Jed leaned down and touched his forehead to hers. "Perhaps," he whispered.

"Jed . . ." she began, but he placed a finger over her lips and shook his head.

"Why fret unnecessarily? Mother will arrive in a few days and you may need your full complement then," he teased. "Besides, everything could turn out just fine. I assure you, you'll serve me best by promising to have a wonderful summer in Europe."

He kissed her cheek, then quickly mounted his horse, waved in Catherine's direction, and was off.

CHAPTER 16

Baltimore City, Maryland
Mid-August 1811

"The carriage is ready," Dudley called up the stairs from the foyer. Myrna made her way down the steps first, with Hannah trudging close behind her. He stood at the bottom step and gently grabbed their heads and placed kisses on their cheeks before they passed through the doorway. His eyes became moist as he noticed their red-rimmed eyes and Beatrice's equally crestfallen face. "I'm going to miss them," he whispered to his wife as her sisters exited the house and got in the carriage. "Most men would be joyous to get their house back, but I'm truly going to miss them."

Beatrice tried to smile, but she was at the very edge of emotion and could barely meet her husband's gaze. "It was a good idea to send us on a shopping trip this afternoon. Another day in this house watching the clock wind down to the hour of my parents' arrival would have driven us all mad."

Dudley nodded. "Hannah seems stoic considering that she has seen the lieutenant nearly every day for four months and will rarely see him at all once she returns to Coolfont."

Beatrice slumped against the rail, motioned for Dudley to close the door, and began to cry. "Oh, Dudley. Hannah is not mourning losing the lieutenant because she is too busy mourning Jed Pearson!"

"Because he never replied?"

Beatrice's guilt bore upon her like an anvil until she could carry the burden no longer. "Because he never got the letter." Seeing the strange look that clouded her husband's face, she hurried to explain. "Myrna asked to be the one to deliver it. Though I didn't know exactly how, I did know her intentions were to keep Jed from reading it until the lieutenant had a chance to win Hannah's heart. But poor Hannah. The tears she cried each day when no reply ever arrived!"

"Oh, Beatrice . . ." he moaned as he shook his head in disappointment. "After the way the Lord has blessed us, how could you have meddled in someone else's happiness this way?"

"I know . . . I know . . ." she muttered. "The only excuse I can offer is that we acted in what we thought was her best interest. Right or wrong, Mother hates the Pearsons. She would disown Hannah before allowing her to marry Jed. Lieutenant Robertson is exactly the kind of man Mother would welcome into the family, and you yourself knew the lieutenant was practically in love with Hannah from the first night they met. We thought by encouraging that pairing, we had found a way for Hannah to enjoy the love of a good husband and Mother's love as well."

"Why should your mother's raving opinions matter?" Dudley shot back angrily.

"You've come from such a loving family, Dudley. You would never understand," Beatrice cried. "We hoped we could spare Hannah from suffering more of Mother's wrath, but now it all seems pointless, seeing how she's developed into a mere shadow of herself these past weeks."

"You simply have to fix it! Tell her the truth."

"I can't. That would destroy her trust in us. We don't know how Jed Pearson would respond to her confessions of love. What if he tells her she is merely a sweet friend? She would be left with no one. I can't do that to her now. Whether or not we deserve her love, we do love her."

"Yet two people who may have been destined to be together might now be separated because of your meddling. Meanwhile, the poor lieutenant wears his heart on his sleeve, falsely believing she cares for him, while fretting that her melancholy is indicative of a terrible ailment."

"She does care for him, Dudley. In time, those feelings may still deepen."

Dudley pointed to his wife. "You are not God! You had no right!" Then he stomped to the front door.

"Dudley!" Beatrice yelled after him, but he waved her off and slammed the door behind himself. Her knees still quaked when she joined her sisters in the carriage for the sweltering ride into town.

Hannah summoned every possible speck of courage to hold her tears at bay as they drove up Calvert Street. She worried about her mother's moods and her father's distance, about losing the freedom she had enjoyed in Baltimore, and about the awkwardness of saying good-bye to Andrew. But mostly she worried about facing her future without Jed.

A few stray tears trickled from her eyes as she clung to the hope that he had not received her letter. In her heart, she believed that, regardless of his feelings for her, he would not have allowed her profession of love to have gone so long unanswered. Still, since her sisters had given her their word that her letter had been hand delivered, she could not imagine why he had not replied. It mattered little anymore. Her parents were coming, and her time in paradise was over.

Even dressed as lightly as she was, Hannah felt perspiration trickle down her neck and into her corset. She tried to dismiss her discomfort as she stared at the people on the crowded streets, wondering whether everyone's life was as complicated as hers or if some people truly were as carefree and happy as they appeared. From the carriage windows, she saw women pushing baby carriages and businessmen dashing in and out of buildings. Then her attention was drawn to the backs of three men walking in the same direction as the carriage.

One was a short, round man, another a man of average height and build, but the third was a tall man with broad shoulders stretched beneath a white shirt and brown vest. It was his thick, wavy brown hair blowing in the hot August breeze that captured Hannah's attention. Although she couldn't see his visage, there was something familiar about his bearing. *Could it be Jed?* She strained to catch a glimpse of his face, but he was farthest from the street and he kept his head turned to look into the windows. As the carriage passed them, the three men entered a jewelry shop.

She tried telling herself she was merely seeing what she hoped to see, but no amount of persuasion could ease her mind. Though she risked appearing foolish if she was wrong, she saw no value in exercising lonely prudence. With each click of the carriage wheels on the brick street, distance and seconds ticked by until Hannah could remain still no longer.

"Stop the carriage!" she called to the driver as she scrambled to gather her skirt.

"Hannah!" her sisters gasped as she opened the door and leapt to the street from the moving vehicle. She tripped, but caught herself, and quickly disappeared into the crowd.

She lifted her skirts and ran down the walkway, staring into the store windows, searching for the jeweler's shop she had seen the three men enter. Her chest heaved, and she longed for a corsetless breath. Finally, she had to stop and lean against a hitching post to settle her racing heart. She could feel the drip of moisture fastening the fabric of her dress to her skin, and she knew she looked a sight. But as soon as she could draw a full breath, she began searching again. As she scrambled along, she smiled broadly, imagining how Jed would scoop her into his arms as he always did. But then he would finally see that she was fully grown, not merely a child to be fretted and fawned over, but a woman fit for marriage. She would tell him that she loved him, and they would be together.

Hannah nearly fainted by the time she found the jeweler's. She slipped inside and scanned the room, her eyes turning wide with disbelief when she could not see the three men. The shopkeeper's wife was so alarmed by her appearance that she rushed over to her and made her sit down. Hannah resisted, struggling first to get her question out between gasping breaths. "Were three men just in here? One a tall man with dark hair?"

"Land sakes, dearie," exclaimed the woman, "catch your breath first and then we'll talk."

"No!" Hannah argued weakly. "I need . . . I need to find them."

The woman looked to her husband. "Were three men just in here?"

He searched for the receipt. "Mr. Samuel Renfro picked up a watch he had in repair. His friend bought a string of pearls, and the other gentleman was inquiring after a cameo."

Hannah's heart nearly stopped beating. "Did they mention where they were going?"

The man scratched his head as he thought, and then he beamed. "The man with the pearls mentioned Philadelphia, but I think they said they were going to eat before heading on."

"There are three or four eateries within a block or two. If they are eating, they'll be there awhile. Sit and catch your breath before you go," the woman ordered.

Hannah smiled in frustration as she rose on shaky legs. "I can't. Thank you just the same, but I just can't. I have to find them. Could you point out the eateries to me?"

The woman shook her worried head. "There's Steinman's across the way." She pointed to a delicatessen across the street, and Hannah noticed meats and cheeses hanging in the windows. "And Botto's restaurant is two doors down. There are two more eateries and a bakery beyond them."

Hannah smiled appreciatively and darted across the street, dodging horses and carriages. She pressed her face against the Steinman shop window, but Jed was not inside. Farther down the street, she saw a swinging sign advertising "Botto's Italian Cooking" and rushed in to avoid Beatrice and Myrna, who had directed the driver to turn the carriage around as they searched for her. As luck would have it, there, seated at a small, round table, she saw two men whose clothing matched that of the men she had seen on the street. The owner greeted her disheveled appearance with some skepticism, and at her insistence, seated her at a table near the doorway within earshot of the men.

"Where is Jed with our pastries?" Timothy complained. "I'm ready to order my entree."

Hannah's heart leapt, and she ordered a cup of tea and toast while awaiting his arrival.

Timothy pulled a black velvet bag from his pocket, from which a strand of pearls spilled onto the checkered tablecloth. "Tell me, Samuel, do you think she'll like them?"

"You're asking the wrong man, Timothy. I chose medicine because it is easier to convince oneself you are too busy to court than to admit that you have no one to court. Ask Jed for his opinion. He seemed quite astute about women's fancies when he inquired about the cameo, and Philadelphia proves he has had more than ample success at winning ladies' hearts."

Hannah felt her skin prickle and her spine chill as she tried to focus on their conversation.

Timothy laughed. "I'm just afraid it's too much. I don't want to frighten her away."

"Ahh. Then take your lesson from the master," Renfro teased. "Surely Jed and Catherine Peltier are proof that feigning indifference only heightens a suitor's appeal."

Hannah was so lost in the woman's name that she barely noticed the arrival of her order.

"You're quite taken with our friend," she heard Timothy remark.

Samuel laughed comically. "The man has the Midas touch with people. Remember when we walked into Getty's Tavern? The old-timers paid me no mind, but Jed left with his pocket stuffed with the names of political contacts. It's no wonder the woman who has fallen in love with him is the daughter of a politician. Catherine probably knows if she reels him in he'd make more than a noteworthy husband. She could likely ride his popularity into the governorship."

Each word made Hannah's throat tighten until she could barely swallow. *Catherine Peltier . . . "The woman who has fallen in love with him . . . he'd make more than a noteworthy husband . . ." Is that why Jed never bothered answering my letter?* She couldn't control her shaking hands.

As she rose, Hannah's legs faltered, and she knocked her cup and saucer to the floor with a crash. Her crestfallen eyes met those of Jed's two friends as she staggered out the door to find the bakery, hoping to catch up with Jed, to have a few moments alone with him. As she hurried down the sidewalk, scouring every sign for a bakery shop, she heard the shout of the restaurant owner calling for her to stop, but she pressed on, disappearing into the crowd. She searched every face for Jed's until she saw him exiting a jeweler's across the crowded street. The very sight of him flooded her with memories so sweet and dear that she knew if she could only reach him everything would be as she knew it should. She waved her hand at him, but his head was lowered as if examining something. The only attention she drew was that of the restaurant owner still chasing her. Her head swung left and right, searching for a break in the busy stream of buggies and carriages so she could cross to meet Jed. Just as she saw an opening, she noticed Jed holding the item of his attention in the air against the sun's light. It was a cameo.

For Catherine? She stalled for a moment. Then, more determined than ever to settle things, she stepped blindly into the street. She saw a team of horses bearing down upon her and heard the driver shout as he pulled back hard on the reins, driving the painful bits into the mouths of the horses. Startled, they reeled back and snorted. Hannah's old fears of Druid returned mercilessly, paralyzing her. She screamed and her arms shot forward in a vain attempt to protect herself, agitating the horses further. They reared and pawed the air wildly, and as they came down, a hoof clipped Hannah, dropping her into the street as a crowd of bystanders looked on.

* * *

Jed looked curiously at the gathering crowd as he entered the restaurant where his friends stood staring out the window. "Your pastries, gentlemen," he said, presenting the bag with a flourish. "Plus, I found the perfect cameo for Frannie's birthday." Noting their interest in the scene outside he asked, "What happened?"

"A young woman was sitting right there." Timothy pointed. "She bolted upright and left without paying. The owner chased after her. I suppose he caught her and called for the sheriff."

"Poor thing," Jed muttered, looking at the uneaten plate of toast and the mess on the floor. "Only toast and coffee? Either she was sick or poor. In either case, what she needs is help."

A woman rushed by, calling for a doctor. Timothy and Jed looked to Samuel.

"I'm not a doctor yet," he stammered. "I don't even have any supplies with me."

"You're likely the most qualified person around," Jed declared as he barreled through the throng, pulling Renfro along with Timothy close behind. As soon as he reached the center of the crowd, his heart skipped a beat. There, lying unconscious on the ground, was a beautiful young woman whose haunting face resembled his sweet Hannah. Jed stared at the face framed by dark hair that had obviously fallen free of the pins holding it piled on her head. She was soaked with perspiration and her complexion was pale, not the rosy palette common to Hannah's face. But the eyes were unmistakably hers, as were the full lips that had always smiled brightly at him. Instantly, he knew with growing soberness that, like Frannie's transformation into a woman, he had also missed Hannah's. And there she was before him.

"Do you know this woman?" Mr. Botto, the Italian restaurateur, asked him sharply.

"Yes," Jed gasped in sorrow. "Hannah . . . Hannah . . ." he cried to her.

"Hannah?" Samuel and Timothy repeated in unison as they gaped at one another.

Jed suddenly remembered Renfro and drew him down, urging him to examine Hannah. Timothy shoved a few coins into Botto's hand and sent him away as he set about to clear the crowd.

"Is she . . . ?" Jed groaned to Samuel. After a long minute, the medical student laid a calming hand on Jed's arm.

"She's got a bad bump on her head and some scrapes and bruises, but she'll awaken as soon as we get some air into her lungs." He began turning Hannah onto her side. "Blast these corsets!" he cursed. Jed covered Hannah with his jacket while Samuel unbuttoned the back of her dress and loosened the ties. The color immediately began returning to her face.

Jed took her left hand and noticed the absence of a ring. His heart soared at the revelation that she was unattached. "Is it safe to move her?" he asked Samuel. "I'd like to get her off the street."

At Samuel's nod, Jed wrapped the coat around Hannah and lifted her into his protective arms. As soon as he raised her up, she took a deep breath and began coughing and thrashing. "It's all right, sweetness. It's Jed. I've got you, Hannah." He cradled her against him. "Jed's got you."

The sound of his voice caused her eyes to flutter open. As soon as she recognized his face, relief washed over her, and she relaxed in his arms, exhausted. Jed was savoring the feel of her against him when she suddenly became rigid, pushing back from him and turning her face away.

"I think I can stand now," she uttered with a muffled cry.

"I don't think you should try just yet," Jed murmured softly, tightening his arms.

"Is there a place where I can sit?" she asked as she buried her face in his pounding chest.

Timothy noticed a hotel on the street corner. "The Lord Baltimore has a large lobby."

Jed carried her to the hotel, murmuring reassuringly to her as tears formed behind her closed lids. He noticed the moistness welling there and panicked. "Are you in pain, Hannah?"

She shook her head and pressed her face into his aftershave-scented shirt. Jed laid her on the sofa and knelt beside her, but she avoided his gaze by leaning back and laying her arm across her eyes. He held her free hand, bathing it with kisses and pressing it against his cheek as he urged Samuel Renfro to examine her thoroughly.

When Renfro pulled Hannah's arm away from her eyes to examine them, Jed saw a curious look pass between them. "Is she all right?" he asked the medical student.

"She's fine. Nothing a little rest and attention won't fix." He winked at her and smiled. "I'm sure you two have much to discuss. Timothy and I will leave you now."

Jed took Renfro's hand in thanks as he walked past him to join Timothy at the door. Then he turned his full attention to Hannah. "Hannah . . ." Jed's voice shuddered and he hid his face to disguise his fear. His voice was husky with emotion when he resumed speaking. "You frightened me nearly to death. Whatever possessed you to run into the street?"

She touched the moistness on his face, then, as if unable to bear the nearness of him, she turned away. "I . . . I need to find my sisters," she mumbled. "They'll be frantic looking for me."

"Shhh . . . soon enough, sweetness," he shushed as he tenderly brushed her hair from her face. "What are you doing here in Baltimore? How did you get separated from them?"

"I ran into a shop . . . for something I . . . I wanted." Hannah's voice broke. "It was foolish of me. Please let me find them," she cried. Attempting to stand, she fell against Jed.

He clutched her to him, breathing in the scent of lilac water on her clothes and brushing his lips along her cheek before setting her down. He pressed his brow against hers. "When I saw you lying in the street, I didn't even recognize you. Then, when I finally did, my heart nearly leapt from my chest. If anything had happened to you . . . I . . ." When he looked into her eyes he thought he saw equal passion reflected there, but her voice was reserved.

"Much has happened in the last year. We've both changed."

"Yes," he sighed. "You're a beautiful woman now. The sweet girl I adored is no more."

"Then it's true . . ." she whispered.

"What is? Oh, Hannah, you can't know how glad I am to see you." He kissed her hands. "I went to Philadelphia to see Frannie and to clear my head. While I was there, I made some decisions. Ohhh," he moaned as he hugged her close, "I can't begin to tell you how much I've missed you. I have so much I want to tell you . . . so many friends I want you to meet."

A small sob escaped Hannah at the reference to his new Philadelphia friends.

"What is it, Hannah? Are you in pain?"

She pressed her eyes closed against the welling tears and shook her head.

"Are you sure you're well? You look at me as if I were a stranger."

"I can't spend time with you, Jed," she managed. "My parents are on their way as we speak, to pick up Myrna and me and take us back to Coolfont tomorrow."

Jed's disappointment was palpable. "Then tonight," he said breathlessly, clutching at her hands. "Offer me this night. I'll call for you at seven. We'll have some supper and . . ."

Hannah lowered her head and shook it slightly. "I already have a commitment tonight."

There was something in her voice and in the hanging silence that sent a chill down Jed's spine. "Are you . . . are you seeing someone, Hannah?" The words stumbled out of his mouth and echoed in his head like a recurring nightmare he struggled against but could not escape. She nodded slightly, and he relaxed his hold on her hand before grasping it again. "But what of our agreement?" he asked with feigned humor. "Neither of us was going to fall in love without telling the other, remember?" His voice quivered and he forced a smile. "You were to introduce me to your intended so I could see if he was worthy of my best girl."

"Yes, and you were to be my dearest love." She looked accusingly at him and then broke her gaze to stare at her hands. "We made many promises to one another, Jed, but time has revealed them for what they were . . . childish pledges between friends."

"Friends?" he muttered weakly. "Yes, of course . . . pledges between friends."

Hannah heard the pain in his voice, and for a moment Jed saw the glimmer that once filled her eyes those years ago, when they were close.

"Isn't that what I am to you, Jed . . . ?"

The stoic momentarily gone, his sweet Hannah returned to him, looking at him with those beautiful, trusting, green eyes. He tried to understand the implication buried in her question when a more perplexing query emerged.

"Isn't that what you want from me . . . just a good friend . . . just your little Hannah?"

Jed sensed a glimmer of longing in her questions, and he leapt at the chance to finally express his affections. He held her shoulders, forcing her to face him, and his brooding eyes searched deeply into hers. "Hannah . . . I . . ." And then a commotion broke the moment.

"Look who we've found!" announced Timothy triumphantly as he and Renfro burst through the door, followed by a panicked Myrna and Beatrice. The women nervously swarmed around Hannah, disrupting what the entire entourage immediately realized had been a private moment. Regretting both the timing of the surprise and the surprise itself, Timothy looked at his increasingly distraught friend and stammered, "They've . . . been inquiring after their sister . . . I . . . just assumed . . . I'm . . . sorry, Jed . . ."

Determined to declare his love for her despite the intrusion of fawning, chattering onlookers, Jed drew Hannah's attention back to him. Then he heard the words that silenced him.

"Andrew will be here soon," announced Myrna. "We told a soldier on the street that our missing sister was Lieutenant Robertson's intended, and he hurried to fetch him here."

Samuel noted the immediate change in Jed's bearing . . . the rounded shoulders and the devastated look on his countenance. He tried unsuccessfully to draw the sisters away, but they could not be persuaded. And so Samuel watched helplessly as the great man shrank before his eyes.

Jed braced his weight to rise. "So you are promised to a lieutenant," he whispered to Hannah as his eyes began to sting. "All I've ever wanted was your happiness, sweetness," he muttered. "Be happy, my sweet, sweet Hannah." Then he hurriedly stood and exited the hotel.

Samuel and Timothy rushed after him, but Jed had melted into the masses on the street. "What just happened in there?" cried a worried Timothy. "Does she love Jed or not?"

Renfro pressed his palms to his temples and moaned, "I don't know. But I'm sure of one thing. Our idle quips about Catherine are what sent her into the street. I fear we unknowingly set something terrible in motion today, my friend, and it may have altered two destinies."

"Then we've got to find him and explain. Good heavens . . . we've got to find him."

Both artillery officers had arrived in time for Dudley to watch Jed's emotional departure, and though Hannah's pitiable state immediately drew Andrew's devotion, Dudley instantly understood the true cause of Hannah's relentless tears. He knew her sisters had finally succeeded in severing a love that neither Jed nor Hannah might find again.

The image still haunted Dudley back at the Snowden home, where Hannah went immediately to bed, unwilling to speak and unable to eat or drink despite her sisters' and Andrew's constant care. Beatrice and Myrna alternated wringing their hands with guilt and praying to God for forgiveness for the havoc they had undeniably caused. They had seen it—the agonized parting gaze between the two people they had deceived. And Beatrice had other worries. Each time Dudley looked at her, she felt ashamed, but a downcast look of dishonor now emanated from him as well. When Dudley could no longer bear seeing tears in the eyes of his protégé and friend who'd unsuccessfully offered his heart to the broken girl, he headed for the front door, prepared to leave. Beatrice stood several feet away from him, pleading for his forgiveness.

"Will you ever be able to look at me again without contempt?" she asked tearfully.

Unable to face her, he lowered his head and replied over his shoulder. "I pray so."

She stifled a shuddering cry. "I never intended it to turn out this way."

"I understand that. It is the casualness with which you toyed with their lives that unnerves me. Soldiers risk their lives in defense of the freedom to choose, and yet you and Myrna casually desecrated the principle. And now you've made me complicit in your crime."

Beatrice looked bewildered. "How?"

When Dudley turned and faced his wife, his expression showed the same look of pain she now carried. "I should run to Jed Pearson and tell him the truth, but how can I?" He raised a shaky arm and pointed up the stairs in the direction of Hannah's room, where Andrew maintained his vigil. "How can I, knowing that I will destroy a young man I love as a brother? This is now my dilemma as well, Beatrice, and all we can do is pray for Jed's ability to forget, and hope that Andrew's goodness will be enough to give Hannah the desire to go on." He turned and placed his hand on the doorknob.

"Where are you going?" Beatrice asked nervously.

"To purge my soul," he answered just before he slammed the door shut.

* * *

Timothy and Samuel scoured the city looking for Jed. They were painfully convinced that they had been the catalyst in the day's debacle, and that knowledge spurred them on to search for their despondent friend, to try to convince him to go to Hannah and set things right.

They knew Jed wasn't one to normally find solace in the bottle, but under the circumstances they felt compelled to search every alehouse and tavern in town. It was nearly dark when they happened upon a tavern near the port and inquired about their friend. The owner of the establishment recognized Jed's description, but his news wasn't favorable.

"He staggered in here this afternoon, as sorry a feller as ever I've seen. A couple of ne'er-do-wells took one look at him and knew they had found themselves a nice patsy, I figure, 'cause after a couple more drinks the three of 'em tottered out of here as if they were old cronies. Then a while later your friend drags himself through that door, all bloodied up and battered with nary a penny on him. The sheriff carted him off to the hospital about two hours ago."

Timothy and Samuel hurried to the hospital, but they were told that a Captain Snowden had come for Jed. Their last hopes lay at the stables, and they went to search for Jed's horse.

"What happened to your friend?" asked the stable master. "His hands were raw and bloody, and his face! Why, he looked like a team of horses had run him over. Captain Snowden offered to pay for his room at the hotel but Mr. Pearson refused his hospitality. He just drew an "x" on his bill, said he'd send payment, and rode off. He could barely stay mounted, poor fellow."

"What shall we do now?" Samuel asked Timothy.

"I have no idea where he would have gone under such circumstances. He may have gone north to wait for Frannie. Her ship's expected home soon. That's what I think he would do, so I suppose that's our best hope. I'll set off immediately. Pray I can catch up to him and get a chance to undo the damage." Timothy mounted his horse.

"I think I'll draft a letter and post it for his home . . . just in case he went there instead," Samuel declared.

Timothy nodded. "And keep your eyes and ears open here in Baltimore as well." Then he kicked his horse and shot off at a hard pace up the north road to Philadelphia.

CHAPTER 17

The Willows
The Following Day

Jed reached the county line just before dark, barely able to hold the reins in his battered and swollen hands. He had tried to defend himself, but after one good sweep from one of his assailant's feet he was on the ground with two pairs of boots stomping his hands until they were useless, and kicking him in the chest until he heard his ribs crack. The effects of the liquor, as well as the beating, left his head pounding, but the ache in his heart dwarfed all his physical pains. He had never planned for any scenario other than ending up blissfully married to Hannah. Now that that dream had been taken from him, nothing else made sense or mattered, and he couldn't even bring the image of the Willows to his mind. It was as if his heart had willed itself to Hannah years ago and, without her, it could never be truly his again. It frightened him that he was also unable to bring the faces of Bitty and Jack or the others, to his mind's eye.

Yesterday morning he had been so excited. His time in Philadelphia had renewed him to the obligation of freedom, and that witness had been amplified as he'd stood in Getty's Tavern and spoken with old-timers who had fought in the Revolution and who abhorred any form of tyranny. He had returned home to the Willows, spending days juggling numbers and crop production figures, and he believed he had formulated a plan to free his slaves and save the Willows as well. He had planned to confer with his attorneys in Baltimore . . . right after lunching with his friends . . . and then he'd found Hannah . . .

Jed's mare slowed, sensing a change in the grip of the reins. As Jed slipped from the saddle, the rough brush scraped his face and hands before he landed on the hard ground, his face in the dirt. He allowed the darkness to swallow him again. Then, sometime later, he felt the velvety nuzzle of his mare as she softly nickered at him. His eyes fluttered open just long enough to see the black and gray patchwork of clouds quickly obscuring the moon. Then the rain began.

The usually blessed rain was now an annoyance, jostling his senses until he could no longer lie still hoping death would pay him a call. As the hard earth turned to mud and began to ooze around his mouth, he spat angrily and sat up. He met the muzzle of his loyal bay mare.

"Death won't even have me, Tildie," he groaned as he labored to get to his feet, struggling three times to get his foot back into the stirrup. Once mounted, Jed released his pack and laid it across his saddle, wrapping the straps around the horn, making a pillow of sorts. Then he wove his battered fingers into Tildie's silky mane and lay low, resting his torso against the pack and Tildie's neck. He let her have her head and she continued on through the night, following the scent of the Patuxent River toward home. Morning broke, and with it came the scorching late-August heat that drained Jed's remaining reserves and wore heavily on his already exhausted mare. It was nearly noon when she turned down the Willows' lane. By the time she reached the porch of the manor house, her legs quivered, but she stood firm until Jed lifted his head and slid off her back to the ground.

Seeing the toll the long ride had taken on his old friend, he rubbed a loving hand over one of her front fetlocks and whispered, "Good ol' girl." Then he succumbed to fatigue.

Jack was in the barn when the riderless mare arrived. As soon as he recognized Jed's bay, he started sprinting for the manor house. With one look at Jed's battered body, still and prostrate on the ground, Jack was seized by the same fearsome shiver he felt that day in Calverton when Jed stormed into the angry mob.

"Bitty!" Jack hollered with a tone that made Bitty's neck prickle. "It's Jed! He's hurt bad!"

Bitty ran through the house and out the front door, letting out a moan as she saw Jed. She leapt down the stairs from the porch to crumple by her master's prostrate form. Abel saw firsthand the depth of her worry over the young man, as if he were her own son. To him, Jed Pearson was just the man who currently owned him, a better man than most white men he had known, but one still inclined to hold men as property. But he'd learned that to his father, Jed was the embodiment of hope, to Jack he was a brother, and to Bitty he was still much more.

She laid Jed's head in her lap and bent over him, gently touching his head and face and calling out his name while Jerome hobbled over and began examining his legs and arms.

"He's mostly just beat up," Jerome said anxiously. "He'll mend with good care."

Bitty called orders to Jenny, who'd appeared at the doorway. "Get me my satchel of herbs and some clean cotton strips! Hurry!" Then she turned to the men. "His mother's away and his father's in Baltimore. We'll tend him. Abel, we need a board, a long, wide one to carry him upstairs on. Where's Markus?"

Jack spoke up. "He left for Georgetown this morning. He took a few horses to the races to see what they'd bring. He won't be home for two . . . three days . . ."

Bitty saw a curious expression on Abel's face, and she quickly snapped her fingers to curtail his thoughts. "Abel, please go fetch me that board." Her eyes were stern though she attempted to keep her voice calm and respectful.

Abel shot her a surprised glance, and she feared where his mind was wandering, but she pointed her arm in the direction of the barn and repeated her request with a firmer voice.

Jerome grabbed Tildie's bridle in one hand and Abel's arm in the other. He took a step toward the barn and said encouragingly, "Come along, son. I'll help you find one." Abel stared down at his wife, resistant at first to his father's tug, but slowly he relented and followed along.

Bitty's heart raced. She knew a difficult day lay ahead. Jed's parents were gone, Jed was incapacitated, and Markus was away for several days. It was nothing out of the ordinary for her and Jack to be directing the daily affairs in Markus's and Jed's absence, but now things were slightly different. Abel had brought a new element of unrest to the estate. Was he thinking of escape? Was that what she'd read in his eyes?

Jenny arrived and brought nearly every other Willows' slave with her. Everyone gathered around, chattering in hushed tones, some crying softly, all too aware that their own destinies were tied to the life of their young master.

Bitty searched through her bag of herbs and pulled out some tins. "Jenny, Sarah's in the kitchen. Fetch me a kettle of boiling water and a teacup." The girl ran off, appearing grateful to be of some service. Bitty saw Abel's oldest son standing in the throng. "Caleb, I need some basil. Could you and Eli go pick some for me?"

As the two boys hurried away, Bitty felt the soft pat of Abel's three-year-old daughter, Helen. "What can I do, Bitty Mama? I wanna help too."

Bitty grabbed the child to her and cried softly into her dress. Then she wiped her tears and smiled brightly. "Bitty Mama needs some marigolds, Helen. You know those pretty yellow flowers you were pickin' the other day? You and Grandy go fetch me a handful of those, hear?" As the two youngest children of her new family scampered away, she groaned inwardly in fear. *Yes, it's going to be a very hard day . . .*

After Abel and Jack carried Jed upstairs and laid him in his bed, Bitty made herb poultices for the worst cuts, and slathered homemade salves on the others. She tossed marigold heads into a pot of steaming water and made Jed drink some of the tea to reduce the swelling in his body. Then she tried to get some warm broth into him. Despite all of her attempts, he refused to discuss his accident and requested that the drapes be drawn and all visitors be banned.

"We gotta get word to your father," Bitty said.

"I don't want him to know about this. I don't want to see him or my mother." Jed looked at his useless hands and instructed, "Send Markus up when he gets home. I'll have him write a note to my parents with an excuse to keep them in Baltimore until I make some decisions."

He fell back against the pillows and stared blankly at the wall. A sense of foreboding washed over Bitty. "I'll write your note for you, Jed. Frannie says my penmanship is real good."

Jed turned to face her. He reached a hand out to her, and she took it and sat on the edge of the bed, his one hand dwarfing both of hers.

He smiled apologetically at the small woman he loved so dearly. "It is good, Bitty. Very good, it's just that . . ."

She smiled understandingly, then admitted with an awkward laugh, "My spellin's not up to par yet."

"They don't even know you can read." Jed smiled as he drew her hand to his mouth and kissed it. "I'm tired now, Bitty. I think I'll rest a while, but thank you for taking care of me."

His eyes were wet, and she guessed the worst pains might be in his heart, things her remedies and poultices could not heal. "I'm gonna be sittin' right outside that door, Puddin'. If you need anything I'll be right here."

A melancholy smile tugged at his lips. "You haven't called me Puddin' since I was sixteen. It was the day I left for the university."

Bitty tucked the covers under his chin and framed his face with her hands. "I didn't think a university man would stand for it." She smiled affectionately as the sadness in his eyes overwhelmed her. "You growed up to be a fine man, Jed Pearson, and I'm proud of you." Her voice broke and as she tried to pull away, Jed drew her to him.

"Do you really think I'm a good man, Bitty?" he asked with sad skepticism. "Are you truly proud of me? Besides Frannie's, your opinion is the only one that matters to me anymore."

She sat down slowly, cradling his battered hand in her lap. "What's makin' you ask me such a question as that? You know I love you. Everyone on this plantation loves you, Jed."

"But are you proud of me?"

" 'Course I am," she replied. "No master is better to his people."

"Master . . ." he muttered, turning his head. It sounded like a curse word to him.

"What happened to you, Jed? You left here yesterday all happy and fired up, and now you seem as though the life had just been squeezed out of you."

"I've lost her, Bitty . . ."

Bitty understood instantly. "You've loved Hannah since you were small."

"Everything I've ever done, everything I've ever planned was for her. I always believed we'd marry and live here on the Willows, but I waited too long to tell her, and she's found someone else." His voice became a pained whisper. "I don't know what to do, Bitty. Without her I have no reason to go on." He turned his head to face the wall.

"What did you do to yourself?" She pointed to the cuts and bruises that colored his face.

"Just a fitting finale to the day my life came to an end."

She placed her hand on his shoulder and spoke, though he refused to look at her. "Times come when you feel like you're at the bottom of a well with no rope and the water is gettin' higher and higher, but you got people dependin' on you. You got to make that your reason for climbin' out."

"Not now, Bitty," he begged. "Please . . . leave me."

She slowly withdrew and closed the door to find Abel waiting for her in the hall.

"We need to talk," he said firmly, pointing down the hall.

"Whatever you need to say to me you can say right here."

Startled by her firmness, Abel swallowed, then declared, "It's time to leave. We can get a two-day start before Markus gets back. We can take the sloop upriver and cross into Baltimore on foot. There are lots of free Negroes living there, and we could blend in until we can make our way farther north."

Bitty had known this was coming. "And what about money, Abel?"

"We'll sell the sloop . . . and you've got access to Jed's wallet."

Bitty had never been so disappointed by anyone, and Abel saw it. "You're right. I *could* take money out of Jed's wallet. In fact, I could *ask* Jed for money and he would up and give it to me, no matter how much it was I asked for. Know why? Because he trusts me, Abel. Know how I know that? Because he already proved it to me when he spent a fortune bringin' your family here 'cause I asked him to. I earned his trust and I won't go and ruin that. See, I may not have grown up with Bible learnin', but somethin' inside me understands right and wrong. I guess it's either in folks or it's not, and I guess when it's not, no amount of good parentin' or teachin' can put it there. I just never figured you were so vacant on the matter."

"It's not dishonest, Bitty. What do you figure Jed owes you for all the work you've given him, not to mention what he owed your parents? The way I see it, he'd be getting off light."

"So, forget that he's busted up, helpless in bed, his heart all broken? Forget that he's loved me in the best way he knows how for lo these many years, and just up and kick him when he's down? Well, I'm just not made that way, and if you are, well then, git on with you."

"Are you saying you'd give up your family for a man who keeps you as property?"

Bitty's tear-filled eyes filled with scorn. "Only two people's ever called me 'property' or made me feel like it, and Jed was never one of them. Now . . . just go."

Abel's shoulders slumped with guilt. "I . . . I'm sorry, Bitty . . . I . . ."

"Please, Abel. If you've got it in your mind to git, then git. I won't ask you to stay."

He watched his wife sink into the chair outside Jed Pearson's door, and he knew she meant to remain there regardless of what he decided to do. He shuffled his feet, making no progress in one direction or another. Then he took a step to turn, hoping she would call him back, but she didn't. In the silence he saw his choices clearly. "What about our vow? You said . . ."

"I know what I said. But you said you'd give this place a chance."

Abel sighed. "It's been a year, Bitty." His voice became more sober. "You realize that if we miss this chance, things could change for the worse, and we might never get another."

Bitty considered how nervous even she had felt at the thought of Jed dying or even losing interest in the Willows. But then she remembered the young man's heart and the feeling she had in his room as he longed for her approval. "He's a good man, Abel. I'm willing to place my trust in him, but only you can answer for your family."

Abel placed his hand over hers. "You're my family now, Bitty."

She closed her eyes and felt the weight of responsibility resting on her shoulders. "What do you want me to say? I can't see into the future, I can't leave, and I can't have you blamin' me for the rest of my life." She wished he would just leave and end the torturous conversation.

Abel took both of her hands. "Why'd I have to fall in love with a stubborn woman?"

"I'm not stubborn, Abel. I'm loyal, and you knew that goin' in. What about your folks?"

"I haven't spoken to my father about my plans, but he suspects that I'm planning to run."

Bitty rose to her feet and stood motionless. "Will you send me word before you go?"

Abel nodded and pointed out the window that overlooked the meadow where the slave quarters were located. "I'll leave a candle in our cabin window if we stay, and if it's dark . . ."

Bitty nodded stoically. "Then I'll know you're gone."

"Is there anything I can do for you before I . . ."

"Would you tell the children I . . ." her voice broke.

Abel dropped his head quickly. "I'll tell them. I'll tell them." And he was gone.

She sat back in the chair and stared blankly out the window, hoping for some sign of Abel or the children. As each hour passed she checked on Jed and found him sleeping so soundly that she sometimes worried whether or not he was breathing. Nightfall came. With resignation she watched out the window and counted little cabin roofs. Darkness consumed the windows under the fifth roof, and her heart sank. She rushed to the window and peered more carefully, and when her second count confirmed the first, she slipped to the floor by the windowsill and began to cry.

Jed listened to the quiet sounds of her sobs from his bed. Only pretending sleep, he had heard the conversation between her and Abel, and he knew he was a factor in the breakup of her family. By rights he could have Abel hunted down and arrested, but he knew how much pain that would cause Bitty. Jed's world was falling apart, piece by piece, and his only wish was that his injuries were sufficient to end his pain.

Morning came but Jed forbade the maid from opening the curtains, and he refused care and food as he began counting the days until he would wither and die. He heard Bitty's neurotic pacing outside his door and called for her in the evening. "Has Markus arrived yet?"

"No, Jed. Not yet. Do you want me to send Jack after him?"

"No, no," he replied. "He'll be here tomorrow. There'll still be plenty of time."

Bitty began to argue with him, and even tried pleading with him, but nothing seemed capable of reviving his spirit. He was wallowing so deeply in self-pity that even she couldn't reach him. For the first time the connection between them seemed broken. She considered what she had sacrificed to stay at the Willows, and for a moment she questioned her decision. However, she knew that he needed her more than ever before, and she couldn't abandon him without a fight.

An idea came to her and she ran to find Jerome. He and Sarah were still struggling with their own loss, doing their best to divert questions from the other Willows residents as they tried to buy their foolish son and their grandchildren some time. When Bitty arrived on their doorstep, pain was evident in their eyes. No words were spoken as Jerome took Bitty's hand and gave it a squeeze. They allowed a few silent moments to pass between them before getting on to the reason Bitty had come calling.

"I want you to talk to Jed, Jerome. You're our only hope right now."

"What can I do? If he won't talk to you, what can I say to him? And now that Abel's run off, well, I'm afraid I might say something that will give his secret away."

"He lost the love of his life and he thinks his world is falling apart. He just wants to die. I know some of your story. You know those feelin's. You're the best person to talk to him."

"I can hardly just walk in there when he's refused company, Bitty."

"Pray to God, Jerome. He'll tell you what to do. That's what you've told me when Abel and I've had problems." Even the mention of Abel's name brought her pain, but she pushed it aside and tugged on Jerome's arm until he followed her. When they reached Jed's door she knocked and entered, despite the fact that Jed had not invited her in.

He knew it was Bitty, for only she would dare such an intrusion. "Leave me, Bitty," he moaned without looking up.

"Jed, Jerome needs to speak to you, so I brought him up." She held her breath to see how Jed would respond and if Jerome would be frightened off by a cantankerous reply.

"No, Bitty! I don't want to see anyone. Just leave me in peace."

Bitty pushed the reluctant old slave forward and kept talking. "You told Jerome anytime he had a question or an idea to improve things on the Willows that he could come and talk to you, man to man. Well, he needs to speak with you tonight."

Jed tried to sit up and argue, but his initial attempt to move sent a sharp pain through his torso. He gasped loudly and fell back hard against his pillow.

Bitty fought the urge to rush to him. The toll of his refusal of food and care showed cruelly in his face. She couldn't bear to see him this way, so she wrung her hands and simply said, "Well, I'll leave you two alone to talk." Then she shuffled out of the room.

Jerome trembled as he waited for some encouragement from Jed. At long last Jed's tired voice mumbled, "Say what you came here to say, Jerome."

Jerome moved near the bed and shoved his hands into the pockets of his trousers. "Mr. Jed, sir," he questioned nervously, "I believe the slaves would benefit from the building of a church."

"A church?" Jed replied flatly.

"Yes, sir. As it is now, we have no place large enough to gather all the people together. A church would give us a place to meet and worship God together, but it could also serve as a gathering place for meetings or when you or Mr. Markus needed to speak to everyone."

"And who would conduct services, Jerome?" Jed chuckled sarcastically. "Imagine what would happen to all of us if a preacher or anyone else came in and saw the Willows' slaves reading from the Bible or singing from a hymnal!"

"I would do it," Jerome said modestly.

Jed rose gingerly on one elbow and looked at the man with quiet wonder. "You stood in for a preacher when Abel and Bitty were wed, but that marriage was more symbolic than legal."

Jerome stood serenely.

"You do have an amazing command of the Bible, Jerome, and your vocabulary and elocution equal most educated men . . ." Jed continued to eye the man closely, too curious now to let his questions go unanswered. "You didn't come to America from Africa, did you?"

Jerome pulled himself up straight and met Jed's gaze. "No, sir."

Jed pointed to a chair, his curiosity now overcoming his malaise. "I would like to hear your story if you wouldn't mind telling me."

Easing into the seat, Jerome let out a long, low sigh as if the burden of remembering his past bore so heavily upon him that it squeezed the very breath from his frail, aged body. He wriggled down into the soft fabric, then leaned forward and placed his bony hands on his knees.

"For forty years I've tried to fade these memories from my consciousness, and I've never spoken of them to any man since I landed on American soil. My wife doesn't even know the entire tale and neither does . . ." He nearly choked at the mention of his runaway son.

"I know about Abel, Jerome. I heard him arguing with Bitty in the hall yesterday."

Jerome tensed and eyed his master carefully.

"I'm not going to chase after him, if that's what you're worried about," Jed said as he adjusted his position. "I don't know what I would have done if this had happened last week, but today . . . it just doesn't seem worth the pain it would cause."

Jerome seemed to shrivel, becoming somehow smaller than he had been a minute before. "I thank you, sir. Thank you," he uttered as his head dipped in gratitude.

Then Jed mused aloud, "I just wish I knew why he hated it here so. Bitty thought he would be so much happier at the Willows than he had been at White Oak."

"Perhaps once you hear my story you'll understand why Abel has hungered so for freedom." Jerome lifted his head and wrung his hands. "It's mostly my fault. I refused to answer his questions, thinking that knowing the whole truth would only make him more bitter than he already was. I was born in Saint Domingue, not Africa, Jed. The Spaniards once ruled our entire island but the French took over in 1697, and they proved to be far worse. They committed horrible atrocities, subjugating my people by flogging, starving, and even burying men alive for failure to comply with their demands. My father could see a major rebellion on the horizon. He felt death was more palatable than French rule, so he stole a small boat and set his family on the open waters. A terrible storm capsized our vessel, quickly taking my mother and sister to their graves, but my father and I hung onto the boat for two more days before he finally slipped into the sea, leaving me alone." His eyes became moist.

As Jerome went on, he spoke to Jed as comfortably as one friend confiding with another. "I was just about to let go myself when a missionary boat from a monastery in Barbados miraculously came by. I was eight years old when the priests found me and took me to live with them. They used me to run errands and maintain the grounds, and in return they educated me in spiritual matters as well as in secular knowledge. I was taught Portuguese, Spanish, and English in addition to my native dialect, and the French I had already picked up. I was taught from the works of the great masters, and at one time I could even play the piano." He chuckled sadly.

"The priests assumed I would enter the seminary. I was twenty, and I accepted that God chose this path for me the day He plucked me from the sea. But then I began to have doubts . . ."

The diversion from his misery was a godsend, and Jed couldn't bear the pause in the story. Ignoring the physical pain, he forced himself upright to ask, "What happened, Jerome?"

A wistful smile tugged at the corners of the elderly man's mouth. "A woman . . . a girl actually. Her name was Elena." He leaned back in the chair, obviously savoring the memory. "She came to market three times a week. I never noticed her until I agreed to the seminary. The priests told me the devil was tempting me away from God's service, and for a year I accepted that and avoided seeing Elena. As the time drew near for me to take my vows, thoughts of her clouded my mind once more."

Jerome shifted his position and leaned forward, staring at the floor. "I spent one evening with her . . . the most wonderful evening of my young life. We steamed fish in banana leaves and ate as we talked about our dreams and watched the sunset. We shared a single, sweet kiss . . . and then I walked her home. That was it, but that evening changed the course of my life forever.

"I told the priests I couldn't commit my life to God as long as I had these feelings for Elena, and they advised me to take my worry to the Lord, which I did. However, I took a bottle of rum with me as I headed to the beach to pray. I prayed and drank and then drank some more until at some point I must have passed out." He laughed sadly. "Again, the Lord directed me to unseen paths. A slave escaped from a ship, and men were out hunting for their runaway. Unable to find their missing captive and evidently unwilling to return to their captain empty-handed they . . ."

Jed gasped softly. "They took you instead?"

Jerome nodded, amused that the man who now owned him seemed so blind to the irony of their current conversation. "Yes. They found me sleeping and clubbed me to keep me from yelling out until they were underway. They stripped me to the waist and beat me so badly I slept for three days before awakening on the sea. I tried, in every language I knew, to explain to the slavers that they had made a mistake, but my efforts only prompted them to beat me more. They warned me that an uppity, educated Negro would likely be executed when we arrived in America, so when Master Stringham bought me I modeled the Africans who had just arrived."

Jed was speechless for several seconds. "You must have wanted to die."

"Oh yes . . ." moaned Jerome as he leaned back in his chair and closed his eyes.

The irony of their situation finally hit Jed, and he cringed. "You must hate me."

Jerome smiled sympathetically. "No. Hate is the very worst master," he smiled. "Hate imprisons the heart and mind as well as the body. I placed my trust in the Lord. I tried to see His purposes . . . why and where He was leading me." He looked curiously at Jed and shivered.

"Who knoweth whether thou art come to the kingdom for such a time as this," whispered Jerome reverently. He felt Jed's eyes on him and met the young man's gaze. He paused before speaking, drawing Jed's complete attention. "Perhaps God is leading you as well."

"Leading me? By having me beaten nearly to death?" Jed laughed sarcastically, but as he considered the old man's own story, he sobered and his brow wrinkled again.

The old man continued, "We are so quick to ascribe the bad things to God, and in our ignorance or arrogance we are also slow to ascribe the good to Him. God is not responsible for everything that happens to us, Jed. *Someone* disappointed you . . . some *men* beat you, but God can still consecrate all these things for your good and lead you if you'll surrender yourself to Him."

"Is that what you did, Jerome? Is that how you survived your own sorrow?"

"I kept praying to God for deliverance. Eventually, He showed me that I had two choices. Either I could mourn the life I had lost and spend the remainder of my days miserable while I waited to die, or I could try to remember that He had always loved me and still did love me, and trust that He would show me His purposes and make me an instrument in His hands. It wasn't easy. At times I cried like a baby and begged for deliverance, but each morning I would commit to make that day count for something. In the end, He heard me. He delivered me here, Jed."

A glimmer of hope appeared and then disappeared from Jed's face. "Tell me honestly, Jerome. Have you ever been able to forget Elena or the life you might have had?"

Jerome met Jed's eyes and paused for several moments. "Not completely, but what I can't forget I use to measure my life today . . . a very different life indeed, but still a fulfilling one. I've known love. Sarah has been a good wife to me, and Abel has always been a caring son. I've been given opportunities to serve God's neediest children. When I see my Lord someday, I think He will be pleased with what I've made of my circumstances."

"And you think God can help me start over . . . to build a life without the woman I love?"

"I don't think you can begin to see what He can do with you."

Jed allowed the man's comments to sink deep into his heart. "Sit a while with me, Jerome?" he asked as he extended his hand to the man. "I have many things to tell you as well."

* * *

Bitty took the quiet passage of each minute as a sign that Jerome could penetrate the young man's locked heart. She wondered about Abel and the children, whether they were safe and if she would ever hear from them again. Forcing herself to look at the darkened cabin that had been the family's home since her wedding day, she thought she saw a light in the window, and then, knowing better, chided herself and looked away. When she turned her head back again, she saw lights in both back windows and stretched her head out of the window to get a better view. Frantically counting the rooflines, she nearly wept when she clearly saw lights in the windows under the fifth roof. Then a voice sounded from the darkened hall to her left.

"Bitty?" Though his features were obscured by the dim light, the contrite voice and hulking form were unmistakably Abel's.

"Abel?" she replied nervously as she stood and faced him.

"The children lit the candles for you. They were hoping you'd see them and hurry home."

"What are you sayin', Abel?" she asked cautiously.

"I'm saying that if you're staying, well then . . . I'm staying too." He sounded tentative as he met her gaze, obviously worried by the lack of emotion shown there. "If you'll still have me, that is."

"Why are you stayin'?" she questioned coolly. "I don't want to wake up every mornin' wonderin' if you're goin' to ask me to pick up and run in the middle of the night."

"I've already lost one wife, Bitty. I won't leave another one behind."

"Duty isn't enough, Abel. Tell me why you're stayin'."

"I love you. If that's what you've been waiting to hear, then there it is. Believe me, surrendering my heart to you has never been the problem."

Bitty's lower lip quivered, but she remained firmly in her spot. "Then what is?"

Abel walked slowly toward her and reached for her, but she was riveted to her spot, awaiting his reply. "The children and I never left the property today. I took them in the meadow by the White Oak fence while I tried to figure out my own mind." His chin fell to his chest and he shook his mighty head. "You need to understand, Bitty. I've been whipped and beaten, and the hope of freedom was the only salve I had to heal my wounds. It was within my grasp today.

"Then dusk started rolling in, and Helen kept crying to go home to Bitty Mama, and the other children joined right in with her. That's when I knew."

Tears welled in Bitty's eyes. "Knew what, Abel?"

"I'm staying because I love you, Bitty, and because I love you I traded my chance at freedom for something else. I traded it for trust today. I trust my wife's judgment, Bitty."

She looked at the slouching shoulders of the man and knew how hard it was for him to depend on someone. Walking into his outstretched arms, she said, "Let's go home, Abel."

CHAPTER 18

London, England
September 1, 1811

Stephen Ramsey wondered what his father would think if he could see him this day, dressed in clothes that cost more than the tenement house where he grew up. Here he was, a dock rat from Liverpool, about to have a private meeting with an aide to the great British naval commander, Rear Admiral George Cockburn.

Ramsey strolled into the exclusive London pub with its elite clientele, scoured the room in search of a particular face, and scowled. Mitchell was late. When the Member of Parliament finally arrived, a few people seemed to recognize him despite the pains he took to avoid being seen.

Ramsey was irritated by his antics. "Stop making a spectacle of yourself," he snarled under his breath.

"I'm sorry. I'm uncomfortable about this meeting."

Ramsey could clearly see the truth of his words in his countenance and bearing. Some could handle it. Some could not. This man was clearly someone unfamiliar with pressure. *Just a while longer,* he thought to himself as he tried to reply matter-of-factly. "Why?"

"Aren't you?" Mitchell hissed. "Dearborn chose the location and chose the time. Look at this room. They have enough officers in here to hold an impromptu tribunal. What if we're being set up? What if Cockburn's aide agreed to this meeting so he can arrest us for treason?"

Ramsey tried to disguise the eerie feeling those words raised in him. A few unsettling seconds passed before he was able to regain his confidence. "That's not going to happen."

"How can you be so sure? You requested this meeting after receiving confidential information I leaked to you regarding the likelihood of war. That is a treasonable offense!" His head drooped forward and he drew his handkerchief from his pocket to dab at the beads of sweat forming on his brow. "Eyebrows are being raised. I'm as skittish as a mouse each time I hear a footfall outside my office door. Look at my hair! I'm nearly fully gray now."

Ramsey leaned forward and growled at his companion, "Pull yourself together!"

The bite of Ramsey's voice quickly sobered Mitchell, but Ramsey knew his colleague was becoming a liability. At times like this he asked himself why he had ever drawn the weakling into his plans, but he knew. Mitchell's previously spotless reputation in Parliament and his penchant for avoiding controversy, coupled with his representation of the angry dock people around Liverpool's Mersey River, had made him the perfect patsy. Lord Liverpool would have been unapproachable and uncompromising, but his commoner colleague in the neighboring district had been easily manipulated—until recently. Now the man's conscience was working overtime. No matter. Ramsey knew he had insulated himself and the Consortium's investors from Mitchell. Any one of them could sit down at Mitchell's own dining table, as some of them actually had, and he would have no idea of their ties to the Consortium.

Mitchell's eyes darted back and forth, scanning the room, and he whispered, "Lord Whittington addressed the House of Commons, warning us to beware of sedition. He's been making inquiries. In fact, his watchdogs have gone so far as to pull the past five years of voting records for some members of the House of Commons."

Ramsey pursed his lips as his cold, blue eyes surveyed the man's new, expensive attire. "You were advised to deposit your money and maintain the status quo."

Mitchell's face fell. "I know . . . I know," he moaned. "I did. I deposited it just as you instructed me to do, but the opportunity to spoil my loved ones enticed me until I withdrew some. What can I do now? They'll be more suspicious if their inquiries cause another change in my habits." He hung his head in shame. "I wish I had never . . ."

"But you did!" Ramsey retorted menacingly.

"Yes! Yes, I did," Mitchell argued back. "But I didn't seek this. Why did you pursue me? Everything I hold precious is at risk now."

"Stop whining, Mitchell. If you play your part well tonight, you will soon be able to withdraw from Parliament and live handsomely anywhere you choose in this world."

"There are some things money cannot buy, Ramsey. Things that require a lifetime, sometimes several noble lifetimes, to earn. Like an honorable name! But, of course, I am speaking of things that hold no value in your world."

Mitchell's comments hit a nerve in Ramsey, reminding him that no matter how much wealth he acquired, he would never rid himself of the stain of poverty, a tarnish he sought to hide behind the trappings of power and material goods. He reminded himself that though he was not a man known openly in accepted political circles, he was, in his own right, a man of influence. Yet there were circles that still remained, and ever would remain, closed to him. But not to his son . . . not for Arthur. He would buy his son the respect he had never been paid himself.

When barely eight, Ramsey's father had dragged him to the docks and apprenticed him on a ship to a Captain Harris, who taught him the import and export business. On each voyage the young Ramsey had invested more and more of his earnings in goods for resale until he was able first to buy his own ship and then later a small fleet. Eventually he'd acquired a wealthy clientele whose names sang out weekly from the front page of the *Times* society section.

It was a simple leap from selling these socialites expensive treasures for investment purposes to advising them about an exclusive and lucrative overseas investment company called the Consortium. Ramsey had convinced them that he was employed by the powerful investment group, admitting to no one on the earth that he was actually the mastermind and manipulator behind its covert actions. It had been an easy ruse to establish, since the only concern of his investors was their return. As long as it was hefty, they trusted his word, caring little about the trail their money took to reach their ledgers. With his keen business acumen and willingness to do what was needed to make a profit, Ramsey, by age fifty, had built himself a secret empire.

He understood Mitchell's fears. Unlike Ramsey, the mild man had not had half a lifetime to insulate himself so he could enjoy the rewards of the business without direct scrutiny. Still, Ramsey knew there were those who suspected that something was awry by the way his own lifestyle had rapidly elevated. That was part of the pleasure derived from his game. He was making a different life for his son while flaunting his success in front of nobles, the likes of whom his parents had served on hands and knees—and he was using the nobles' very money to do it.

"You do understand your role today," Ramsey coached.

"Yes, yes. I am to introduce you as a concerned constituent who is in possession of information and services that could be crucial in the event that war breaks out with America."

"Correct. Once the introduction is made, make some excuse to leave."

"So," huffed Mitchell, "I am not to know what service my influence has rendered?"

"Do you really want to know? Could you sleep if you knew what havoc I am preparing to help His Majesty's military unleash on the States?"

Mitchell shuddered and closed his eyes. "No . . . no. Dear heavens, no."

CHAPTER 19

Philadelphia, Pennsylvania
September 1811

The Murdock School already bustled with returning students when Catherine Peltier and the Wilmington entourage arrived, much to the surprise of Mrs. Murdock. "Did Catherine apply for enrollment this semester?" she inquired of her assistant.

"No," fretted Miss Tipton to the school's matron as Catherine and four of her debutante friends checked in. "Last spring she implied she was to be wed to Francis Pearson's brother."

Grace Watson, the sixth Wilmington student, heard the conversation and stopped cold in her tracks. "I wouldn't mention that name to her," she whispered. "I've heard that Frannie's brother wrote to her shortly after his departure, thanking her for her sweet company while declining her invitation to visit Wilmington. He encouraged her to pursue other suitors, as much as telling her he was not pursuing her. But," she added conspiratorially, "she had written her parents letters soon after meeting him last spring, assuring them that a proposal was forthcoming, and they had, in turn, spread the news to all their Wilmington friends! When the Peltiers picked her up from school, instead of telling them the truth, that Mr. Pearson had refused her, Catherine kept up the ruse all summer, pining over his anticipated arrival. And when he didn't show, she still held her tongue to the truth, playing the part of the scorned innocent while painting him a scandalous rake. She forfeited all her vacation plans, pining over him, and ended up having an absolutely dreary summer."

"What shall we do when Francis arrives?" murmured Miss Tipton.

"Find Catherine a bed in any available room for now. As far as she and Francis go, well, we'll cross that bridge when we come to it."

* * *

Fifteen minutes later, Frannie Pearson exited a carriage in the company of Mr. Timothy Shepard. "Thank you for telling me about Jed and Hannah. Poor Jed. He loved her so much," Frannie said.

"Samuel and I think she dashed into the street after overhearing our quips about Catherine. Still, it puzzles me that she would become riled by such a report if Jed was merely her friend, particularly when she is being courted by another. Personally, I believe she cares for Jed as much as he cares for her. I only wish I had been able to find him to tell him so. I assume he at least received Samuel's letter explaining why she really raced into the traffic, but we've had no word from him, and we fear he desires no further contact from us at this time."

"Do you think he made it back to the Willows?"

Timothy Shepard heard the worry in her voice, and his own face clouded with sadness. "He was badly hurt, but the stableman said he rode off in a hurry. He didn't come to Philadelphia, so where else could he have gone?"

"If only I had been here instead of abroad! I need to write to him immediately."

"I'm sure he will contact you now that you're home. He didn't want to discuss it with us, but you two are so close. I know it's you he'll come to." Timothy touched the back of his hand to Frannie's cheek. "You have a way of making a man feel whole when he is with you."

Frannie blushed and looked away. "I'm sorry, Timothy. I haven't been good company, especially in light of your kindness . . . meeting our ship at the dock yesterday. I'm overwhelmed by it all, particularly by your letters. I read every one at least twice. They are beautiful."

"It was not kindness that motivated me, Frannie. I selfishly wanted to see you before I left for New York, and I wanted to give you these." He pulled the velvet bag from his pocket.

"Oh, Timothy . . ." she resisted as he clasped the string of pearls around her neck. "I can't . . ."

He hushed her softly. "Please, Frannie. Indulge me in this last thing."

Frannie lowered her head demurely and Timothy tipped her chin upward to where his soft lips met hers. Tentative and nervous, she nonetheless allowed the innocent advance.

"I love you, Frannie," he whispered to her. "I'm not asking you to say it to me in return. I know you are not ready for such a commitment. I just ask that you think on the things I wrote in my letters and tell me you'll agree to write to me this fall and allow us to see what may come of it all."

She wiped at her eyes and nodded. Smiling, he began to step away. He paused to stare at her another moment and then returned to her, drawing her to him once more.

"All right, Timothy, we'll see where things go," she agreed, and as his carriage pulled away she felt the door to her heart open slightly.

Several girls' faces were pressed against the upstairs windows, swooning over the scene. As soon as Frannie crossed the threshold, they hurried down the stairs, flooding her with questions.

She closed her eyes and waved everyone off for a few seconds while she caught her breath. Then she made her way into the parlor amidst the flurry of her schoolmates' questions.

"What do you want to know? Europe was wonderful!" she sighed.

"Tell us about Mr. Shepard," a girl pressed. "You two seemed quite cozy."

Frannie blushed at the one topic she preferred not to discuss. "Jed gave him our itinerary a few weeks ago, and he came to the docks every day until our ship arrived."

"What lovely pearls," another schoolmate tittered. "Does this mean you two are officially courting?"

Frannie smiled thoughtfully. "I don't know what we are quite yet. We've really only spent a few weeks together—last spring—and now he's on his way to New York to study the law. He did the loveliest thing though. The night before we sailed, a courier delivered a box of twenty-two letters to my stateroom. Each one was from Timothy. He must have written one every night after we met. They were lovely, and I got to know him while we were apart."

"And what of your brother, Jed?" asked one of the non-Wilmington girls. "It appears that only one university man fell in love last spring." The girl giggled maliciously.

Frannie's smile quickly faded. "I haven't spoken to Catherine yet . . .

and I've been out of the country so . . . you should ask her those questions yourself."

"Yes, ask Catherine." The young woman in question descended the staircase heavily, one deliberate step at a time, her eyes riveted on Frannie. "Ask poor, foolish Catherine who waited for a promised visit from a man who duped her into believing he loved her."

"Catherine, Jed never said any such thing. You were in pursuit of him."

"Had I known the family history, I would have been more guarded. My father made a few inquiries and uncovered some very interesting facts about the philandering Pearsons."

Frannie leapt onto her feet. "How dare you!" she replied in furious defense of her brother. "You weren't a target, Catherine, you were a fool, a fool for misconstruing courtesy and friendship for love when Jed clearly told you before leaving that he was not of a mind to court anyone at this time. You wasted away a summer knowing he was indisposed with business that rendered him too occupied to even write. Timothy told me just this evening that Jed scratched a note to you out of courtesy and told you to pursue other suitors."

The girls' attentions turned to Catherine as they awaited her rebuttal. Catherine merely dodged the comment, hurriedly regrouped, and tried another tactic. Dripping with empathy, she said, "How can you stand there and even mention the good name of poor Mr. Shepard? Perhaps I should warn him."

Frannie looked momentarily confused before her expression turned to all-out panic as she realized who Catherine's intended target actually was. "Don't, Catherine . . . I beg you," Frannie muttered. She surveyed the room for support from the girls, who were salivating for more gossip.

"Does Mr. Shepard know that you have left a trail of broken hearts behind you, Frannie?"

"Mr. Shepard knows everything, Catherine. But my business is none of your affair."

"What a fortuitous choice of words. What was it, Frannie? One engagement broken by a jilted lover, and one man hunted by the law . . . or was it one engagement broken because of a lover who is hunted by the law?"

Frannie clenched her fists and took another step in Catherine's direction. "I was the innocent party in both instances, Catherine."

Catherine looked at her condescendingly. "How many times can you cry victim?"

"How many times can you slander another to turn the scrutiny away from yourself?"

Mrs. Murdock and Miss Tipton had heard the raised voices and stood in the background, listening to the commotion just long enough.

"Girls!" Mrs. Murdock cried sharply. "This is absolutely enough. Now, all the rest of you get to your rooms. I don't want to hear another word of gossip on this or any other topic!"

As her audience began to withdraw, Catherine pointed her finger in Frannie's direction. "Mrs. Murdock, Francis Pearson is here at your school under false pretenses. She didn't come here for an education. She was sent here to hide from a scandal!"

Frannie's stomach tightened as she watched the ravenous expressions of her "friends."

"That will be quite enough, Catherine!" Mrs. Murdock warned.

"Ask her!" baited Catherine, who became further emboldened by the lingering girls' interest. "She won't deny it. Ask her!"

"I said that will be quite enough!" Mrs. Murdock commanded forcefully.

The girls nearly trampled one another as they raced from the room. But the look of disappointment on Catherine's face brought Frannie no comfort as the old feelings of hopelessness began to wash over her.

Catherine began to slink up the stairs, but Mrs. Murdock halted her. "Remain where you are, Miss Peltier. I am not finished with you yet."

Catherine's eyes were glued to the floor.

"Neither of us is in a position to serve as Miss Pearson's judge or jury. However, your churlish behavior is a sufficient violation of the school's honor code to warrant dismissal. I am therefore asking you to pack your bags first thing in the morning. Your parents are still in town tonight, I believe. I'll send Mr. Brewster to their hotel with the news this very evening. Furthermore, to prevent you from sharing any more of your malicious gossip, Miss Tipton will be your personal chaperone for the evening. Understood?"

Catherine began to argue, but one look at Mrs. Murdock's angry face made her think better of the idea. She nodded compliantly and headed dejectedly for her room.

Once the room cleared, Mrs. Murdock placed her hands on Frannie's shoulders. "I'm sorry this happened tonight, Francis. I'll send Catherine away, but gossip is as hard to retrieve as a dandelion's seeds. I'm not sure we can ever stop the idle chatter that has commenced tonight. I'm not asking you to leave, but you might find it easier elsewhere now. In either case, it's your decision to make. Stay in Miss Tipton's room tonight, and give us your decision in the morning."

Miss Tipton helped Frannie drag her bags into the woman's first-floor apartment, then closed the door behind her. Frannie's head was spinning. A few acerbic phrases had destroyed the fragile new life she had begun to rebuild. She spent a fruitless moment pretending that things could settle down, that she could continue at the school. She had never desired to be a "Murdock" woman, with all the folly that that entailed, but she had begun to feel safe and welcome at the school, and now she did not. She knew she could no longer remain there without cringing every time she heard someone snicker, and she refused to live like that.

Frannie made her decision. She opened Miss Tipton's bedroom window and had dropped two of her satchels to the ground when she heard a knock at the door.

"Francis? It's Mrs. Murdock. I just wanted to be sure you are all right before I turn in."

Frannie froze momentarily but there was no hesitancy in her resolve. She remained silent until she heard Mrs. Murdock's door close. Then she lowered herself out the window, dropping four feet to the soft grass below, and walked to the corner where she hailed a passing carriage.

"The Indian Queen Hotel, please," she directed the driver as she stared stonily out the window. She considered heading to her mother's room, to ask if she could accompany her home tomorrow, but she couldn't bear seeing the disappointment in her mother's eyes, so she asked for a room of her own.

As soon as she entered her hotel room and closed the door, panic hit her. What would she do and where could she go? Jed would take her in, but what would her life be like? She couldn't bear the scrutiny of the gossipy locals, and yet she refused to live as a recluse, reducing her beloved Willows to a comfortable prison. She touched her pearls and thought about Timothy Shepard, but insecurity now replaced her joy. *How could the world have changed so completely in an hour?* She had told him everything about Frederick and Duprée, and like Jed and Markus, he had wanted to thrash Frederick and hang Duprée. But that was months ago when the deed seemed buried in the past. She was unsure how he or his politically minded family would feel about such a scandal that could be exposed again at any time. The thought of being dismissed for an indiscretion wrongfully attributed to her was too painful to bear. In all honesty, she cared for Timothy. But because she was not sure she loved him, she decided against placing her security solely in the hope of a man's affections, at least for now. Instead, she considered her assets.

Although she was a woman of some means, her resources were insufficient to sustain her indefinitely. She would need work, but what employment could she secure with her limited skills? She fretted over the dilemma until exhaustion drew her into a restless sleep.

Arising late, long after her mother had left for Baltimore, Frannie called for a carriage to take her to Southeast Square, to the somber spots she and Jed had visited on their last day together. She watched the mourners at the potters' field and visited the mass grave of the Revolutionary soldiers, a place that had filled Jed with patriotic resolve. Unlike his revival, she felt the weight of her burdens press down on her, and for an hour she succumbed to the gloom.

A barefoot Guinea woman passed by, dressed in a simple dress and a tattered black shawl. A sling filled with Johnnycakes hung from her rounded shoulder, and a small jug was tied to her waist. She approached Frannie with a compassionate smile and presented her meager offerings. Frannie shivered with shame that she, who possessed more than her share of the world's good fortune, should have allowed self-pity to break her. She smiled gratefully at the woman, took a pinch off a proffered cake, and offered thanks. Suddenly renewed, she picked herself up and headed back toward the hotel.

A sweet sound floated deliciously on the air like a waft of fresh bread, nourishing her soul. A piano, a violin, and a dulcimer played unfamiliar tunes that seemed strangely welcoming to her, so she stopped for several minutes to listen. Sometimes the melody was performed by a solo soprano, and sometimes she heard the harmony of a choir. Though she couldn't discern the French words, she knew the messages were happy ones. She was drawn toward the source until she eventually found herself on Spruce Street, standing outside two Tudor-style buildings painted azure blue and trimmed in red and gold. Two large placards hung on the buildings' walls. The sign on the smaller building read *L'Académie de Musique,* while the sign on the larger structure, the place from which the music drifted, read *Le Jardin des Chanteuses.*

The front doors of both buildings were protected by arched red awnings, but the golden door of Le Jardin des Chanteuses was also framed by paintings of songstresses dressed in exquisite gowns with jewels and feathers in their hair. Soon Frannie peered through the wide-open door and dark interior to the front of the building where brightly lit lanterns illuminated a stage. It overlooked a large, open room filled with small, round tables and chairs. The soprano-voiced woman, whose blonde-haired, blue-eyed image was reflected on one of the paintings beside the door, now stood on the platform. Heavy velvet drapes hung above her head and descended in graceful arcs to the left and right, framing her slight figure in shades of red. The drapes were secured to the walls by thick velvet cords that two men hooked and released to open and close the curtains.

The men and the woman playing the instruments, sat in chairs on the floor below the stage. Another man sat in the back row of seats barking orders to the stagehands, the musicians, and the other performers who hid behind the curtains, peeking through the fabric when the director shouted their name.

"Genevieve," the man called in a voice laced with French intonations. "You are supposed to open with this number tomorrow evening, yet you still don't know the words and you are missing the lower notes. If you can't sing the song, I will find someone else who can."

The singer threw her hand to her hip and rolled her eyes, paying the director little mind.

"You think I am joking?" he argued. "Just because you can sing doesn't mean you don't have to work. I can find another singer like that!" he threatened with a snap of his fingers. He heard a sound from behind him and turned, squinting into the sunlight that streamed through the open door. Shielding his eyes with his hand, he eventually made out the form of an attractive woman in a green and black dress. He smiled appreciatively and hurried to her, bowing and taking her outstretched hand as he placed a courtly kiss upon her knuckles.

"Mademoiselle," he greeted with a wink and a nod, "welcome to Le Jardin. Henri de Mordaunt at your service." He bowed and smiled again, and Frannie felt completely flustered.

"I . . . I am so . . . so sorry for disrupting . . ." she stammered as she tried to pull away.

"Mais non!" he replied sweetly, his accent growing thicker with each word. "It is never a disruption when a beautiful woman enters a room. What brings you to Le Jardin today, Miss . . . ?"

Frannie's wide eyes darted nervously from person to person. "Miss Pearson, Francis Pearson. I'm sorry for interrupting. I heard the music and I followed it, but please, forgive me."

Again, she tried to pull away. Instead of releasing her, however, Henri de Mordaunt began leading her down the aisle toward the stage. "You like music?" he asked.

"Uh . . . yes . . ." Frannie replied skeptically.

"Do you sing or play?" he probed further as he took another step toward the stage.

"I . . . I sing a little, but mostly I play . . . the piano." Then, realizing the purpose of his questioning, she recoiled and pulled away forcibly. "Oh . . . no, no, no!" she protested. "I didn't mean I *sing* when I said I sing . . . I mean I sing, but I'm not a singer. That's what I meant."

Henri's smile persisted. "Perhaps you are a singer who has never taken the opportunity to be heard. Are you a soprano or an alto?" he asked as he pointed to the stage.

"No, no, no!" Frannie resisted, shaking her head. "I could . . . I could never get up there."

Henri leaned back and tugged at Frannie while pleading, "Come, Francis. How does one know what one can do until one tries?" He swept the room with his arm. "There is no obligation in trying, and you are among friends." Then to the group, he inquired, "Isn't she?"

All the people in the room as well as those behind the stage offered enthusiastic encouragement, including the diva named Genevieve, who extended her hand to Frannie and said in a hearty country drawl, "Come on up here, darlin' and let us hear ya sing."

Genevieve's conspicuously American dialect shocked Frannie, but the woman's kindness flooded her with comfort. Frannie looked into her welcoming eyes and pled, "I've never . . ."

"It's all right. Don't be frightened," encouraged Genevieve as she extended her hand to Frannie. She led Frannie to the center of the stage and whispered in her ear, "Just imagine that yer in yer own kitchen singin' as ya wash yer dishes. Now what tunes do ya know?"

Panic washed over Frannie again. "I . . . know a . . . few tunes from *Philadelphia Harmony,*" she offered weakly.

"Hymnodies," Genevieve mused. "No, I don't think the musicians will know them. How about 'Drink to Me Only with Thine Eyes'? Do you know that one?"

Frannie nodded slightly. "Yes, yes, I do know that one."

Genevieve patted her on the back and bellowed the tune's name to the musicians. When the music began, Frannie froze. Her eyes fluttered in fright as she fought to recall the words. Genevieve stood beside her and began to sing along, and soon Frannie sang with enough confidence that Genevieve dropped out.

She moved away from Frannie and smiled approvingly to Henri, who also seemed impressed and pleased. At the end of the first verse, Genevieve added her soprano descant. The beauty of the two women's harmony astounded even Frannie, who was suddenly enjoying the game, and comfortable enough to match the soprano's power and volume.

As they concluded the song, Le Jardin's staff applauded and the two women hugged and bowed to their fans. Genevieve raised a curious eyebrow at Henri and said, "She's got a good strong alto voice, Henry. Good breath support, too. She'll do all right."

Henri ran onto the stage and began pumping Frannie's arm enthusiastically. "Very good job, Francis. One of our altos left us recently, and we've an open spot in the chorus. The job pays room and board and twelve dollars a week, more if you are willing and able to teach lessons at the Academy next door or if you are willing to serve meals in the restaurant between songs. If you move into a soloist position you would naturally earn more. We also provide your wardrobe, but our rules are very strict. No fraternizing with the guests except in our parlor after the show or if you are invited to join a party at their dining table. And curfews must be strictly adhered to. We are a quality establishment, Francis, providing entertainment and musical lessons for the finest and most prestigious families in Philadelphia. As such we must insist that our entertainers maintain the highest levels of decorum. Do you understand?"

Frannie nodded while her mind calculated the wages. "How much more does the position pay if I teach piano lessons?"

Henri smiled. "The Academy charges a standard of fifty cents per half-hour lesson, and the Academy keeps half. How many lessons you teach depends on your popularity and skill. If you are in demand, some students will pay more to secure your time, and you are free to keep whatever you can charge above the Academy's twenty-five-cent share." Henri saw the interest in her eyes and encouraged her curiosity. "A popular teacher can make more teaching than she can singing. A good teacher and singer can double her wages very quickly. Are you interested?"

"You say room and board is included?" Frannie asked.

"Yes. Cast members share rooms, and lavatory facilities are down the hall. Meals are served in the kitchen at eight, twelve, and five o'clock. I believe the girl who left us was Genevieve's old roommate. Her space is still available, is it not, Genevieve?"

Genevieve smiled warmly. "It most certainly is. Shall we move your things in?"

Frannie bit her lip as she considered her decision. The old Frannie would have mocked a vocation that dressed women in frippery and flounced them about a stage, but as of yesterday her situation had changed. She had become a new Frannie, and though she knew she was risking more controversy if she agreed to join the company, her indignation over the unfairness of her situation emboldened her. *What would Jed say?* she wondered. He was not one to run from a fight, but neither was he one to incite one. Frannie knew her protective brother would drag her home rather than see her draw further fire. Looking at the welcoming faces of the Le Jardin cast, she felt truly wanted. *Perhaps in time, after I've proven myself . . . perhaps my family will understand.* She smiled at Genevieve. "Yes." She nodded happily. "I believe I'll stay."

* * *

Mrs. Murdock knocked on Francis's door to no avail. Fearing that the poor girl had done herself in, she called upon the gardener to remove the door from its hinges. Her fear promptly shifted to aggravation when she realized that Frannie had simply run off, leaving most of her things behind. By afternoon Mrs. Murdock had sent for the sheriff, and new rumors began flying as the girls contrived elaborate tales explaining Miss Pearson's disappearance. Everything was considered, from a simple escape to a romantic elopement between her and the dashing Mr. Shepard. Just as the Peltier contingent was about to embark for Delaware, a carriage arrived. The driver delivered a handwritten note from Frannie to Mrs. Murdock thanking her for her fairness the previous evening and requesting the remainder of her belongings. She included a forwarding address. As Mrs. Murdock read it, she began to feel faint, then, drawing upon wisdom gleaned from years of experience, she quickly drafted a reply.

Dear Francis,

I am much dismayed by your current decisions, and deeming them to be the result of an overwrought mind, I grant you the courtesy of not immediately reporting your situation to your parents. I advise you to see me immediately, child, lest your actions give credence to Miss Peltier's accusations.

Mrs. Murdock

* * *

Frannie and Genevieve spent the afternoon becoming better acquainted as they awaited the arrival of her things from the school so they could get her settled in. "Can I ask you something?" Frannie began.

"Anything, sugar," Genevieve replied as she sat on the corner of Frannie's bed.

"Are you really French?" chuckled Frannie.

Genevieve laughed softly. "What gave me away? Was it my fine French accent?"

"So is anyone in the company actually French? Is Henri?"

"He is, actually . . . at least his father was, but his mother was an American, born in Virginia. A fine piano player, I'm told." Genevieve leaned in close as if sharing a secret. "Henri's real name is Henry, named after his mother's father, but everyone here has French-ified their name to add some ambiance to Le Jardin. Anyway, Henry's father was a French chef, a friend of L'Enfant's—you know, the French architect who designed Washington City? They opened a little bistro in New York that catered to foreign dignitaries and such. Mr. De Mordaunt cooked and his wife entertained by playing the piano and singing. When the capital moved to Philadelphia, they up and followed the government. Then after Henry's father died, he took over and expanded the business. And, voilá! Le Jardin and L'Académie was born!"

"So, is Genevieve really your name?"

The blonde woman batted her eyelashes and placed a dramatic hand to her forehead. "Little ol' Jenny Potter from Cutter Springs, Pennsylvania? Land sakes, no! Genevieve is my stage name. We all have 'em. Henry says it gives us a little anonymity . . . helps keep the customers at a distance, so to speak, but mostly he thinks it gives the place some . . ."

". . . ambiance . . ." laughed Frannie. "So I guess I'll need a new name too."

"Oh, yes. We're all supposed to be French or European. We sing mostly French folk songs, and if we sing something not traditionally French, we're supposed to make it sound French." As she stood up and mocked a stylish French walk, Frannie roared with laughter. "What shall we call you . . . hmm . . ." she pondered. "I've got it! How about 'Francesca'?" She dramatized the word, drawing it out for seconds while it resonated on her tongue. "I'm not sure if it's French or Italian, but it sure sounds fancy enough."

"Francesca . . ." Frannie repeated as she looked in the mirror. She nodded approvingly. "I like it. Yes, I'll ask Henri if Francesca will do."

Jenny sat back and stared at Frannie seriously for the first time since their meeting. "So what's yer story? Yer too well dressed to need work. You look like one of our customers."

"Aren't you all here because you love to entertain?" Frannie asked, dodging the question.

"Well, sure," Jenny answered meekly. "Wearing pretty dresses and singing is better than bein' someone's servant, but isn't the dream of every woman to have her own place someday?"

"Is that your dream, Jenny?"

Jenny lay back on the bed and stared at the plastered ceiling. "When Henry caught me singing for pennies on the street and offered me this nice job where I get gussied up, I thought I was finally somebody special. I thought some rich man would think so too and carry me off to my own fairy-tale ending, but I found out it ain't like that. Sure, the customers'll invite you over to their table to smile at their clients or to pretty up the scenery, but once they walk out that door they look down their noses at us. That's why Henry's rules are so strict. He's a good fella, he is. He's just tryin' to protect us from any foul talk or rumors. And so I gave up those dreams of bein' rescued by some rich man and decided to make my own dreams come true until the time true love finds me. I figured it out some months back. I realized that you can't really plan your life unless you're willin' to make your own dreams come true. That's what I'm gonna to do. I've saved up over seven hundred dollars, and when I reach two thousand I'm gonna buy me a little grocery shop. A nice respectable life while I wait for love . . . and in case it never arrives."

Frannie lay down on the bed beside Jenny and realized how similar the two of them really were. "What about your roommate . . . the one who married and left the company?"

"Theresa? Bless her heart. Yeah, her dream did come true, but it weren't a customer that carried her away. She married the man who delivered milk to Le Jardin. This place blessed her twice. It brought her John and a nice nest egg to boot. She took her savings and invested all of it on a tip she overheard a guest—a banker—tell his clients. She hit it big enough to double John's herd. Now that's how you make a success of your singing career, if you ask me."

There was a knock on the door and Jenny got up to answer it, returning with a note which she handed to Frannie. "The driver brought this to you."

Frannie scowled after reading the note. "It seems if I want my things, I'll have to face my schoolmistress."

The driver returned her to the Murdock School, where a disappointed Mrs. Murdock was waiting on the front porch with Frannie's bags. The initial meeting was tense, but Frannie held her ground, doing her best to alleviate Mrs. Murdock's preconcieved notions about Le Jardin and the nature of Frannie's employ there.

"I don't like it, Francis, and I certainly don't approve of your decision, but I'll delay sending word to your parents until the semester's end when I refund the winter's tuition. You have until then to tell them the entire truth, or be assured that I will."

So, in agreement with Mrs. Murdock, Frannie began her career at Le Jardin. She began by singing in the chorus and small groups and serving meals between songs. But teaching piano lessons was her mainstay. As Henri predicted, her fees increased in response to the demand for her time. In wonderment she watched her savings begin to grow. Henri outfitted her with several beautiful gowns in the color green that would become her signature on stage. He also assigned her an occasional solo. Unlike the more fashion-conscious soloists, Frannie sang without the breathing restriction of a corset, and Henri selected musical numbers that complemented her earthy tone and vocal power. Within a month her portrait was featured on the gallery outside the doorway, and her salary was increased as well. Capitalizing on Jenny's experience, Frannie began procuring business tips from the wealthy clients who relished conversing with the free-thinking sportswoman. These she parlayed into prudent investments.

She also engaged in a bit of subterfuge, sending Le Jardin's driver by the Murdock School from time to time to pick up her mail, while maintaining the pretense of residing at the school in her correspondence to her family. It was a temporary ruse she intended to maintain until she could speak to her family in person.

That opportunity presented itself when a note arrived from her parents inviting her home for Christmas, and she pledged to disclose the secret of her career choices at that time. By then she would have a sufficient portfolio to validate the success of her decision. The news would still meet with mixed reactions, she knew; she suspected that Jed and her father would be angry with her at first, while nonetheless finding her financial report of some merit. Her mother, on the other hand, would see her entrance into the entertainment world as another stamp of "trollop" upon her already sullied reputation.

The night of November fourteenth, Frannie was riding on this wave of measured optimism. She had finished her set of six French folk songs when the waiter brought a note to her, as he did most evenings, inviting her to join a table for supper. She was led to a table from which three smiling gentlemen rose and bowed. Walking toward them, she had noticed a man staring at her from a darkened corner of the room. As she greeted the gentlemen, she peered into the darkness in hopes of identifying the face focused so intently on her. The three men fawned favorably over her performance, and she tried to be gracious and cordial. Still, she couldn't shake the chill that ran down her spine each time she glanced at the table with the lone seated figure.

Unable to bear it any longer, she excused herself to confront the man. However, just as she stood, as if anticipating her intentions, the man also rose and made his exit from the door and around the corner beyond her view.

CHAPTER 20

Coolfont
Late November 1811

Two months had passed since Hannah and Myrna returned to Coolfont in funereal silence, each of them suffering a death of sorts, leaving all their love and possibilities in Baltimore. Myrna's were left the moment Mr. Baumgardner told her he would be so encumbered with work that it would be months before he could slip away to Coolfont. Hannah's were ripped from her in a hotel lobby as Jed Pearson departed through the door.

Myrna returned to her submissive, flat persona, moving ghostlike through the motions of life while Hannah slept late, hiding from the world under her goose-down comforter as long as possible each day. When guilt finally drove her from the confines of her room onto the veranda, she would sit and stare silently as the green, supple world turned brown and brittle.

Oddly enough, though Susannah didn't know the cause of her daughters' malaise, it stirred something maternal in her, and she began soothing her girls with motherly affection. Each morning she delivered trays of delicious cakes and fruits to the girls and sat at their bedsides, brushing their hair and reading to them from cherished books. Though Myrna was a woman by all accounts and Hannah well past the age where such tending was expected, the two daughters drank in their mother's love like water upon parched soil. In connecting with her, they were able to enjoy their father and the love of a family for the first time in memory.

Two disturbing elements marred this blissful season. First, Susannah became increasingly possessive of her daughters, allowing no one to tend to them but her. She even became wary of their loyalties to Beatrice, who had made two trips to Coolfont to secretly deliver stacks of letters from Andrew and Mr. Baumgardner. Her paranoia also led her to dismiss Selma from the house and into the dreaded fields. Second, a sudden sense of foreboding made Susannah constantly fret over her daughters' futures, and she would wander about wringing her hands and muttering about needing to find a way to protect her girls. For these reasons both Hannah and Myrna had vowed not to speak of the men they had met or the adventures they had shared, fearing that somehow they might banish the magical spell upon which their current peace was so precariously balanced.

Buoyed up by this newfound sense of familial happiness, Hannah and Myrna began showing some interest in life again. Hannah saddled Druid and set off for a long ride on a new course, reveling in the feel of the brisk wind as it whipped her face and tousled her hair. Time became irrelevant to her, and she rode until the early colors of sunset tinting the sky alerted her to the lateness of the hour. Fearful that her tardiness would make her mother frantic, she hurriedly turned Druid back toward the manor and drove him hard.

Myrna had heard a ruckus in the yard below her window in the afternoon and looked out to see her mother standing on the walkway without a shawl or coat, scolding a servant who was attempting to return her to the house. A sharp look and a threat from Susannah sent the well-meaning servant scrambling for cover, leaving Susannah free to continue traipsing down the one-hundred-yard path to the barn. There she stopped and swiveled left and right, presumably calling Hannah's name, before she returned again, religiously counting each footfall.

Myrna watched her mother become more emotionally unraveled with each trip to the barn. She groaned inwardly as she hurried to her, hoping to comfort Susannah and cajole her into coming inside, or at least to distract her before her brittle nerves shattered again.

"Come in, Mother," she encouraged. "You'll catch your death out here."

Susannah regarded Myrna as if she were only slightly more than invisible, continuing her muttering and counting as she paced up and back, her eyes darting wildly all the while.

"Please, Mother," she pled again, taking hold of Susannah's arm. "Lean on me."

Susannah Stansbury recoiled sharply. "I can't leave," she muttered. "A good mother never leaves. She protects her babies . . ." she repeated over and over as she paced and counted.

"Mother, Hannah was so excited to ride Druid. She'll be back soon, you'll see," Myrna said reassuringly. "Come inside and sit with me a while. We'll have some tea and scones. Doesn't that sound lovely?" She began to lead her mother, and Susannah, seemingly mesmerized by Myrna's invitation, began to follow, until another worry crossed her mind.

She stopped suddenly, grimacing in derision. "There's no time!" She began to rapidly tap her head as her eyes resumed their wild darting. "I have to make plans. I have to protect my girls . . ."

Myrna sighed in frustration and decided to take a more straightforward approach. "Mother, tell me what you must protect your daughters from? Perhaps I can help."

Riveted by the notion that someone was paying attention to her concerns, Susannah settled her eyes on Myrna and cocked her head sideways like a collie's. She drew her hands up in front of her as if in prayer and pointed them, emphasizing each well-pondered point. "Father told me a good mother never leaves . . . she plans for her children's safety and future. She must protect her babies." Her pacing resumed. "I've left those duties to others. That was a very bad thing to do . . . very bad! No one can love my babies like their mother," she emphasized in a pitiful, whining voice. "They're nearly grown. Who will tend and protect them when I'm gone?"

A menacing look crossed her face, frightening Myrna.

"I can't trust anyone here . . ." Susannah whispered cagily. "First it was Charles Kittamaqund, hiding in the woods, always watching, and now it's the slaves. They've always hated us. They're just waiting to catch us off guard. Then they will rise up and murder us all!" She pounded her fist against her hand. "I stay up all night keeping guard. I can't rest . . . I keep a vigil. I never sleep." Her voice now became singsong and childlike. "I just walk, walk, walk . . ."

"Please, Mother, let's go inside . . ." Myrna pleaded as she again tried to lead Susannah.

"You're just like your father," growled the mad woman, ". . . pacifying and coddling me." She wagged her finger in Myrna's face. "You're part of the conspiracy, aren't you?" she accused sharply. "You're all in on it, except for Hannah. I have to protect Hannah from everyone."

Susannah thrust all her weight into Myrna, nearly throwing her daughter off balance. Myrna, the stronger of the two, quickly regrouped and wrapped her arms around her mother, holding her fast and speaking softly to her in a tearful voice until Susannah calmed down and rested against her middle child.

The insane woman began to whimper. "Please, let me care for my babies before the voices begin again." Her tears began to flow. "I have to make my plans now . . . before the voices return. Before Selma sends her slave magic into my head to take my love away again. She wants my girls to love her best. Then she will turn on my babies and I won't be able to protect them."

Myrna clamped her eyes tightly against her own tears. This glimpse into her mother's twisted, tortured mind was too vivid. Like the antique kaleidoscope in the parlor, her mother's love and perspective were so distorted that reality was barely recognizable. Myrna had never understood the demons her mother battled or the concerns that had driven her strange behavior and prompted the havoc she had wreaked. Father had . . . her poor father had.

Willing to do anything to soothe her weeping mother's anguish and restore the peace, Myrna compromised on a promise she and Hannah had made to remain silent regarding the lieutenant and Mr. Baumgardner. "Hush, Mama. You needn't fret over Hannah and me anymore. Our marriage prospects look very bright and secure." Susannah's head shot up.

"You met someone in Baltimore?" she asked, pleasure brightening her face.

Myrna decided to feed her mother a few more details, hoping Hannah would understand. "Yes. Beatrice and Dudley hosted a dinner party, and we met some very nice gentlemen."

"Ahhh," Susannah beamed. "Dudley Snowden. I selected him myself for Beatrice. I knew he would take good care of her and provide well for her security. I chose well, didn't I?"

"Yes, you did, Mother." Myrna breathed a sigh of relief, hoping that the mention of Dudley had diverted Susannah from requiring further details regarding her and Hannah.

"Did you and Hannah fancy anyone in particular?"

"Hmm?" stalled Myrna.

"At the dinner party . . . did you and Hannah fancy anyone in particular?"

"There were a few whom I believe will call on us this holiday season."

Susannah sat expectantly as Myrna sputtered along, offering random tidbits about the dinner party and news of the city. Suddenly, the young woman realized that she had painted herself into a corner from which the only escape was to lie to her mother—which was unthinkable—or to completely violate her pact with Hannah. She chose martyrdom, providing details about Harvey Baumgardner while hoping those disclosures would satisfy her mother's maternal inquiries.

"A lawyer?" beamed Susannah. "And one invested in government! He must be very well connected. That would place his wife in fine circles, Myrna," she gushed. "And what is he like?"

Surprised at how satisfying this mother-daughter interaction felt, Myrna plunged in happily. "He is a plain-looking man, but I don't mind. He is fortyish and his hair is thinning, but he is humorous with a quick wit. I'm never bored in his company."

Susannah nodded with manic enthusiasm. "Older can be better . . . yes, older can be better. An older man is settled, not as prone to philandering."

"Yes, let's go in now, Mother. You're chilled to the bone. We'll talk more inside."

Susannah lay down on the walk and placed her head in her daughter's lap. "No, no. Let's stay here until Hannah comes home. Just wrap your arms around me, dear, and I shall be warm enough. Tell me more about your Mr. Baumgardner."

Myrna looked for anyone she could send to fetch her father, but no one could be found. She could hardly blame the slaves for making themselves scarce around the house, now that she understood the threats her mother muttered against them. She brushed her hand through her mother's tangled tresses and continued detailing the time spent in Mr. Baumgardner's company. When she could find nothing more to relate, she again tried to coax her mother into the house, but the woman still would not budge from her post.

"Tell me about Hannah. Did she fancy anyone?"

Myrna's heart began pounding. *Jed Pearson.* She hesitated to answer, and the worried craze returned to Susannah's voice as she began to rise from where she lay.

"Didn't anyone fancy our Hannah?"

Myrna pressed her mother back across her lap and closed her eyes, praying for guidance. "There was a young lieutenant," she mumbled, nearly choking as she watched Hannah walk from the barn.

"A lieutenant?" Susannah repeated with pleasure. "Just like Dudley . . ."

"Yes, Mama. Very handsome and a gentleman in every definition of the word."

Hannah looked on worriedly as she approached the scene. "Hello, Mother. Myrna, why are you and Mother out here in the cold? She's nearly blue."

Myrna shot her sister a stern, scalding look, though her voice remained calm and reassuring for her mother's sake. "Hannah, Mother insisted on maintaining a vigil here for you because she was so worried about you. She refused to go inside, and I've had to tell her stories about our visit to Baltimore to keep her nerves settled."

"I'm so sorry, Mother," Hannah said as she knelt beside her, placing an apologetic hand on her shoulder. "Druid and I had such a wonderful ride . . . I guess I lost track of time. When I returned, I couldn't find any of the hands near the stables, so I had to cool him and tend him myself. Let's go inside now and I'll make you both some tea."

"No . . . first I want to hear about your lieutenant."

Hannah swallowed hard and glared at Myrna, who shot a defiant look back at her.

"Yes, Hannah. Mother was pacing for hours, worried sick about her daughters and their futures. I assured her that our prospects look bright. She simply wants to share in our happiness."

"Yes, Hannah," Susannah pressed. "Tell Mama about your lieutenant."

Distraught over Jed, Hannah hadn't bothered to open one of Andrew's letters. "We're . . . we're merely friends, Mother," she stammered, looking to Myrna for help.

"It's true, Mama," her sister conceded. "He's smitten but she is too young to reciprocate."

Hannah cast her eyes down, willing to deny her aching heart's ability to love rather than endure a lecture about Lieutenant Robertson's husbandly merits.

"Seventeen is not too young! Not too young at all in today's world. If the young man is well positioned and steadfast, he can make a good marriage with a young bride. Yes, yes . . ."

"She's not of such a mind yet, Mama," Myrna interrupted. But Susannah seized upon the notion as if with talons.

"I'd much rather see her married to a fine soldier with a bright future than to have that scoundrel Jed Pearson hovering around her, sullying her chances for a good match."

Hannah gasped so loudly that it startled both her sister and her mother. "Please excuse me," she muttered as she scrambled to her feet and ran off into the house.

Myrna heard sobs break loose before the door closed, and suddenly Susannah was on her feet, rushing after Hannah. Myrna held her back, making excuses for Hannah's sudden retreat. "I think the ride was too much for her today. You know how vigorous a run Druid can give. Perhaps it was just too much for her first ride after such a long time away."

"Yes, yes . . ." Susannah replied, glaring in the direction of the stables. "That's it. Too much work. It's too much for my poor dear, Hannah. Far too much . . ."

* * *

When the two girls were finally alone, Hannah challenged Myrna. "How could you?"

Myrna hung her head in shame and sadness. Nevertheless, after she had detailed the afternoon's events, Hannah realized that her lateness had left Myrna in a difficult situation with few choices.

"I can't bear it, Myrna. If she forces Andrew upon me, I will die. I have no interest in love at this time, and I can't imagine that my heart will ever be open to anyone again."

Myrna wrapped her arm around her younger sister. "Forever is a very long time to mourn, Hannah, but we have bigger concerns on our hands now."

"How bad was it with her this afternoon?"

Myrna's eyes welled up with tears. "She is completely paranoid. She believes the slaves are planning to rise up and kill us all, particularly Selma. She believes Selma uses slave magic to send evil voices into her head to 'take the love' out of her."

"That's ludicrous!"

"Yes, to a rational mind. I knew she believed Charles Kittamaqund was always watching her. She begged Father to chase him off, but he convinced her that Charles was here to protect the dead or some such nonsense. Now she has transferred her fears to the slaves. You know the sounds of footsteps we hear at night? It's Mother. She walks the halls, afraid to sleep, keeping a vigil over us in anticipation of the slave revolt she believes is coming."

"How could Father have borne it all so long?"

"I don't know, but like him, I'd rather pacify her and enjoy a few moments of her love than send her away. I am starved for Mother's love, Hannah. Don't you feel that way also?"

"Yes . . ." she replied mournfully. "I long for every scrap of affection she casts my way."

Myrna took her sister's hand in hers. "Like Father, I will do almost anything to keep her happy and content for as long as I can."

Hannah nodded. "I am agreed."

A soft knock sounded on Hannah's door. "May I come in?" a timid voice asked.

Hannah opened the door and found her mother wrapped in a warm quilt with a bed cap covering her graying auburn hair. "Warmer?" she questioned as she adjusted her mother's wrap.

"Yes. Your father takes fine care of me, but I missed the company of my girls."

"Come in and sit a while with us, Mother," offered Myrna as she patted the bed.

Susannah caught her reflection in the mirror on Hannah's dressing table and was startled by it. She gingerly touched the glass to verify that the ashen face staring back at her was indeed her own. "I am running out of time . . ." she muttered.

Myrna dashed to her side and embraced her. "It's evening, Mother. It's the fatigue from a long day, that's all. Sit here and we'll show you how young and beautiful you still are."

Susannah sat in the wicker chair before the table and smiled hopefully as Hannah removed the cap from her head and combed through her hair with her fingers. "See how much better you look just by removing the cap? White washes you out. Let's give you a little color."

She pulled a drawer out, forgetting the stack of unopened letters that lay tied in a ribbon in the bottom. Susannah caught sight of the bold, manly script on the top envelope that bore a military insignia. "What are these?" she inquired with childlike curiosity.

Hannah quickly snatched the rouge from the drawer and slammed it shut. "Let's try this, Mama," she suggested weakly as she heard the drawer opening again. Susannah lifted the letters from the drawer and read the name of the addressee. *My dearest, Miss Hannah Stansbury . . .*

"My dearest?" she exclaimed. She scanned the return address. *Lieutenant Andrew Robertson, First Artillery Division, Maryland Army Corps.* She looked up at her young daughter's wan face and swooned, "Hannah, you are in love!" She clasped Hannah's hands in hers and gave them a joyous shake. "This is an answer to my prayers . . . to see both my girls safe and protected. You must write to him and tell him you love him before your separation discourages his attentions."

Susannah remained completely oblivious to her daughter's frozen expression.

"Hurry, darling. We'll have a steward deliver it today. And Myrna, you must write Mr. Baumgardner as well. Your father and I will want to meet both gentlemen as soon as possible!"

Hannah looked to her sister for support, and this time Myrna did not falter. "Mother, the letters have never been opened. See? Hannah is not ready for such an attachment."

Susannah's head cocked oddly to the right as if she were listening to someone.

The sisters' fearful eyes met in the mirror. "Mama," Myrna began as if she were speaking to a child, "Hannah doesn't love Lieutenant Robertson. She doesn't want to encourage him."

The smile left Susannah's face as a far-off gaze came into her eyes. "He loves you. That should be enough. Besides, you have all of us to shower your affections upon."

"I can't marry someone I don't love, Mama," Hannah cried.

Susannah wandered to the bed and sat gingerly, fumbling with the binding on the edge of her quilt. "Well, of course, you can, Hannah.

My papa always told me, 'Marry early before a rogue comes along and steals a piece of your heart.' He said some women never recover from the ache caused by that missing part. I was a good girl. Not like poor Mama. The rogue got to her first."

The girls were stunned.

"Papa said Bernard was a good man and a hard worker. He told me the best marriages were based on security, and after nearly thirty years of marriage, I'm quite sure Papa was right."

Nervously, the girls went to her and sat on either side of her. "But you came to love Papa, didn't you, Mama?" Myrna asked hungrily.

The same glazed look remained in Susannah's eyes as she answered, "Oh yes. That's why I pushed him—to make him great. He hovers so carefully over me and my health . . . it was the only gift I had to give him in return." She placed one hand on each of her daughters' faces. "That's what I want for my girls. You see, men's greatest fear is that they will love more than they are loved in return, but a man who will shower devotion upon his intended will eventually win her heart."

Hannah stared at her hands in silence.

"Write the letter, Hannah," Susannah encouraged.

"I'm not you, Mama. I just can't. Let me live here with you and Father. I'll watch over you and keep you in good company if Myrna and Mr. Baumgardner eventually wed."

"It's not the natural order of things, dearest. You need a home and family of your own."

"Please, Mama," she pleaded. "Everyone I love is here. I have you and Father to cherish and I have Sel . . ." She hesitated, remembering Myrna's warning. "Druid . . . I have Druid for company. Please, Mama. I cannot write and profess feelings for the lieutenant that do not exist."

Susannah stared at her daughter as if seeing her for the first time. Then she rose and headed for the door. "A mother knows best . . ." she said, closing the door.

* * *

The following day Susannah's distant, tense manner returned. Her daughters tried to resurrect her more tender nature, but she was like a soldier, leaping from her chair at every sound, then extensively investigating its cause. Her constant scrutiny of the servants was more intense than ever. The next morning, before dawn had fully broken across the winter sky, Hannah heard a ruckus in the backyard. She looked out the window to see the overseer dragging Selma across the yard in the direction of the whipping post. Flying down the stairs in her nightgown, Hannah screamed at full voice and bolted out the door, drawing Myrna and her father behind her.

Susannah Stansbury stood by the post, grabbing her head, rocking back and forth and yelling, "Stop her! Stop her!" as she pointed in Selma's direction.

"Mother! What are you doing?" screamed Hannah so bitterly that Susannah cowered. She shoved her way between Selma and the men, who turned to Susannah for direction.

Bernard hurried to his wife and wrapped his arms around her. "Let her go," he ordered the men as he pointed to Selma. "Never touch a slave unless I order it, do you understand?"

The men released her in rough fashion, muttering as they sauntered away. Susannah pressed her face into her husband's robe, still holding her head and rocking madly to and fro.

"Make them stop, Bernard . . . the voices in my head . . . please make them stop."

Looking pitifully at his girls, he sheltered his wife as he led her back into the house and put her to bed. Hours later Susannah struggled in her sleep, whimpering, "Don't leave, Mama . . . not in your pretty blue dress," over and over while Bernard sat at her bedside trying to comfort her. Myrna and Hannah kissed him and offered to take a turn beside her, and after he reluctantly left to rest, the pair knelt by her, now frighteningly aware of the depths of her illness. Myrna took the Bible and headed for the rocking chair in the corner to read aloud.

"Father was in the Beatitudes, but there's also a marker in Acts. Where should I begin?"

"Either is fine," Hannah answered halfheartedly. "Something in Acts—chapter three caught my attention earlier, but I love the Beatitudes. Read from Matthew."

When Myrna reached the end of chapter seven, she repeated the last two verses. "'And it came to pass, when Jesus had ended these sayings, the people were astonished at his doctrine: For he taught them as one having authority, and not as the scribes.' You've studied the Bible in greater detail than I, Hannah. Who were the scribes?"

Hannah thought for a moment. "I believe they were court officials. However, after Israel fell, the scribes became teachers and interpreters of the law."

"Like a reverend?"

"I suppose so. They were teachers, without the authority to perform priestly duties."

"'. . . he taught as one having authority, and not as the scribes.' So education wasn't enough to give them authority back then. Interesting. Divine authority must not matter anymore. Reverends now get university degrees or become licensed by the state. That must be sufficient today."

"Why should it be?" Hannah curiously countered the idea.

Myrna scowled at her sister and began to close the book, but Hannah bade her to continue. "Read on, Myrna, and listen to what it says in chapter eight." She listened carefully, waiting for the verses anticipated. "'And when Jesus was entered into Capernaum, there came unto him a centurion, beseeching him, And saying, Lord, my servant lieth at home sick of the palsy, grievously tormented. And Jesus saith unto him, I will come and heal him. The centurion answered and said, Lord, I am not worthy that thou shouldest come under my roof: but speak the word only, and my servant shall be healed. For I am a man under authority, having soldiers under me: and I say to this man, Go, and he goeth; and to another, Come, and he cometh; and to my servant, Do this, and he doeth it. When Jesus heard it, he marvelled, and said to them that followed, Verily I say unto you, I have not found so great faith, no, not in Israel.'"

Hannah's eyes lit up. "Do you think it is merely coincidence that this story about the centurion's power of authority is so closely placed to the verse describing the Lord's authority?"

"What are you implying?"

"Read on first, a little further."

Myrna complied. "'When the even was come, they brought unto him many that were possessed with devils: and he cast out the spirits with his word, and healed all that were sick: That it might be fulfilled which was spoken by Esaias the prophet, saying, Himself took our infirmities and bare our sicknesses.'"

Hannah held her hand up to signal Myrna to stop. "Has the Reverend Wilcox been out to see Mother lately?"

"I cannot recall the last time I saw him come by. Since Mother and Father no longer attend, I suppose he has removed them from the membership rolls."

"Did he ever attempt to cast the torment from Mother, or did he ever try to heal her?" Hannah whispered, so as not to wake Susannah.

Myrna was aghast. "That's blasphemy, Hannah. Such miracles ceased with the Apostles."

"But why, Myrna? Surely God loves us today and sorrows over our pains. Perhaps we simply lack the faith of the centurion, or maybe we have lost the *authority* needed for such miracles."

Myrna stood abruptly to end the conversation. "I'll not listen to another word, Hannah."

"Why is it blasphemy to inquire about such things, Myrna? Didn't you just read in Matthew chapter seven, 'Ask, and it shall be given you; seek, and ye shall find; knock, and it shall be opened unto you'? Doesn't James tell us to 'Ask in faith, nothing wavering'?"

Myrna clamped her hands over her ears and refused to listen. Suddenly Susannah began ranting and begging again for the voices to leave her, so Hannah cradled her mother's head in her lap and spoke softly to her. Then, as her mother began to settle, she challenged Myrna. "Could the people in scripture have been more beset by evils than she is? Like me, don't you wish someone had the power and authority to act in the name of God to come here and cast them out or heal her from her afflictions?"

Her face contorted in sorrow and her voice riddled with frustration, Myrna asked, "What good does it do to wish for things that can never be again?"

Myrna watched her sister's countenance soften from willful resolution to peaceful understanding. "What is it?" she questioned Hannah timidly.

"Myrna . . ." Her voice was ethereal. "What if those verses not only speak of powers that once were . . . but of authority that will be again? Turn to the marked page in Acts, chapter three."

When Myrna reached the verse, Hannah recited the words. "'And he shall send Jesus Christ, which before was preached unto you: Whom the heaven must receive until the times of restitution of all things, which God hath spoken by the mouth of all his holy prophets since the world began.'"

"It speaks of a restitution of all things, Myrna. That must include the authority and power to heal the sick!"

Myrna hung her head, torn between the words Hannah had recited—with their possible new interpretations—and the rigid constraints of what she'd been taught all her life.

"Think about it, Myrna! That must be it! Can you feel the right-ness of it in your heart? Perhaps this restitution has already begun! Wouldn't you surrender everything to find out?"

Just as the idea began distilling in Myrna's heart, Susannah reached her arms out to her girls, inviting them to lie beside her on the bed. The moment of spiritual enlightenment was lost as the enticement of a place in their mother's arms lulled them away. After a few minutes their father entered the room, looking gaunt and trou-bled. He opened the door and seemed surprised to see the girls lying beside his wife. Leaning against the doorjamb, he looked at Susannah, grave disappointment showing in his face.

"Girls, leave us, please," he said firmly.

The unfamiliar tone in his voice drew the girls' immediate attention, and the pair bolted upright. "What's the matter, Father?" asked Myrna.

"I need to speak to your mother. Please leave us." His voice was stern and sorrowful.

Fear gripped the girls as they considered what scenario could evoke such emotion from him. "You're frightening us, Father. Tell us what has happened," Myrna begged nervously.

"Oh no . . ." Hannah groaned. "Say it isn't Selma! Tell me Mother didn't order the overseers to harm Selma." She ran to her father and melted into a heap at his feet.

Myrna rushed to Hannah, but her eyes were riveted on her father's face, searching for some sign regarding the heinous accusa-tion. "Is it true, Father?" she wondered incredulously.

"Is this what you wanted, Susannah? To terrify your daughters . . . to break their will?"

Susannah sat up and cried for her girls, extending her arms to them.

"Answer me, Father, please," Hannah pleaded. "Is Selma all right?"

Bernard glared at Susannah's display of innocence, growing angrier. He bent down and lifted Hannah to her feet and pressed her close to him. "Selma's fine, dearest. Selma's fine."

She lifted her tearstained face to read her father's eyes. "Really, Father?"

Susannah called out across the room, tears of pain in her own eyes. "Come to Mama, Hannah. All I want to do is protect my babies. Mama would never do anything to hurt her dears."

Hannah felt so guilty for having accused her mother of such an atrocity that she left her father's embrace to find forgiveness in her mother's. Susannah wrapped her arms around her, uttering words of loving absolution in response to Hannah's pleas for forgiveness.

While Hannah's relief over Selma's safety dispelled her concerns regarding the cause of her father's anger, Myrna was not so quick to allow the matter to rest. "Then what is it, Father?"

Myrna's distress seemed to break her father's will, and his anger gave way to emotions far more terrifying.

"Perhaps if I had intervened earlier," moaned Bernard.

"Father!" Myrna demanded more forcefully. "What did Mother do?"

Bernard grabbed at his hair. "I barred the windows to keep you safe, but I denied the threat you might pose." He looked at the floor and cried, "Oh, Susannah . . . how could you?"

Hannah gathered enough courage to ask Susannah herself. "Mother, what did you do?"

A look of wonder washed over Susannah as if she alone knew a secret. "Did you know that baby eagles can become so comfortable in their fluffy nests that some are afraid to fly? Their mothers begin removing the soft lining until all that remains is the framework of the nest. If they are still afraid to take to the skies and soar, she begins pulling out the sticks until they barely have a thing to perch on. Eventually, they are forced to fly or fall." Her expression became childlike. "Imagine how terrified they must feel . . . as if they have been betrayed. Eventually, instinct does take over and they realize that they were meant to soar. Then they understand . . . their mothers were helping them become what they were always meant to be."

"What have you done, Mother?" Hannah repeated.

"See? You're angry. You've already made up your mind to be angry without trying to understand that it was for your own good," she whimpered as she withdrew behind the covers.

Hannah softened her voice. "Please tell me, Mother. What did you do for my own good?"

Susannah looked for understanding from her husband, but instead found his cold stare bearing down on her. She turned her attentions to Hannah and tried to summon the clarity to explain her reasoning.

"He was standing in your way, Hannah. He was keeping you here."

Hannah's brow furrowed at the use of the pronoun *he*.

". . . besides, he was far too vigorous for you. Now you'll be free to pursue other interests, to write to Lieutenant Robertson so you can leave Coolfont and build a home of your own."

As Myrna heard her own words from the previous day now spoken by her mother, she knew what she had done. Horrified, she found herself Hannah's betrayer for the third time.

"I don't understand," muttered Hannah absently.

"It's Druid," Myrna uttered as realization struck. She began sobbing. "Mother's killed Druid. Hasn't she, Father?"

Bernard rose and reached his arms out to Hannah, his expression calming somewhat as he realized his girls needed him. "Yes, dearest. Your mother slipped out of the house last night. She grabbed Mobey's gun and . . . He's gone."

Hannah was too numb, too wrung out to move as she realized she pitied her mother more than she hated her. But as she saw Myrna collapse on the bed, she knew her sister was also terrified at what other insanity might await them as their mother's condition continued to crumble.

Susannah smiled at her family. "I've taken care of all the details, Hannah. Druid cannot monopolize your time, Selma is in the fields where she cannot impose upon you, and Father and I have each other. Now you two girls must marry. That will complete my duty, and I'll have been a good mother. I must see to my duty. Agreed?" she asked with a wild-eyed grin.

The girls stared in concert.

"So . . . you'll each write to your gentlemen today?"

The girls looked at one another in dazed amazement. Myrna's expression warned Hannah that any other type of life had now become more desirable than remaining in Coolfont's land of the macabre. They looked to their father, who seemed to have given up—completely at a loss as to what to do. But his silence clarified that he would not encourage the girls to stay.

"Do I need to extend myself further to lead you along?" warned Susannah.

Myrna spoke first. "No, Mama," she replied obediently in a trembling voice. "Can we return to the city? It would make courting ever so much easier."

Susannah paused for a moment to give the notion some thought. Seeing the sense in the plan, she nodded her agreement. "Hannah, are you also clear on your responsibilities?"

"Yes, Mother," she replied numbly.

"Yes, Mother, what?" inquired Susannah sharply.

Hannah bowed her head, believing that she had no other options to guarantee the safety of those she loved. She took one shuddering breath and stated, "I'll write to the lieutenant today."

"Excellent." She spread her arms to gather her daughters. "Then all is as it should be."

CHAPTER 21

The Willows
December 1811

Jed saddled Tildie for a brisk morning ride. Clouds of steam blew from her nostrils with each exhale, and she, like her mended master, seemed fit again and ready for a hard ride. He headed down the lane at a brisk pace toward the river. Some thought the Patuxent didn't present well in the winter when her bright green foliage turned to muted tones of beige and gray, but there was something clean and crisp in the chilled air and in the crunch of the frozen grass as horses' hooves broke each frosted blade. For the first time in months, Jed felt alive. He had feared he would never love the Willows again, never be able to care about her without the hope of Hannah coming to live there. But Jerome had helped him trust that God would lead him, and when fall began painting the farm red and gold, Jed had slowly begun to have hope.

Horse and rider blazed along the river trail to an outcrop of land where the construction of a mill was planned. Unfortunately, the workers feared the spot, believing it to be haunted by the ghost of an Indian. Some claimed they had seen him; others claimed to have heard him singing some melancholy chant at night. As a boy, Jed had been so badly frightened by the stories that his father threatened the whip to the back of anyone who dared repeat the tales. Now, years later, the stories still persisted. With the morning mist rising from the frost-laden ground, Jed had to admit that there was something mysterious about the spot.

He smiled contentedly. It would be a year or two before the Willows' mill would grind its first grains, but the hope of it made him dare to believe that other good things awaited him and the farm as well. He turned Tildie and sped back toward the meadow, to another project of which he was immensely proud. A small frame chapel was under construction here, its four walls and the overhead joists already in place. With Jerome supervising this project, Jed felt his people, including Abel, were happier than he had ever before seen them.

Jed turned the horse again and urged her into a gallop in the direction of the tobacco fields. He surveyed the acreage that had been lovingly tended over the previous months and smiled contentedly as he recalled the buoyant spirit that had touched them as they all worked together, master and hireling, slaves and free men.

He guided Tildie past the house and toward the barns, then tied her up and strolled past the smaller building where long tables stood in preparation for the tobacco seeding that would take place in a few days. If all went well, the seedlings would be a foot tall and ready for transplanting into the prepared field by May. As Jed calculated the long growing season, he thought about America's uncertain future. He knew that if Senators Clay and Calhoun continued to stir the debate in Congress, the country would likely be at war before the leaves could be harvested.

Pushing the thought away, Jed sneaked into the main drying barn, where Markus was inspecting the previous fall's harvest. "How do they look?" Jed asked, startling his friend.

Markus recovered and held up a mahogany-colored leaf. "I think slower curing produced a better leaf. This tobacco is sweeter and more pliable than any I've ever seen."

"We're weeks past the main sale, though. Do we still have a buyer?"

"I contacted our loyal customers and promised them a special crop this year. They agreed to hold back on their purchases to accommodate us. Even if we're too late to sell it all this season, next year they'll clamor to order our leaves in advance."

Jed winced. "I'll be glad when the mill is finished and we can begin to diversify."

Markus nodded his agreement. "Once we shift to grains, we can use every free acre. Horse breeding could be lucrative as well. We have several orders for our quarter horses."

Jed smiled and patted his friend on the back. "We've nearly got a real farm running here now, Markus. We haven't done too badly for a couple of pups and a handful of workers."

Markus laughed. "Most of the credit is owed to that handful of workers you mentioned. Jerome is a treasure trove of knowledge, and the people follow him like Moses. You've got more than a farm here, Jed. You've nearly built yourself a town."

The rapid approach of a horse caught their attention. The rider hanging onto the horse for dear life was Bartholomew, the fiftyish Negro butler who managed Jed's parents' Baltimore home. Jed had never seen the man on horseback in his entire life and his legs grew weak as he considered what the man's arrival portended. He mounted Tildie and shot off down the lane to grab the reins and slow the uncontrolled gelding. Once he had taken hold of the reins, the poor butler dropped gratefully to the ground.

"Oh thank you, Mastuh Jed. The man at the docks handed me this wild beast when I got off the boat . . . nearly killed me. I barely made it here to give you the message."

"What message, Bartholomew?" Jed queried nervously.

"It's your fathuh," he gasped. "Your mothuh done found him passed out across his desk. She sent me to fetch the doctuh and then told me to come straightway and bring you home."

A chill shot through Jed. He had never considered his parents' mortality. To be sure, there were strains in their relationship, but he had never considered losing either of them. "Was she able to revive him?" Jed asked frantically as he steadied himself against Tildie.

"No suh, least ways not whilst I was around." The thin, graying man began to shudder. "He looked awful poorly, Mastuh Jed. All gray and limp. Poor Mistuh Pearson."

Jed stared blankly at the ground as Markus rode up. When he raised his head his face was slack and pale. "It's my father . . ." he muttered weakly.

Markus instinctively took hold of the reins to Bartholomew's horse. "Go pack, Jed. I'll see to him and his horse."

Jed nodded and hurried to the house to throw a few items into a satchel. Bitty noticed the ashen color of his face as soon as he crossed the threshold.

"Jed, what's the matter?" she asked as she reached a loving hand up to his shoulder.

"It's my father," he replied numbly. "He may be dying . . ." He hurried up the stairs before the sting of tears overcame him. He passed his parents' wedding portrait and gently touched the image of his father, and as he did he allowed his fear and sorrow to overtake him. As he worried about his mother, his concerns also turned to Frannie and how she would handle the news, particularly in light of the rift that had developed between her and their parents over the past year. Once packed, he hurried downstairs to his office and began to pen a hurried note to his sister. After writing a few words, he stalled and reconsidered. He hurried outside and found Bartholomew waiting with Markus, who was astride a third mount and holding Tildie's reins.

"I'll ride down with you two and bring Tildie home."

"Thanks, Markus," Jed said. "I don't know how long I'll be away . . ."

"We'll manage. I'll send you word from time to time. You do likewise, all right?"

Jed nodded numbly.

"What about Frannie? Do you want me to . . . ?"

Jed shook his head emphatically. "Not yet."

"But if the worst comes to pass, she'll never get home in time to . . ."

He shook his head. "She won't make it home in time either way. Let's pray there'll only be good news to tell."

* * *

Baltimore's weather befit Jed's errand—a bone-chilling drizzle misted the city. Finding their city home's front door ajar, he called anxiously to his mother as he shook the wetness from his coat. She didn't answer immediately, and he hurried from room to room, finally finding her asleep in his father's study, curled up on his leather sofa beneath his wool coat. "Mother," he said calmly as he gently awakened her, "how is Father?"

She burst immediately into tears, giving Jed his answer. He sent for the doctor and spent hours by his mother's side, trying to comfort her while the weight of the Pearson family fell fully upon his shoulders. After the doctor sedated her, Jed steeled himself and numbly began attending to the details of the funeral and managing the estate. He penned the distressing note to Frannie and sent it to the Murdock School by private courier. Next he selected a casket and burial clothes for his father, then stopped by the lawyer's office to see to the will. Last of all, Jed went by the newspaper offices to place notices in the papers announcing his father's passing, closing each article by channeling all future business questions to him at his father's main office on Calvert Street.

It was late afternoon when he returned home to find his mother still sedated and asleep. He could bear neither the quietness of the house nor the physical presence of his father in every space and smell. To escape, he headed to Calvert Street to attend to necessities there. His father's secretary, Mr. Carpasian, a pepper-haired and dark-eyed round man, was making long lists as he reviewed ledgers and receipt books. When Jed walked in, the man leapt to his feet, nearly paying obeisance to the son of his employer whom he clearly esteemed as his new superior.

"I knew you'd be coming by, sir. I have everything ready for your review . . . tables, ledgers, receipts . . . everything is in perfect order."

"I'm sure it is, Mr. Carpasian," Jed stated wearily as he climbed the oak steps to his father's office. "I'd like a brief overview of our assets and a list of our immediate obligations."

"Of course, sir. I have them right here," the man stammered as he lifted a pile of leather-bound ledgers. "Every unit is leased and all rents have been paid up-to-date except for a few tenants for whom your father made special circumstantial provisions. The bills and expenditures are listed inside, and there is the question of St. James Episcopalian Church."

"St. James Episcopalian Church?" Jed repeated as he hung his frock coat on the coat tree.

"Yes. It's an old arrangement that precedes my employ, but your father stipulated that I was to make monthly deposits of thirty dollars into the church's account."

"Have we any idea by whom or why this fund was established?"

"No, sir, Mr. Pearson, but I could investigate it for you."

Jed sat on the edge of the desk and rubbed his fingers deep into his weary eyes. "Please do, but be discreet, and continue to make the scheduled deposits until I say otherwise."

"Yes, sir. If you'd care to sit, I'll get the ledgers and review the other accounts for you."

Sit down? In his chair? Jed hung back momentarily, then gingerly touched the leather chair long molded by the weight of his father's body. He stared through misty eyes at the family portrait that hung on the opposite wall. It had hung over the living room sofa at home until a more recent portrait had been commissioned. He had never given this old piece a second thought, and here it was, placed like a captured memory amongst his father's treasured memorabilia. An Indian bonnet and pipe sat on a ledge, two treasures of a peace accord the first American Pearson had struck with Chief Four Eagles when Jonathan was still just a poor tutor on a few acres of disputed land. Lastly, a roughly pressed, silver Spanish coin, otherwise known as a piece of eight, hung under glass, proof of the lottery that had secured the Willows' future. But Jed suddenly realized that his father had left footprints of his own along history's path. Though the eye first caught Grandfather Pearson's musket hung beside a framed letter from President Washington for his daring service in the Revolutionary War, a second glance revealed a framed discharge letter for the grand man's son—Jed's own father—along with a sketch of father and son in Revolutionary garb.

Jed had never understood his city-loving father, never accepted that his own ties to his grandfather's pioneer legacy ran through the very sinews of the man he had smugly dismissed. Now that he could finally understand, he was too late. He heard the sound of Carpasian's returning footsteps and quickly blinked and coughed to hold his emotions at bay.

As Mr. Carpasian briefed him on the business assets and liabilities, Jed's mind strayed. He toyed with the old hickory pipe and fingered the loose tobacco that half filled the humidor. After the two men had spent an hour reviewing the company's current standing, a picture formed, detailing how his father had spent his last few weeks.

Apparently, he had been worried about his neglect of the business and had recently made monumental efforts to get his affairs in order and address all the concerns at each of his properties. Jed was surprised to see that his historically profit-oriented father had forgiven large debts to a few delinquent tenants who had fallen on hard times, even rewriting their leases and granting them a year's free rent to allow them to get back on their feet. Even though he had paid off all his creditors, he was still able to leave his wife their home, free of any mortgage, and a sizeable portfolio to assure her a comfortable, secure future. All in all, Jed could see that he had done everything in his power to leave his affairs as simple and orderly as possible for his family, prompting Jed to wonder if he had known he was ill for some time.

"Will there be anything else, sir?" Mr. Carpasian asked.

"I'd like to go through his correspondence . . . to send word of his passing to those outside the reach of the local paper's readership."

"Very well, sir," Carpasian said as he hurriedly opened a file drawer lined with folder after folder. "All his correspondence is listed alphabetically from the most recent to the oldest."

"I can see that. Thank you." Jed scanned the room, noting anything else he might have a question about before releasing the man for the day. "And what about that carton over there?"

Mr. Carpasian stooped and began to tote the box away. "It's just an odd assortment of old newspapers your father had saved for personal reasons, mingled with other odds and ends. As he grew more fatigued, he tossed everything that wasn't pressing, but which he intended to reexamine later, into this box." He turned matter-of-factly and then, remembering something of greater curiosity, he turned back around. "You may want to look through it, Mr. Pearson. Last April, a woman delivered a random stack of mail to the office . . . advertisements and charity bills for donations that were bound up and addressed to 'Mr. Jonathan Pearson.' I told the woman your father was away. I asked her if the enclosed materials were of such a pressing nature that they should be opened at once, but she replied that they weren't urgent. And then she inquired about you, asking when you would next be in the city. I told her I had no idea and she left. Your father glanced at the material in late May or June, but he set it aside with the intention of making donations to a few of the organizations at a later date. He always meant to get around to it. His heart became so tender at the end . . ." He stopped short. "Perhaps I'm just being sentimental. I'm so sorry, sir. Allow me to just take these away now."

Mr. Carpasian began to exit, but similar sentiment in Jed couldn't part with a task that his father had intended to see to. "On second thought, please leave the box. I still may want to make a few donations in my father's name."

* * *

Jed regretted Frannie's absence from the funeral but was glad to spare her the pain of watching his mother hover in that anguish-filled state between wife and widow, waiting to say good-bye yet unable to move past grief. The service was a glowing tribute to his father's life, and the church was filled by many members of Maryland society who had regrettably "lost contact" during the past year. Jed had neither the energy nor the inclination to challenge them at such a time. It required all his attention to simply keep his mother from throwing herself into the grave. Never before had he understood how completely conjoined the pair had grown over the years. He wondered what would become of his mother now that her shield and support was gone.

As sleet fell from gray skies, Jed stood by the graveside while distant relatives and acquaintances paid their final respects. Stewart Stringham dared to attend, along with Frederick, who arrived with his new wife in tow. A mousy, quiet woman with tight, curly black hair secured with pins and combs, her short round figure contrasted sharply with the Stringhams' tall, reedy forms. Jed mused how the emotionally detached pair reminded him of the childhood rhyme about Jack Sprat and his wife. Stewart offered an obligatory gesture, a closed-eyed nod, to note the Pearsons' loss, but Frederick's face showed true compassion as he lifted his forlorn head momentarily to greet the man who had been his friend and nearly his brother.

Jed marveled how a few moments had altered the courses of their friendship and lives. He wondered if Frederick regretted what he had lost, and he noted how fate may have placed them on similar, parallel paths again, each forever destined to mourn the loss of their one true love because of a single missed or miscalculated moment. Jed blinked hard and squeezed his mother tighter, trying to focus on his duty as a group of neighbors from the Patuxent continued by.

"Lovely funeral, Jed," one neighbor commented. "At the very least, it can always be said that Jonathan had a son he could be proud of."

The man passed by before Jed had a chance to throttle him, but seconds later another fine friend offered a similar indelicate remark. "Dear Jonathan. I suppose his poor heart couldn't take all this Francis business."

Having had enough of funeral etiquette, Jed pulled his mother away from the line and into her carriage. All the way home he wondered what had prompted such a latent rash of judgments against Frannie, especially since the gossip had ceased and her parents had welcomed her home.

At home, he had just settled his mother back into bed with another dose of elixir when Bartholomew called for him. Jed descended the stairs to find the undertaker standing in the foyer with a bundle in his arms.

"I wanted to drop your father's personal effects by. His pocket watch and cuff links are in the satin bag, along with the contents from his pockets from the night he died." With a brisk nod, the man was gone.

Jed walked into his father's study and held up the suit coat his father had worn his last day on earth. He pressed the fabric to his face and breathed in the familiar scent of pipe tobacco and cologne. Suddenly he was transformed into a little boy, standing beside the washstand while his father applied dabs of the scented alcohol to Jed's own cherubic cheeks and throat. His eyes grew moist and he instinctively reached for the stylishly folded handkerchief that still jutted from the jacket's front breast pocket. He dabbed at his eyes and reverently rubbed the white cotton fabric between his fingers before placing it in his own pocket. Shaking the satin bag onto the table, he saw his father's watch and cuff links slide out. He picked up the timepiece and traced the etched initials *JEP* on the cover. He wondered how many times he had begged his father to let him push the button that released the latch, as if he were performing an enchanted act by simply opening it. Time after time his father would play the game, snapping the watch closed and cheering with awe when its face was miraculously revealed again.

He picked up the cuff links and placed them in the palm of his hand, opening and closing his fist tightly over them as if wishing he could magically convince them to transport him back to another place and time, a time when he lived such simple love and was able to express it. *What happened?* The separation had been so subtle that summer before he left for the university. Though sixteen, he feared living so far from the familiarity of home and family. He had been unable to express it and so, rather than appear immature and childish, he had become stoic and detached. His father, assuming his son needed room to grow, stepped back further. It was in that quiet realignment that the emotional distance increased between them. Jed still needed the counsel of a man, but unable or unwilling to admit his need to his father, he allowed the opinions of scholars and historians to mold his values. As they whittled him into their own image, his view of his father became distorted until he could no longer clearly remember the great man of his childhood.

Jed pressed his fists to his eyes and begged God to tell his father in death what he had failed to assure him in life . . . that he loved him, honored him, wanted to be like him, and would strive to be as patient as his father had been when his own sons came along. *Please, God. If there is a heaven, let me see my father again so I can tell him these things myself someday.*

He gathered up his father's trinkets and began to slide them into the bag when he noticed an envelope tucked inside. It was addressed to his father and postmarked Philadelphia, though no return address was listed. Jed opened it and pulled out a handbill from a theater in the city. As he inspected it more closely, the hair stood on his arms.

Le Jardin des Chanteuses was printed across the middle, while the images of four women filled the corners: *Genevieve, Mariselle, Bernadette, and Francesca.* Each caption contained the name of one of the women. Jed's eyes were riveted on a single image and name. He closed his eyes and shook his head in disbelief. *Why, Frannie?* Another troublesome question came to his mind. *Who sent this?*

Jed headed upstairs to bed, quickly succumbing to the bone-weary fatigue he had denied for three days, though a recurring dream disturbed his peace: over and over he saw his bedroom door open, revealing his mother standing over him, kissing him goodnight.

When he awoke in the morning, he went to check on his mother. She was nowhere to be found, though her nightclothes and wrapper lay discarded on the floor beside her unmade bed. He headed down the stairs, repeatedly calling for her, but the only reply he received was from Bartholomew.

"She's still in bed, Mastuh Jed."

"No she's not, Bartholomew. Are you saying you haven't seen her at all this morning?"

"Not a glimpse. Cook hasn't seen her neither. She's waitin' breakfast on huh."

Jed remembered his dream from the previous night. He ran to the front door and found it unlocked and ajar. "Have you been out this door today?" he asked Bartholomew.

"No, suh. Just the back door is all."

"No, no, no!" Jed muttered as he raced to get his coat and several blankets. He ran the three blocks to the cemetery yard where his father's fresh grave was now covered by a blue drape. He recognized the fabric of the winter blanket kept on the back of the parlor sofa for nights when the fireplace's warmth was insufficient to handle the winter chill. He hurried to the graveside and lifted the heavy, saturated corner of the woolen fabric. There, under the frozen fabric and pressed into the soft, moist earth, was his mother's frail, blue-tinged form.

She did not awaken as he carried her home in his trembling arms, nor did she make any effort to return from the ethereal plane. Hours passed, and as her fever rose and her body shuddered, she opened her eyes momentarily and looked into her son's tortured eyes.

"I never got to say good-bye to him," she whispered, and then she slipped into a deep sleep from which no medical protocol could awaken her.

For four days Julianne Pearson lingered in the realm where the body and spirit struggle to remain together. Jed sat near her side, reading to her from her favorite book of verses and then moving on to a worn copy of the Bible he found in her bedside table. He had never seen a Bible in their home except for the large family heirloom that served more as the family record than as a sacred tome. He lifted the cover and read the inscription penned inside:

April 13, 1782

To Our Dearest Julianne on the Occasion of Her Sixteenth Birthday.

Darling, as you arrive at the dawn of womanhood, you are everything we dreamed our little girl would grow to become. The time has come for you to have your own copy of God's word so you can prepare to raise a family in Christ. Hold fast to that which you already know to be true. Follow the counsel in Proverbs three, verses five and six. "Trust in the Lord with all thine heart; and lean not unto thine own understanding. In all thy ways acknowledge him, and he shall direct thy paths."

Submit cheerfully to His will, Julianne, and He will lead you back to Him. God bless you, dear.

Love,

Mummy and Daddy

Jed read the inscription over and over, wondering what had led her from such a devout past to a life where the mention of God was rare and reserved for special occasions. He read the verses again and again from the book of Proverbs, particularly the line that said, "And he shall direct thy paths." He thought about Jerome's ominous counsel: "I think God is leading you."

The words had chilled him. "We are so quick to ascribe the bad things to God and in our ignorance or arrogance we are slow to ascribe the good to Him as well. God is not responsible for everything that happens to us . . . but God can still consecrate all these things for your good and lead you if you'll surrender yourself to Him . . . I don't think you can begin to see what He can do with you." It was the first time Jed had imagined that God even knew him.

Is that what your parents were trying to tell you too, Mother? Jed wondered. He noticed the worn edges of the Bible's cover and pages, evidence that it had not simply sat in a drawer, but that it had been read many times over. *But when?* He wondered if she had pulled it out in quiet moments after his father was fast asleep, secretly nurturing the seeds of faith. Jed wondered momentarily why she had denied this part of herself, but the answer came to him with assurance: because it was not of value to his father. The sadness of the idea swept over him.

Jed heard the sound of voices downstairs. Before he could stand, Frannie bounded through the door, wailing in disbelief. Jed rushed to her, wrapping his arms around her to calm her shuddering. "I'm so sorry, Frannie."

"I thought I was coming home to comfort Mother . . ." she sobbed. "What happened?"

"She muttered something about not having had a chance to say good-bye to him. She'd slipped out in the middle of the night. By the time I found her the next morning, she was nearly frozen, and then pneumonia set in. She's barely had a lucid moment since."

Frannie broke free of his grasp and flung herself onto the bed and across her mother's legs. "Mama . . . Mama . . ." she cried.

Jed knelt beside her and wrapped his arms around her again. He laid his head on top of hers and whispered in a voice husky with emotion, "Just dwell on the time you spent together this summer, Frannie. Remember posing with her by the Seine. Hold onto those memories."

* * *

The hours passed as Julianne Pearson's breathing became more labored, and the doctor arrived to help ease her final hours. She drew her final breath with each of her hands clasped in the hands of her children while faithful servants watched from the doorway.

Jed made his second trip to the undertaker's in a week's time to attend to the grisly details of another funeral. Two days later, sister and brother stood by Julianne's graveside, arms and hearts linked, receiving friends and family as they released their mother into the eternal care of that great God upon whom Jed found himself increasingly reliant. He wanted to dispense with the post-funeral gathering, but Frannie pointed out to him that it would likely be their mother's favorite part. Though he hoped that the postmortal soul was concerned with items of greater consequence than which hors d'oeuvres were served and who attended, he had to admit that in her mortality, these social details would have been of preeminent import to his mother.

Realizing that the person who sent the handbill was possibly among the "close personal friends" in attendance, Jed watched carefully as the people filed by, always remaining close by his sister's side, demonstrating clearly where his loyalties lay. He felt relieved that the most disparaging people confined their disapproval of his sister to nods or silence; compared to the effusive praise and condolences showered upon him, though, Frannie clearly felt the visitors' censure. Nonetheless, she bore it all with dignity and grace, and Jed was never prouder of his sister.

Again, the Stringham contingent attended, but this time Stewart made a deliberate point to pause and offer a discourse chronicling his long admiration for Julianne, taking special care to note her forgiving nature and longsuffering, particularly in regard to her children. Jed stood stone-faced throughout the dissertation and watched Frannie issue such a cold, hard stare that the man seemed to slither from the line, despite his earlier bravado. Frederick and his wife, Penelope, barely lifted their eyes as they each uttered words of sympathy, leaving Jed to marvel that Stewart had found a woman for Frederick to marry who was even more browbeaten than his own son. As they stood uncomfortably before Frannie, Jed could only imagine what was going through all three of their minds. Penelope looked into Frannie's face, measuring the woman her husband had loved. It was clear she had also examined herself and found herself lacking, as she dipped her head and lowered her eyes again.

Frederick's face was torture personified. His lips remained parted as if a speech lay on the very tip of his tongue, longing for any encouragement to leap from there to Frannie's heart. Francis Pearson's eyes remained blank and distant, as if she were regarding him from miles away. When his wife moved past, he reached for Frannie's hand and searched her eyes for a response.

"Hello, Frannie. I'm here if there is anything . . ."

Frannie's hand hung limp and unresponsive as she replied, "Penelope needs you."

Jed was saying good-bye to the last of the people leaving the cemetery when the undertaker approached Frannie to discuss the details of her mother's interment.

"We're ready to lower the casket, Francesca. Would you tell Mr. Pearson?"

It took a moment for Frannie to register hearing her Philadelphia stage name, but she recovered and quickly challenged the man. "What did you call me?"

"Are you only using that name at Le Jardin?" the man asked timidly.

Frannie lowered her head and whispered fearfully, "How do you know about Le Jardin?"

The man shrugged his shoulders. "The handbill in your father's coat pocket. I just assumed . . ." He stopped speaking as Frannie turned and left without a word.

"The handbill in your father's coat pocket . . ." Frannie kept repeating those words, torturing herself with exaggerated notions of what her notoriety had done to her family. *Everyone must already know!* She remembered the silent stares of the mourners as they passed by her in the line after lavishing praise upon Jed. *Jed! Jed must already know too!* She measured every word he had spoken and every gesture he had offered her. If anything, he had been excessively protective of her. *Excessively protective?* She cringed. *Yes, Jed knows.*

Soon everyone in the house had gone to bed, leaving the two siblings alone. Jed had busied himself with details to avoid the topic he dreaded raising while allowing Bitty to fret over Frannie. As his sister sat staring into the fire, he finally had to face how quiet and melancholy she had been since leaving the graveside, and he knew the time had come.

Sitting down beside her, Jed placed an arm loosely across her shoulders. Her head fell limply into the crook of his elbow, though a distance continued to separate the pair.

"Perhaps you should get some rest, Frannie. You've had a hard day."

"Hard days would seem to be the norm rather than the exception."

Jed decided to pursue the opening she had offered him. "Are things difficult at school?"

Frannie turned to face him. "I know that you have been informed about Le Jardin."

As his head fell back against the sofa, he closed his eyes. He looked at his sister, the weariness evident in both of their eyes. "I just found out the other day."

"The handbill?" she asked.

"Yes, the handbill. Why didn't you tell me? If you needed money I would have—"

"I meant to tell everyone at Christmas," she said defensively as her eyes began to tear. "I knew Mother would disapprove, but I truly thought you and Father would hear me out. It's a very respectable establishment. Catherine found out about Duprée and defamed me in front of everyone. I needed a safe place while I formulated a plan. I didn't intend to stay, but I love it now. And I love my friends, Jed. They are true friends. They are as good to me as family."

Jed pressed her hands to his lips. "You know you have placed yourself in the line of fire."

She stared back into the fireplace and considered his warning. "I know, but again, it is without merit. I would be comfortable having anyone come to Le Jardin and see me perform."

He blew out a rush of air. "Then that's all that needs to be said." But Frannie knew he was still worried about her.

"Is it? The undertaker told me the handbill was found in Father's coat pocket. I—I am not afraid of people wagging their tongues behind my back, but . . ." Her voice broke and her lips began to tremble. "The one thing I cannot bear is the thought that . . ."

Alarmed at how upset she seemed, Jed questioned, "What is it, Frannie?"

"Jed, do you think seeing that handbill caused Father's heart attack?" she sobbed.

He drew her against him and whispered in her ear, "Of course not."

Frannie pushed him away to study his eyes. She wanted the truth, not mollycoddling or hollow solace. ". . . because if it did, then I killed Mother too!"

Jed framed her face with his hands and stared soberly into her eyes. "Listen to me, Frannie." He enunciated the next words slowly. "You did not harm your parents! Do you hear me? I went to Father's office to put his affairs in order, but there was nothing to do. He had already organized everything. I felt then and I feel more so now that he knew he was ill and he was doing everything in his power to make his eventual passing easy for us, particularly for Mother."

Frannie wiped her eyes and searched her brother's face to be sure his words were sincere, and he saw relief begin to brighten her countenance.

"Father was sixty-four and he had lived a full life, Frannie. We both knew he drank too liberally and he rode and played as hard as men half his age. I am convinced he knew when his body wasn't feeling as it should. Sending you two to Europe gave him the opportunity to get his affairs in order without Mother becoming suspicious. He knew she would be devastated. He even forgave over nine hundred dollars in past-due rents a week before he died. Yes, I am convinced he knew he was dying and was trying to leave this earth in God's good graces."

Jed smiled reassuringly into Frannie's hopeful eyes, and his voice softened. "I've also learned a few new things about Mother . . . things I never knew before. She gave up a large part of herself for Father, and she simply couldn't face life without him. Nothing you or I could have done would have filled the void he left in her life."

Frannie nodded and let her head drop against his shirt as her tears moistened the cotton fabric. He held her and rocked her until her crying quieted, and then he dried her tears. "So what will you do now? Head back to Philadelphia or remain here to irritate your accusers?" He smiled.

"I've been thinking about it all evening. I'm going to buy or build a grand home right in the most exclusive part of Baltimore City, Jed."

Jed laughed cheerfully. "Frannie, it may take months to get Father's will probated, and even then it may not amount to sufficient resources for such a lavish lifestyle as that. And you don't have such funds in your personal account."

"I don't mean to build today, Jed, but someday, when I'm finished singing at Le Jardin. In the meantime, I've been saving my wages from teaching piano lessons and singing."

"Frannie, Mozart couldn't earn enough teaching piano lessons to build such a house."

"It's what I am *doing* with my wages . . ."

Jed's eyebrows arched in worried curiosity. "Please assure me it is legal."

Frannie laughed, enjoying the moment. "Quite legal, brother."

"Tell me what have you have done now. I dare not even guess."

"Let's just say there is more than one way to get an education. You may well be coming to your little sister for a loan someday. But don't fret," she teased comically, "just as you offered all you have to me, so will I gladly share all my wealth with you as well." She grabbed his chin as she withheld her grand secret. Finally, as his frustration with her games became evident, she explained. "The business titans who make up a portion of the clientele at Le Jardin freely share stock tips and investment advice with me. My portfolio is quite impressive, Jed. I have stock in two banks and shares in the Pennsylvania Power Company. They plan to install gas pipes that will bring light and heat to every home in the city. Imagine that! Street lights and homes where lamps burn without need of refilling . . . and I will be one of the early pioneers in the industry!"

Jed smiled appreciatively. "And where will you build this grand house?"

"Someplace very visible. I want to assure the local gossips that they did not run me out. I want them to know that Francis Pearson is coming home in grand style."

Jed smiled admirably at his sister. "You've got pluck. I'm proud of you. You never let anyone control your destiny. Even when fortunes turn on you, you carry on."

"I hid my tail and ran some . . . until I turned and realized how much I fancied my tail!" She chuckled softly and then sobered. "A man came into the club one night. I couldn't make out his face, but something in me knew he was familiar and that his intent was malicious."

"Perhaps I can shed some light on your mystery," Jed sighed. "Our dear friend Catherine—well, her father made some broad inquiries regarding our family this summer. It seems Stewart Stringham's wife is from Wilmington. Stewart was more than willing to give Catherine's father an 'unbiased' report."

Frannie gasped. "Somehow I always knew it was him."

"It seems that after Catherine was dismissed from the school, her father wrote to Stewart again, piquing his curiosity about you. Stewart knew you hadn't come home, and he had heard rumors that you were being courted by a promising young attorney, the son of a man running for Pennsylvania's highest office. He couldn't bear the thought of you marrying better than Frederick. So he went to Philadelphia, stopped by the school as a dear family friend and . . ."

"And got my forwarding address," Frannie finished with awe. "Well, I have to give that weasel credit. How did you get all this information?"

Jed smiled mysteriously. "How do I get all my information? Bitty's sister Priscilla pieced it together and told it to Bitty, who told me. Does knowing all that persuade you to rethink any of your plans?"

"Not at all. In fact, I am more resolved than ever."

"And what about Timothy? Does he know about your new career? It might not bode well with the conservative political circles in which his family travels."

Frannie became thoughtful. "What you said today about Mother—about her giving up things—is timely. I care about Timothy, Jed, but I'm not ready to give myself to anyone. That may consign me to live alone for a number of years, but I am prepared for that." For the first time since she'd arrived, she was reminded of Jed's own aloneness, and she broached the topic. "Timothy told me about your meeting with Hannah." She took his hands in hers and stared at the scars and discolorations that still remained from the beating he took that day. "She reacted like a jealous woman, Jed. Have you considered the possibility that she loves you in return?"

"Timothy and Samuel apprised me of their theory." He looked at Frannie. "I was there, right beside her. I would have . . . seen it. No, she's in love with someone else, and I'll not mar her happiness."

"Self-doubt rendered you unable to read her before. You also refused to see that she was a woman when others could. I'd remain open to the possibility until the wedding bells chime." She rubbed her small hand over his scarred ones. "Just tell me honestly. How are you?"

Jed feigned a smile, signaling that the topic was still unapproachable, even to her.

"Would you see Renfro and Timothy if they called on us over the holidays?" she pressed.

"Yes, but I'd like to pretend that day never happened. Would you explain that to them?"

"Of course." She laid her head on his shoulder, and nothing more was said as they drifted off into the first hours of restful sleep either had known in days.

* * *

The Willows contingent headed back to the farm, leaving Jed and Frannie alone to sort out all they had been through. Christmas was a somber affair, cheered only by the monetary gift sent to Mr. Carpasian and the shopping and wrapping they did for the servants' gifts, which brought Jed and Frannie particular pleasure. They spent a few days enjoying one another's company, playing cards and checkers, reading aloud to one another by firelight, and attending the plentiful concerts in the city. As they returned home one evening, Bartholomew whispered in Frannie's ear. She hurried into the parlor to find two guests waiting anxiously for their arrival.

"Timothy! Mr. Renfro!" Frannie squealed excitedly after the butler withdrew. "You got my messages! I wasn't sure when you would be coming, but I told Bartholomew to be sure to make you comfortable when you did."

"He treated us like kings," laughed Samuel Renfro as he patted his jutting belly.

Timothy Shepard extended his arms wide to Frannie and folded them around her. He pressed his face close to hers, but when the length of the embrace grew too long for her comfort, she patted his back and pulled away.

"Are you sure Jed will receive us?" he asked nervously.

"Quite sure. Just refrain from apologizing for the past. He prefers to simply move on."

Jed passed the doorway and Frannie hurried to his side and drew him into the group. The first few seconds were awkward as all three friends struggled to build a bridge of conversation that would carry them beyond their last meeting. Frannie was the great conciliator.

"Jed, Samuel is once again a permanent Baltimore resident! He was accepted into the first class of the Baltimore College of Medicine. They've even hired him as a teaching assistant."

Jed extended his hand warmly and said with a smile, "I thought this class wasn't to sit until fall."

"It won't," Renfro replied, "but I am arriving early to assist with administrative matters."

"A professor?" mocked Jed playfully. "I'm impressed . . ."

Frannie hurried on, drawing Timothy in. "There's more good news, Jed. Timothy has been hired to work as an assistant to Senator Andrew Gregg from Pennsylvania! He'll be close by also, right there in the heart of government. Isn't that wonderful?"

The two men eyed one another for several seconds. When Jed finally extended his hand to his college chum, Timothy clasped Jed to him heartily. Having crossed the emotional abyss, the entire foursome retired to the sofas to chat and reminisce.

"I was so sorry to hear about your father's passing," Renfro said to Jed. As the two men began a discussion about the frailties of the heart, Timothy turned to speak quietly to Frannie.

"You must have thought your world had crashed down upon you."

"For more reasons that you could possibly know, but I think Jed is having the harder time. As he goes through our parents' personal papers, he is realizing that there was far more to them than we were ever privileged to know. He seems tormented by that discovery."

"I suppose that is true for most of us. As soon as we believe we are grown, our priorities shift away from the love of our parents to building a life and home of our own."

Frannie tipped her head and breathed deeply in anticipation of Timothy's next segue.

"I have missed you terribly," he whispered quietly, but Frannie quickly raised her hand to halt the conversation.

"Much has happened since we said good-bye. There are things I need to tell you."

"About Le Jardin?"

Frannie was dumbfounded. How far had her infamy traveled? "How did you . . . ?"

"Miss Peltier felt it her duty to warn me that I was . . . involved with an *entertainer*." He emphasized the word, interjecting a scary tone into it.

Frannie fell into momentary shock, then she laughed loudly. "Her gall knows no bounds. And how was the news received at the Shepard home? I doubt your father was pleased."

Timothy's smile indicated that his father did not yet know.

"And he needn't be told, Timothy. At least not at this time. I feel numbed and drained by all that has happened. I can only offer to be your dear friend, if you've a mind to accept that."

Timothy took her hands in his and nodded his understanding, though disappointment was evident in his face. "Then I shall consider myself the dearest friend of an entertainer, for however long it requires for me to win her heart."

* * *

On January fourth, as Frannie's carriage waited to return her to Philadelphia, she and Jed watched their two friends ride off to begin their own new adventures.

"Do you have enough blankets to keep you warm?" Jed asked as he pulled the cloak tighter around his sister's shoulders.

"You've stuffed the carriage full," she teased. "I wish I could stay and help you go through Mother's and Father's things. I hate to think of you settling all this alone."

"The staff will be a great help. So, we're agreed to keep the house for now? You're sure?"

"Until I have my own city home, I would feel better knowing we have this one," Frannie declared.

"I feel the same. Then I'll leave Bartholomew in charge of things here."

"What will you do about Father's business affairs?"

"I'm going to spend a day or two attending to some details . . . making donations in Father's name to the charities he had intended. After that I think I will leave the day-to-day operation to Mr. Carpasian and just meet with him occasionally to go over the books." He playfully adjusted her cloak again. "Since you're a business tycoon and my prospects look bright, I see no reason to close down the company and put the man out of work in the dead of winter."

Frannie knew the time for parting had come. "When will we see one another again?"

"After speaking to Timothy, the real question is *where* will we see each other? Will we be in the United States of America, or will we be standing on the most recent British conquest?"

"And you are still determined to fight?" she asked pointedly.

"It will be every man's duty. However wise or foolish the timing might be, the cause is just. As long as Britain continues to harass us, we cannot feel fully free. The greater fear is that if the British succeed in conquering Napoleon, thousands of additional troops would be freed from that front to battle us, and what prize will they seek? They will want Washington City, and with the Willows lying almost directly between the capital and Baltimore, I am in this on three fronts."

Frannie groaned. "I can't stand any of this. Perhaps I should stay with you."

"Ride on to Philadelphia, Frannie. I'll feel much better knowing you are safe there. I'll write to you regularly, and you do the same, and let us pray that when this is settled, justice will have prevailed."

CHAPTER 22

Baltimore, Maryland
Mid-January 1812

Mr. Carpasian picked up the paper, his hands nearly trembling with excitement. "Are you certain of these figures, sir? I mean . . . is it your intention to pay me this amount of money?"

"Only if those figures are agreeable. I want you to be happy in both salary and situation."

Carpasian grabbed Jed's hand and nearly shook it off. "Oh, yes, sir! Yes, sir. I'd be very happy . . . ecstatic, actually. I'll be as loyal an employee as ever there was, Mr. Pearson."

"I'll be around quarterly, but unless there's a problem, the day-to-day operation will be yours. After I sort through this box of correspondence and sign a few checks, I'll be on my way."

"Very well, sir. Oh, I did some checking on the St. James Parish account. It was established in the winter of 1781 by your grandfather. Odd how the bank manager clearly remembered the date, though he seemed uneasy about discussing the particulars of the agreement. He did promise to have a clerk pull the records, however. We should know something soon."

"Thank you, Mr. Carpasian."

"Of course, sir." Carpasian nodded as he closed the door behind himself.

Jed began sorting through the muddled mess in the box his father had left. The top few papers were, indeed, pleas for donations from charitable organizations, but the rest seemed to be newspaper classifieds and handbills from theaters and restaurants from April 1811.

April . . . When he still dreamed of a life with Hannah.

He rustled through the clutter, removing the charitable requests before setting the box out to be discarded. A flash of lavender caught his eye, and for a moment a familiar happiness rushed over him. *Hannah wrote on lavender stationery!* He chided himself for thinking of her and set the box aside, but try as he did to ignore it, he knew he would be overcome with regret for not having at least looked.

He wasn't sure if he wanted it to be a letter from Hannah or not. Trying to contain his anticipation, to prepare himself for another disappointment, he slowly combed through the pile. He wondered if he was becoming as insane as Susannah Stansbury, grasping at such a crazed notion. The impossibility of it calmed him, and reason began to drive his fantasy away. He almost withdrew his hands a second time, but just then he came upon the item and saw the penmanship. It was unmistakably Hannah's!

He snatched the envelope from the box and nervously opened it. He saw the date, *Sunday, April 14, 1811.* His eyes scanned each line warily, reveling in the familiar script while worrying what news had prompted her to write. Before reading a single word, he hurried to read her closing, *Your dearest Hannah.* He pressed the envelope to his lips and repeated the words.

He questioned the wisdom of reading the letter and reopening old wounds. But even if he was never to have her for his own, some glimpse into what had befallen their association . . . some insight into what had made their last meeting so strained and odd . . . would at least satisfy his need for resolution. With reluctant anticipation, he returned to the first page and began to read.

Dearest Jed,

I have missed you so. Mother is still obstinate in denying me the privilege of writing to you or receiving correspondence from you, and though I have tried on several occasions to post mail to you through subterfuge, she has foiled each attempt and I have paid dearly for my disobedience. It is only because I am summering with Beatrice and Dudley that I am able to disobey Mother on this singular occasion and pen one letter to you . . .

He felt sick. She had written . . . she had even been punished for writing, and yet she persisted in her attempts. He could scarcely imagine what punishment had been meted out.

In the page and a half describing the sullen state of affairs at Coolfont, Hannah's gentle forgiveness for her mother shone through. She then mentioned a dinner party Beatrice had hosted that very evening, at which Myrna had supposedly found her one true love. Jed read and reread the paragraphs, knowing Hannah well enough to see that she was circling around something without directly addressing it.

The next paragraph described Beatrice and Dudley's fondness for their circle of friends. Again Jed sensed that she was avoiding something. The closing paragraph hit him like a shot through his heart.

> . . . *my sisters are intent on pairing me off before Mother and Father carry me back to Coolfont. Beatrice and Dudley have hand selected a young lieutenant as my first suitor. He is a fine-looking man with a gentle bearing and solicitous heart where I am concerned, but he is not you. Why is it that the one man whose opinion matters most to me still sees me only as a child? Please call for me at Beatrice's home. Either define for me, clearly, what love you feel for me so I can stop measuring all men against you, or tell me I am right to love you as I do no other. Please do not delay, Jed.*

> *Your dearest Hannah*

Jed flew from the office of Pearson Properties so explosively that Mr. Carpasian feared his new employer might soon suffer the same fate as his father. Down the street he ran, five blocks, past his parents' house, and seven more to the Snowden home. With every step he kept repeating the lines that pushed his racing heart onward: *Tell me I am right to love you as I do no other. Please do not delay, Jed.*

"I'm coming, Hannah," he pledged to the icy, January wind. His heart raced as did his mind, carrying him back to that final day in August when Hannah had rebuffed him so. She had written her plea in April and he had never replied. *She must have felt her profession of affection had been cast aside as childish folly.*

He needed to see her, to look into her eyes and tell her why he had never responded, to assure her that her feelings for him were equaled and even surpassed by his own love for her. Then he needed to explain why he had stalled in declaring these things. He would tell her she was right—that he had falsely placed valor and honor over passion, regarding her as a child when she had matured beyond his understanding. That had been his error, but that had been his only error. Someone else was to blame for the treachery that had kept them apart.

As he stood on the Snowdens' porch, his heart pounded and he had no idea how he would begin. He imagined that Hannah would open the door and leap into his arms. Failing that dream, he hoped he would not throttle whoever else had the misfortune of standing in his way.

He pounded so rapidly and fiercely upon the door that the Snowdens' butler shook as he timidly cracked it open, permitting a view of the mistress of the house, who, upon identifying Jed, went pale and quaked as if she were about to faint.

A booming voice sounded from an upstairs room. "Beatrice! What is all that racket?"

Beatrice swallowed hard to clear the lump from her throat. "Just someone at the door, dear," she answered with false calm. She quickly dismissed her butler and peeked through the cracked door. "You shouldn't be here, Jed."

He hadn't expected a royal welcome from Hannah's oldest sister, but Beatrice's cold reception now placed her on his list of suspects. "I've come to see Hannah," he declared.

Beatrice slipped onto the stoop and nearly pulled the door shut behind her. "She has not returned from spending the holidays at Coolfont, but . . . I'll tell her that you've called for her."

Jed thrust the letter at the woman. "Just like you delivered her letter to me?" he charged. "After nearly nine months I found it buried in a heap of rubbish in my father's office!"

The woman gasped, revealing at least some complicity in the letter's delay. "Please, Jed. Your arrival here will only cause more heartache. Hannah is engaged to be married."

The kick of the words made him stumble back. They echoed around and around in his head, taunting him and pricking at his heart with each reverberation. His hands dropped from where they had shaken the letter at Beatrice. "But she loves me," he said mournfully.

The sight of watching such a proud man diminish before her eyes was unbearable to Beatrice. She placed a compassionate hand on his arm and with utter sincerity she replied, "Much has happened since the night she penned that letter to you."

Jed's pain returned to fury at the mention of the passing of time . . . time he was denied . . . time that was purposely stolen from him, and he shrugged off her kindness. "Clearly it has, since as of April last, Hannah's letter professes her love for me and begs me to hurry and rescue her from a planned union you and Myrna were pressing her into! And who is her betrothed? Could it be the selfsame lieutenant you arranged her to meet at your dinner party? She loved me then, Beatrice, and I will not leave here until I hear from her own lips that she does not love me still!"

With each revelation, Beatrice seemed to shrink further. She pressed her hands upon Jed's chest, pleading for him to leave. Then the door opened, slowly revealing Dudley's anguished face. "It is enough, Beatrice. Jed, please forgive our lack of hospitality and come in."

Jed's eyes stared down with derision upon the uniformed rescuer who had shown him kindness the night he was beaten. But Dudley's compassion seemed equally suspect now, and Jed glared at the artillery captain's insignia. "So you were in on it too . . ."

"Only after the fact, Jed," Beatrice declared as she rushed to her husband's defense. She began to weep. "Dudley is dismayed by the scheme which has caused great distress between us."

"Tell me why you did it. I realize that your mother has always harbored some prejudice against my family, and must have added the appalling rumors about Frannie to her list of reasons I was unsuitable for Hannah. But she is a mad woman, Beatrice, and everyone knows it. I have always found you to be a lady in every sense of the word, and more pleasantly disposed toward me. Why then did you agree to this treachery?"

Beatrice staggered into the parlor and dropped into an armchair, allowing her head to drop into her hands. Dudley hung his head but remained in the doorway, unable or unwilling to comfort his wife. His wife's words had never been truer; a distance had settled into their marriage as a result of the treachery, and his guilt and regret had nearly consumed him each time he saw Hannah and Andrew together, knowing they had been consigned to a marriage with boundaries, imposed upon them by the will of others. "Tell him, Beatrice. Finally, let truth prevail over lies."

She looked painfully up at her husband, the sting of his indictment searing her heart. She invited Jed to sit, but he refused, and she nodded her understanding. "It was I who agreed to allow Hannah to write you that one letter, and I fully intended to see it delivered. Someone else devised the plan to delay your receipt if it."

Her hairsplitting infuriated Jed. "You say you intended to honor your promise to deliver the letter? Then the 'courier' had to have been Myrna. Am I correct?"

Beatrice nodded her hanging head.

"I assume that being *good Christian women,* you two sought a way to deliver the letter to spare your souls the damnation of an outright lie, while at least delaying my receipt of the note in the hopes that your candidate might eventually win her heart. Are my suppositions accurate?"

His sarcasm made Beatrice feel like the most profound of sinners. "Painfully accurate."

"Myrna discovered that my father was in the country when she delivered the box. That began the delay, and she probably assumed that when he arrived and opened it, he would consider the entire box little more than refuse and discard it without further regard. Neither of you could foresee that my dying father's heart was very charitable when he returned to the city. So, ironically, the very rubbish Myrna collected actually appealed to him. When he passed away last month, I inherited the box. You see, Beatrice, despite your efforts to cheat honesty and feign piety, Providence assured the letter's rightful delivery to me."

Beatrice's expression showed her shock. "I am so sorry, Jed. I didn't know about your father. I have been so indisposed of late . . . I haven't glanced at a paper in weeks."

"I knew," admitted Dudley. "I read the accounts of both your parents' deaths and was tormented by the thought that in such an hour of grief, you needed Hannah more than ever. Yet, so many lies and lives were entangled at that point . . . I couldn't free enough of my conscience to go to her and tell her the truth."

Jed's eyes brightened with hope. "So you admit it then! She does still love me!"

Beatrice looked at him with shining eyes. "You will always be her one true love, Jed, but it is not as simple as that."

"Of course it is!" he insisted.

Beatrice rose to face him. "Jed, our mother is very ill and growing worse all the time. Despite that fact, there is one truth that alters all others. No matter how abusive or neglectful a mother might be, a child hungers for her love. Mother threatened to disown Hannah if she married you, and though Hannah would have impetuously chosen a life with you, Myrna and I knew in time she would beat herself with guilt and longing. Our intentions were not selfish, Jed. We had hoped to find a way to win her both the love of a good man and Mother's love as well."

"I could have filled her life with love enough to compensate for her mother's lacking!"

"No, Jed," countered Beatrice softly. "No one else can ever fill that void. That became evident just this past fall. As horrible as she has ever been to Hannah, she began showering love upon her girls. It soothed an aching hunger in each of us that no other love could satisfy, so much so that Hannah is willing to forgive Mother of every injustice. She's even had Andrew take her home often since their engagement, and why? Because she drinks in every drop of Mother's proffered affection."

Jed ran his trembling hands through his hair. "Why are we in this position? What evil could I have possibly committed to provoke your mother to loathe me since my first breath?"

"It wasn't you, Jed. You inherited her hatred of your grandfather along with his fortune."

Jed couldn't believe his ears. "My grandfather? What crime did he commit that was so heinous as to warrant such a grudge? Did he buy her land? Snub her father? Kill her cat?"

Beatrice could hardly answer. "She holds him responsible for her mother's death."

The shock stole Jed's very breath. "She believes what?"

"It's true, Jed," Dudley stated. "I've heard her say as much myself."

Jed turned on him. "Did she spout this absurd rubbish in one of her muddled dreams?"

"It's real to her, Jed," Beatrice said in Dudley's defense. "That's all that matters."

"It is not all that matters! Not if you are telling me that my prospects of ever being with Hannah rest on her unsubstantiated delusions!"

Beatrice shook her head. "Now you understand the dilemma Myrna and I acted under."

Jed looked at her incredulously. "No matter! I cannot accept that life with a man she does not love, and the crazed affections of a madwoman, are fair compensation for denying her the love of the one who has adored her since she was a child." His voice broke with emotion. "Even in the days when you and Myrna treated her as an outcast, my letters were her refuge. And when your mother and father were cold and indifferent to her, it was to me that she turned for comfort. Consider this, Beatrice. Long after your mother is dead and gone, Hannah will still be bound in a marriage of your choice, not hers, and to a man you consigned her to through lies and deception. Can you honestly deceive yourself into believing that this is what is best for her?"

"It has gone too far now, Jed. Other lives are at stake. The lieutenant is as unaware of the deception as were you and Hannah. He is a good man, a colleague of Dudley's who is much revered by our family. Hannah is resigned to the arrangement and has come to fancy the lieutenant."

"Resigned? Fancy?" He looked at Dudley. "Would you have wanted to settle for such anemic passion? Tell Hannah the truth and let her decide."

Beatrice leapt back in. "She will choose you now, Jed, but I can also assure you that in choosing you she will lose all association with her parents. And if she does that, in the end her remorse will destroy your love." She shook so badly that she could hardly remain standing. "Regret has eroded the love in our own house. That is why I can speak on the matter with some authority."

Dudley couldn't bear it any longer. He strode over to his wife and placed a supportive hand on her arm. "Our problems are the result of our choices, Beatrice, and somehow, we will find a way through them. Knowing that our destiny lies in our own hands, how can we deny Jed and Hannah the same privilege? He is right. The truth must be told."

He turned to Jed, the heaviness of his own burden evident. "Hannah's intended, Lieutenant Andrew Robertson, is as a brother to me. I can assure you he knows nothing of this intrigue. He knows Hannah loves you, Jed, but like Hannah, he believes you love her only as a dear friend or brother and that you are involved with a woman you met in Philadelphia. So you see, he has already agreed to accept the role of second fiddle because he is also devoted to her happiness. I know I have no right to make any request of you, but as one man to another, I ask one favor of you. Before you go to Hannah, visit with Andrew first, and if, after meeting him, you believe telling Hannah the truth is in her best interest, then you may do so with our blessing. And I give you my word that we will do everything in our power to smooth whatever wake may follow."

Dudley went to his desk where he scribbled a note and offered it to Jed. Jed stalled while he peered into the man's eyes. Believing his words to be honest, he took Dudley's proffered hand and then strode out of the Snowden home without further comment.

The garrison penned on Dudley's card was located in the stronghold named Fort McHenry, a few miles outside of Baltimore on a peninsula that jutted into the Patapsco River. Jed stepped from his carriage and crossed the bridge that led from the Baltimore Road uphill to the ravelin, where young soldiers stood guard. A sentry questioned him, and when Jed showed him Captain Snowden's note, he was escorted over a footbridge to the sally port. He was stopped two more times after this main entrance to the bustling fortress before reaching the building where the officers were headquartered. A young corporal eyed him curiously while announcing Jed's arrival to Lieutenant Robertson. Seconds later the lieutenant's door opened. The man who exited was not a strutting, bombastic peacock in uniform; rather, he was a young, fair-haired fellow with an amiable manner and an endearing smile, a man who warmly offered his hand, greeting Jed as if they were old friends. Jed recalled Hannah's description of him in her letter, *He is a fine-looking man with a gentle bearing and solicitous heart . . .* Her description was accurate, and Jed felt his resolve slip until her final comment reverberated in his mind: *But he is not you.* Steeled again in his cause, he stoically shook the man's hand, denying the initial urge to like his present foe.

"Mr. Pearson, I am delighted to make your acquaintance. Please come in." The lieutenant looked at his young secretary and said, "Corporal Cole, please hold all my messages."

He offered Jed a seat in a worn leather chair, the only other piece of furniture in the room aside from the lieutenant's own chair and desk, upon which maps, charts, and papers lay. Jed caught sight of a letter from the United States Department of War entitled, "The Probability of a British Attack on Washington and Baltimore Cities," which Lieutenant Robertson quickly slid under a pile. Jed now noted the pressure his rival was living under, suddenly regretting that he had come at all, and sorry he hadn't simply insisted on seeing Hannah directly in the first place.

"Please excuse the mess, Mr. Pearson. Things have become quite hectic of late."

"I can see you are occupied with weightier matters, Lieutenant. I apologize for barging in without an appointment. I'll be going." He turned for the door, hoping the gentleman would not insist he remain, and disturbed by an unexpected feeling arising from his begrudging but increasing appreciation for his rival's character. To his discomfiture, the lieutenant hurried over to him and placed a hand on his shoulder.

"I know why you've come, Jed, and I can assure you that nothing in the world bears more critically upon me than this particular matter."

Jed turned slowly, his face twisted in confusion. "You know why I've come?"

Robertson sat on the edge of his desk as he again invited Jed to sit in the leather chair opposite him. "I was at the Snowdens' that afternoon in August . . . the day you rescued Hannah. I had heard about you previously, of course." He laughed sadly. "I'm sure you know that Hannah credits you and your letters for making her the woman she is today. She rose to your expectations of her. I thought you were as a brother to her and I thanked you every day for all you had done for her. After that day in August, seeing her lying in bed, shattered and shaken and wanting only to die, I knew you were far more than a brother to her. I knew she was in love with you."

His head sagged, then lifted. "The only detail I missed was discovering how you felt about her." His eyes met Jed's. "Hannah thought you were in love with another. The only obstacle lay within me. Could I accept that I would never be the man she truly wanted?"

Jed's voice was condescending. "You asked her to marry you. I assume you reached a compromise on that matter."

The lieutenant's embarrassment showed. "For one such as Hannah, yes." He nodded. "Yes, I would abase myself and accept my fate. Does that surprise you, especially coming from a man trained to fight, a man trained to seek victory and eschew defeat?" he laughed in self-derision. "When Hannah's love is the prize, I find I am more a prisoner than a conqueror."

"You've erred in one important bit of information, sir," Jed replied sternly.

Robertson straightened and nodded again. "Your friends' prattle was incorrect, wasn't it? There is no other woman."

"Never," Jed replied unequivocally. "Not one day in my entire life have I ever loved anyone but Hannah. I withheld that information from her out of propriety because I first knew I loved her when she still needed time to examine such feelings." Jed confessed tenderly as he stood, "I tried to deny that she had become a woman, fearing to press my feelings upon her until she was mature enough to know her own mind. I waited too long, but I intend to correct that error."

Lieutenant Robertson stood and faced Jed. "Then we have a problem, sir."

Jed cocked his head in disbelief and pulled Hannah's letter from his pocket. "Are you saying you will not withdraw your proposal, knowing what you now do?"

"I cannot."

"Perhaps you will change your mind when you read this. Hannah intended for me to receive it in April, but I was conspiratorially denied its receipt until this very day." Jed handed him the letter and pointed to the final paragraph.

The lieutenant winced slightly as he read it, refolded it, and handed it back to Jed.

"I have already accepted all of this, Mr. Pearson, and I feel your pain, believe me. Were I selfishly fighting for Hannah, I would withdraw and pave the way for you to be with her. However, I remain steadfast in my commitment to her because I believe marrying me is in her best interest."

Jed raised his hands in the air and laughed incredulously. "Is there no reasonable mind left in this city that believes two people who love one another have a right to be together?"

"Please, listen to me," Robertson pleaded with pained eyes. "You have only dealt with these revelations for a few hours. I have been tortured by them for months. You fail to factor in the most bizarre but incontrovertible detail. Hannah's mother . . ."

"Hang Hannah's mother!" Jed closed his eyes in frustration and paced to clear his mind. "Hannah's mother is of no concern in this matter!"

"You are wrong. Perhaps there was a time, even a few months ago, when her mother's abuse may have left Hannah willing to walk away from her. That is no longer the case, and you are partly accountable for the circumstances that have altered your fate."

Jed stared blankly at him.

"When Hannah left Baltimore, I was certain I would never see her again. I wrote to her every week for months after she returned to Coolfont, receiving no reply. Then she suddenly began encouraging my interest. I was wary at first, and with good cause. Do you know why she finally replied?" He raced on without pausing for Jed's response. "Your August meeting so completely devastated Hannah that her visible pain cracked the icy shell surrounding Susannah Stansbury's previously locked heart, finally permitting some semblance of motherly love to leach from hers and into Hannah's. Even after the woman's last unfathomable cruelty to Hannah . . ."

Jed cringed and interjected, "What unfathomable cruelty?"

The lieutenant's eyes showed sorrow. "You didn't know? Of course . . . how could you have?" He paused and stared at the floor for a moment. "Druid . . . Mrs. Stansbury shot and killed Druid, believing him to be a threat to her daughter's welfare. Surely you knew how much that horse meant to her, and yet, Hannah's hunger for her mother's love remained so great she forgave her even that great injustice. That's when she wrote to me. *Why then?* I had to ask myself. I concluded that it was because she is willing to endure anything to ensure her mother's association . . . even marriage to a man she does not love but who, unlike you, has her mother's approval."

Jed's jaw was clamped tightly. "What of the day when Susannah is dead and gone, when she discovers that the man she loved and who clearly loved her in return once stood before you and declared himself? Will a few years of crazed maternal love be worth the betrayal of all who should have acted in her best interest but who instead denied her a voice?"

"Either way, Mr. Pearson, we are both already ruined men. Whichever of us loses her hand to the other will spend the remainder of his days inconsolable. The victor, though, will spend his days in equal pain, for that man will know that he was unable to make her truly happy."

"I don't believe that," Jed argued. "I am prepared to do anything to bring her happiness. I've planned my life around her happiness."

"I believe that is your intention, but we will each fall short of our desire. If she marries you, she will be denied the affection of her parents. Though she may never speak of her sorrow, you know what her guilt will do to her. She will mourn that she wasn't there to nurse them during illness or to ease their passing from this earth. She will lament that her children were unable to see where she grew up or to know her parents. No matter what other happiness you bring her, knowing that you were unable to grant her these simple joys will be your eternal penance."

Jed felt the sting of his words. "And yours?" he asked sarcastically.

Lieutenant Robertson shrank in humiliation. "My penance will be, as you have already said, to admit that I consciously denied her the right to know how it feels to be truly in love." He grimaced before facing Jed. "I will be able to protect her while still allowing her unfettered access to her parents. I can even protect her beloved Selma by bringing her to live with us, and I will shower her with love every single day—but despite all this she will never be truly happy."

He walked nearer to Jed and spoke man to man. "She will wonder what her life would have been like if she had married you. As she carries our children, I will wonder if she wishes daily that they were flesh of your flesh instead of mine. She will dream of you at night and I will watch her heart break every morning when she awakens to my face on the pillow beside hers, when I know she is wondering what it would be like to awaken to find you there in my place."

Jed swallowed hard, feeling the sincerity of the man's pain, though the reality of his own burned in his stomach like bile. "Please don't ask me to stand down and then feel pity for you because she won't love you. Not when you will be the one to hold her in your arms and father her children. Your life will be none the worse, because you are right about one thing—once Hannah has given herself to someone, she will consecrate herself to fulfilling her vow. Outwardly she will deny her own happiness to make the life of her family heavenly. It is how she is made. It is the character trait I have most admired in her." His voice was raw with emotion as he thought back to the day when they took their horseback ride, when he'd told of the kind of home she would make.

"It's true," agreed the lieutenant. "Everything you've said is true."

"The only right thing to do is to tell Hannah the truth and allow her to weigh the consequences and choose her own happiness. Surely you see that," Jed reasoned.

"She will likely choose you, you know, so be certain that that is the best course for her in the end." The lieutenant closed his eyes and breathed out a long, low sigh. "I've tried so hard and so long to look at this from every angle that my mind is now like a whirlpool, consuming all reason. I no longer know clearly what is right or wrong. I only know I cannot withdraw."

Jed groaned in anguish but Robertson hurried to finish his thought. "To do so would leave her with only two choices, to be denied association with her parents or to be alone. I won't do that. The matter and the consequences lie in your hands. Consult your conscience and then do what you must, sir. If you go directly to her and she chooses you, I will offer you no resistance."

Jed turned for the door as a chill ran through his body. *The matter and the consequences lie in my hands.* He kicked at a spot on the wooden plank floor as he cursed his fate again. It should be so clear. She loved him and he loved her. Why should anything else matter?

But he knew the lieutenant was right. Susannah hated him, and in her current state of mind, she would transfer that hatred to her own daughter if Hannah betrayed her. He cursed the aspect of life that allowed other people's choices to affect one's destiny. That was all he could do, unless he could settle the matter of Susannah's hatred. He turned back around and faced his rival, his own face taut as he moved inches from the lieutenant's. Tightening his jaw and closing his eyes in disbelief at what he was about to do, he almost choked on the words as they left his mouth.

"Stall your marriage for at least one year. I will be watching to see if you are acting in her best interest or in your own. If I find that you are not a man of honor, sir, or if I find a way to soothe her mother's enmity toward me, I will tell Hannah everything and claim what is mine. If in a year's time, however, I believe Hannah is truly happy with her choice, then I will stand down."

CHAPTER 23

The West Indies
Late May 1812

Duprée had been running for two years, and the unrelenting watch for his assassin had worn him thin. He watched cagily as the British naval officer approached, leaving his four comrades standing near the door. The demeanor of the man reflected nothing but disdain for the mercenary, and Duprée knew that his debt had not been forgiven.

Deciding to face his fate with strength, he leaned back and grinned. He would not cower or plead for mercy. He did not know if this officer could be bought, but he had nothing to lose. Even as the uniformed man pulled out a chair and took a seat, he considered that option.

"Sebastian Duprée . . ." the officer began with a smirk. "A great many people would like to put a rope around your neck. It seems you have made far more enemies than friends these past few years, and the time has come for you to pay the piper, as it were."

Duprée smiled as innocently as possible, leaning back against his chair. "You must be mistaken. I have nothing to account for. I forfeited the deed to my late father's New Orleans plantation. I am sure my creditors are enjoying the view from the southern balcony. My debt is paid."

Unaffected by Duprée's claim, the officer leaned forward and sneered, "Not exactly, my friend. Your creditors claim your debt exceeded the property's value. My notes indicate that you agreed to provide certain services in the States to your lenders as partial payment. They do not feel you have honored the agreement, and I have been sent to arrest you."

Duprée laughed out loud. "You and I both know you cannot arrest me. The other terms they set were services outside the confines of the law. They wouldn't dare charge me in a public court for failing to complete these services because it would expose them." He leaned back again. "No, they want something from me, but all they have to secure my services are idle threats. Go home and tell the men who sent you that I consider our arrangement satisfied."

Duprée awaited his fate in eerie silence. Though he had never met any of the principal investors in the consortium, he knew full well from the power and influence they wielded—including the ability to dispatch naval officers in their stead—that they must include men in the highest echelons of Europe, and perhaps its governments as well.

The naval officer was no novice at dealing with mercenaries and privateers. He knew they were primarily drawn from the dregs of society—liars, thieves, and murderers. But since the toll of the war with Napoleon had been heavy, such paid spies and anarchists were necessary to unsettle the enemy and to gain advantages that would minimize the losses to the regular military. "While living in Maryland, you committed crimes against a white woman, a crime punishable by death. Your creditors transferred your debt to the military. As you know, tensions are high between our two governments. It may be in our best interest to return you to Maryland to stand trial on these charges as a gesture of goodwill between our two nations."

Duprée's bravado quickly faded. He fought the despair creeping into his mind and slapped another smile on his face. "I am a very resourceful man. The Consortium could have killed me long ago, but they know I am far too valuable. They sent me to Virginia three years ago to identify ports where illegal slave boats could dock and set up auctions. Then they gave me a thousand dollars to establish a similar operation in Maryland. I spent eight miserable months in the oyster pit of the Patuxent River, mapping every tributary for them so they could move their boats in and out safely. I soon realized I had simply traded one form of slavery for another, so I started looking for a way to outrun my creditors and—"

The officer leaned forward and interrupted him abruptly. "Do you still have them?"

Confusion showed on the Creole's face. "Have what?"

"The maps. The maps of the Patuxent River. Do you still have them?"

Duprée smiled wryly. "I do. I've been holding on to them as collateral against my debt. I'll give them to you in exchange for a document from my creditors, absolving me."

The naval commander nodded his head. "Do not rue the day your creditors assigned you the task of mapping Maryland's rivers. That assignment may be your very deliverance."

Cocking his head, Duprée stared at the man, suddenly becoming taciturn and thoughtful.

"I have the duty of securing privateers," the officer continued. "I am particularly interested in men familiar with the Potomac and Patuxent Rivers and the Chesapeake Bay."

Duprée's eyes bulged with excitement as he began to see the plan. "You're going to attack Washington City and Baltimore!" He smacked the table and laughed with pleasure. "You'll need my maps. The Patuxent is treacherous. It can rise or fall ten feet in yards of water, and the oyster beds can destroy the hull of a ship if she gets hung up. I've charted almost every mile of that river and what I haven't person- ally charted I copied from the ferry captains' maps."

"When you hand over those maps, I'll arrange for your debt to be satisfied in full—"

The wily Duprée slapped his hands on the table again and beamed.

". . . but I cannot erase the charges held over you by the American courts. Instead, I can offer you another arrangement."

The Creole's smile faded quickly as mistrust filled his eyes. "What sort of arrangement?"

The officer leaned forward and smiled wryly. "I have some business to conduct along the Patuxent. Business well suited to a man of your natural . . . talents and abilities. If the tensions between the two nations result in war, Britain will be victorious. Those who assist us in achieving that victory will be aptly rewarded. As a hero of the new nation, you, Mr. Duprée, would not only have all current charges against you dropped, but you could end up a very wealthy man . . . perhaps even owning much of the land you saw as you charted the river."

Duprée's sly smile returned. "And what must I do to earn this great reward?"

The officer extended his hand to the former slave. "All in good time. All in good time."

CHAPTER 24

Baltimore, Maryland
June 1, 1812

Hannah heard the muffled sounds of tense voices filtering down the stairs when she and Andrew arrived at the Snowden home. She gave her fiancé an apologetic look and headed into the parlor to play the piano, offering her sister and brother-in-law a polite indication that they were not alone in the house. She played on for several minutes, noticing no change in the volume or intensity of the conversation. Then she noticed a look of worry cross Andrew's face.

"Perhaps I should be going," he whispered to Hannah as he rose.

"I'm sorry," said Hannah, glancing up the stairwell. "I have no idea what the matter is."

"Will you be all right? I hate to think of you sitting all alone here in the parlor."

"I'll be fine," she assured him as she walked him to the door. "I have a good book. It will keep me in quite good company until Myrna arrives."

"How are she and Mr. Baumgardner getting on?"

"Well enough."

"Well enough . . ." muttered Andrew, drawing the words out long and low.

Hannah caught the disappointed tone in his voice. A strain had settled between them over the past few weeks, and it could no longer be ignored. "Is something on your mind, Andrew? You've seemed distracted this evening. More so since we've arrived home."

Andrew sputtered as if he had something ready to burst from his lips, then he stated, "I'm fine, Hannah. I'll just be going."

The relief that washed over her face when he announced his departure nearly broke his heart. Uncertain, he stalled his exit and turned to face his raven-haired fiancée. "Are you happy, Hannah?" he asked nervously.

She halted with her hand on the doorknob, longing for him to leave so she could be alone with her thoughts for a few minutes. Such moments had become so rare recently. Myrna and Beatrice hovered over her constantly, and Dudley's solicitous concern bordered on bothersome. And then there was Andrew's daily fawning since their engagement. It had been difficult enough writing the letter to him that opened the floodgates of his attentions; it was harder yet to feign affection for a man who so fully deserved to be loved and cherished.

Hannah had been honest with Andrew the night he proposed. She told him that though she was very fond of him, she did not love him. She was surprised at how sedately he had received her admission. He simply asked if she thought she could find someone to marry that she could love more, to which she had replied, "No." After accepting the fact that she would never marry Jed, she had prepared to marry no one. But then Andrew painted a contented picture of their future life, accepting that his primary asset was her mother's approval. Hannah accepted his proposal, seeing their union as more a merger of minds than a uniting of hearts. She had thrown the best of herself into the relationship, hoping that if she honored the union, God would bless it and soften her heart. Instead, she had found so much more. Her own happiness grew from the grateful way he received each kindness she showed him.

Still, one of the hardest things for Hannah was the way her happiness was constantly being scrutinized by everyone, as if she were some sort of barometer of joy upon which all others' happiness depended. Now, it was being assessed yet again.

"What cause would I have not to be happy, Andrew?" she answered his earlier query with her own question.

He turned his head to the wall in frustration before meeting her unsure gaze, then spoke softly. "I simply want the very best for you, Hannah. I hope you know that."

"Why do you persist in interrogating me on this?" she whispered as she headed outside.

Andrew stopped her near the door. "Have you noticed that whenever I ask you if you are happy, you always respond with a question, as if you are avoiding the topic altogether?"

Hannah sighed loudly and gazed at him, pausing to sweeten her words with kindness. "It is because I've never known much of happiness, Andrew, but right now I am as happy as I have ever been. My relationship with my parents is as sweet as I have ever known, I have the daily association with my sisters and Dudley, and no man could be more attentive than you. I am trying to be deserving of the sacrifices you make in my behalf. So yes, Andrew, I am happy."

He smiled, though his eyes still reflected melancholy. "I know you have not seen much of what a happy marriage can be, but I have, Hannah. My parents are as in love today as ever. I don't think they ever settled for 'getting along well enough,' and neither should we." He glanced up at Dudley and Beatrice's window. "Even happily married people have difficulties, but if they have invested the best of themselves in that union every day, they will have a firm foundation that trouble and difficulty cannot rend."

"I'm doing my very best, Andrew," Hannah said through shining eyes.

He pressed his fingers to her lips. "I am not asking more *from* you Hannah. I want to give more *to* you . . . to help rebuild the security you lost these last months. I realize we do not share the same association you once enjoyed with Jed, and I'm not attempting to replace him. I only want you to know that I would like to be a friend to you as well as being your husband. I don't want to rush you. I know such friendship develops over time. I also know that writing one's thoughts can sometimes open a more intimate conduit than speech. Perhaps we too could allow fondness to grow between us if we wrote more and visited less."

Hannah was surprised by her feelings. When Andrew first mentioned Jed's name, she felt as if an icicle had been plunged into her chest, chilling her already numbed heart even further. As he hinted at withdrawing, a new fear gripped her. "Something's wrong."

"Nothing bad. Changes are on the horizon, and I may not be able to see you so frequently. I think the change might be a blessing in disguise."

He smiled but Hannah was not convinced. "You are being reassigned, aren't you? Oh, Andrew. Where are they sending you?"

For the first time he felt wanted by her. "I am not being relocated," he explained, pulling her close. "Changes are occurring, and my leave may not be as liberal as Dudley has allowed."

Hannah's face went ashen. "Dudley's being reassigned! Oh, Andrew. That's it, isn't it?" Andrew's silence confirmed her words. "But you're not leaving?"

With closed eyes, Andrew kissed her forehead, quietly thanking God for her concern. "I promise you, I will still be near, watching and worrying over you every day I am not here."

"And we'll write?"

"Yes. Every day. I want to know everything . . . your dreams and plans and the silly trivia we forget to share when we're near. I want you to share your fears with me as well. Let your heart guide your pen and together we will build a foundation that can withstand any adversity."

Hannah wished she could tell him her dreams, the recent ones that frightened her so and left her more confused every day. His sincere request to know the deeper things of her heart wrapped her in security, and Hannah willingly allowed the swell of emotion to carry her away. She tilted her head back, offering her lips to him. She felt the warm softness of Andrew's mouth gingerly touch her own.

As quickly as their lips met, Andrew willed himself to withdraw them. "Search you heart and perhaps you will find just a portion of the longing I felt in that moment." He wrapped his arms around her, whispering her name in her ear. "I love you, Hannah." It was uttered as softly as a breeze across a tender leaf. He had not expected any gesture in return. It was enough to simply say it with her arms clinging to him. As he began to release her, he felt her arms tighten around him, clutching him to her. Then the utterance was breathed into his ear that was as renewing to him as holy writ.

"I'll miss you, Andrew."

It is a beginning, he thought happily and closed his eyes.

* * *

Hannah spent two hours staring idly at the flickering images cast on the pages by the oil lamp. Her mind replayed her conversation with Andrew, and she found herself truly longing for him. A few times she turned her attention to the sounds coming from Beatrice and Dudley's room, the voices arguing a while longer before Beatrice began to cry softly. Myrna arrived home from the theater with Mr. Baumgardner and quickly dismissed him when she became aware of the tension in the house. Hannah offered no insight into the reason for the couple's drama, and soon the voices completely died out and the younger sisters headed upstairs to sleep.

Hannah turned down the crisp sheets on her bed, the fresh scent bringing a certain comfort that rarely accompanied her sleep, at least not since the nightmares had begun—the haunting dreams that left her frenzied and drenched in sweat, crying out in fear. Twice Dudley had rushed in, once with gun in hand, prepared to defend her against whatever assailant provoked her screams. Despite the obvious reality of her fear, it was soon apparent that the torment came from within, leaving her defenseless. She had tried to dismiss the dreams as the manifestations of an anxiety-riddled mind, but as they continued to haunt her night after night with increasing ferocity, she began paying closer attention to them, attempting to recollect the images when she awakened. In the beginning she would wake with only a repeated cracking sound ricocheting through the dark abyss of her memory. Then, more recently, she began to recollect what it was that prompted her panic. *Utter blackness!*

The recollection made Hannah's knees weaken. Feeling vulnerable—powerless—she dropped beside her bed, clutching her coverlet in one hand and reaching for her Bible on the bedside table with the other hand. She thumbed to the fourteenth chapter of John, verse eighteen, a scripture she had found days ago that had brought her immeasurable comfort: "I will not leave you comfortless: I will come to you."

Over and over she repeated the words in her mind until the promise felt personal to her. Nevertheless, just as she would begin to feel a measure of peace wash over her, she would be swept away by another agony. Jed was lost to her. Dudley, her protector, was leaving.

And now Andrew was forced to withdraw. Myrna was consumed by her own affairs, and Beatrice, poor Beatrice, had burdens enough without Hannah adding her own to her sister's load. She had only her faith in God to carry her.

Hannah pressed her face into the coverlet, rocking back and forth as tears began to well. She cried out to God, begging Him to make it known to her if her prayers were reaching heaven. Once again, she again considered a question that repeatedly haunted her. *Has the restitution of all things begun?* She raised her head to the ceiling and cried aloud, "Please, Lord . . . show me."

For nearly an hour, she wrestled her fears there, kneeling across her bed. She used her last bit of energy to drag her body onto the mattress before exhaustion overtook her. Her sleep was peaceful for a time, with dreams sweetened by the promise of comfort she had gleaned from the Apostle John. Then, somewhere in her subconscious mind, she heard it again, the cracking sound. Her pulse began to race in anticipation of what was to come. Soon the thick, choking blackness crept toward her, consuming the light bit by bit and burying her beneath it until she was isolated and alone. Her breathing became rapid as she struggled against the dense murkiness surrounding her. Then a new component entered the night terror. Far away, shouts of frenzied voices, some filled with rage, some with fear, echoed in the perimeter of her mind.

Despite her attempts to break through the exhausted haze that bound her, holding her prisoner to the images, she could not. She felt the panic rise in her throat again as she prepared to scream. Suddenly, a personage appeared in her dream. Although Hannah couldn't identify the male form, she somehow knew he brought peace and safety. His arms were outstretched, reaching for her. She heard him calling to her, soothing her. She tried to isolate his voice from the others in the cacophony as she struggled to make her way toward him, to see his face and to have his arms envelop her. But just as she drew near, a noise awakened her and the image was gone.

She clamped her eyes shut, trying to summon the face and voice back, but her efforts availed her nothing. A sound in the hallway drew her back to consciousness and she nearly cried in frustration. Thumping sounds receded down the stairs and into the street. Then she heard Beatrice's mournful weeping and a light tapping on her door. Throwing her summer wrapper around her, she turned the bolt on the door. Before her stood a red-eyed, completely bedraggled Beatrice.

"Did I awaken you?" Beatrice asked between shudders.

"No, no," responded Hannah as she pulled Beatrice into her arms and drew her into the room. "Poor dear. Why are you up so early? It's barely past dawn."

"Dudley's gone," Beatrice said in disbelief. "He's been reassigned. He's known about it for weeks but he didn't tell me until last evening . . . and now he's gone."

"Where have they sent him?" Hannah asked, brushing her black hair from her eyes.

"Detroit. There's trouble brewing with the British along the Canadian border, and William Eustis, the secretary of war, ordered more troops there." Beatrice's final confession broke her resolve and the tears began again. "Dudley volunteered to go."

"He volunteered?" Andrew had not disclosed that information to Hannah.

"He made excuses for his decision. He said they needed seasoned officers and he felt it was his duty to offer. But he volunteered weeks ago when we were having some . . . difficulties." She blew her nose and wiped her eyes. "He was so tender and caring toward me last evening. I truly believe if he had the power to change his decision he would have."

"I'm sure you're right," offered Hannah. "How long is his assignment?"

"That's the reason he postponed telling me. If the president signs the declaration of war, he could be gone for months . . . perhaps even years, with only occasional visits home."

The reality of military life brought Hannah up short.

Beatrice stared blankly at the wall. "When he proposed to me, he told me he would soon resign his commission. We talked of so many possibilities, from owning a small shop like his parents once did to buying a small farm. We still hoped to be blessed with a child before we grew too old, but now we will barely see one another."

Hannah wrapped her arms around her sister again, feeling unequipped to offer any reply.

"I'm so grateful we had last night," Beatrice cried as Hannah tightened her embrace. "I thought he didn't love me anymore. At least I know he still does. At least I have that."

Hannah stared at her in shock. "All couples have disagreements, Beatrice, but certainly there was nothing grievous enough between you to make you think he no longer cared."

The woman couldn't face her sister. "There was, Hannah. May God forgive me, there was. I committed no moral indiscretion, but there are other ways a spouse can undermine trust in a union, and I only hope Dudley will one day see me as righteously he once did."

"He's a good, Christian man, Beatrice. He understands forgiveness. Surely no one who understands the mission of Christ as Dudley does could withhold forgiveness from another."

Beatrice smiled sweetly at her sister. "You understand forgiveness, don't you, Hannah?"

Hannah smiled back, brushing an errant strand of dark hair from her sister's face. "Probably not as fully as I should, but I think I understand it enough to know that you of all people should deserve clemency for an error."

"Why do you say that?"

"Because I know your heart. You are not wicked or mean spirited. It's not your nature. I believe God takes those things into account."

"You truly love me, don't you?" Tears began to fall down Beatrice's face.

Hannah smiled playfully as she dabbed at her sister's tears. "Silly girl. Of course I do."

"I don't deserve it, Hannah. I'm not as good as you believe." She looked carefully upon her sister's face and frowned. "You look exhausted. You didn't sleep well either, did you?"

Hannah stared at her hands and shrugged.

"The nightmare?"

Hannah's head dipped and she nodded silently as her sister's hand reached for hers.

"Was it the same?"

"Nearly. But this time I saw a man coming toward me through the stifling darkness. I couldn't make out his face, but something in his bearing seemed familiar and it calmed me."

"Hannah, you've been tormented by this horrid dream now for several months. Dudley thinks you should speak to someone, the reverend perhaps."

Hannah clenched her sister's arms, causing Beatrice to wince in pain. "You have to promise me that you won't say a word to anyone else about this, Beatrice. Please, promise me!"

Beatrice carefully pried her sister's fingers from her arms. "What has you so worked up, child?"

"Please just promise me you won't speak to any ministers about my nightmares. Please!"

"What fear binds you so?"

Hannah's eyes bored into her sister's. "Beatrice, do you think God would speak to me in my dreams? I mean, do you think He would use them to answer my prayers or send me a warning?"

A smile broke across Beatrice's face. "Is that what this is about?" she laughed softly. "No, Hannah, I don't think God is sending you messages in your dreams." She raised her hand to brush along her sister's disheveled hair. Her voice was filled with good-natured humor intended to comfort her sister. It was clear, though, that Hannah was anything but comforted.

"God spoke to Samuel in a dream, and what of Joseph of Egypt?" Hannah continued. "God spoke to him in dreams and gave him a gift to interpret the dreams of others to save nations." Her words spilled out with rapid frenzy. "Couldn't He communicate with us . . . warn us as He did His children in ancient days?" Hannah's head slumped against her own chest.

"What is it, darling?" Beatrice asked as she scooted closer, trying to calm the young woman. "Why are you so set on having God be the author of your dreams?" Beatrice lifted her sister's chin with one finger as Hannah's tears fell from her dark lashes. Her eyes showed anguish, and as she spoke, the tremble in her voice chilled Beatrice to the bone.

"Because if God is not sending these images to me, I may be a damned soul."

Beatrice's mouth fell open.

"They are frightening images, Beatrice. The reverend once accused me of being a rebellious soul. Myrna thought I was blasphemous for even considering some new ideas lately. What if they're right? If God is not using these dreams to warn me, then what if I am possessed of a devil like those poor tortured souls in the Bible?"

Beatrice drew her close. "Hannah, you are the least devilish person I know."

Hannah looked into her sister's eyes for several long, silent seconds, dreading the fear she saw growing there. "Then the only other alternative offers me no more comfort." She began to cry softly.

"What, Hannah? What is it?" her sister asked with alarm.

Hannah looked into her sister's troubled face. "What if I am becoming mad? What if these dreams are the prelude to the same sickness plaguing Mother?"

A knot formed in Beatrice's stomach at the mention of the very worry Dudley had expressed the previous night. She drew Hannah even closer. "No, no," she argued as she shuddered with fear. "You're not going mad, Hannah!" It was more an order than an observation. "Don't even say such things. It's not that at all. It can't be. Not to you, my angel. Not to you."

Hannah caught Beatrice wiping away her own tears. She looked into her sister's dread-filled face and pressed her further. "Remember how Mother had those horrid imaginations that Selma was somehow stealing her ability to love from her? If it's not a warning from God, what else can it be but the tormenting of madness . . . or the devil?"

Beatrice scrambled to find a possible explanation that would soothe her sister's fears as well as her own worries. "Let's just think logically about it. Heaven knows, dearest, we have both been consumed by troubles aplenty and seeking solace. Perhaps your mind is simply jumbling up all your worries and projecting them into your dreams. The darkness may just be your mind's way of dealing with all the upheaval."

"And the cracking sounds and the voices?" asked Hannah hopefully.

Beatrice's face contorted as she tried to make sense of these elements. "I don't know, Hannah." Her sharp voice belied her worry. "This whole thing could be some expression of your concern for Andrew. Maybe you love him and worry about him more than you realize."

"Do you think so?" Hannah wondered, her eyes pleading.

"I feel sure that is it," Beatrice replied, trying as hard to convince herself as Hannah.

"Of course, you're right," Hannah conceded weakly. "I'm making far too much out of a simple nightmare. That's all, right? Of course . . . Forgive me? I'm such a fool at times."

"We are about at our limits." Beatrice closed her eyes and kissed the top of Hannah's head.

"Thank you for being so understanding, Beatrice," Hannah said somberly. "My time with you has been among the happiest of my life. And look at what you have done for Myrna! Her grin is nearly a permanent fixture. Whenever Mr. Baumgardner is around she is either giggling incessantly or smiling like a jack-o-lantern."

"Now that does worry me. It is almost too much, I'd say. No one is that happy and that completely entertained at all times. It's as if no man had ever tied a cravat or told a joke before. At this rate she will smile her lips off before the wedding and he'll be unable to kiss the bride!"

Hannah covered her mouth to stifle her laughter and Beatrice joined in, pleased for the opportunity to share a moment's release. As the mood settled into a more contemplative one, Beatrice broached the topic she had hinted at earlier.

"What of Andrew? Do you truly care for him? Have we pressed him upon you, Hannah?"

Hannah paused before answering. "I wouldn't have chosen him myself, but he is a fine man."

"And Jed Pearson?" Beatrice inquired carefully.

An undeniable look of anguish deadened Hannah's eyes momentarily before she buried it again. "I have faced the truth that Jed loves someone else, and though a part of me will always love him, misplaced passions are as wasted as diamonds in the sea. Andrew knows I withhold a piece of myself from him that I have already given to another, and yet he still wants me. I doubt I could do better than such a man."

Beatrice quickly changed the topic. "So have you two set a date for your wedding?"

Hannah stared at her hands. "No. His assignments are also altered by events in Washington City, and he will not be as free to call any longer. We're going to write and allow things to proceed gently. We are in no rush to the altar."

"Not like Myrna and Mr. Baumgardner?"

Hannah rolled her eyes playfully. "I believe the two of them have agreed on a date, and I believe it will be soon. They were engaged in quite a bit of whispering and giggling last evening when he dropped her off."

"Giggling? How completely out of character for them!" Beatrice joked sardonically, hoping as she did so that she would one day be able to say the same of Hannah.

CHAPTER 25

On the Road to Washington City
Early June 1812

The thundering of his horse's hooves on the road occupied Captain Snowden's thoughts for a time. Soon, however, the cadence became so rhythmic that his troubled mind drifted back to the previous evening and the dreadful timing of the news of his reassignment. He had known for weeks that his hasty offer to take a battle assignment had been accepted, and though his regret was almost immediate after tendering his papers, he was, nonetheless, being sent north.

Skirmishes along the Canadian border were becoming more frequent as the British sold arms to Indians and thus increased their influence over hostile local tribes. Dudley knew it was ludicrous to hope to defeat the British armada on the seas, and nearly as foolish to believe that the meager and underequipped American ground forces could withstand the British army. But voices in the government, namely those two war hawks, Henry Clay and John Calhoun, had a plan to land a critical blow to the British economy: they'd set their eyes on stopping the redcoats in Canada. Desiring more than merely to secure the borders, their fiery rhetoric inspired other representatives to call for the removal of Britain from the whole of North America. Now, most of Washington City was chanting the battle cry. Denying Britain trade with a valuable colony—when coupled with the trade calamities the French had dealt them—might break the behemoth's back, the war hawks felt. But that would require an invasion across the border, and Dudley knew that meant a bloody conflict from which many soldiers would not return.

Therein lay Dudley's anguish. He was a soldier, trained to lay down his life in defense of his country. As such, he was not afraid to perform his duty. Marriage, though, had changed something in him. He could no longer look at his assignment through merely strategic eyes. Once his foolish anger had abated, he knew he must factor Beatrice's suffering in the cost of his deployment. Although he would still do his duty, he knew he owed her a bit more of himself than he had given her lately. He had withheld his affections from her since discovering her treachery, and only recently had he been able to admit that his withdrawal had been more about his own guilt and complicity than about hers. He could have mended the deceit—told Hannah and Jed the truth himself—but he hadn't. And why hadn't he? Because, like Beatrice, he wanted a particular outcome for the people he loved. Instead of acknowledging his own flawed reasoning, he had thrown his own guilt onto his wife's back and allowed her to carry the bulk of it.

After the anguished meeting with Jed, Dudley began to own up to his personal involvement in the deceit, and he slowly began doling out kindness to Beatrice, which she had received with grateful penitence. He winced at the memories, knowing he had never completely absolved her. When he had made some sweeping comment about his "part" in the affair, Beatrice had quickly rushed in, bathing him in absolution. He now knew that he had never confessed sufficiently to set her free of her own guilt, especially if he were to pass away on the battlefield. At that moment, he vowed to spend the rest of his days begging God's forgiveness and dedicating himself to righting the wrong committed against his wife.

Dudley thought about their final hours spent with each other, nestled together in the marital bliss he had foolishly denied both of them for so many months. Things could have been so different. They could have been expecting a child by now, or he could have at least left his wife knowing she was cherished, with the assurance that her love was his sustaining force during this campaign. Instead, he had prattled on about deposits and securities, should he not return, with only a few tender moments left to soothe the ache in her loyal heart. He smiled as he formulated a plan, deciding to send her a letter and a gift from Washington City, and from each stop along the way, so that with the receipt of each token, she might more fully realize the depth of his love for her.

Heading into the city, Dudley searched for the office of the secretary of war. The capital had not changed dramatically since he had visited some three years earlier for the inauguration of President James Madison. Though L'Enfant's sprawling, wheel-shaped city was still sparsely populated, its more than eight thousand residents now exceeded the population of its rival, Georgetown. With the entrance of the president's fashionable wife, Dolly Madison, some changes were underway. Her sorrow over leaving beautiful Philadelphia with its cultural and social opportunities had been highly advertised; in characteristic form, however, she had used her irrepressible charm and resplendent style to begin developing a vision of Washington City's potential. Already her efforts were beginning to leave their mark on the nation's capital.

Dudley smiled at the constant caravan of work crews mending the beautiful but structurally flawed President's House. Though architect Benjamin Latrobe was primarily involved in the construction of the elaborate Capitol building, he made his opinions known regarding the problematic leaking roof and gutters of the President's House. Still, Dudley had no doubt the vivacious and adored Dolly Madison would make it a place of beauty and honor, inside and out, before her husband's service ended.

A high stone wall now encompassed the mansion, while brick buildings flanked it east and west. To the east lay the building hosting the treasury secretary and his staff; on the west lay the offices of the navy, war, and state departments. Dudley was quickly dispatched to a room down the hall, where he spent five terse minutes with an aide to Secretary Eustis, whose office was filled with tense, scrambling men shuffling maps and papers from room to room. Hearing whispers of a war vote in the halls, Dudley knew the hawks were pressing hard for the president to sign the declaration of war. He picked up his orders and waited until he was outside the office and away from the confusion to read them. Suddenly the purpose of his strange, faraway assignment was clear: he was serving as much as a courier bearing bad news as he was a warrior. Dudley rubbed an anxious hand across his tight brow and read on. He was to take the Patowmack Canal from

Georgetown to Cumberland and then travel on to Ohio, where he would meet up with a garrison of Ohio militia forces being deployed to Detroit.

At the realization that a battle seemed imminent, his muscles twitched like an animal preparing for flight. His thoughts turned to Beatrice once again, prompting him to head down Pennsylvania Avenue to a curio shop, where he purchased pearls for her. He moved to a bench under an elm tree and pondered carefully before writing her a brief note.

Dear Beatrice,

Each mile that passes reminds me more fully of what a fool I have been. I love you, darling. Please forgive a thoughtless old soldier for squandering our precious time together. Be assured that you are ever on my mind, and though I don't deserve it, it would bring me immense comfort to have you tuck me into your kind thoughts as well. Until we are together again . . .

Dudley

He posted the parcel and sought to ease his melancholy in the company of an old friend, heading toward Georgetown to an ivy-covered pub convenient to the canal. He peered into the dim light inside, hoping to see the blue-eyed face of his father's friend. His eyes found their mark, and his face broke into a wide grin. But once Dudley entered the establishment, the visage that caught and held his attention was not that of Light-Horse Harry Lee, his father's old Revolutionary chum, but that of another man seated against the far wall, a man from his more recent past—Jed Pearson.

Light-Horse Harry rose to greet the grown child of his old war comrade. Dudley returned his enthusiastic embrace and quickly exchanged greetings and news, though his eyes constantly darted back to gaze at Pearson, who suddenly showed a spark of interest. Harry led his friend to a small table and ordered a round of drinks, while Dudley excused himself for a moment and slowly made his way to where Jed sat.

"Hello, Mr. Pearson," he began nervously. "I was surprised to see you sitting here."

Jed eyed him as if he were nothing more than a gnat.

"Few people even know it's tucked in here," Dudley stammered uncomfortably.

Jed took a long draw on his ale. "Must I clear my travel plans through you Snowdens?"

His voice was acrid and bitter, with a sad tone that tore at Dudley's heart, and the captain shook his head apologetically. "Please forgive me, Mr. Pearson."

As he turned to leave, Jed stood abruptly and called after him. "No, Captain Snowden. Please . . . forgive me." His voice was thick with pain and regret. "I have no cause to treat you this way. Your intentions have been honorable."

Dudley showed a hint of an understanding smile and continued his withdrawal.

"Captain Snowden?" Jed called out again. "May I ask one favor of you?"

Dudley turned, grateful for the exchange. "Anything. But first I need to clarify something. I cannot leave this thing as it is between us. Right or wrong, Beatrice is no more guilty than I, and however you feel about the way we have violated your life, you must know . . . I had as much opportunity to remedy it as she, and therefore I deserve your equal scorn."

Jed's faced became taut and grim, but Dudley continued.

"One final point, Mr. Pearson. I know you went to see Lieutenant Robertson. He told me of your agreement. He said you handled the situation with the utmost honor. I simply wanted to tell you, man to man, that Hannah will have done equally well with whichever man wins her hand."

Jed searched Dudley Snowden's face, trying to determine the sincerity of the comment. "My motives were not completely unselfish, Captain. I bargained for a year of delay so Hannah can come to know her own mind, and so we can each test the character of the lieutenant. But I do not anticipate losing Hannah. Be assured—I will win her parents' approval. In fact, prior to coming to Georgetown, I was in Baltimore scouring courthouse records and visiting relatives to disprove

Susannah Stansbury's crazed claims regarding my grandfather. I've also been checking up on your candidate, the lieutenant, to determine for myself what manner of man he is. But the truth is, I have found nothing and no one able or willing to either prove or disprove Mrs. Stansbury's claims . . . and so far, your lieutenant has proved to be what you have described him to be. Nonetheless, right is right, and I am determined in my quest to claim what Providence intended for Hannah and I to have, though the next few months may alter all our lives in ways we cannot foresee anyway."

"Never were truer words spoken," Dudley concurred quietly, then paused. "And the favor?"

Jed nodded, remembering his request. "It is on this very topic. That gentleman you greeted . . . is he the famous general known as Light-Horse Harry?"

"He is."

"Would you introduce me to him?"

Dudley looked curiously at the young man.

"He and my grandfather served together in the Revolution. I'd like to hear his appraisal of our chances if this conflict turns to war. I've heard he has unique opinions on the subject."

Dudley pursed his lips and responded, "Come. I'd be glad to make the introductions."

The three men spent an hour as Henry—or Harry Lee, as he was known during the war—recounted war stories involving the ancestors of the two younger men. After the laughter had settled down, Harry's mood grew quiet and contemplative. "I was a young buck when I served by your father and grandfather, but now I am as old as your father was when I served by him, Captain Snowden." He looked from Dudley to Jed. "Are either of you men fathers?" When they shook their heads, he explained his question. "Well, I am. My youngest son is only five and a half . . . we call him Robert E." He leaned back in his chair and sighed. "I worry about the world we will leave to children like my little son if we engage in a war with Great Britain right now. I don't believe we can win it, gentlemen. I don't like to murmur against my leaders, but it's my honest opinion that we will meet with defeat if we attempt to fight the British at this time. They will not make the same mistakes that cost them the Revolution. They have adapted their tactics to our terrain and conditions, and as unequaled as they are on the sea, the alliances they are developing with the Indians could make them indomitable on the land as well. In either case, it will surely not be a gentlemen's contest."

Jed's attentions shifted between Dudley's lack of response and Harry's warning. "Have you made these opinions known to the government?" he asked.

The Princeton-educated soldier smiled sadly, his bravado dimmed by the comment. He suddenly looked considerably older than his fifty-six years. "I've tried. They will not listen." He shot a knowing glance at his military friend, who hailed the waitress for his bill.

Jed knew Lee was a battle-tested, decorated hero who had not only served as Virginia's governor for three terms, but who had also served in the Continental Congress. His book, *Memoirs of the War in the Southern Department of the United States,* was a highly regarded account on battle strategy. "Surely they will listen to you. I don't understand."

Dudley touched Jed's shoulder to change the direction of the conversation, but Harry smiled his thanks and waved his friend off as he turned to face the wide-eyed young man beside him. "I appreciate your patriotism, Mr. Pearson, but I'm afraid I have already exhausted my influence in Washington. You see, I had a few grand plans that failed, and I ended up in debtors' prison a year after my little Robert was born. The same fate befell my good friend Robert Morris. I am, in a few blunt words, an embarrassment to some, and simply unwise to others. On the matter of informing the powers in Washington City of the Brits' strengths, well, I have a dear friend, whose son, Alexander Hanson, is a newspaper publisher. He is a vocal member of the antiwar Federalist Party. This group has attempted to make their case in the public forum, but they fear for their lives. The patriotic sentiment in the nation runs too high and wild to listen to opposing views. To be truthful? I'm not even sure war can be avoided any longer. The British will not back down, and we are certainly not of a mind to tolerate their incursions. My only wish is that we had more time to prepare, but I've seen the troops moving. Something is already in the works."

Dudley's quietness suddenly caught Jed's and Harry's attention. "You know all too well of what I speak, don't you old friend?" Harry asked.

The captain checked his pocket watch but remained composed and unforthcoming. "I hate to leave good company, but the hour of my departure is at hand. I've a boat to catch."

"You're taking the Patowmack up to Cumberland?" Harry questioned.

Dudley paused before nodding.

"And then northwest to the Canadian border, I'd wager. God speed, friend."

Harry and Dudley shared a long, emotional embrace. Volumes were exchanged in the parting glance between the two warriors who each knew the price of valor. Harry's eyes remained fixed on those of his military brother, but his words were directed to Jed. "He's a man caught between vows. In honoring the one, he neglects the other. 'Tis a hard road a soldier must walk, between love and honor. I know it well, and it breaks my heart to see another man trod it."

Dudley turned to Jed. "It is as you said: the die is already cast. May God bless us all."

He shook Jed's hand before turning and heading out the door. Harry and Jed remained standing for several seconds as they watched him disappear into the crowds on the busy street. They sat, and an eerie sense of quiet overtook them as the precarious reality of the future sank in. Harry took a long draw on his ale, looked at Jed, and spoke, his voice low and heavy. "So what brought you to Washington City, Mr. Pearson, business, politics, or pleasure?"

Jed shook his head to bring Harry's question more clearly to his mind. "Business. I own a plantation on the Patuxent, and I brought some of our horses to Georgetown to sell."

"Ahh!" commented Harry. "The races!" Then he looked puzzled. "I thought the fertile fields along the Patuxent were famous for tobacco."

"They are. Tobacco is our primary crop, but we're attempting to diversify."

"What is such a man doing here, peddling horses during a plantation's busiest season?"

Jed now took refuge in his glass. "I've turned the operation over to my foreman. I have no interest in the farm at present." He quickly drew from his glass again.

Harry stared long and hard at his companion. "Loneliness is like a mole on your back. You can't see it, but it follows you wherever you go."

Jed looked at the man curiously. "Did Dudley . . . ?"

"No . . . no. He's not one to prattle," Harry answered quickly. He pointed to Jed's eyes. "It's obvious enough. I've carried that burden myself, so I know its mocking look well."

Jed carefully turned the conversation. "Tell me more about this coming firestorm we're facing. I plan to join the Maryland militia if war is declared."

Harry's head shot up as an idea formulated in his mind. "You're in no hurry?"

"None at all."

"Then stay with me for a few days. I'll give you a first-rate tour of our capital while she is still ours. Then follow me back to Virginia, to Alexandria, for a few days. I'll show you some of the most beautiful horse farms in the world. Perhaps you can do some business as well."

Jed accepted the offer, and the days getting to know the man and his country passed pleasantly enough, though few of Harry's old comrades involved in the new government would accept his invitations to dine with the pair. Harry and Jed laughed over old stories, growing quiet and nervous, however, when the topics of war or the discussions in the Congress were broached. When Jed worked the name of his friend Timothy Shepard into the conversations, he discovered that the engaging lawyer had already garnered the respect of many in the capital's tightly-knit circle. In fact, Jed soon discovered that his friend was not only serving as an assistant to Senator Gregg from Pennsylvania, but that his charm and organizational skills had made him a favorite of the First Lady as well, placing him on frequent loan to her while she organized the private presidential papers and acquisitions that had accumulated since the nation's birth.

Jed even managed a quiet evening alone with his old college chum. To his dismay, once they had reminisced and shared personal updates, the conversation became stilted, making it appear as though the tense capital climate had made Timothy just as secretive as the city's politicians.

"Really, Timothy," Jed groused, "all this cloak-and-dagger behavior is infuriating. The news is bandied about in the papers every day. We are just two friends engaging in a discussion of the day's news. What harm is there in that?"

"I am privy to things that are not open to the public forum. If they were to leak out, I could be called up on treason!" he whispered with agitation.

"All right, all right. I suppose a good friend of a government clerk should be just as willing to spot a penny for a paper to get his news as the next man."

Timothy raised his eyebrows and gazed at the table. "Just be careful which paper you are caught reading," he muttered as he lifted his cup to his lips.

"What's that?" Jed inquired curiously.

"Yesterday a man bought a copy of the *Federal Republican and Commercial Gazette,* a notorious, antiwar publication printed in Baltimore. Two men who were headed to enlist in the militia saw him sitting on a bench on New York Avenue reading the paper, and they beat him to a pulp and nearly destroyed the newsstand that sold him the paper."

"I hope they were charged!"

"I'm sure they were. Battery is battery, and despite the inflammatory things that paper writes, the law still upholds freedom of the press. But our citizenry is growing increasingly intolerant of naysayers and predictors of gloom and doom."

"That's Hanson's paper, isn't it?"

Timothy seemed surprised by his friend's information. "Yes. How do you know that?"

"Harry Lee mentioned him." Jed again broached the forbidden topic. "Lee has reservations about our ability to win a war against Britain at this time. He believes we are much more heavily armed with hope and patriotism than with ships and armaments."

Timothy's jaw set tightly and he thumped his fist against the table. "When a nation's back is pressed against the wall, patriotism and hope may be its greatest assets."

"So, you agree with his grim assessment of our military situation?"

Timothy breathed deeply and stared at Jed, then leaned forward to reach for the sugar, as if adding more to his cup. As he did so, he whispered, "Many think William Eustis made a better military surgeon than secretary of war. But our success will depend on our men on the battlefield, and though we may not be as well supplied as we would like, we have other distinguished assets."

"Assets more essential than ships and guns?" Jed queried sarcastically.

"If not more essential, then at least equally fundamental. I willingly place my trust in the Corps of Engineers trained at the Military Academy. They have been strengthening our fortifications and harbor defenses. Some of the best military minds in the world have dedicated themselves to defending this nation. And, let us never forget the spiritual advantage of defending one's own soil. We are fighting to preserve our own land, not to conquer another."

"The Indians could claim that same position, Timothy. In fact, Britain is using our incursion into their tribal lands to whip up their anger against us."

Timothy Shepard closed his eyes and sighed. "It's true. There is one thing General Lee says with which I completely concur. This will not be a gentlemen's contest." He leaned back into his seat heavily. "This struggle may well rip our nation apart. It has already divided us geographically. The merchant-driven Northeast is primarily distressed over maritime concerns. They swing with the Federalist Party and away from war with the British naval power. On the other hand, the South and the Northwest are indignant over the redcoats' arrogance and their arming of the Indians. They hunger for war and side with the Democratic-Republicans." He leaned back and surveyed his friend. "You are both a merchant and a landowner, right in the British crosshairs. With which opinion do your loyalties now lie, Jed?"

"What are you implying, Timothy?" Jed responded abruptly.

"I just want to know if your scorn for Lieutenant Robertson has tainted your opinion against the entire United States military, that's all."

Jed's face tensed in anger before he brought himself under control and became more contrite. "I am able to separate my personal affairs from my political ones. My opinions on war with the British have nothing to do with my affections or my purse. They were forged years ago and remain steadfast. I do not know if we are justified on each point of the cause—I'll leave that to God and the politicians to sort. However, after spending time in Philadelphia and especially after the night we spent in Getty's Tavern in Gettysburg, I became certain of one thing—the principles upon which this nation was founded are divine. Freedom . . ." he paused contemplatively, "is a divine virtue. God has a purpose for this free society. Regardless of whether or not state law requires military service of its men, I am willing to fight and, if necessary, die to maintain that freedom. As long as we are a sovereign nation, we can rise above our greed and baser interests. I fear, though, that without liberty, God will not manifest His purposes here, and we will pay the price for our infidelity to this democracy."

The two men fell silent, finally clear that they were united on these basic principles. "You should write an editorial to that effect. Your name has clout, Jed."

Jed shook his head emphatically. "And what of you, Timothy?" he said, quickly changing the subject. "Will you be joining the militia here in the capital?"

"I cannot. Since I have inherited property in New York, I am excluded from service here. But so many clerks and aides to the Congress are required to enlist in the militia, I may well serve my country best by simply remaining in the city and continuing to perform my duties."

Jed nodded his understanding.

"And what of the Willows? Will you turn the operation over to Markus if you enlist?"

"Markus will likely serve on the sea as a privateer. He is perfect for the post. He knows every tributary in this state and in Virginia like the back of his hand. He's an able seaman as well as a crack-shot. Civilian sailors of his caliber are being called up into the regular navy. We will see what fate has in store for him."

"But the Willows . . . ?"

"I am entrusting its care to Bitty and her father-in-law, Jerome, with Frannie acting as my representative. I have papers being drawn up to secure the futures of all the Willows' workers."

"Freedom papers?"

"In the event of my death, they will all be granted their freedom and a parcel of land."

Timothy chuckled sarcastically. "For so hefty an inheritance, some slaves might be tempted to put a bullet through their master's back."

Jed did not return the humor. "With Hannah lost to me, they and Frannie are all I have in this world, present company excluded.

If my friends consider me of so little value that they would do me in for a parcel of dirt and a piece of paper, what good is my life anyway?"

"And Frannie agrees to these terms?"

"She has done well for herself. She will fight to preserve the Willows against intruders, but she will agree completely to the terms regarding the workers."

"And what if you survive this war and return to find only a burned-out, vacated heap?"

Jed remained quiet as he pushed his seat away from the table. "I only know that for now the place holds no happiness or solace for me. It haunts me, and I want only to be away from it."

"Is that why you are burrowed here in the city, in Harry Lee's company?"

"Most people think we will soon have our answer regarding the war. The papers say President Madison is pressing Congress to come to a rapid decision. If Congress does, he should sign the declaration of war immediately, and I will be a member of the Maryland militia. I therefore think my stay here will be brief."

"A word between friends?" Timothy whispered as he offered his hand to Jed. "It will."

* * *

After a few days in Washington City, Harry Lee turned his horse south and headed for Alexandria with his young Maryland guest in tow. They passed a nearly vacated town in northern Virginia, where Harry swept his hand along the horizon of unkempt streets and said, "This was to be my legacy to my dear first wife, Matilda—a beautiful city, the heart of commerce into the Ohio River Valley. George Washington had a vision of taming the Potomac River so trade could spread throughout the western regions of the country, so the Patowmack Company was formed. This little canal venture opened the door for the Constitutional Convention of 1787."

"It did?" inquired Jed curiously.

"General Washington was truly a visionary man," Harry said admiringly. "He was a general then. He needed the cooperation of both

Maryland and Virginia to make the canal a reality, so he convened a meeting at his home in Mount Vernon. It was so productive that a similar convention was held a few months later to discuss trade. This series of meetings became the framework for the Constitutional Convention."

"And Matildaville?"

"She is a dying city. The Potomac is a treacherous river. Construction and operation costs bankrupted the Patowmack Company. I lost nearly everything, and sadly, so did many of my friends who invested on my word and reputation."

"But the canal is still moving goods east and west. The dream was a good one," Jed protested.

"Yes, the dream was good and the engineering was sound, but the canal loses money every day, every trip. Rumors circulate about someday digging a canal on the Maryland side of the river. I hope it happens. I would like to see George Washington's vision realized."

"You've lived an amazing life in fifty-six years," Jed marveled.

Harry smiled modestly. "I was once a cocky spirit, but time has taught me humility. I have known and lost much in this life . . . money, love, power, influence. Love is the most priceless of them all." Harry suddenly seemed unable to get home quickly enough, so they mounted their horses and headed south.

They pushed on hard for Alexandria and Harry's home, where his wife Ann and his many children awaited, including his precious young Robert E. Lee. They stopped along the way only to make a few brief introductions for Jed with some plantation owners who specialized in fine horses. When they arrived at their destination, Jed found Harry's Alexandria home comfortable and snug. Stepping from room to room felt like touring a historical museum filled with memorabilia from heroes of the Revolution. Jed marveled at the hefty role Light-Horse Harry had played in the war, and then shuddered at the thought that this great man had been cast aside when military and financial troubles plagued him, as had Robert Morris of Philadelphia. Considering the transitory nature of fame and fortune, Jed agreed with his friend's philosophical conclusion that of all the treasures of life, love was the most important.

That notion brought him little comfort as he considered his current loveless situation. Nevertheless, seeing how deeply Harry had loved Matilda, and how, despite great misfortune, he had struggled to rebuild a new life with a new love—Ann—it seemed cowardly to Jed to turn tail and run from life.

From the comfort of Harry's Alexandria home, Jed spent the next few days touring several grand plantations in northern Virginia. Their dependence on and treatment of their slaves was as much a subject of his interest as were their exquisite horses. Jed felt a giddy sense of happiness in knowing he was digging himself and his people out from under the burden of that lifestyle. He bought several beautiful mares and a fine Arabian stallion from a plantation that had once prided itself on its deep ties to British royalty, but which now proudly flew an American banner from its upstairs balcony. Change was in the air everywhere. Jed was ready for it, and Harry sensed it.

With his newly purchased prized horses in tow, Jed prepared to head back to the Willows. When Harry offered his new young friend a parting handshake, his head was cocked as if in thought, and his face bore a quizzical expression. "I'd like you to join me and my friends for a game of whist sometime. My friends make an impressive assembly. I'll send word to you."

Jed nodded politely and gave a parting wave as he bid adieu to his host and headed for the Patuxent and home. Two days later, on the evening of Thursday, June 18, Jed arrived at the Willows. He had barely stabled the horses when the news arrived by horseback courier declaring that President Madison had signed the declaration of war. In the distance Jed could hear the sound of gunfire as angry residents of the Patuxent region, long wearied by Britain's harassment and incursions, expressed their willingness to go to battle.

It was not a universal sentiment. By Sunday morning, a firestorm had erupted over the antigovernment rhetoric littering Alexander Hanson's editorial in his paper. The already intolerant majority had now reached its boiling point as the lawyer-turned-politician, now turned editor, attempted to use his newspaper to pummel the government. Nearly rabid with his cause, the self-appointed political watchman stood alone among his journalistic peers, slandering the war and those who pressed for it, placing him squarely in the crosshairs of the erupting fury until their wrath could no longer be contained.

On Monday, June 22, Jed soon learned, Hanson's enemies headed to the Baltimore office of his *Federal Republican,* breaking into the building and not only destroying the presses, but venting their anger in such animosity that they literally destroyed the building. Luckily, Hanson, a Georgetown resident, was away at the time, and his co-editor had slipped out before the melee erupted. But the rioters' delirium had not yet been satisfied. After destroying Hanson's building, the violence spilled into the streets.

While most of Baltimore accepted the incident as Hanson's traitorous due, Jed Pearson received the news with a sickened heart. He had never met the man, and he did not agree with his vehement one-sidedness. Despite that, he felt he was watching the unraveling of the very fibers of freedom that the young nation was supposedly engaging in war to protect. He worried about the state of mind in Baltimore, and especially about the safety of a certain young resident by the name of Hannah Stansbury.

CHAPTER 26

Heading North, Ohio Territory
Mid-June 1812

Dudley Snowden posted notes and gifts to his wife nearly every day until he hit territory too wild and unsettled for reliable postal service. Baltimore seemed suffocating to him as he passed through stretches of Ohio's virgin timberland. It was only the thought of Beatrice that brought the busy, burdensome city to mind. Perhaps it was the complicated interweaving of their lives with her complex family's that tainted the thought of continuing on there, or perhaps it was the ashes of their sins that made him long for a fresh start. In either case, a fresh start is what he felt they needed to find happiness together again.

As he passed long stretches of green, dotted only with an occasional rustic homestead, Dudley's mind was filled with possibilities. It was far too untamed for Beatrice's sensitivities, but there was something invigorating about the thought of building something . . . together. He had laid down seventeen hundred dollars for their town house in the city. It was already fully furnished when he asked for Beatrice's hand, leaving her little to do except for purchasing a knickknack here and there. She had been happy simply to be married and independent from her family. Now Dudley felt she would also benefit from building her own nest, particularly if children came along.

He smiled at the prospect of fatherhood, a thought that had frightened him once. It was the fear of a man who had looked himself squarely in the mirror, counted himself plain, and then, believing it unlikely that he would ever be blessed in love, dedicated his lonely heart to the battlefield. He had told himself he was better off alone and unfettered by anyone who might mourn his death than romantically encumbered like the dashing soldiers whose striking appearance won them the hearts of whichever women they chose. Then he had met Beatrice, a woman who likewise thought of herself as plain and unlovable, and together they were a perfect match. After that, life and living became more precious to him than medals and glory.

This would be his last campaign. He had already submitted his letter of resignation from his commission, effective at the end of this assignment. If he survived to do so, all he wanted was to begin anew and again see the look of love and wonder wash over his wife's face at his appearance. It would be such a joy to see the disappearance of the fear and remorse that had come to burden her countenance whenever he'd lately entered a room. He closed his eyes against the pain and focused on the beautiful scenery, allowing the hope of a brighter future to ease the discomfort of the past as he hurried along.

The Ohioans, whose company he had joined, were besieged by one problem after another. On July sixth, midway through the state, word arrived that on July second the American schooner *Cuyahoga* had become the first British conquest of the newly declared war. Loaded with supplies, the schooner was transporting sick soldiers from General Hull's Detroit command. Word of the declaration of war had not yet reached the ship's crew, and as it sailed up the Detroit River past the British garrison of Fort Amherstburg, a small force of native Indians, British soldiers, and British sailors rowed out and took command of the vessel with little resistance. Completely appalled at the development, Dudley left the company of the militia and hurried on alone to deliver his critical message from the Department of War to General Hull, commander of Fort Detroit. He followed the trail that wound along Lake Erie to where it narrowed into the Detroit River and headed north. As he approached the city at daybreak, he saw the pinwheel-shaped Fort Detroit rise from the lake mist—set a short distance from the river and surrounded by a series of streets and houses that likewise appeared shrouded in a damp haze.

Three poorly dressed soldiers standing on the parapet shouted Dudley's approach. A rider came out to check his papers and then escorted him inside the fort's wall. The fort had survived numerous conflicts in its nearly seventy years of service, its shabby appearance serving as a timeline of each battle. Five columns of structures lined the interior of the fortress, providing housing and stores for upwards of two thousand souls, though, from the look of the tattered, mismatched uniforms that hung on the frames of weary men, it appeared the stores were currently quite meager.

Dudley was escorted to the northeast corner of the fort, where the commandant's house was located, and was led into the general's office to await General Hull. A sketch of the commander standing beside President Thomas Jefferson hung on the wall. Dudley was not astonished by the connection. He knew President Jefferson had appointed the Yale-educated Revolutionary hero to be governor over the Michigan Territory in 1805, but he also knew that Hull had stirred up many enemies among the Indians as he attempted to secure land concessions from the First Indian Nations. As a result, Hull had found it necessary to seek protection for the territory, fearing an Indian uprising that could lead to massacres.

Dudley tried to not let Washington City gossip influence his opinion of his new commander. He knew General Hull's appointment to the post of Brigadier General of the Army of the Northwest ran concurrently with his appointment as governor. It was a concession offered to him after he was overlooked for the position of secretary of war. He hoped these posts would give him sufficient leverage to assure cooperation from the government, but Dudley's news from Secretary Eustis would dash those hopes. Aside from the final companies of Ohio militia currently on route, no further assistance of armaments, stores, or ammunition were planned.

"Captain Snowden, welcome to Fort Detroit," offered General Hull amicably as he pulled his blue suspenders over his shoulders, returning the salute offered to him by his newest officer. "Please excuse the lateness of my rising," he apologized as he slid into his blue officer's jacket festooned with gold buttons and white herringbone trim along the breast. "I'm afraid this company is still exhausted from slicing their way through the Michigan forests." He adjusted his spectacles over the bridge of his nose and began to read the documents Dudley handed him.

Dudley stood at attention, watching as the plump-cheeked general's face grew somber. The man rubbed at his pointy nose and hunched his shoulders, making them appear even rounder. "Very well then," he said with a sigh. "So how many men is Ohio sending?"

"A few hundred, sir, but their numbers change daily as the sick drop off and new men join their ranks."

"And how many days behind you are they?"

"It's hard to say, General. A few weeks . . . maybe more. They are a poorly outfitted group, traveling on foot and hunting for food as they travel. Their progress is unsteady."

The general nodded his understanding as he removed his glasses and rubbed his fingers deep into his eyes. "I understand. Well, the corporal will show you to the officers' quarters."

Dudley was escorted out in a perfunctory manner. The corporal led him to the officers' quarters, located in a drab log-and-frame building boasting few accoutrements above the general soldiers' quarters. The officers' beds were lined up singly along each wall, with wash-stands and trunks assigned to each "compartment." Only two beds of the thirty or so in the room were vacant. Dudley opted for the one near a seemingly amiable man in his mid-forties. He was sitting up, partially dressed in a uniform very similar to the general's. The officer was engrossed in the previous day's mail, reading it by a small shaft of light breaking through a nearby window. As Dudley set his satchel down, the man opened a sweet-smelling parcel and withdrew part of the contents. He broke a bit off of the treat and popped it into his mouth with a contented sigh. Looking at Dudley, he smiled and extended the parcel in his new roommate's direction. "Fruitcake?"

Dudley smiled back and declined with an appreciative wave of his hand. "Thank you all the same, but I couldn't deprive a man of one bite of something so precious from home."

"Already missing the wife and family?" the officer asked know-ingly as he stood and offered his hand to introduce himself. "Captain Stephen Mack of the Michigan militia. I understand such feelings."

Dudley shook the man's hand as he replied, "Captain Dudley Snowden from the Maryland First Artillery Company. Did you say you're part of the Michigan militia? But isn't your family here in Detroit?"

Captain Mack shook his head. "No. My family is still back in Vermont. I haven't seen them in eighteen months, and it was two years since I'd seen them before that. I came out here in eighteen hundred to build a homestead and get a successful business started. I felt it best to allow them to continue in Tunbridge, in the society of family, until I had established a proper home here. It's taken a mite longer than I expected, so I understand a man's longing for his family. Twelve years out and I have only occasional letters to mark my own family associations."

Dumbfounded, Dudley tried to make a lighthearted quip. "And a fruitcake . . ."

Captain Mack smiled and offered his package again. "This? This isn't from my wife. It's from my sister, Lucy, bless her heart. She and her little family are as poor as church mice, but she never fails to remember her brother. Are you equally blessed with good sisters, sir?"

"None of my own, Captain, but I've been blessed with sisters-in-law, one of whom in particular could be no dearer to me if we were joined by blood. Poor, dear, Hannah . . ."

His voice trailed off and Captain Mack caught the worry there. "Illness?"

As he removed his gloves and jacket, Dudley marveled that the stranger, friendly as he was, cared to pursue the topic, and he stared at the man in wonder. There was a hardness about his lined face and hands that spoke volumes about hard work and exposure to the elements. His voice, however, portrayed softness and caring, and his bearing, though confident and commanding, also seemed gentle and warm. Dudley liked him immediately.

"Illness? Not really, at least not of a medical sort. Life has been cruel to her, and now I am worried that my absence may be as hard on her as it will be on my wife."

The bugle cry of reveille sounded from the parapet. Every bed came alive as sleep-deprived officers leapt to their feet and into whatever uniforms they possessed. Captain Mack, nearly fully dressed, quickly repacked his mail and fruitcake in a box and slid them into his trunk. He tapped Dudley on the shoulder and spoke with a wink, "You've been riding all night. You're due some shut-eye. You rest up now and join us this afternoon. I'll introduce you to the ranks, as fine a bunch of men as you'll find in any fort. Hopefully we'll make short work of the British along our line and soon be home with the ones we love, eh?"

Dudley attempted to protest and join the company, but Captain Mack persisted until Snowden relented and curled up under a blanket. Though his body rested, his mind continued to wrestle with worries about home and Beatrice and Hannah.

* * *

The morning sun streamed through the small, translucent window by the time Dudley awoke. He quickly dressed and hurried out into the parade grounds near the fort's parish church, where several hundred men were gathered. Unsure of his assignment, he approached General Hull's house to receive his duties. Spying Captain Mack descending the porch and striding back toward the officers' barracks, Dudley hurried to catch up to him.

"Shall I drill the troops?"

"We've more important duties right now, Captain Snowden. We're pushing on to Canada in two days, and we need to ready the men and our supplies for the invasion."

"But more Ohioans are on their way."

"The general feels we can't wait for them. When the *Cuyahoga* was captured, his plans for the campaign against Fort Amherstburg were on board. We assume the enemy knows our intentions."

Dudley saw the worry on Captain Mack's face as the man stared absently at the ground.

"We must take confidence in General Hull's stellar reputation," Mack continued unconvincingly. "He is well respected as a man of sound judgment and courage. We've plenty of real concerns to address without worrying about absent troops and captured plans."

Dudley's brow wrinkled with unease. He was too new to the fort to have an assessment of his own, but the innuendo was serious. "And . . . what is the current plan?"

"We'll cross the river from Detroit and strike at Sandwich, thirty-five kilometers north of Fort Amherstburg. Once we've established our position there, we'll attack the fort. It houses the King's Navy

Yard and the Indian Department. Once it's ours, we'll greatly hinder their ability to build and repair ships in the northern quadrant, and we just may be able to lessen their influence over the Indians as well."

Dudley nodded in agreement. "How can I help?"

"The general is drafting a proclamation as we speak, warning the Canadians to lay down their arms. I am handling the inventorying of our supplies and assigning men to load the wagons for the campaign. Why don't you assist Lieutenant Colonel Miller in equipping the men? You'll find him near the powder magazine inventorying the artillery and gunpowder. We must be ready to strike quickly and decisively."

* * *

Initially, everything went according to plan. The Americans crossed the Detroit River on July twelfth and pushed onward, their mere arrival causing the Essex militia stationed in Sandwich to scatter, thus providing Hull's troops ample opportunity to embed firmly in Canadian territory. Filled with bravado, the soldiers jeered at the British retreat by firelight. Although Captain Mack and the other officers favored cautious optimism to vaulted egotism, they smiled at their disheveled troops, dressed in filthy, mismatched garb, but full of jubilance. The regulars were attired in old, worn blues that had seen many days of marching and drilling, and some men were obviously clad in old Revolutionary dress pulled from old trunks. Volunteers wore anything from buckskin to farm clothes, some with nothing more than a shako hat or a gun belt to identify them as part of any organized military body. Despite their appearance, the officers realized that their show of spirited optimism would be needed in the days ahead. Sure enough, only four days later, Hull's forces encountered the enemy again at the bridge over the River Canard, the final natural barrier that stood between the American forces and Fort Amherstburg.

Dudley noted that while Hull's forces numbered about 2,500 men, 300 or so were volunteers, and members of the combined Michigan and Ohio militias numbered another 1,600, leaving just 600 regulars. But despite their mixed levels of training, they effectively routed the British, driving them away from the bridge and leaving the Americans a relatively clear path to Amherstburg. The ballyhoo of triumph sang from the men as they hungered to push forward and capitalize on the day's victory. But as the officers awaited Hull's signal to lead their companies on, they saw hesitancy in their general.

Captain Snowden's anxiety over the commander's indecision transmitted itself into his horse, causing the animal to prance nervously and whinny eerily. He signaled his men to hold as he urged his horse alongside that of his fellow officer, Stephen Mack.

"We should press on while we have the advantage," Dudley said quietly.

"I agree, but our commander is not confident about that course of action." Mack's words were clipped and forced. "He is counseling with his senior advisors, and rumor has it that he will order us to make camp here while he *reevaluates* the situation."

"Reeval . . . ?" Captain Snowden forced his tongue to silence as he sat astride his mount, awaiting the decision. Shortly, Colonels Cass and McArthur rode up to Mack and Snowden, avoiding eye contact with the troops.

"We are currently on land belonging to Monsieur François Baby," Colonel Cass began. "We are commandeering the farm, and General Hull is setting up headquarters inside the main house. Send word to the other officers to have their men stand down and make camp round about. There will be a senior officers' meeting in one hour in the general's new quarters."

The colonel allowed his eyes to make brief contact with the two captains, and the lack of confidence demonstrated there sent a chill down Dudley's back. He dreaded the blow this news would be to the men who had made the difficult mental and emotional preparations for battle, and who might interpret their leaders' delay as doubt of their readiness. Doubt was deadly in war, and Dudley knew he needed some way to redirect their attentions into a positive vein. Once the tents were up, he ordered the men to clean and check their muskets, though none had fired but one round since leaving Fort Detroit. When the men had finished that drill, Captain Snowden called his band of thirty men to follow him to the outskirts of the makeshift camp. As they passed restless, idle soldiers who little more than an hour ago had been steeled for battle, his heart sank and he stepped up the pace of his own men and hurried past.

Once in a clear field by the river, he drilled his men in proper artillery formations. It was quickly obvious that less than half of his assigned company had ever had any formal military training. Using those few to train the others, he tried to build camaraderie and trust among his group. Then he reviewed the proper technique for loading the musket efficiently and quickly.

In the voice the normally soft-spoken man reserved for only this post, Dudley barked, "Men, I know some of you have rifles of your own. I wish we could outfit you all as well, but for now, learn to love your musket. Consider it as precious as your wife." A titter of laughter broke through the line of soldiers, and Dudley smiled inconspicuously, pleased they were at least with him in spirit. "Be a good husband to her. Never lay her aside. Never treat her as less than precious. Give her the best of your care and attention at all times, as your life will depend on it."

The untrained soldiers looked at him with a cockeyed glance.

"How many of you men are married?" Dudley called out briskly. A few raised their hands awkwardly. A touch of humor entered Dudley's voice. "After our drill the rest of you ask these men about the value of a man's life when he doesn't treat his wife well, and you'll soon understand what I am saying." Again the ranks filled with laughter.

Captain Snowden's voice again sounded commanding. "You will each carry sixty rounds of ammunition in your leather magazine pouch at all times. Each day I want a fresh count of your munitions. If you are short, prepare additional cartridges until you number sixty. Is that clear?"

The men responded with a decisive, "Yes, sir."

"I know that all of you have fired a musket, but that doesn't make you trained soldiers. Lieutenant Baldridge will now demonstrate the proper technique for efficiently preparing a cartridge."

At first the young artilleryman went through the motions slowly. He filled a square of paper with a round lead ball and gunpowder, then twisted it into a paper cartridge. He held this up in the air and the men sniggered derisively at him. The lieutenant raised a curious eyebrow at Captain Snowden, who smiled calmly and nodded for the

young soldier to proceed with the demonstration of "drilling." He
fired his gun and deftly proceeded to reload. Taking out the cartridge
he had just filled, he tore it open with his teeth, put some gunpowder
into the pan on top of the gun, then poured the remaining
gunpowder and the ball down the muzzle of the gun. In a motion as
smooth as could be, he forced the ball down with a ramrod and fired
again, firing and loading four rounds in a minute. The ranks fell
silent in awe.

"It's a dance, gentlemen . . . smooth, graceful, requiring perfect
timing. You and your 'wives' must become a team, able to likewise
complete the motions three to four times in a minute. Do not waste
your precious ammunition in practice, but go through each of the
motions until you can do so successfully. When you have each
demonstrated to the lieutenant that you have mastered the task, this
company may return to camp for supper—and not before. We train
as a unit, we drill as a unit, and we will fight as a unit. Understood?"

Again a decisive and proud, "Yes, sir," echoed back at the captain.

"Very well then. Carry on, Lieutenant."

Dudley smiled as he turned his horse and returned to camp.
Regardless of what the other companies were feeling, he knew that for
this hour at least, his men still felt like soldiers. And he hoped that
the news from the senior officer's meeting would announce their
departure for Amherstburg while they still felt that way.

As soon as he passed the last stand of trees separating his men
from the grounds surrounding Monsieur Baby's brick home, he
caught sight of the senior officers exiting the building. The general's
decision was obvious. Captain Mack posed a question, the reply
causing his head to shake in disbelief. Several of the senior officers
engaged in a heated dispute with Lieutenant Colonel McDonnell and
Major Glegg, two of General Hull's senior advisors. Captain Snowden
stood apart in the company of several other captains who had gathered, awaiting the final word. Eventually, Mack made his way in their
direction. He tried to force the grimace from his face and display a
matter-of-fact bearing, but no one could deny the incredulity underscoring his words.

"In light of the capture of the *Cuyahoga,* which carried the
general's personal documents, including the plan for the attack on

Amherstburg, the general feels it prudent to stand down for a time to test the integrity of our communication and supply lines, to be sure the capture of our intelligence items has not allowed the British to compromise them."

"Of course, they will be compromised," one captain argued. "How could they not be? All the more reason to press on while the advantage is with us."

"Wasn't it his son's idea to separate the general's personal papers from him and place them on that boat with sick soldiers and the musical band?" another muttered angrily.

"Gentlemen!" Captain Mack growled. "Let us keep the morale of our troops foremost in our minds. Murmuring will do nothing but harm these brave men. We are to drill them to keep them battle ready while we await word concerning the outcome of offensive strikes said to be about to ensue at Buffalo, Niagara, and Kingston. If they can weaken the British defenses elsewhere along the border, we will quickly follow with our strike at Amherstburg."

"And when are these battles planned? Tomorrow? Next week? Next month? If our supply lines are compromised, how long does the general think we can hold this position?"

Captain Mack pulled himself up straight and stared down at the rebellion percolating through the officers surrounding him. "Gentlemen, you have your orders. Now see to your men until further word arrives."

As the murmuring band departed, Mack's shoulders slumped in defeat. "Are you a religious man, Captain?" he asked Dudley when the others were gone.

"I'm not a zealot, but I think of myself as prayerful."

The officer's hand rested upon his friend's back. "That is our best defense tonight."

* * *

Hours later, after the men's voices had faded into sleep, Dudley made a final pass by his sentries before turning in. He saw a form in the distant moonlight, kneeling under a stand of trees. Fearing one of his men had fallen ill, he approached, softly calling out as he made his way closer. To his astonishment, the form that rose and faced him was that of Stephen Mack.

"Are you ill, Captain?"

"Only in spirit."

"Excuse me?" Dudley replied.

"I sought seclusion to pray."

Dudley stammered in embarrassment for having disrupted the man's privacy.

"No need, Captain Snowden," Stephen Mack laughed good-naturedly. "I find it curious . . . the discomfort men feel about the subject of prayer."

"Despite my own leanings toward faith and God, I suppose I don't often ascribe religiosity as being common to most military men."

"It should be. Who needs the guidance of the Almighty more than one about to face his brother in combat? Freedom is a sacred principle, wouldn't you agree?"

Dudley nodded silently as he considered the comment. "Indeed it is."

"I am simply a militiaman, an entrepreneur who soldiers for a cause. When that cause is won, I will return to my home and my business ventures and resume my civilian life, complete with Sunday services and time to sit by the fire and study from the Good Book."

"I take it faith has been a big part of your upbringing?"

Captain Mack sat on the ground and smiled upward at Dudley as he also took a seat. "My mother's influence. My father was possessed of a God-fearing spirit, but he didn't allow it to lead him until he tired of pursuing his phantom dreams of riches and glory. With women it seems to be more inherent. I don't believe it is as frequently so with men."

Dudley reflected on the women in his own life and smiled accordingly. "I agree that women are more susceptible to godly things, but I believe it is manifested as differently in them as it is in men." He leaned in to emphasize his words. "Take my own family for example. My wife, Beatrice, is the epitome of piety and love. She bridles her passions while occasionally garnishing her thoughts with humor. Then there is my sister-in-law Myrna, who is a God-fearing woman. But religion is like a whip in her life, keeping her submissive and wary at all times. And then there is Hannah . . . my sweet angel,

Hannah. She is quite the opposite. Her faith seems to set her free. She fears no one and nothing, even daring to upset traditional religiosity by posing question after question in pursuit of knowledge about the nature of God. She attributes everything good in her life to God and somehow accepts even her dreadful misfortunes as divine tutorials, turning them into more good things which she in turn attributes happily back to God as well." He shook his head and laughed sadly, obviously longing for his family. "They are each a marvel to me."

Mack's interest was piqued. "Your women remind me of my sisters. Lovina and Lovisa—twins—both found great solace in prayer. They were pious ladies, given to much exhortation and hymn singing, and yet their lives were short and difficult of health. My sister Lydia was much like your Beatrice, good, sweet, kind . . . willing to enjoy the good things of life, but your Hannah reminds me of another sister, my Lucy."

"The fruitcake baker?" Dudley smiled.

"Yes," Mack replied with a nod and an echoing smile. "The same."

"Amazing the feelings of protectiveness they stir even from so far away," Dudley mused.

"What worries beset you about your Hannah?"

Dudley paused, unsure how to properly express his concerns. "Her life has always been surrounded by difficult circumstances, but she somehow managed to maintain a cheerful countenance despite them. Yet recently she suffered a tragic loss." His voice became husky. "Soon afterward she began being tormented by disturbing dreams. Several times I ran into her room in the middle of the night, having been summoned by her frightful cries. She could barely remember the scenes that terrified her so, being able to recall only the feelings that accompanied them. As obviously upsetting as they were, she somehow believed that there was a message buried within them that, if unlocked, would prove to her good." He closed his eyes and shook his head sadly. "Her mother is stark raving mad, and I fear Hannah is beset by the beginnings of the same malady. I fear my departure and the loss of her security may add to her psychosis."

Stephen Mack's brow furrowed slightly as if in deep thought. "Why are you so quick to assign madness to her visions?"

"I told you about her mother . . ."

"Yes, but is either Beatrice or Myrna similarly affected?"

"Well . . . no," stammered Dudley, "but neither do they have these dreams."

"Neither do they have such an intimate relationship with God. I wouldn't be so quick to ascribe madness to what may be inspiration. If a woman so close to God thinks that He has a hand in her dreams . . ."

Dudley looked dubiously at his friend. "You don't mean to say that you believe in heavenly manifestations, do you?"

"You're questioning the wrong man on this matter. Both of my twin sisters went to their graves attesting to having experienced separate but undeniable heavenly encounters with Deity. And you'd be hard pressed to convince my sister Lucy that God seals the heavens to His children. Her husband, Joseph Smith, and his family have had similar experiences at the veil between this world and the next. Lucy will tell you of the miracles she has seen wrought through the power of prayer and faith. In simple words, Captain, I believe we may be living in a day where the fulfillment of prophecy is about to unfold."

Dudley looked skeptically at the man he had earlier regarded with respect. "Prophecy?"

Captain Mack remained earnest. "Do you believe that the Lord will come again? Do you believe in the foretold Second Coming?"

Dudley sputtered as he considered a topic he had rarely regarded as more than mystical.

"I do," Captain Mack testified boldly. "Don't you think He would begin to prepare the hearts and minds of some of His children to receive His work when it commences? You see, I believe He is softening hearts and guiding those of His children who are already willing to listen and believe."

Dudley was astonished, and yet something in the man's words comforted him and seemed right, particularly in light of Hannah. "You have given me much to think on, Captain."

"Commit these ideas to prayer, friend. I cannot say for certain that your Hannah's dreams are similar to those of my sisters, but neither would I advise you to rule out the possibility."

CHAPTER 27

Baltimore, Maryland
July 18, 1812

The Stansbury sisters sat in the Snowdens' parlor sewing pearls on Myrna's wedding dress and chatting amiably about the wedding that was fast approaching. Suddenly Hannah tightened her grip on the fabric as sounds grew louder and the voices settled in.

"Hannah!" The worried voice was Beatrice's, who noticed the strange expression on the face of her sister. "It's all right, Hannah. You're not alone! We're here, Hannah!"

Even Myrna laid the concerns of her mangled dress aside, focusing her energies on reaching into her sister's terror to retrieve her. "We're right here, Hannah. Can you hear us?"

But Hannah knew their proximity would do her no good. The darkness soon swallowed them up and their voices as well, rendering her utterly alone. She felt her fingers clawing at the bodice of the dress, struggling to draw a full breath and to slow her racing heart. She became weak and knew she was succumbing to the fear, but she couldn't fight any longer. She begged God to free her from the clutches of whatever bound her, or, failing her rescue, to receive her to Himself. Then she heard a gentle voice and the accompanying sense of comfort.

On previous occasions she had thought it was a heavenly being, an angel or some such personage with an unrecognizable but familiar bearing who had come to rescue her. This time she felt certain she knew the voice, and though her rescuer was mortal, she thought him no less heaven sent. She reached out, trustingly, for his arms. He drew her to him and she buried her face in the crook of his shoulder as he carried her through the dense haze. They were huddled together as they made their way, until beyond a certain point light broke through the murkiness. She lifted her head to gaze into the face of her rescuer and then she awoke.

Hannah wrestled in the bedcovers, begging the image to return, but it was gone. She bolted upright to clear the fog from her mind, to focus clearly on the unidentifiable but familiar voice. She found herself alone and discovered the twists in her sheets where her hands had clutched the supposed wedding gown. Again her pillow and nightdress were sweat-soaked. But it was of no matter. Beatrice had been right. The blackness was the symbol of her distress, and someone was coming to rescue her from it!

She slid from the bed and straightway went to her desk to retrieve her journal from the drawer. Carefully, she added this night's dream to the other entries that catalogued her journey into what she had come to believe was either her complete madness or devilish possession. She had stopped discussing her dreams with either of her sisters, who, despite their preoccupation with Myrna's nuptials, were so distressed by Hannah's recent decline that Hannah could only bear giving them falsely cheery reports of restful sleep. Only in her journal had she chronicled the truth of her fears in an anxious scrawl. But this morning was different, and with a light heart, she wrote with bold, happy strokes. She had dreamed the dream again, but this time she had received her answer!

Hannah bounded down the stairs, refreshed and glowing. Her sisters rushed in upon her, relieved to see the morning color return to her hollow face and a true smile dancing on her lips.

She plopped into her chair at the table, calling out to the servant, "Martha, I believe I will have three griddle cakes this morning, if you please . . . and two sausages as well."

Beatrice reached a loving hand across the table and gave Hannah's a squeeze. "It's wonderful to see you eating again."

Myrna agreed enthusiastically. "I thought we were going to have to alter your bridesmaid's dress again. You've become as thin as a rail."

Martha presented Hannah's plate like a trophy, setting it down before her with great panache. "And iffen you wants anythin' else you jest ask, and Martha will fix it up fer you."

Hannah beamed at the woman who had fretted over her diet or lack thereof every morning since the dreams began. "I slept wonderfully. Thank you for worrying so. Now enough of me. What news have you two this morning? Myrna, are we finishing your gown today?"

"Done!" she replied. "Beatrice and I sewed the final pearls on the sleeves last night."

Hannah's face fell. "I'm sorry. I let you down. I must have nodded off."

Beatrice rushed in sweetly. "Don't berate yourself. Watching you enjoy a few moments of peaceful rest on the divan last evening made our work pleasant and swift, and when we were finished we helped you up to bed."

Hannah blushed and dipped her head. "I don't even remember that, but I dreamed about working on the gown." She blushed again. "Oh . . . I love you both so, and you have been so good to me. It will be a lovely wedding, Myrna. My only sadness is that once Mr. Baumgardner carries you away, our lazy mornings together will be ended for some time, since you will be living on his country estate for the remainder of the summer."

"But you do like him?" the bride asked eagerly.

"Very much," Hannah quickly answered. "He's very entertaining."

Myrna's face momentarily contorted. "Do you think he's too entertaining? Does he appear foolish and silly? I mean, I, of course, love his sterling wit." She quickly began nervously sawing her sausages, lifting her head frequently as she awaited her sisters' responses.

Sweet Beatrice rushed in. "I think men tend to mellow after marriage. To my thinking, it would be much better to have a man mellow from too much frivolity, settling into a nice sense of humor, than to have a man be barely possessing of humor and end up old and dour."

"Exactly my thoughts!" replied Myrna with a wave of her knife.

Beatrice shot Hannah an amused smile, and the three settled back into breakfast.

"Have you heard from Dudley today?"

Beatrice quickly swallowed, pleased to give an update. "The mail hasn't arrived yet this morning, but all his previous letters have been so lovely and sweet. And the gifts! The man has showered me with trinkets from his travels on the road to Detroit. His last letter said

General Hull was deploying them over the Detroit River and onto Canadian soil. He warned me he might not be able to get a letter posted for some time once they engaged the British."

Her voice became thin at the mention of battle, causing Hannah to regret having raised the topic.

But Beatrice jumped back in to fill the silence. "Did I tell you that Dudley has made great friends with a captain in the Michigan militia . . . by the name of Stephen Mack, I believe. Captain Mack has spoken so beautifully about Vermont that Dudley wants us to make a trip there, possibly to buy a little shop or farm. In fact, Captain Mack offered to have us stay with his family. Wasn't that lovely of him?" She hurried on, finding solace in incessantly speaking about her husband. "Dudley fell in love with the Ohio area, but he thinks it would be too untamed for me after Baltimore life. He believes Vermont might be a nice spot for us to begin again. It has a nice sound . . . Tunbridge, Vermont."

She dabbed at her eyes with her napkin. Beatrice's emotions had lately been uncharacteristically on the surface. There were many reasons for it, her sisters knew. Their period of sisterly bliss was about to end, or at least would be greatly altered by Myrna's marriage. Dudley was gone to war, and Hannah's health had borne heavily upon the eldest sibling. Hannah was determined to turn the household attentions away from her health and onto her sisters.

"Well, Vermont sounds lovely! If you move, I will go along and help settle you in."

Myrna gasped at the thought of being left out of the plan. "Yes," she then agreed limply. "And Mr. Baumgardner and I will visit to get away from the Maryland heat and humidity."

The three sisters wondered what lay in store for each of them beyond July. Hannah smiled secretly in her heart. She had faced her fears and seen the dream's meaning. Help was coming.

CHAPTER 28

London, England
July 19, 1812

Ludgate Hill was sweltering, discouraging all but the direst in need from waiting on the hot stone steps and streets for the exit of wealthy worshippers from the late service at St. Paul's Cathedral. London's finest citizens, including many members of both houses of Parliament, streamed through the doors, gasping at the unseemly heat, barely noticing the alms seekers. Some of the ladies kept coins at the ready for London's poor children, while several members of the House of Lords, most notably the beloved Lord Whittington, sought out the heads of families, offering news of work and handing out pound notes—enough for a father to buy his babies bread, milk, and cheese for supper. Lord Whittington had a way about him. Though certainly elevated above the populace, he always looked the recipient in the eye and made him feel like a man despite his circumstances. It was not always so with the other wealthy men, many of whom jutted their offerings out blindly as if they were handing hay to a cow, as was the case with the two men making their way across Ludgate to a secluded spot under a shop awning. They had each offered token coins as if it were part of a ritual required to pass, but they neither looked at nor spoke to a single person, despite the fact that one of the men was Parliament's own—assigned to represent those he ignored.

"So, Mitchell, I hear my gift was appreciatively received," bragged Stephen Ramsey as he tapped the ram's head handle of his umbrella against Mitchell's chest.

Mitchell returned a subtle nod, unflustered by his friend's bravado. The strain of the recent intrigue had lined his face beyond his forty-one years. In truth, his hair was now as gray as it was blonde, but he was satisfied that the reward had been worth these small sacrifices.

"Rear Admiral Cockburn has lauded your generosity in transmitting Duprée's debt to the service of the Crown," Mitchell confirmed.

Ramsey sniggered. "I'm happy to serve the Crown when it serves my interests as well."

"And the people, Ramsey," Mitchell interrupted with immediacy. "We must not lose sight of the fact that we are doing this primarily for the sake of the people of the Liverpool area."

Ramsey stared at the man, then laughed incredulously. "Have you pacified yourself with that tale so many times that you've actually come to believe it? Delude yourself if you must, but we both know who will prosper most if Duprée's efforts prove successful."

Mitchell squirmed. "Cockburn must find him an able seaman to rave on about him so."

"Seaman?" Ramsey looked into Mitchell's face until he was convinced the man truly was either completely daft or completely foolish. "Oh, Duprée can handle a boat capably all right, but Cockburn doesn't want him for his talents at sea. He wants him for his brutality on land."

Mitchell's face went ashen white, and Lord Whittington, scrutinizing the curious pair from afar, noted with interest the severe change in his colleague's appearance.

Ramsey pressed on, leaving the member of the House of Commons without the comfort of ignorance. "Cockburn needed a man on the ground in Maryland to incite havoc, to stir up slave revolts, and to plunder the Tidewater area to divert the local militias away from the primary targets. Duprée threatened to expose us if I prosecuted him legally, so by turning him over to Cockburn, I get my revenge on his insolence and he serves my interests in a most lucrative way."

"Let me remind you that all I agreed to do was stall a few key votes! I may have prospered while serving my neighbors' needs, but I want no part of murder and pillaging."

Ramsey sneered at Mitchell. "The gift is already unwrapped my friend—legally, and as you said, with the military's gratitude. Who can fault us if the war's brutality plays nicely into our investments?" Ramsey opened his umbrella as a sunshade and took a step into the light.

"We are not finished here!" declared Mitchell sharply as he reached for Ramsey's arm.

Ramsey stared at Mitchell's hand, his eyes burning like a branding iron, until the man could no longer bear the scrutiny and withdrew it. "My son has arrived, and there are other eyes upon us."

Mitchell made a casual scan of St. Paul's and saw young Arthur Ramsey in the company of Lord Whittington and the earl's ten-year-old-son, Daniel. Though a conversation was ensuing between the earl and Arthur, without question, the lord's eyes were riveted on Mitchell and the older Ramsey. "Good heavens!" Mitchell gasped as he offered a weak wave in the earl's direction.

"Settle your nerves!" barked Ramsey under his breath. "We're just two worshippers sharing a conversation after services—lest you allow yourself to fall apart and draw suspicion."

"And what shall I do?"

Ramsey smiled at him as if he were an idiot. "I'm going to claim my son and pay my respects to the earl. Do whatever you like. Your usefulness has expired and our association is ended." His voice was cold and final as he walked away, leaving a dumbstruck Mitchell behind.

Ramsey smiled at his life's treasure, his twenty-four-year-old son, Arthur. A refined, dignified Cambridge graduate, he was both the source of his father's pride and his primary bother. He looked more or less like his father; he had the same square jawline and strong nose that gave his face the look of a common man. His hair, though, was chestnut-colored like that of his pious mother, the daughter of one of Ramsey's wealthy investors. Although she was plain by her own rights, Ramsey accepted that the best of her had made their way to Arthur. Ramsey knew the very best of everything he would do or become was embodied in his son, but he also understood the resistance Arthur felt toward his father's work. Soon after Ramsey's wife had come to understand the nature of her husband's business, she dedicated herself to raising their only child to be God-fearing and honorable—simply to spite him, or so Ramsey believed. The piety she had instilled in Arthur had drained the lad of monetary ambition, leading him in the direction of the clergy and further and further from his father.

As Ramsey approached Arthur and the Whittingtons, he inserted himself into the conversation. "My Lord Whittington," he greeted, bowing.

"Mr. Ramsey . . ." the earl bowed in return. As he rose, his eyes were riveted on those of the entrepreneur, whose cocky bearing was so different from that of his heir. "You have a fine son in young Arthur here."

Ramsey smiled wryly and placed one affectionate hand against the back of his son's day coat while giving Arthur's silk cravat a tug with the other. "Thank you, sir. His mother and I are quite proud of him, though we worry his Cambridge mind will starve to death on minister's wages."

Arthur flinched at the familiar tone of disappointment in his father's voice and tensed as he whispered under his breath, "Please, Father . . . not now."

Lord Whittington kept a protective arm around his own son, Daniel. His compassion for Arthur's situation prompted him to jump in encouragingly, placing his other hand gently on the young ministerial student's shoulder as he rebutted his father's sarcasm. "Lucky is the man whose son learns early that there are other, more important things in life than wealth alone."

"Yes . . . my lord," Ramsey agreed with a hint of scorn. "How fortunate for each of us, nobles and commoners as well, to have sons whose lives will be dedicated to serving others." He bowed again in mock self-deprecation, rushing in with a note of apology. "Though I draw no comparison between our lowly family and the house of the Right Honorable Earl of Whittington."

The earl noted the smug air and waved tenuously, bidding the man to rise.

Ramsey continued with a sideways glance at the earl's son. "Again, my apologies, my lord. I didn't mean to imply that your own son, the young Viscount, will be considering trading his castle for a parson's bunk. After all, if the nobility were to lower themselves to the level of the commoners, who then would lift up the lowly masses?"

Lord Whittington stifled his retort as a mercy to Ramsey's son.

"We should be going, Father," Arthur sputtered. "Dear Lord Whittington, please forgive us for taking leave so suddenly, but we must go." Then he guided his father away.

"Arthur's father doesn't like us, does he, Father?" asked the earl's son.

"Don't be troubled about it, Daniel. There will always be those who will look upon our station and see only the privileges and not the responsibility we bear because of it. All we can do is help whom and where we can and leave the rest to their own means."

"I'm not sure I want to be a noble, Father. Not if people will judge me harshly for it. Isn't that why the colonies rebelled? To be rid of the monarchy and the nobles?"

The earl knelt down to face his troubled son. Compassion swelled over him as he placed his hands on the sensitive boy's shoulders. "It is true that some of our citizens believe they have found a better way, and they have rebelled against the Crown. We are engaged at this hour in a war to reunite our peoples, but regardless of the outcome, the House of Whittington has always stood loyally by the monarchy. Will we allow a rude man to divert us from our duty?"

Daniel's large eyes shined with pride. "No, Father."

Lord Whittington embraced his son, burying his face in the collar of the lad's coat. "That's my brave boy. Now run along and join your grandmother by the carriage and I'll be there presently." As his adoring eyes followed his son to the carriage where the Dowager Countess of Whittington stood, he again spied Mitchell. The lord's mood instantly shifted.

Mitchell had busied himself making brief, pointless conversations with people as he awaited the appropriate moment to approach his colleague in Parliament, hoping to make a plausible excuse for the scene that had played out between himself and Ramsey. Seeing the way Arthur guided his father away from Lord Whittington, Mitchell perceived that the conversation had not gone well. He attempted to disappear back into the crowd, but the earl had made eye contact with him and was already moving in his direction. Mitchell dipped his head and searched his memory for the story he had concocted, but his mind went blank as the earl reached him.

"Mr. Mitchell."

"L . . . L . . . Lord Whittington," he offered weakly with a pale nod of his head.

"Is that Ramsey chap a friend of yours?" he asked pointedly.

"He is . . . he is just . . ." Mitchell stumbled awkwardly. "We've met a few times."

Lord Whittington watched the Ramseys enter their carriage and his eyes followed the vehicle as it disappeared down Ludgate Hill. "It is indeed difficult to believe that such a man could be blessed with a son like his Arthur," he mused aloud. He turned to drive his point home to Mitchell. "It is only out of respect for the lad that I have not launched a full-scale investigation into Ramsey's doings. The man is an opportunist, pure and simple, and you'd do well not to sully your own reputation and that of Parliament by associating with him."

"I don't believe the chatting of two parishioners after services is a matter of state."

Lord Whittington raised one eyebrow. "If it is that simple," he replied skeptically.

Mitchell felt every nerve in his body twitch. "What are you implying?"

The earl's eyes were deadly serious. "No implications, just a series of observations. The monarchy is troubled, and two months ago an assassin cut down our prime minister. We had all expected that in our current session we would pass the antislavery legislation for which he so boldly fought. Our nation should lead this fight, but instead there has been much stalling."

"Are you pointing your finger in my direction?"

Lord Whittington didn't yield. "There's been a marked change in your voting record of late and," his eyes shot to the expensive cut of Mitchell's suit, "other changes as well."

Mitchell's hair rose on his arms and neck. "I refuse to stand here and be subjected to your innuendos!" He turned to leave, anxious to end the discussion before his resolve failed him. Whittington's hand held him fast in place and he felt the earl's hot breath on his ear.

"Just know, my friend," the lord whispered, "that rumors are circulating about unsavory dealings between your friend and a member of His Majesty's Navy. Yes, we must win this war with America, but we must do it with honor, in a manner that unites our two peoples and without further undermining the integrity of the throne. Our national security may depend on it, as the eyes of the world are upon us . . . just as eyes are upon you . . . and have been for some time."

The Liverpool native's face fell pale. "I've done what I felt was best for my constituents. If you had proof of any wrongdoing, we would not be standing here playing cat and mouse. You of all people would have charged me formally. You have nothing."

The earl's face became pallid with disappointment, and his voice took on a steeled edge as he realized the fall of a once good man. *"Had* nothing, Mitchell. You've made my point."

The look of disillusionment on the earl's face made Mitchell feel dirty and used, and what followed forced Liverpool's representative to recognize the depths to which he had plunged.

"What could a man like Ramsey have offered you to entice you to sell your soul and risk fouling a name so previously honored and highly esteemed?" the earl asked in bewilderment. "What will you say to your family? What legacy have you left for your sons?"

The earl turned to walk away in disgust, but looked back to make a final, painful point. "We each pledged our very lives to this noble work, Mitchell. You've now helped unleash a plague on the States that will either stain Britain indelibly or bring God's intervention against our military. What could have possibly been worth such a price?"

CHAPTER 29

The Willows
July 21, 1812

Bitty stared down the lane as she waited for Jed to return from yet another hunting trip with Jack and Markus. She understood the cause of his current restlessness, having seen the light go dim in his eyes after the day his horse had dragged his beaten body home. It wasn't the beating—he was strong and had mended nicely. It was the heartache that had made Jed vulnerable. Jerome's words had helped him pick himself up and carry on, but the light in his eyes had never fully returned. Then, after his last trip to Baltimore, something had further extinguished the fire from his once mischievous but whimsical eyes.

She shook her head with worry as she walked over to the sideboard where two letters from Philadelphia sat unopened. Since Jed had posted no letters in return for his sister's previous three mailings, Bitty assumed Frannie was likely worried about Jed as well.

I ought to just write her a letter and tell her to git herself home to speak with that brother of hers, thought Bitty. "Land sakes." She stopped short. "I can straighten him out myself!" And as she wiped her hands in her apron, she resigned herself to talk with Jed when he returned home. She missed him—it was as simple as that. *Not so simple to Abel,* she thought. That was still a troublesome situation. Although Abel had settled in to life at the Willows, he frowned upon her motherly affection toward Jed until his mistrust had made him as suspicious of the Willows' master as he had been of Stewart Stringham.

Bitty looked out the window across the vast expanse of the Willows' front lawn that spread left to the main barns and right toward the fields of tobacco. She saw her father-in-law, Jerome, directing the laborers as they tended the maturing plants. She worried that standing all day in the sweltering sun was too much for a man of his age, but he seemed to relish the trust Jed had demonstrated by placing him in charge in Markus's absence. Unfortunately, the additional confidence placed in Jerome seemed only to accentuate the chasm of trust between Jed and Abel.

Bitty spent the rest of the afternoon sending baskets of vittles to the workers and watching for any sign of Jed. As soon as she saw dust stir along the lane, she sent her basket of sweet breads on with two of her stepchildren and grabbed the hems of her skirts so she could make a fast entrance into the house. After running a moist cloth over her dusty face, she grabbed the bread bowl and began measuring the ingredients for biscuits. She quickly mixed the dough and then tossed it onto the breadboard to knead.

While in this busy mode, Bitty watched for the first movement of the door, a signal that the young man she loved as her own had returned. Her eyes moved back and forth from the dough to the door in a nervous rhythm as the aggravating minutes ticked by. Unnerved by his delayed arrival, she wiped her hands on her apron and headed toward the window to check on his progress. When a pair of large hands covered her eyes, and Bitty screamed in surprise, spinning around with her fists clenched. Once she caught sight of Jed's beloved face, his thick arms swept her up.

"I finally managed to sneak up on you!" he laughed heartily.

Momentarily forgetting how cross she was over his long absence, she simply enjoyed the comfort of knowing he was all right. Finally, she noticed the contrite but smiling faces of Markus O'Malley and her brother Jack standing behind Jed and she knew she was about to be affectionately bamboozled. Before they could begin spinning excuses for their long absence Bitty pushed away from Jed and placed a reproving smack against his chest as he set her down.

"Got some of that sugar fer yer own kin?" Jack asked with outstretched arms.

Bitty shot him a sideways glare, fighting hard to hold a smile at bay. "Don't go thinkin' that a hug and a kiss will make everything all right. Whilst you three have been out bein' scamps, others have been doin' your work and mindin' things."

Markus and Jack each held up arms weighed down with salted rabbit and fish. Jed nodded in the direction of a pile of wild birds on the floor, gutted and ready for plucking.

"We've been busy too. This meat will add some nice variety," Jed said hopefully.

Bitty put her hands on her hips and counted the kill. "Three of you, each good shots, out there for two weeks, and this is all you brought home? They don't make enough wool for you to pull this lie over my eyes."

Jed looked at his companions and smiled sheepishly. "Maybe not," he confessed, "but men need to get away from time to time, Bitty. Being cooped up here drives me crazy now."

As Jack and Markus felt the mood shift, they gathered up their kill and headed to the smokehouse, leaving Jed and Bitty alone. Bitty returned to her biscuits, working the dough until it was a flat, floured circle. She was "mullin'," as she referred to her spells of deep thought, and Jed felt certain his recent unsettled behavior had caused her many such moments.

"I knew you'd be comin' home today," she began. "I saw you had militia duty comin' and knew you'd be back to tend to that."

"You're upset with me," Jed muttered as his hand slipped over her flour-covered one.

"Times is I don't even know you anymore. You're allowin' things to change you. One day you're off chasin' after idle gossip and the ghosts of the past, and the next you're off gallivantin' like some fool. A man can't just run from what troubles him, Jed. Least of all, it's not the way you're made. How can you ever hope to build anythin' if you run when times git hard?"

Jed flopped into a chair and allowed his head to slip onto his chest. "Maybe I don't care about building anything anymore. Maybe I'm ready to just carve the whole estate up like my family intended in the first place, give everybody a piece, and call it quits on trying to pretend the Willows is anything more than just miles and miles of dirt."

Bitty slapped her hands hard against her thighs, sending a cloud of flour ceiling bound. She strode over to Jed's chair where, despite his seated position, he still towered over her petite frame. Undaunted by their difference in size, she rose up, gritted her teeth, set her jaw firmly in place, and pointed her finger straight into his chest. "You couldn't hurt me more deeply if you took me out back, stripped me to the waist, and laid a lash across my back."

Jed shrank with shame at her expression.

"Now you listen to me, Jonathan Edward Pearson," Bitty declared as she pulled him to his feet and dragged his frame through the back door so he could see the laborers in the fields. "You might hold the title to this land, and even the title to the people who work it, but what the Willows is and what she can become belongs as much to every one of those people as it does to you, only they got no voice in the matter. Only you can give 'em a voice, and if you run this place into the ground or carve it up and sell it off, even if you free all those people and give 'em each a chunk of land to boot, if you do all that and pull out, leavin' men like Stringham to buy up the rest, you'll be sendin' 'em off like lambs to the wolves, and you know it. They need you right now, Jed, just like you need them."

She pulled his head down closer to her as her eyes began to shine. "You've said it yourself. Aside from Frannie, you've got no one else but these people right now, people who toil and sweat on *yer* land, not because they fear you, but because they love you . . . because you've shown 'em some measure of kindness and given 'em a dream of a real home. But if you go 'round fussin' and spewin' about *yer* troubles, and then threaten to dissolve what they've gived their lives to build, well then, you'll sure enough kill 'em."

Jed leaned heavily against the doorpost and sighed, rubbing his fingers into his eyes. He drew Bitty to him with one arm and laid his head upon hers. "I'd never do that, Bitty. I was doing just what you said . . . fussin' and spewin'." The pair both laughed. "I'm glad I have you to set me back on track when I get lost. A man needs a woman's perspective at times."

Bitty dabbed at her eyes with an apron corner. "And sometimes he just needs to get away from things and think." She patted his side as they walked back into the house, chastening herself for pressing so hard on the young man upon his return. "So how long do you plan on stayin' this time? Frannie's been worried." She pointed to the two envelopes from Philadelphia.

"I don't know. I suppose it all depends on what news the militia has waiting for me. If we're still not being deployed into full-time service, I'll try to stay close to home for a while."

"And Markus and Jack?"

"I know it's been selfish of me to carry them both away while leaving the burden of the tobacco resting so heavily upon Jerome. How is he?"

"Fine . . . fine," Bitty answered in a sad singsong as she went back to mulling over her biscuit dough. "He's supervisin' Abel and a few others on breakin' ground for yer mill right now. He thrives on responsibility. *All* men need to feel they're valued."

Jed caught the hidden message. "Abel's helping with the mill, Bitty?"

Her head came up protectively. "Why does that surprise you?"

"I'd like to make things better between the two of us. Do you think he'd like to come along on the next hunting trip?" He smiled affectionately, knowing the trust he'd be implying by offering to place a gun in the hand of the man who, of all the people on the entire estate, cared the least for him.

Bitty ran to him without wiping the flour from her hands. Palms against his chest, she looked into his eyes. "Do you mean it, Jed? Would you do that?"

"You know I'd do anything for you, Bitty."

"Bless you, Jed. Nothing would make me happier than to have you two become friends."

* * *

While Markus and Jack headed into the tobacco fields, Jed headed to the dock area to check on the mill's progress. He helped the crew of men dig for an hour while Jerome spun stories. Jed noticed the admiration in Abel's eyes as his father freely shared the wealth of knowledge that had long been locked inside him. Abel filled in the gaps where his father's aged memory showed lapses, and Jed marveled at the extensive knowledge Jerome had secretly imparted to his son in complete defiance of his previous owners. It became ever more apparent to Jed that no politics or whip could enslave a man's mind.

An individual did that to himself, and he found new respect and empathy for the frustration Abel had experienced over his lifetime.

After an hour, Abel's shovel hit something solid. He switched to an axe, and the mighty swing produced a dull thud and then a cracking sound. *Wood?* Jed wondered in awe. With the old legends reverberating in his mind, he sent everyone but Jerome and Abel to the tobacco fields. He and Abel continued digging until an old coffin was revealed. While Jed climbed down to investigate, Abel and his father moved away from the grave and Jerome began uttering a prayer. The axe had left a hole in the wooden box, revealing a swatch of decayed, blue fabric. Jed saw three letters, *SBM,* etched into the top of the wood with the date *1781 A.D.* inscribed below. He ran the curiously familiar initials through his mind but could match them to no known relative.

He'd been studying many family records of late, and making inquiries among tight-lipped relatives regarding Susannah Stansbury's claim of his grandfather's complicity in her mother's death. Today's incident also seemed to have no bearing on his search, but then a squeamish feeling momentarily washed over him as he remembered why the letters seemed familiar. He considered how many times had he studied his grandfather's portrait, pondering the three initials painted deftly on the locket? *What were they . . . ? SAB . . . a mismatch.* He was oddly relieved that the engraved initials added nothing to his search for answers, for neither had they strengthened Susannah's wild claims. He sighed as he studied them, realizing he was forced to admit that he was also no nearer to proving her wrong, and with each passing day, his hope of ever being with Hannah was fading.

Jed climbed back out of the grave and said, "Let's cover it back up and wait for nightfall so no one else finds out. We'll move it down the property and bury it with a marker. Tell no one. If news of this gets out, the ghost stories will begin again and we'll never get the men back down here to build this mill."

Abel looked nervously at his father and back to Jed. "You want to move the dead?"

"Just a short distance. And we'll fashion a proper marker this time."

The father and son remained dubious about the chore as they helped Jed cover the coffin. They finished just as the supper bell rang, calling the workers in from the fields. Jack and Markus fell in close to Jed and followed along to the hollow, where large kettles of rabbit stew stood ready for serving. Markus and Jack took their plates and sat under a tree as Jed briefly recounted the coffin's discovery, outlining the night's chore to them and the need for silence.

Jed ate and laughed alongside the dark-skinned children, joining in games of "Blind Man's Bluff" and "Spear the Hoop" until the fiddles came out and dancing commenced. By dark, fires were lit and everyone gathered around in a tight circle. Jerome again stepped to the forefront to lead his little congregation in a brief worship service.

"I think I'll grab a little shut-eye before we dig up that coffin," remarked Markus, who stretched and groaned as he worked a knot out of his back. "Walk back to the house with me?"

"No," replied Jed thoughtfully. "I think I'll sit and listen to Jerome's sermon a while."

"Sermon?" chuckled Markus. "Don't tell me he's convinced you he's a preacher now!"

"Maybe he is and maybe he isn't," Jed answered. "Jerome says that in the Bible men were called by God to preach, not licensed by the state. I've never known anyone who knows the Bible better than he, and no one loves to read and teach from it more than he does either."

"You do still realize that he can't legally serve as a minister, don't you?"

"Yes," Jed responded with a smile, "but maybe he has been given a calling to teach and preach. In any case, I enjoy his interpretation of the scriptures. They make me feel . . . I don't know . . . hopeful, and if there's one thing we can all stand an extra helping of right now, it's hope."

Markus clasped his friend's shoulder. "Fetch me later, Jed."

Jed offered a quick wave to Markus before turning his attention to the gray-haired slave whose presence never failed to captivate the crowd of anxious listeners.

"We have all worked hard today, and we can all lay our heads down tonight knowing that soon the harvest will come when we will see the fruits of our labors, and that is a good feeling."

From the gathering came the soft sounds of voices affirming Jerome's words.

"Jesus taught by using symbols familiar to His disciples. He will teach us the same way. Today, as I was working in the dry earth, I watched the children herding the livestock, and I was reminded of these scriptures from Isaiah, the fifty-third chapter, verses two through six: 'For he shall grow up before him as a tender plant, and as a root out of a dry ground: he hath no form nor comeliness; and when we shall see him, there is no beauty that we should desire him. He is despised and rejected of men; a man of sorrows, and acquainted with grief: and we hid as it were our faces from him; he was despised, and we esteemed him not. Surely he hath borne our griefs, and carried our sorrows: yet we did esteem him stricken, smitten of God, and afflicted. But he was wounded for our transgressions, he was bruised for our iniquities: the chastisement of our peace was upon him; and with his stripes we are healed. All we like sheep have gone astray; we have turned every one to his own way; and the Lord hath laid on him the iniquity of us all.'"

The image of the suffering Christ filled Jed's thoughts as the words *All we like sheep have gone astray; we have turned every one to his own way* ran repeatedly through his mind. He considered the turmoil of the new nation and his own personal turmoil that had prompted his faithless tirade earlier. Then he contemplated the phrase *And with his stripes we are healed.*

Removing himself from the gathering, Jed pondered the upcoming militia drills that were preparing him to leave for war. He considered his place in the universe and his reckoning with his Creator. Suddenly, he felt compelled to seek God, and in a cluster of evergreens near the house, he fell to his knees and let his thoughts run to God and godly things. He posed his questions regarding the purpose of life until finally a peace settled over him, assuring him of a plan for each and every person on the earth. Armed with that assurance, Jed began inventorying his many blessings as a sense of gratitude displaced the remaining slivers of selfish hurt.

He jumped as he felt a hand on his shoulder, compromising his solitude. Turning to grumble at the intruder, Jed's eyes met the intense, onyx stare of "the ghost" of the Willows.

The man bent a blanketed arm to point to himself. "Pearson's son knows Charles?"

Jed scrambled to his feet and nodded, half frightened, half mesmerized by the old face. Charles pointed back at Jed. "You uncover grave. I hear and come quickly. You must not do this." He shook his head with deliberateness. "Woman rest there. Must not move her."

Jed was momentarily speechless, then questioned timidly, "May I . . . ask . . . who she is?"

Charles stared into Jed's eyes as if considering the request. "Let the dead rest. Hannah . . . Sun Woman . . . she *your* woman?"

The young man's face became taut with pain as his head shook in sadness.

"I hoped . . . you . . . Sun Woman . . . bring peace to your lodges," Charles said, disappointment in his tone.

"Peace . . . lodges? Do you know about . . . ?" Jed stopped and looked askance at the man, recalling Susannah's claim that his family had killed her mother. "You were my grandfather's friend. Do you know anything about him and the McClintocks?"

Charles's face softened at the mention of the surname of the woman he had helped bury so long ago. "Go to Hannah. Make peace so the dead can rest. Then Charles can follow his people to the Delaware." And as silently as he'd arrived, he was gone again.

Go to Hannah . . . make peace, Charles had counseled him. He longed for nothing more, but how should he proceed?

* * *

Jed barely slept all night, a regrettable way to begin four days of bivouacking with the Patuxent militia. Abel brought a linen sack filled with stores and a few of Bitty's hot biscuits for the ride. As Jed took them, he looked Abel in the eye and extended his hand to the man.

"You and your father were right about the grave, Abel. We're not going to move it."

Abel looked askance at Jed and nodded slightly as he gingerly shook his hand.

"I guess I'm like Bitty. I tend to mull things over before I take good advice, but I appreciate getting it. I hope you'll always feel inclined to share your opinions with me."

Abel continued to eye Jed with skepticism.

"When I get back I'll be making another hunting trip into the mountains. There's plenty of game up there. Would you join me?"

Abel squinted and then his eyebrows arched in pleasant surprise. "I would," he replied simply. "It's been a while since I've even held a gun, let alone fired one."

"Take this and practice while I'm away," Jed said as he pulled his musket from its sling.

Abel stepped back in protest, but Jed nodded and persisted. "I still have my rifle."

A look of pride crossed Abel's face as he held the symbol of trust in his hands. Jed mounted Tildie and extended his hand again in farewell, and this time Abel took it quickly.

* * *

The Patuxent Regiment of the Maryland militia was a mixture of backwoods crack-shots, freemen, and farmers of varying degrees of wealth. Mingled within their ranks were a few old veterans. Once assembled, however, they were of one mind and one purpose. Jed was warmly greeted by the men as he came into camp. In addition, he found the association with his neighbors comforting in light of the war talk simmering around each fire.

When Frederick Stringham rode into camp, Jed was pleasantly surprised. For some reason he hadn't expected the family to honor the January 1812 law that had called for all able-bodied white male citizens of Maryland between eighteen and forty-five years of age to perform militia duty. Somehow, Jed was comforted in knowing that at least in this one area, even his unscrupulous neighbors felt equally threatened and desirous to be part of the community. Still, he felt a twinge of sadness at the lost friendship.

Frederick and Jed nodded as they passed, each feeling the curious scrutiny of other neighbors upon them. The two made it a point to be cordial but separate throughout the four-day exercise. When the hour came to be assigned to groups, Jed carefully watched as the men were divided, purposely positioning himself to be excluded from Frederick Stringham's company.

By law the men could be drilled for only three hours without refreshment and for no more than six hours a day. Despite the restriction, and because most of the men felt as Jed did—that the reported skirmishes along the Canadian border were simply a prelude to the sought-after prizes of Washington City and Baltimore—they remained clustered in groups long after they were dismissed. During these impromptu gatherings they discussed weaknesses along the riverfront and defensible points that could be exploited to their advantage.

On Saturday morning, the son of the militia commander came riding in with a memo. His father's face grew pale as he read it. Within minutes, word of war news drew the militiamen to the commander's side like moths to a fire.

"We've received word from the Canadian front, men—bad news. The Indian chief Tecumseh has been rallying warriors from various tribes in an effort to eject all Americans from what they consider to be their land. They call this alliance the First Nations Confederacy, and it's rumored that their numbers have reached eight hundred and grow larger every day."

Murmurings swept through the assembly as each man considered the terror the Indians could inflict upon the settlements and forts thinly scattered along the northern frontier.

"It gets worse. Fort Mackinac has surrendered. Some three hundred whites and seven hundred natives of various tribes moved throughout the village, taking all residents as their prisoners. Lieutenant Hanks, the officer in charge of the fort, didn't even know war had been formally declared, so finding his small garrison of sixty soldiers completely outnumbered and unprepared for such an engagement, he took the prudent course and surrendered to avoid an all-out massacre."

Jed suddenly remembered Dudley Snowden's recent transfer to the Canadian front. "Are the names of the men captured or taken prisoner listed? I have a friend deployed near there."

"Pray he hasn't been sent to Detroit," remarked the commander. "It's rumored that Tecumseh and his First Nations warriors are headed that way."

Jed felt a chill run through him.

The commander stepped onto a stump as his voice boomed above the men's heads. "Men, by law we are only required to drill four days between March and December, but I believe we can all see the handwriting on the wall. The Department of War has failed to communicate with their outposts, and they have yet to formulate an overall strategy. Secretary Eustis still denies that Washington City is the ultimate target and therefore has made no additional provisions to further protect the city beyond the institution of the local militias. If the British are willing to inflame the Indians, even those who were once friendly to our settlers, then there is no telling what other savagery they may wreak upon us to achieve a victory. There are rumors of traitors amongst us, even now, whose loyalties remain tied to the Crown. If such men aid and abet the British, we could see slave revolts here that would rival the Indian attacks up north. Gentlemen, we may be the only hope for our area. We may not be able to stop the British from attacking our capital, but we must at least defend our homes and families and make every attempt to slow the redcoats down. I am dismissing you until our next scheduled drill, but if any of you desire to muster before that, or if you hear news that would give us reason to gather our company sooner, send word to me at my home and I will send runners to each and every one of your farms. Until then, God speed."

A sudden sense of urgency filled Jed and others in his company, each quickly packing and then driving their horses at top speed down the road from Bladensburg to their farms. A few miles from his home, Jed saw Frederick stooped beside his gelding, picking a stone from its left front hoof. Out of courtesy he stopped to check on his neighbor. "Everything all right?"

Frederick recognized the voice, looked up, and smiled awkwardly. "Just a stone."

An uncomfortable silence hovered until Jed spoke. "Shall I ride along . . . to be sure he can make it home?"

"Uh . . . I'm sure he'll be all right, but thank you."

Grateful he'd declined the offer, Jed responded, "Well enough, then. There won't be any more houses to stop at for help soon . . . just long stretches of open fields."

Frederick nodded soberly. "I was just thinking about what Lieutenant Peyton said today. There's so much land to protect, with only a handful of people per thousand acres to keep watch."

Jed measured his old friend's words carefully. "In times like these, a man needs to trust his neighbors more than ever."

Frederick stared thoughtfully at Pearson. "I agree."

"Is there any reason for White Oak and the Willows to be under any particular caution?"

Hearing the implication in his neighbor's voice, Frederick stalled as he ran an approving hand down his mount's fetlock, then mounted her with a delicate skill Jed had forgotten the man possessed. He turned to his old friend. "Jed, no matter what you think of me, I hope you would know that I would never willingly allow any harm to come to your family or to the Willows."

Jed's eyes dropped from Frederick's somber face to stare at the ground as if searching for his reply there. "There was a time when such reassurance would not have been needed."

"I miss those days," Frederick muttered sadly.

Jed raised an eyebrow in response. "Well, if you feel you'll be all right, I'll be on my way." He tipped his hat, pulled Tildie's reins, and gave her a stern kick. Frederick watched dejectedly as Tildie stirred up the dirt along the trail and the pair disappeared ghostlike into the dusty haze.

Frederick took extra care with Branson, his gelding, walking him carefully the rest of the way home. He arrived at the main horse barn Saturday evening at dusk, when the fireflies were just beginning to flicker above the grass line. Removing the saddle and bridle, he waved the stableman off, preferring to tend to the horse himself. He needed a few minutes to collect himself before heading into the small frame house that he and Penelope shared. *Shared* was the wrong word. Frederick cringed with guilt over the travesty he had committed in binding the timid woman into a loveless union that was more of a business merger than a marriage.

Penelope was a good person—a plump, plain, egoless girl who believed her own opinions and needs were of such small consequence that they were never voiced. Stewart had struck a deal that essentially exchanged the prospectless Penelope for an impressive dowry of three female slaves who would serve as her attendants, and for a stable full of fine quarter horses that added nicely to Stewart's stock. Initially, the woman was willing to accept any arrangement that would free her from her father's disappointed gaze, and Stewart had done a fine job of convincing Frederick that a quick marriage would issue Francis Pearson such a retaliatory scalding that he would gain great respect along the river for the move. But the truth? As kind and unde-manding as Penelope was, after anticipating a union with the spirited Frannie, no woman—particularly not one with such a dull manner—could ever interest him. Aside from performing his wedding night obligation to consummate the marriage, he had avoided all intimacies and bonding with his wife. His was a cruel twist of fate, but his cold response to his emotionally disenfranchised wife was something he could address, even improve, perhaps. However, since seeing Frannie at the funeral, his inclinations toward his wife had lessened even further, while thoughts of his first love tore at his peace of mind.

He gazed at the house like a condemned man staring off at the gallows. His relief was palpable when the stableman told him a carriage had come that morning and ferried both Miss Penelope and his mother to his wife's home in Virginia for a visit. *At least she and Mother are friends.* A pang of guilt momentarily lessened his joy. He knew what a cad his father-in-law believed him to be. Oddly, his cold treatment of Penelope had somehow inclined her father's heart toward her, and she had finally won the pleasure of being her daddy's girl.

Before slowly closing the barn door, he picked up his gun and the deerskin haversack that held his ammunition. He thought he heard a rustle in the trees that separated the property upon which his house stood from the cleared, landscaped lawns that surrounded his father's more palatial home. A horse whinnied and a whispered voice sought to calm it. Then Frederick heard another rustle as a form slipped from the trees and onto the porch of the White Oak mansion.

Quickly reopening the barn door, Frederick slid protectively behind the cover it provided, then cocked the hammer of his rifle and crept in the direction of the house, his eyes scanning quickly in all directions. The intruder was nowhere to be found. Suddenly Frederick saw shadows moving across the dimly lit window of his father's office, and he crept silently onto the wraparound porch and made his way outside the room. His palms were sweaty and his breathing shallow and rapid, requiring all his self-control to avoid gasping and alerting the trespasser to his position. Pressing his slim body against the shutter that framed the window, he listened to ascertain the nature of the intruder's intentions. He told himself not to move from the position lest he expose himself and succumb to the prowler as well. Despite his intentions, the strange vocal inflections tugged at his curiosity, luring him from his safe place. He quickly stole a glance at the man whose demeanor was anything but hostile.

He was in his mid-twenties, Frederick presumed, and dressed in a finely tailored suit. His complexion was too light to be Negro and too ethnic to be white. Frederick knew this was the rumored mulatto man named Duprée who had eluded the authorities since attacking Frannie. The friendly exchange he heard between his father and the felon nauseated him. Suddenly, every one of his unproven suspicions beat upon his fragile peace of mind like a hammer.

He had denied the nagging doubts that pointed the finger of suspicion at his father's recent actions. Why had Stewart made such efforts to powerfully position himself along the river while remaining aloof from the society of his neighbors? Having stepped back and evaluated the debacle at Calverton, Frederick could now see that his father had carefully twisted the day's events to assure the end of his engagement to Frannie, and worse, the sullying of her reputation.

Frederick pondered Lieutenant Peyton's ominous warning about the British inciting the fear of Indian massacres to press even hardened soldiers into surrendering. He could only imagine the venom that would be unleashed by turning slaves upon masters, and he knew the number of runaways had increased recently, with people saying they had seen an exotic man skulking around their property days before the escapes. At the bivouac he had even heard men warn one another to keep their eyes out for traitors who might swear allegiance to the Crown in return for amnesty and protection. Frederick knew his self-seeking father fit the profile of such a man, but in truth he'd never dreamed that his father could side with the British when it was he who'd signed the papers registering Frederick for the militia.

He covered his ears with his hands to drown out the sounds of the negotiations taking place beyond the glass, and tears stung his eyes.

Whatever last shred of decency that remained somewhere within his father had now been compromised. Frederick knew that a decision now rested upon him. As the men exited the room, he heard laughter fade, and he slid beyond the corner to wait discreetly for the door to open. His father scanned the area before offering the spy a parting handshake and a final promise of agreement.

Frederick instinctively raised his rifle without knowing at whom to point it. *Both are traitors,* he told himself. *But one is my father.* He hesitated as a lifetime of intimidation again stole his will, and then something happened. As the man Frederick assumed was Duprée slipped into the tree line, he saw his father's expression turn from camaraderie to enmity. He wondered what Duprée would have thought if he had turned and noticed the look his father wore as he gingerly removed his handkerchief and meticulously scrubbed the hand he had just offered Duprée as a token of allegiance. He knew that expression. It was the same expression his father had shown him at the Calverton auction and at the Cattail Inn. It was the same look he had used the day he told Frederick he was too weak to run White Oak, pressing and pressing him until he succumbed to his father's will, the price of which was the loss of Frannie. Fury roiled in him.

As the sound of Duprée's horse faded away, he slung his arm through the rifle strap and slipped quietly behind his father as the traitor turned to enter the house. He placed one hand over his father's mouth and used the other to wrench his arm back and up until he heard a muffled cry erupt from beneath his fingers. He shoved his father past the entryway mirror, where he saw the terrified reflection of the man who had always held him in derision and for whose respect he would have given nearly anything. Suddenly, the taut age lines around the eyes and mouth and the graying hair that framed the thin, leathery face made Stewart Stringham appear weak and shockingly mortal. For the first time Frederick felt the rush of his own manhood in his father's presence.

He knew his father had shooed the servants from the house to ensure the privacy of his meeting, and it pleased him to have another advantage over the man whose destiny he now would control. Frederick pushed Stewart through a back doorway and into the windowless pantry. Once inside he shoved his trembling father to the ground and warned him in a voice, so filled with contempt that it was unrecognizable, to sit on the floor with his hands behind his head. Having positioned his father, Frederick closed the door and struck a match to light the candle on the shelf.

With his first glimpse of his captor, Stewart seemed both horrified and relieved. Seeing the emotions flit across his father's face, Frederick knew he would need to keep his wits about him or the old man would somehow twist the situation as he always did until his own thinking was so confused that he would capitulate.

"Frederick!" Stewart's voice dripped with condescending affection. "Why the intrigue?"

"Don't play innocent, you traitor!" Frederick seethed, pointing downward at his father. "I know who that man was, and I know what you have agreed to do!"

Stewart's face showed no emotion, as if Frederick's revelations were of no consequence whatsoever. "Good," he replied nonchalantly as he lowered his hands from his head to his lap.

Frederick's head reeled. "Good? Are you mad?"

Stewart looked disappointedly at Frederick as if the dolt had again fallen short of the mark. "I thought you said you knew the situation."

Against his will, Frederick's mind slipped into an old defensive posture, and he had to catch himself to restore his sense of reason. "I know you are making an alliance with a known felon and a traitor! I know you are agreeing to cooperate with the British against your own neighbors to save yourself at their expense. That is what I know, Father!" His chest heaved with emotion, and it required every particle of his integrity to hold fast to right and discard the wrong as his father attempted to counter his logic. He pulled his rifle over his shoulder and aimed. "I also know that I could call for the sheriff right now and have you arrested. Better yet," he whispered madly, "I could drag your traitorous carcass to the Willows and allow your neighbors to have a go at getting the details of your sedition from you. These are the things I know, Father!"

For a moment Stewart Stringham actually seemed cowed. His expression became more contrite and his bearing shrank like a grape withering in the sunlight. Then his demeanor changed so visibly that one could almost see the idea enter his wretched brain.

"What offends you more, son? My treason . . . or the fact that the man I am in league with is Duprée? *You* chose to believe that Francis Pearson had committed an indiscretion against you. *You* announced the end of your engagement. No one put a gun to your head to force you to marry your third cousin. *You* agreed to do it to save face and to secure your control of White Oak. But tonight you faced the reality that Duprée really is the unequaled reprobate Miss Pearson claimed him to be." Stewart's voice gushed with false empathy. "That's what pains you, isn't it, Frederick? You forfeited your chance to marry the woman you loved, and now you are trapped—yes, ensnared like a helpless cub—in a loveless marriage with a woman you cannot bear to touch. I can understand your hurt. I forgive you for taking your anger out on me. A father understands . . ."

As Stewart talked, Frederick lowered the gun as if it had become too heavy to carry. His free hand rushed to his head as if to tear the mangled interpretations of truth from his mind. Then he raised the gun again at his father and yelled, "No!" in a voice so crazed that Stewart scooted into a corner and hid beneath his raised arms. "You! You did it all. I see that now."

Frederick stomped about the narrow pantry floor as pieces of the puzzle fell into place. "All of it! Your infatuation with ruining Jed Pearson, your attempts to turn me against Frannie, all of it. But the worst of it was the way you made me believe it was always my idea, or somehow . . . my fault." He knew he was rambling now. He still couldn't prove anything, but he knew too many pieces fit together in a sick sense for the others not to also have a place in the tale.

"Why did you never speak of your Revolutionary service, Father? When most men of your age burn the candlelight recounting their tales of fighting the British, why have no such stories ever passed your lips? Was it because you served even then as a spy? Had you sold your soul to the Crown even then in exchange for the fortune with which you bought White Oak?"

"You ignorant, impotent pup," Stewart blurted out. "You speak of patriotism as if it were a term devised by Franklin and Washington. Before these men were born, England was our mother! Her arms brought me here, and it was to her that I owed my first allegiance. Many of my peers felt this way long after shots were fired at Concord."

"Yes, but did those men lurk amongst their freedom-seeking neighbors proclaiming one philosophy while secretly serving to undermine it?"

Stewart's taut jaw flexed angrily.

"Did you sit at your flag-draped window and shoot your neighbors in the back as they marched past, Father!"

Stewart leapt to his feet and pointed a shaking finger in his son's face. "Say what you will, but my only crime is in having had the foresight to remain loyal to the side I knew would win in the end. You think the War of Independence ended with the Treaty of Paris? Well, King George was a madman when it was signed, and most of his advisors knew that. I knew the day would come when Britain would return to claim her rightful territories, and that those who had remained loyal to her throughout this democratic experiment would be rewarded. Yes, I played along, tolerating the childish toddling of this ridiculous government. But I also did everything in my power to keep us separate enough to place us in a position to be singled out when the Crown came seeking loyalists. I knew they would need only one ally in each district, a powerful ally, and I did what was needed to make sure they would come to me."

"By being the most obvious coward and traitor?" Frederick spat.

Incensed, Stewart knocked the gun aside and grabbed Frederick by his lapels, his graveled voice tinged with fear. "Call me what you will, but they are coming, Frederick, and with a brutality that you cannot begin to fathom. They will not lose another contest with this upstart nation. They plan to burn everything that stands in their way, and the only hope of surviving this assault is to cooperate. I do not fund them nor do I form their policy, but I have secured our survival by offering White Oak as a base of operations for Duprée's raids, and someday, when White Oak is the last surviving plantation in this area, you will thank me."

Frederick pushed Stewart back against the shelves. "Then what was the point of signing me up for militia duty? Am I just another sacrifice for the cause?"

"No, no, son," Stewart argued more gently. "It was necessary to comply with the law and keep the eyes of scrutiny from bearing down on us. Duprée understands that."

Frederick's head spun as he sought to regain some semblance of the surety he had when he began this confrontation. "And you can conscience such a move without even raising a warning to your neighbors?" He felt sick to his stomach as if he were about to retch. "Well, I cannot. I made a vow . . . to Jed . . . this very afternoon."

"What sort of a vow?"

"We vowed as neighbors to watch over one another's properties."

Stewart shook his head soberly. "You have simply made a vow to a dead man."

Frederick's eyes opened wide in horror. "What are you saying?"

"Duprée has been given a particularly free hand in managing the preparation of this area for battle. A personal vendetta will be waged against the Pearsons and the Willows. No one is meant to survive the assault he will bring down upon that plantation."

"Not even Frannie?" Frederick could barely form the words through his trembling lips. When his father remained emotionless, Frederick let out a guttural groan and slid to the pantry floor.

"And when will this begin?" he asked with a broken voice.

"No one knows the time frame."

"We must warn someone," cried Frederick. "You could meet with the governor. Do it anonymously if you fear retribution. For heaven's sake, Father, you will be a party to the massacre of hundreds of your neighbors. How will you ever be able to live with that?"

"If Duprée hears so much as a whisper of warning leave your lips, he will turn his wrath equally upon White Oak and us. You cannot save them, Frederick. Instead, you'll end up dying with the Pearsons. Besides, men like Alexander Hanson have been warning the government for weeks. What has it gotten him? His 'friends and neighbors' destroyed his printing press and annihilated his offices, and for what? In the sacred cause of patriotism! If the government refuses to give heed to him, what credence do you think they will give to the ranting of an old farmer? Accept it, Frederick, and choose sides, but choose quickly. I can provide a means for your survival, but only if you do exactly what I say. Do you understand?"

Frederick rocked back and forth like a child, his soft moans echoing in the confined space as he struggled to grasp the horrific facts. Stewart couldn't bear the pitiful scene playing out before his eyes, forcing him to face the ugliness of the future events he had consented to help set in motion. Therefore, he was grateful for a scratching sound, presumably of a mouse, that gave him an excuse to leave the larder to fetch a broom with which to chase the rodent.

Frederick pulled himself up and leaned against the door for several seconds before he trusted his legs to bear his weight. As he staggered across the yard to his house, he felt haunted by the spirits of the men and women who would come back to this place and cry out for vengeance against those who had withheld their warning. He pressed his hands to his head and stumbled into his house, caring little about what would happen to him. The world he knew was now over.

CHAPTER 30

Baltimore, Maryland
July 26, 1812

Hannah's pen was poised above her journal as she finished reviewing her most recent entry:

> *The dream played out as it has before, beginning with the oppressive darkness. But it no longer held me in jeopardy because I anticipated that reassuring voice, and then the arms which lifted and conveyed me away from every trepidation. But then a new element entered my vision.*
>
> *After my protector carried me to safety, another voice called my name. I recognized it immediately, but I refused to grant it a place in my happy interpretation because I had already secretly ascribed a name to my rescuer. But night after night, the undeniable voice returned, until the face that accompanied the voice was made manifest to me. It was Andrew's.*
>
> *At Myrna's wedding, Andrew was my loyal, doting escort throughout the day's festivities. As we stood as attendants, watching Myrna and Mr. Baumgardner exchanging vows, I felt Andrew's gaze upon me. I knew he was leaping forward in his mind to the day when we too would stand and pledge our troth to one another. I glanced in my parents' direction, and saw my father beaming with his arm securely wrapped around my mother. He seemed overcome with joy as he watched the pleasure play across Mother's momentarily placid countenance, and I knew the meaning of my dream.*

Jed was my rescuer, having saved me from the darkness of my miserable childhood. Then, as brothers must, he passed me off to another, to Andrew, with whom my future now lies.

It is time for me to lay aside all my childhood fantasies and give thanks to God for showing me my path. Somewhere in my mind I have withheld a portion of myself from Andrew, holding out hope that Jed would return to claim me. But it is to Andrew that I have given my promises and pledged myself, and it must be to Andrew that I now turn my loyalties. I find it curious that, having accepted this new interpretation of my nightmare, it did not return to me during last night's repose. This leaves me to assume that dear Beatrice was right about my nightmares all along. They were merely an extension of my troubled mind, and now that I have properly sorted out my feelings and my duties, they will likely no longer trouble me at all.

* * *

Hannah scolded herself mildly for sleeping late and therefore missing the church service at the local Episcopal church. By the time she dressed in her blue cotton dress and headed downstairs, the mantel clock was chiming eleven times. She searched the parlor and the dining room but found no sign of Beatrice. A covered dish set at her place at the table, holding bacon slices, three griddlecakes, and a spoonful of corn pudding. The food was warm, probably resulting more from the temperature in the room than from the recentness of preparation. Hannah took a forkful of corn pudding and nibbled on a slice of bacon as Martha directed her into the back garden where she found Beatrice sitting in an Adirondack chair under the maple tree, scouring the morning paper.

"There's a lovely piece in the society section about the wedding," Beatrice commented.

"You gave her a wonderful wedding, Beatrice. You must be exhausted. I overslept, and I have to admit it was delicious."

"I agree, but *we* gave her a wonderful wedding, Hannah. I couldn't have planned it without your help. Even Mother and Father enjoyed themselves."

"Have you received any word from them?"

"No. I wish they would have stayed here last night, but Father was so impatient about getting Mother home . . . I imagine they pressed on all night rather than staying at an inn."

Hannah leaned back and smiled. "Mother looked beautiful, didn't she? And Father . . . I can't remember the last time he seemed totally at peace."

Beatrice pursed her lips in momentary shame. "I often wondered how he managed to remain with her when he easily could have had her committed, but he wouldn't hear of it. He has been utterly devoted to her. His situation forced his hand at times, but I've learned so many lessons about love and marriage from his example. He gave his all to honor his vows. I choose to believe the Lord will reward that manner of love in eternity."

Hannah marveled at her sister's comment. "That's a beautiful sentiment, Beatrice, but where did you get such a notion? You're not normally one to question church doctrine."

Beatrice laid the paper in her lap. "I keep hearing the preacher's words in my mind. 'I now pronounce you man and wife until such time as you are parted by death . . .' They were the same words pronounced at my own wedding. At that moment they meant nothing—the limits were meaningless. When I saw the way Father looked at Mother, the most powerful thought came into my mind. For some, it might be enough—a union that lasts a lifetime and nothing more. But for others, for those whose love fills more than a lifetime and for those whom life has cheated, there must be something more, something that transcends death, something that allows love to continue where death and sickness have no claim."

Mesmerized, Hannah breathed, "Be careful, Beatrice. You're beginning to sound like me." She clasped her sister's hands within her own. "What prompts this train of thought?"

Beatrice shook her head to dismiss the question. "So tell me about this delicious night's rest you've had. Are the dreams gone now?"

Hannah eyed her sadly. "Confide in me, Beatrice. Something is troubling you."

"So your dreams . . . were you not troubled by them last night?"

Hannah relented and allowed her sister to channel the discussion away from herself. "I saw it through to its conclusion last evening, and now I understand its meaning."

Beatrice thought she detected a note of regret in Hannah's voice. "And . . . ?"

Hannah widened eyes. "It was as you said all along—something my mind created to avoid the commitments I've made with Andrew." Hannah was surprised by her sister's melancholy silence in response to the news. "I thought you'd be pleased."

"If that is what you believe it means, then I am pleased for you to have your answer."

"What's wrong, Beatrice?"

Beatrice smiled sadly. "I began to favor the notion that your dreams were from God."

Only Hannah could ever know what that statement would have meant to her a day earlier.

"Instead, it seems I am the one looking for hope and you are becoming pragmatic," Beatrice continued, her disappointment now penetrating Hannah's stoicism.

"This really isn't about my dreams or even Myrna's wedding, is it? What's really on your mind?"

Beatrice beat her fists against her skirt. "I don't want to talk about what is on my mind. My mind is filled with fear and sorrow." She slid down into her chair. "I want to feel God's assurance wrap around me. I want peace and goodwill on earth." She crumpled into a ball.

"Have you received word about Dudley?" Hannah questioned as she hurried to her sister's side.

Beatrice opened the paper to the front page where the headline read, "Forts Fall in Fear of Massacres," and then she handed the paper to Hannah as she tried to disguise her worry.

They had not heard from Dudley in weeks. He had prepared them to expect long periods without word, particularly if he were engaging the enemy. Knowing that reports such as this would be littering the local papers, Hannah realized his silence boded poorly for his situation.

"Fort Mackinac may be hundreds of miles from Dudley and Detroit," Hannah offered hopefully. At her suggestion, Beatrice ran into the house with Hannah following closely behind. She searched the map on Dudley's wall for the red circle labeled *Fort Detroit.* Then they searched for the location of the surrendered Fort Mackinac. Their hearts fell when Hannah's finger found the spot.

"It's only a few days' march away from Fort Detroit," Beatrice gasped.

"Don't panic. Let's think . . . We could speak to Andrew. Surely he'll have information."

"I tried to corner him on the matter yesterday. All he could or would tell me was that he had no reports of any engagements between Dudley's garrison and the British."

"All right," Hannah stalled. "What about that Captain Mack that Dudley wrote about?"

"His family lives in Tunbridge, Vermont." Beatrice sounded even more disheartened.

"Why don't we write to them and see if they have received any word? Perhaps the two companies have been separated. Perhaps the captain's family has more recent news."

As unreasonable as it sounded, Beatrice was willing to grasp hold of the smallest glimmer of hope. She hurried upstairs to get the letters. "Here it is!" she cried as she read the paragraph out loud. "I am enclosing the captain's address as well as that of his sister, Lucy Mack Smith. Captain Mack assures me she will gladly help us survey the community for a location suitable for opening a shop. You may wish to employ her services as an artist as well. Her oilcloth paintings sell for use as tablecloths, curtains, and wall hangings in the area. Perhaps you could begin a correspondence with her and preview the area through your dialogues."

Beatrice set the letter down, then looked at Hannah thoughtfully. "I'm going to first write Captain Mack's wife to see if she has any further information regarding our husbands' company. I'll post the letter tomorrow morning," she said, waving her hands nervously. "I wish there was something more I could do."

"We'll pray, sweetness," Hannah sighed, stroking her sister's hair. "And we'll give thanks that Dudley doesn't have to worry about us the way we are worrying about him."

"Yes. At least he knows we're safe here in Baltimore. At least we can offer him that."

CHAPTER 31

The Willows
Monday Morning, July 27, 1812

Jed had returned home from militia duty on Sunday afternoon in a melancholy mood, then locked himself up in his office with Markus until the wee hours of the morning. Bitty had been worried when she saw the lamps burning in Jed's office window until late into the night. It was somewhere near two in the morning when she finally saw Jed's bedroom lamp go out and Markus slipping from the house in the direction of his own snug cottage.

Bitty pulled the shades down the next morning and let Jed sleep late, until nearly noon. So worried was she about his erratic schedule of late that she would have let him sleep on even longer. However that hope was dashed by the sound of a horse's hooves pounding down the lane, followed shortly thereafter by Bitty's reluctant rapping at Jed's door to announce the rider.

"Jed? Are you sleepin'?" she called softly. "Timothy Shepard is here for you . . . but if you're still restin' I'll just have Jack send him away."

Jed had ignored most of the message until hearing the name of his friend, at which point he jumped from his bed and slid into a pair of trousers. "Offer him some breakfast, please, Bitty, and tell him I'll be right down."

He dressed hurriedly, taking the time only to brush his long, dark hair back and away from his eyes. Glancing in the mirror, he felt far older than his twenty-two years. His face was dark from four days of stubble, and his body ached both from fieldwork and the long days of marching and crouching over maps while devising battle plans. He knew, though, that it was more than that. The weight of the unknown was bearing down upon him, as well as the responsibility he alone bore for every life on the Willows.

Looking over at the rolled parchment on his nightstand, Jed felt a sense of contentment. He and Markus had discussed it until nearly dawn, and he was planning to meet with Jerome directly after breakfast to go over the document. Now, however, that meeting would have to wait until he tended to whatever business had brought Timothy to the plantation. He slipped his suspenders over his white shirt and quickly slid into socks and boots and bounded down the stairs to the foyer where the front door still hung open, displaying Timothy's weary frame. Jed hurried out the door to greet his friend with his arms outstretched and a moon-sized smile across his face. He wrapped his larger frame around his guest like a bearskin and greeted him joyously.

"Timothy! Let me take a look at you!" He pulled away to survey the changes Washington City living was wreaking on his old friend. His clothes were dirty and threadbare, his eyes ringed with dark circles. "Living among the powerful men of government has not made you a man of fashion. You look positively dreadful!" teased Jed. "Has our government gone bankrupt? Are there no wages to be paid to faithful civil servants like yourself?"

"Very funny," laughed Jed's weary friend as he surveyed his own dusty attire. "Money I have. It's time I lack. When I do find a few hours to myself, the last thing I care to do is to head off to some emporium to shop for fripperies." The fatigue in his voice under-scored his words.

"Well, then I feel extremely flattered that you would share some of your scant free time by visiting me. Why didn't you let Bitty bring you inside so she could give you a bite to eat?"

"I am exhausted," Timothy admitted, "but I have concerns far greater than fatigue. I need to speak to you . . . alone, Jed. How long I stay will depend on our conversation."

Jed led the way into the house and back to the kitchen where Bitty was scrambling eggs. She eyed Timothy as he followed Jed into the room, as he seemed to regard her with odd curiosity. Jed sidled over to his surrogate mother and placed a loving arm around her and a kiss on her head. Immediately the tension eased from her tiny, taut body. He whispered in her ear and she cast a final, doubtful look at the guest before handing Jed her spoon and heading outside.

Jed knew the unconventional relationship he and Bitty shared seemed paradoxical to the antislavery Pennsylvanian. "If I had known you were coming, I would have had Bitty set out a fine brunch. Since you require secrecy, you'll be treated to eggs à la Pearson instead."

"I believe your maid and I got off on the wrong foot just then," Timothy chuckled.

"Bitty?" Jed replied with a tinge of annoyance in his voice. "Bitty isn't my maid, Timothy. She's as near a mother to me as anyone could be. In most ways, this is *her* home, and I do best when I remember that." He laughed uneasily, hoping to break the tension.

Timothy marveled at the response. "My apologies. I didn't mean to sound impudent. It's just not how most Northerners expect Southern plantation owners to manage their slaves."

Jed tensed as his annoyance increased. "They are my *family,* Timothy. Aside from my sister, Frannie, they are the people I love best and most in this world, and the people I believe love me best as well. Beyond that, I cannot explain it further." Jed unceremoniously plopped a large scoop of eggs onto his friend's plate.

"I'm sorry. I seem to constantly irritate your sensibilities. I apologize, Jed. Perhaps I should just get on to my business. Have you heard from our mutual friend General Lee lately?"

"Our *mutual* friend? Light-Horse Harry?" Jed replied inquisitively. "How do you know him? I never introduced the two of you, did I?"

"Not directly," Timothy replied as he wolfed down a large spoonful of eggs. "You mentioned me to him, though. He asked for me throughout the city and then used his association with you to meet me. He was a pleasant enough chap, so I agreed to a lunch with him. His opinions on the war differed from mine, but he seemed reasonable and private about them at the time. His name is now being rumored in Washington City, and the talk is not good."

Jed's confusion was apparent. "Dudley Snowden introduced me. Then I spent a few days with Harry, touring some Alexandria horse farms while he spoke of his past. We shared some political conversations, and then at our parting he offered me an open invitation to sit in on a game of whist sometime, but that's the only association I have really had with the man. As I said, I think he is a good man, but that's really the extent of our contact."

Timothy raised one eyebrow. "He offered you an invitation to join in a game of cards? Is that all he said at your parting? Did he mention the name of the host?"

Jed rehearsed the brief conversation again in his mind. "He said there would be a prestigious assembly of players and that he would like me to meet his friends."

"He extended a similar invitation to me," Timothy said with note of mystery.

Jed laughed sarcastically. "Forgive me, but I cannot see how an invitation to play cards has become a matter of political intrigue."

"I do not think his invitation had anything to do with a game of cards. I believe he was attempting to arrange a meeting with his antiwar friends . . . to recruit us, so to speak."

"I don't see a correlation," Jed stated dubiously as he poured mugs of fresh milk and slathered strawberry preserves on slices of hot bread.

"First of all," Timothy answered between bites, "there are rumors that Hanson has secured another property in Baltimore, on Charles Street."

"Alexander Contee Hanson? The newspaper editor whose editorial ended up getting his offices razed?"

"The same. He is relocating his *Federal Republican* newspaper to this address. Apparently, he printed another inflammatory, antiwar paper in Georgetown and plans to distribute it tomorrow in Baltimore. While his antiwar focus will continue in future editions, this paper is intended to attack Baltimore's leadership."

"That sounds like madness on his part. By infuriating those who control the police and the local militias, he will be left completely unprotected."

"Exactly. While he is acting within the framework of the law, he must know he is placing himself and his supporters in harm's way. Harry Lee is rumored to be one of those men."

Worried, Jed winced and became more focused.

Timothy continued with a sigh. "Hanson has become a symbol both for those who disagree with the war and for those who see this issue as a defense of free press itself. Word of his return to Baltimore has trickled to sympathizers in that city. They will make their stand with him alongside several of his personal friends and family members. There are also several notables in the group from the Washington City area—a physician, a lawyer, and a professor, as well as several other former soldiers. By far his most critical and influential supporter could be Harry Lee. In such a dangerous situation, with the odds stacked so highly against you, wouldn't you want Light-Horse Harry by your side?"

Jed recalled the stories the men swapped in the capital, tales such as Harry's miraculous command of seven brave men at Valley Forge and how the little band of fearless patriots routed two hundred British cavalrymen. Jed answered thoughtfully, "He was a great soldier and a true American hero, but that was over thirty years ago. He's now a weathered, nearly broken man."

"But he inspires people. Having him on one's side would tip the scales somewhat."

"All you have are rumors and assumptions. Do you have any proof that Harry is making a stand with Hanson?"

"I know for a fact that Mr. Lee left Alexandria a few days ago, headed for Baltimore."

Jed couldn't deny the curious timing, and Timothy became emboldened by his silence. "As the rumors mounted, I asked myself why Lee sought me out so painstakingly. Hearing that he also tried to get you to meet his friends makes me feel certain I am right. I believe the general is trying to be sure that Hanson has an influential group of men assembled at the right time to give the appearance of support for his cause, and I don't like being used in such a manner."

Jed weighed Timothy's interpretation of the situation against his understanding of the venerable war hero. "Nor would I, but that doesn't sound like Harry Lee. He does, as you have said, possess alternate opinions on the war, but he is also very guarded concerning where and with whom he shares them. There could be another reason he has gone to this effort, Timothy. Perhaps he is trying to assemble a cadre of influential men to *prevent* a repeat of what happened a month ago."

Timothy cocked his head to one side and considered that idea. "Would he purposely place himself in danger for such a reason?"

Jed's face twisted in worry. "No matter his politics on this war, he is a diehard patriot. I have felt his reverence for the Constitution and the men who struggled over it. I do not doubt that for some reason he feels his presence there at this moment is worth the personal risk."

Timothy glanced at the clock. "While I maintain no doubts about the efficacy of this war, I would do my part to prevent a riot over it, but the alleged card game is set to begin shortly."

Jed glanced at the clock as well. "As would I, but as you've noted, even if we ride hard, we couldn't reach Baltimore before first light."

A brief look of relief washed over Timothy's face. "Perhaps Providence is watching over us. Nothing but trouble awaits us there anyway. Right now, short of anyone in a British uniform, I cannot name a man more reviled than Hanson. I fear for his very life and the lives of anyone in his association if he generates another antiwar protest in Baltimore. It is not an exaggeration to fear that this protest of Hanson's could incite the entire city!"

As they pondered the sanity of leaping into the political inferno waiting in Baltimore, Jed opened his eyes wide in alarm. "What was that address?"

"Forty-five Charles Street," Timothy replied as Jed's face turned white. "Why?"

"We must hurry, Timothy! That address is only blocks from where Hannah is staying!"

With a large gush of air, they leapt to their feet simultaneously. Jed grabbed his hat and pointed to his friend. "Head to the stables and ask Jack to ready our two horses. I'll ask Bitty to pack two satchels. Then I have a brief matter of business to attend to. How long can you be away?"

Timothy's jaw tightened as the risk of their decision weighed upon him. "I have a few days. If this situation becomes so severe that I cannot return in that time, my tardiness will be the least of our worries. You understand the risk we are taking, don't you?"

"Completely!" Jed exclaimed as he hurried from the room.

After Bitty filled the satchels with biscuits, sandwiches, peaches, and jerky, Jed asked her to find Jerome and bring him to his office.

Jed was bent over the desk signing the final documents when the pair quietly entered the room. Jerome held his worn hat in his hands, while Bitty wrung her hands with worry at the serious expression on her young master's face.

"Please sit down. Jerome, I need your help with something. And Bitty, I want you to hear all this too. Jerome may need you to help him."

Jed continued talking as the pair eased into two chairs. "I understand how personally my safety impacts everyone at the Willows. Because of that, I have had my attorneys draw up these papers to protect every Willows worker in the event that something should ever happen to me."

Bitty didn't utter a sound, her eyes staring into Jed's as he walked to her and placed a supportive hand on her back. "Bitty, you reminded me of this just the other day, though I've been working on such a plan since having a long talk with Jerome on the matter."

The elderly slave nodded numbly, recalling the conversation the two shared at Jed's bedside after the nearly fatal beating he'd endured.

"I am still not convinced that emancipation in this political climate is in the best interest or safety of our people, but I do want to begin preparing for that day. I want each person who has worked to build the estate to not only have their political freedom, but economic freedom as well, including the opportunity to have a livelihood and to own a tract of land. I've discussed all this with Markus and he understands the plan. There are special provisions in there for him and for you and Jack, Bitty, since we've been together the longest, but I think you'll find that everyone will be treated well. This is the future we want us all to work toward."

When Jed placed the rolled parchment into Jerome's weathered hands, the older man's lips trembled. He looked as if he were handling a sacred scroll. When he read the paragraph that listed the names and ages of each slave on the estate under the heading *Those to Be Emancipated,* his finger gingerly ran over every name, presumably allowing their faces to come to his mind. He carefully rerolled the parchment and glanced at the other document Jed now placed in his hands. Sadness erased the previous look of joy from his face.

Bitty had begun to tear up as soon as Jed had spoken, but when she saw the change in Jerome's expression she became confused and fretful. "Why the long face, Jerome?"

Jerome stared quietly into Jed's face as understanding passed between the two men. Then Jed turned his attention to Bitty.

His voice was husky as he spoke. "I hope I am allowed to grow old and watch the fulfillment of this dream, but as this other document states, if I . . . if something were to happen to me, your emancipation would be immediate. No one could ever sell you. Deeds of land would be apportioned to every person who remained to help Frannie maintain the farm. She'll prevent the Willows from being lopped up and sold off to the likes of Stringham, but she'll need you, Bitty, to help her get through."

Bitty's soft cries made her small frame tremble, and Jed leaned toward her. He gave her shoulder an affectionate squeeze and hurried on while he could still speak. "It's probably safest to have Markus handle these affairs, if the time comes. I'm leaving for Baltimore right away. I have urgent business there—business that may put me in jeopardy, but I couldn't leave without knowing your welfare was secured."

Jed extended his hand to Jerome, and the man reverently returned the documents to him. His eyes, like a child's on Christmas morning, followed the papers as Jed placed them in the safe and secured the latch.

"I think it would be best for now if we keep the details of these arrangements between us," Jed indicated. "We know how quickly news travels from plantation to plantation. I'm not sure how our neighbors will respond to the news."

Bitty leapt to her feet and wrapped her arms around him. "Oh, Jed!" she cried.

"This is what you've been praying for, isn't it, Bitty?" he whispered in her ear. "I just want you to be proud of me." His voice broke, and for a moment they were all reminded that beneath the trappings of manhood, he was still barely more than a boy.

"This is a very good thing, Jed," she wept. "But you gotta know . . ." She framed his handsome face in her hands as she brushed dark curls from his eyes. "Bitty's always been proud of you. In every way that matters, you are my child. If not by blood, then by love."

He smiled down on her as he struggled to maintain his composure. "Thank you, Bitty," he whispered shakily. "It helps to know I have someone watching for me, praying for me to come back home." His face dropped into the crook of her shoulder while she wrapped her arms around his thick neck.

When Jed rose he quickly wiped a discreet arm across his eyes and Bitty gave him a stern but loving glare. "I'll be here, Jed Pearson. Bitty loves you. She'll always he here watchin' and waitin' for you to come home."

* * *

An odd mood emanated from Jerome and Bitty, who vacillated between moments of giddy grinning to periods of deep melancholy, prompting anxious chatter among the remaining Willows slaves. Not even their deep affection for Jack and Abel could lure the secret from them, despite the men's constant prodding. Nevertheless, neither of the trusted pair understood the seriousness of the hornets' nest Jed and Timothy were riding into. Late in the evening, Markus entered the kitchen, sharing in their joy but anxious because of the reason for Jed's timing. Only then did Bitty and Jerome understand the direness of Jed's situation. The Irishman and Bitty spent the evening wringing their hands and pacing, while Jerome prayed earnestly for Jed's safety.

It was into this charged environment that Abel burst that night, pounding furiously on the kitchen door until an unnerved Bitty threw it open.

"Abel? What's the matter?"

"We've got trouble, Bitty. Is Markus in here?"

"Yes," she replied, instinctively rubbing her hands over her arms where the hairs suddenly stood on end. "What's the matter? You're scarin' me."

"Seems your secret's out, and it's stirring the people up."

Bitty turned abruptly, meeting the skeptical eyes of Markus and Jerome. When she turned back around to question Abel, further hurt showed in his eyes. Bitty knew that her proud, sometimes difficult husband had interpreted being shut out from Jed's circle of trust as proof of Jed's lack of faith in him. She took his hand and pulled him into the kitchen. "What secret are you talkin' about, Abel?"

Abel scrutinized their faces. "Are you telling me you don't know?"

Suddenly, Markus was on his feet and as tense as a coiled spring. "Out with it, Abel," he called from across the room.

Abel took a deep breath and spoke. "Duprée's back." Bitty immediately panicked, and Abel scooped her into his arms.

"Where? Who made the report?" shouted Markus with venomous ferocity.

"He was at White Oak last night. Priscilla's boy was looking at a batch of baby rabbits born under the larder. He heard Stringham and his son arguing about a man named Duprée."

Just then Jack burst through the doorway, heaving for want of breath. "It's worse than we thought," he gasped as he fell into an empty chair.

By his side instantly, Marcus demanded, "Is it really Duprée? What did you find out?"

Jack nodded while he sought to control his racing heart. "I snuck over to speak to the boy after dark. It was Duprée all right, and his wrath is aimed at the Willows." The worry in his eyes chilled Bitty to the bone. "We've got to get Jed back right away, and Bitty, we've got to get word to Frannie. Say whatever you need to to get her back home. I'll tell you all I know, and afterwards I think we'd best organize ourselves until Jed gets home."

CHAPTER 32

Baltimore, Maryland
Monday Night, July 27, 1812

It didn't take long for angry readers of the *Federal Republican* to head for Hanson's office, where Hanson and his supporters had begun gathering since morning, armed and ready to deter the few dozen agitators they thought might show up for a little rabble rousing. By twilight, however, when the assemblage had swelled into a mob of several hundred, Hanson realized that the public's fury had far exceeded his estimation. Undeterred, the publisher and Maryland state delegate bellowed his intention to defend his property with force if need be—a statement which, unfortunately, only served to inflame the crowd further.

Hanson soon directed the defense to the care of General Lee, who had already assessed their situation. "The law is on our side. Let us be sure it remains so," he warned Hanson. "Men, do not fire unless it becomes absolutely necessary."

As the size of the mob continued to increase, so also did the intensity of their actions. They began to hurl stones, breaking the windows and then bursting open the shutters of the first and second stories of the building. General Lee directed a defensive volley to be fired from the upper story, over the heads of the people in the street, to frighten them away without injuring them. Then he primed the men to wait out the night, praying the mob would lose interest and disperse. All the same, he knew the crowd's venomous anger had reached a pitch that would only be satisfied by the shedding of blood.

The moon's position told Lee that it was somewhere around ten o'clock. He wiped a wrinkled hand across his eyes to clear the fatigue from them—there would be no sleeping tonight.

* * *

A full moon and dry road made the journey to Baltimore swifter than Jed and Timothy had expected. It was slightly before midnight when they arrived in the city, and they heard the sounds of the melee before they even rounded the corner, drawing them directly to 45 Charles Street. A clamoring crowd surrounded the scarred, windowless building, around which was strewn glass, wood, and chipped brick from previous assaults. Musket shots peppered the front of the building and the front door had been battered down earlier in the day, indicating the ferocity the conflict had reached at some point. Although their arrival occurred during a brief break in the violence, Jed and Timothy saw men still wielding guns and rocks. Hearing a lone man beating an unnerving drum cadence, they both knew it was only a matter of time before that primal rhythm would incite the crowd again and draw more assailants to join the angry mob.

Jed and Timothy tied their horses a block away from the building, then surveyed the human mass from the outer perimeter. They were astonished that neither militia nor police were present to dissuade the mobsters and protect those in the house. The pair worked their way through the crowd until they were within twenty feet of the brick wall that surrounded the house. Here and there, never questioning one man too long, they began to ascertain the current mood of the crowd and the situation within the house.

"What's all the ruckus about, brother?" Jed asked a man wielding a fiery torch.

"We've got that traitor Hanson and his turncoat friends holed up inside that house."

"I see a lot of guns in the crowd," Timothy began with another man. "Are the men inside armed as well?"

"Oh, they're armed, all right. They drew the first blood, but they'll not draw the last." The man leaned in closer and spoke in a voice filled with incredulity. "Some say Light-Horse Harry, the Revolutionary War hero, is inside. Imagine that, him casting his lot with a traitor like Hanson!" he spat.

Jed spoke to an older man in homespun. "I'm surprised the militia hasn't shown up." He knew he had to tread carefully.

"Some official came around about ten o'clock or so and asked everyone to leave, but no one paid him any mind." The man turned at the sound of dogs barking and walked away.

Jed moved on as well. He heard loud laughter nearby and sidled up to a small group.

"And, here's one for the books," one obviously inebriated member of the group slurred. "Notes was sent to Brigadier General Stricker who lives on this very street. D'ya know who he is?"

The other men shook their heads.

"He commands the entire Maryland militia. All five thousan' of 'em! He knows we're here, and yet he ain't so much as showed his face tonight. Then again, what soldier's gonna defend the rights of them that blasts them in the paper?"

Suddenly a single voice rose above the cacophony of others. "Gentlemen, I am Dr. Thaddeus Gales, a man like many of you, who shed blood for this democracy! Shall we allow a handful of traitors to make a mockery of our sacrifice?"

His words whipped the men around him into a frenzy. As one, they rushed the front entrance of the house. The deafening sound of musket fire rang out and dropped several of the attackers to the ground. Men pulled the bodies back to a safe position as the crowd drew back. Someone cried out, "Gales is dead!" Jed and Timothy held their breaths, expecting anything from a return volley to a full-out riot, but what occurred next was completely unanticipated. The drumbeat stopped and the crowd fell quiet for a time. Jed and Timothy dared to breathe normally, hoping the momentary truce was the prelude to the crowd's decision to end the standoff and return to their homes. Then, with no warning, a few men reescalated the conflict and raised the frenzy to a new level.

Some agitators dragged a fieldpiece from an alley. Jed saw Light-Horse Harry in a downstairs front window, sword in hand, ready to lead a bayonet charge if anyone tried to fire the cannon. The crowd began chanting again for the blood of the men inside. Then the cry sounded, "Soldiers are coming!"

A few dozen mounted soldiers rode to the front of the crowd, where a major stopped and shouted to them. "Please listen to me! I am your friend, your personal and political friend. On my honor as a soldier, I promise that if you disburse, I will take all the prisoners into custody! I am here to take possession and secure the party in the house."

Jed held his breath as the offer drew loud, mixed reviews. The officer attempted to secure an agreement for surrender from Harry and Hanson's men, but Harry refused the offer. Again the drumbeat commenced and the crowd of agitators continued to swell. Jed and Timothy knew it would be madness to try to enter the house, but as they considered that very option, the stress, fatigue, and hunger of the past eighteen hours coerced Hanson's men to negotiate. Major William Barney struck a deal that quieted both the mob and Harry's men for a few hours, and he stationed dragoons around the perimeter of the house and fence to prevent any further escapes.

While the crowd's appetite for revenge was temporarily appeased, Jed and Timothy knew they faced their best opportunity to spirit Hannah to safety.

* * *

Hannah was sound asleep in her upstairs bedroom when she heard the screaming voices beginning to resound in her head. She willed herself to be calm and not to fear the darkness that would follow. But she heard a new sound—the crashing of glass and raucous laughter echoing as if coming from below. Then the darkness began. She had become strong from facing the dream so many times, and though this scenario was not proceeding exactly as previous dreams, she resisted the urge to give in to the terror, awaiting what had always followed next, the sound of the comforting voice and deliverance. But it had been weeks since she had last faced the dream. In that time she had stripped herself of belief in the signs she had hoped were hidden there, ascribing logic in their place. On this night, with or without logic, peace and comfort did not come.

"Hannah!" Beatrice called as she pounded on the door. "Hannah! Open the door!"

Hannah fell from her bed onto the hard wooden floor, completely disoriented by the rush of reality into her dream. "Beatrice?" she moaned in a quivering voice. "What's happening?"

"Hurry, Hannah!" she whispered in a panic. "Let me in!"

Hannah scrambled anxiously across the floor, still completely disoriented by the absence of the soft glow normally radiating from the street's oil lamps. She heard the eerie sounds of crazed laughter and angry shouting and wondered how she could be living out the terrors from her sleep. When she reached the door, she felt along the polished wood until the brass knob filled her palm, but she was shaking so furiously she could barely find the strength to turn the knob. As soon as she did, Beatrice's full weight crashed against the wooden barrier, forcing it open against Hannah's crouched body.

The pair tumbled into a tangled heap, each struggling in the darkness to free herself from the foreign legs and arms grasping blindly in the air. After several manic seconds, the two women were huddled in one another's trembling arms.

"I must be going mad," cried Hannah as she rocked back and forth in her sister's arms. "My nightmares are coming true."

The sounds of gunfire made the women jolt upright and scream. They pressed themselves more deeply into the corner of Hannah's room beside the desk where she had sat so many mornings, scribbling down memories of such horrors. But she was awake, and for some reason, she found precious little comfort in finally accepting that truth.

"What is happening, Beatrice? Have the British attacked Baltimore? Are the First Nations Indians upon us? How can we defend ourselves?" the normally brave young woman sobbed.

With each query her voice rose in pitch and volume until Beatrice began to worry that Hannah's fears would force her into that same realm that held claim on their mother.

"Please light a lamp, Beatrice. I need some light," Hannah begged in a low moan between sobs.

"I know you're frightened. I am too, but while we can't see our assailants now, neither can they see us. The darkness cannot harm us.

Remember your dream, how the darkness was followed by a voice that led you away from danger and carried you into safety?" Beatrice denied her own fears to keep her voice even, and eventually she felt Hannah's body relax.

"It was a misinterpreted dream," groaned Hannah. "A romantic thread my mind clung to to avoid facing my fears and responsibilities. But I have put that dream away."

A notion came to Beatrice. She didn't know if it was true or not, but at that moment, truth was not her primary concern. Hope was, and she set about to keep hope alive. "Hannah, maybe you were right all along. Maybe your dreams were inspired and I just didn't understand."

"What are you saying?" Hannah questioned expectantly. "Do you believe Andrew will come and save us?"

Beatrice sputtered, finally managing a reply. "I'm simply saying don't give up. Your nightmares taught you to be brave. Don't surrender to fear now. I need you to believe that we will be all right."

* * *

Jed stood among the bushes on the opposite side of Calvert Street, staring wistfully at the dark Snowden home. It had seemed like a beacon to him the day he'd approached it with Hannah's letter in his hand. An hour later, as he headed to Fort McHenry to meet with her intended, no light could have penetrated the darkness that surrounded him. It felt so this night as he stood outside on the darkened street, staring up at the window where slept Hannah, another man's betrothed.

Timothy stood silently beside him. Jed knew he still agonized over his supposed part in Jed's heartache, so he placed a forgiving hand on Timothy's shoulder and the two men stood guard together, surveying the street for would-be assailants that might become a threat to the woman who still unknowingly held Jed's heart. Jed's agony grew worse as the hours passed. And the longer he gazed upward at Hannah's window, the rounder Timothy's slumped shoulders became, until Jed finally released him from the torture, sending him back to Charles Street to check on Harry's situation. An hour later when he returned, Jed stood against a lamppost whose rock-shattered lantern lay broken in a kerosene puddle around his feet.

"You're standing in kerosene, Jed."

"Am I?" Jed responded flatly as his attentions remained riveted on the upstairs windows, shifting from one to the other, looking for any sign of Hannah.

"The situation is much the same for now," Timothy reported. "But, there will be a military intervention at dawn if the attempts to secure the signatures of two magistrates on the authorization papers are successful. The entire situation could become incendiary at the slightest provocation. I can see no peaceful resolution at this point. Blood has been drawn, and the majority is crying for vengeance against Hanson's entire crew. I don't see how the mayor or the courts can uphold the law and still prevent Baltimore from unraveling."

Jed remained stoic throughout the report, and then his head dropped. "I had nearly decided to rush into that house and carry Hannah off to the Willows and safety, but now I worry that the streets pose even greater danger. I don't know what to do."

Timothy laid his hand on his friend's back. "Who can predict how the next few hours will unfold? I need to send word to Washington City. This could spill over into broader areas."

"Then there's something else I think you should do as well, Timothy. Bring Samuel here."

"Renfro?"

"Yes. I think it folly to believe the day will pass without more injuries."

"In that event, don't you'll think he'll be needed at the hospital?"

Jed looked sadly into his friend's eyes. "I'm afraid some won't make it that far."

Timothy nodded his solemn understanding and headed off to find Samuel Renfro.

Jed noticed beads of sweat trickling down his back, causing his shirt to cling to his body, attesting to the stifling heat that further stoked already inflamed tempers. Several times he took cover within the bushes as riffraff ran by, anxious for a bird's-eye view of the melee on Charles Street. Once he nearly left the camouflage when a drunken pack of ruffians ran down the street, pausing at various properties, adding to the mayhem by slinging rocks at windows, and hooting loudly for all Federalists to "come out and receive a taste of what Hanson and his lot were bound to get in the morning." They stopped in front of the Snowden house, where one of the thugs picked up a sizeable rock and cocked his arm back, preparing to smash an upstairs window. The bush rustled as Jed prepared to leap from his hiding place. Distracted by the noise, the hooligan turned erratically and looked left and right, finally dropping the rock and scurrying away, with his nervous cohorts close on his heels.

As the first light of dawn began to break across the eastern sky, the number of people on foot and horseback passing Jed in the direction of Charles Street increased. He noticed movement in the shrubs along the perimeter of the Snowden house, and his heart nearly skipped a beat. He crouched low, moved two houses down, and then crossed Calvert. Slipping through the Snowdens' neighbor's yard, he inadvertently set the dog to barking again. Luckily, the dog had barked so frequently that night that no one was inclined to check on the cause. Jed neared the property line that bordered the Snowdens' lot and saw a man's shape moving across the back porch, jiggling knobs and trying the integrity of the window latches. Jed stood and ran full throttle across the lawn, thrusting his entire weight into the smaller, leaner form, and dropping it face down into the grass.

His prey was agile, and despite the obvious disparity in their sizes, Jed found him a challenging opponent. The smaller man twisted his body wildly, throwing Jed off to the side. He brought his knee up sharply into Jed's middle and for a second, Jed lay stunned on his back while the other man scrambled to his feet. Jed noticed the yellow hair of his foe and thought the face looked familiar. But he took no time in gathering his wits about him, sweeping his leg across the other man's feet and landing him on the ground beside him. The pair spun and ended up on their knees engaged in an arm-to-arm struggle when they caught the first full glimpse of one another.

"Pearson?" the familiar voice sputtered.

"Who's asking?" Jed replied without loosening his hold.

"Lieutenant . . . Andrew Robertson . . ." the irritated voice replied, immediately releasing his grip.

It took all Jed's control to unlock his hands from Robertson's collarbone, giving a little shove as he did. Knowing the enemy did not make him a friend.

Robertson sat back, struggling for breath, allowing his weight to rest on his hands, propped behind him. "What are you doing here?" he asked with annoyance.

Jed glared at him. "What are *you* doing here? There's chaos in the streets just a few blocks away. Why aren't you and your men protecting the public?"

The words hit a sore spot. "We were forbidden to intervene." Robertson shook his head in shame and tugged at his shirt, drawing attention to the fact that he was not in uniform. "I urged my commanding officer to allow me to come to town on a matter of personal duty." He nodded in the direction of the upstairs windows. "I needed to make sure they were safe and secure."

Jed's jaw tightened and he fell back onto the grass, eyeing the lieutenant. "You can return to attending to your other duties now, *Lieutenant.* As you've seen, I've been here all night, and I have no intention of leaving. If things go awry, I'll do what I think is best."

The lieutenant stood and brushed the dirt from his trousers and muttered, "Of course you will." He turned and began to walk away, then slowly turned and stared at Jed in utter frustration. "I've been circling the house all night, but I made this garden my base, and do you know why?"

Jed felt his body tense and clenched his fist instinctively.

"Because nearly one year ago, after your unexpected meeting with Hannah, she was so despondent she wanted only to die. I kept a vigil by her bedside except when I came down to this garden to pray for God to place into her heart some will to live. Eventually she found it again, without you, and I've pledged every minute of my life since then to her happiness."

"You've known her how long? A year?" Jed asked in a voice that sounded as if summoned from the bottom of his soul. "Multiply that by every minute of her life and every breath I've taken since she was born. That will be but a fragmentary measure of what she means to me."

The lieutenant lowered his eyes and shook his head in aggravated wonder. When he brought his face up to meet Jed's, he growled in response, "Then why didn't you tell her?"

The question hit Jed like a kick in the gut.

"Do you know how many times I've wished you had uttered a single word of those unexpressed feelings?" the lieutenant went on. "*You alone* had the power to spare all of us the agony of our current situation!" His volume set the dogs off again. He lowered his voice and continued on. "Why didn't you simply tell her that during all those beleaguered moments and impassioned breaths?"

"I've already explained," Jed stammered. "Propriety kept me . . ."

The lieutenant's hand formed fists which he now pounded against the stale night air. "Blast propriety! You've used that excuse long enough to avoid facing the truth!" he snarled.

"You know nothing about this," growled Jed in return.

"It wasn't Hannah's age alone that kept you mute. Even as you feared other suitors would take notice of her, you continued to treat her as a child. Have you ever asked yourself why?"

Jed wanted to choke the man so he could not finish.

Robertson pointed an accusatory finger in his direction. "I do not deny for a second that you loved her, that you still love her and ever will. But admit to me this night—and to yourself, for once—that the reason you never acted on your feelings for Hannah was because of her mother's contempt for you. In fact, your affection for Hannah actually drove her mother away from her!"

Jed's jaw was set so tightly that an ache began piercing his head as the lieutenant went on.

"Do you know what our courtship has been like, what Hannah has desired above all? To visit and picnic with her mother and father. Just to have association with them. These are things she can enjoy in my company." The lieutenant's voice softened while his eyes implored Jed to consider his next point. "Could she ever with you?"

He wanted to scream. *Can no one else see that I am a victim too?* Jed wondered in agony.

Robertson lowered his head and stared at the ground. "As long as she remained a child, time was your ally. You could enjoy her company until her mother either accepted you or passed away. But in a single season she abandoned her prolonged childhood and became a woman, and time was no longer your friend. You were faced with a choice, and for a moment, when you agreed to stand down, you chose to do what was best for Hannah."

Jed's legs felt limp and weak. He couldn't bear the man's presence any longer.

"What has happened to make you now change your mind, deciding instead to choose what is best for you?" He turned and began leaving the garden.

Jed's chest heaved with emotion as he glared at the lieutenant, feeling as if his rival had splayed and eviscerated him. Now, with nothing left to lose or hide, he warned his attacker. "If you know me so well, then you must know I will not squander this opportunity."

The lieutenant paused, took a few more steps away from the garden, and then paused again. With tight lips and eyes that seemed to bore into Jed's soul, he said, "Six months ago you trusted me to act in Hannah's best interest. Tonight, I'm repaying you with the same trust." And then he was gone.

* * *

Jed maintained his restless vigil until morning. Though his body ached with fatigue, his mind busily rehearsed everything Robertson had said. Finally, at first light, Timothy returned. "I expected you hours ago. Where's Renfro?" Jed demanded irritatedly.

"There were so many casualties from yesterday's skirmishes that even the medical students were being employed in the hospital. He promised to come as soon as he is free. In the meantime he offered us the use of his room to rest. I suggest you take advantage of his offer."

"And you?"

"I stole a few minutes' sleep while waiting to speak to Samuel. I failed to find a courier to carry word to Washington City, so I should deliver the news myself. I'll come to the Willows as soon as I am able. Hopefully, the world will have returned to normal before we meet again."

Jed and Timothy parted company as the first signs of morning activity showed in the awakening city. Jed eyed the Snowdens' butler, George, who cautiously surveyed the street before hurrying out with his broom to clean the broken glass from the walk and the bricked street. Once the chore was completed, the impeccably dressed Negro servant headed in the direction of the market with a basket in tow. Knowing that the women were likely awake in the house filled Jed with an overwhelming urge to knock on the door and speak to Hannah. Before he could act upon his impulse, the chaos began again, driving the notion from his mind.

The first sign that something new was awry that Tuesday morning was the swell of voices as a crowd moved in the direction of Charles Street. Men and boys ran past Jed's position, cutting through side streets to reach the point of interest, babbling about the arrival of the militia. Jed felt torn between his post as guardian of the Snowden home and his worry over Harry. He heard the incessant drumbeat and the cadence of hundreds of marching feet that served to rally more nosey riffraff from every corner of the city. Three times Jed left his post to run to a point where he could watch the swelling crowds. However, he was soon unable to make any sense of the sea of humanity closing in around 45 Charles Street. It was after nine when he saw George returning. He approached the man so quickly that the butler nearly dropped his basket to the ground in fright.

"Did you see the crowd assembling on Charles?"

The butler's eyes narrowed in suspicion, and he excused himself and tried to move around the large man who blocked his way.

"Please, sir," Jed pled. "Could you just tell me what you saw?"

The butler eyed Jed curiously, recognizing the face but unable to ascribe a name to it. "The militia's there now. They hauled them men outta the house and walked 'em ta the jail."

"Could you see the men? What was their condition?"

Again the butler scrutinized Jed's face. "Mebbe you should speak with the missus."

"I had a friend in that house. An older gentleman. Please, I just need some word on his condition."

The butler stalled before answering. "I didn't see no faces. The militia lined up and walked the prisoners down the center, but people threw rocks and such at 'em ever' step of the way to the jail. It was near onto a mile. They're inside now, but some surely was hurt."

Jed's heart sank in fear for Harry, but the chance to get word about Hannah suddenly consumed him. "And the ladies of the Snowden house . . . are they well this morning?"

A look of recognition swept over the butler. "You came askin' about Miss Hannah a while back, didn't you? She's up. Should I tell her yer askin' for her?"

Faced with the chance to actually see Hannah, Jed's heart began to race. He had arrogantly assured Robertson of his readiness to plead his case to her, and though he had rehearsed her rescue over and over in his mind, their long separation now weakened his confidence. *What if she has fallen in love with Robertson now?* The doubts began again, but this time Jed did not surrender to them. Instead, he rehearsed his plan in his mind once more, forcing himself to make Hannah's safety paramount. "No. I need to go now. I just wanted to be sure they were all right," he assured the butler, though he planned to return and secrete the women away.

He hurried along to Renfro's address. A tiny German woman, cloaked in a white pinafore, greeted him warmly. She sent him up to room 7, where he found a scrawled note inviting him to eat what he could find. He downed a slice of bread with a slab of cheese, followed by a mug of water that was warm from the heat. Then he fell exhausted onto the bed.

It was early afternoon when he awoke to the sound of a chair scooting across the wooden floor. When he was finally able to focus, he found Samuel Renfro draped across the table.

"Samuel!" he apologized, staggering to his feet. "Come and lie down in your bed."

"No matter," the portly young man said with a weary smile as he waved his friend off. "I barely arrived and thought I'd eat a bite, but it seems my plate served me better as a pillow."

"Any word on the situation?"

"Tensions are dangerously high, Jed. There is speculation that despite the mayor's pledge to die protecting the prisoners and their rights, the crowd will storm the jail tonight and mete out their own justice. The mayor asked General Stricker to call the militia in to protect the prisoners. He's also promising those calling for their blood that none will be allowed out during the night."

Jed let out a rush of defeated air and fell into a chair. "Perhaps if I raise bail."

"Judge Scott denied them bail."

"Then what avenues are left to us?"

Samuel shook his head in worry. "All we can do is pray that men's godly natures rule them, and be prepared to move if and when an opportunity presents itself."

While Renfro slept, Jed formulated a plan. He visited his office manager, Mr. Carpasian, to inform him that he was arranging for a monetary draft from the business account. As Jed prepared to leave the office, Carpasian offered him information that nearly tore him from the task at hand.

"I have the information from the bank manager regarding the St. James account," Carpasian said in an unusually confidential tone. "The original beneficiary was an Episcopalian minister named Reverend McClintock, who passed away in 1802. It seems that weeks before your grandfather's death, he witnessed a codicil to the reverend's will, stipulating that the funds he was paying to the reverend be extended for an additional period of twenty years and diverted to the church following the reverend's passing. The sum of the deposits thus far exceeds sixteen thousand dollars!"

Jed's eyes grew large. "Why would my grandfather sanction such a strange bequest?"

"Mr. Pratt, the bank manager, remembered the account. Perhaps you should talk to him."

"McClintock?" repeated Jed. *McClintock is Hannah's middle name and her mother's maiden name . . .* He shuddered as old tales and new truths began to collide.

Jed went immediately to the bank. After cashing the bank draft against the Pearson Properties account, he asked to speak to the bank manager, Ichabod Pratt. As soon as the ancient, weathered banker recognized the young heir, he assumed he was there about the St. James account and began to rant.

"I'll tell you what I told your father. Please just let the dead rest. Each time I arrange those transfers I am reminded of the part I played in destroying a family."

Jed felt his skin prickle. "The deposits to St. James Church? I don't understand."

The man rubbed a trembling hand against his brow. "There simply are no reparations equal to some wrongs . . . no compensation for some losses. Money cannot mend everything."

"You are speaking in riddles, sir. Who was thusly wronged and what was their loss?!"

Pratt's lips trembled. "So many . . ." he said as he wrung his hands. "We all thought we knew best. But poor Sarah was never the same afterwards, and we were all to blame."

Jed knew he needed to tread carefully with the frenzied man. "To blame for what, sir?"

Mr. Pratt looked as if he were on trial. "He was a man with no prospects and a reputation as a rogue. We considered him unfit for one of our own, and our disapproval influenced her parents to forbid her from seeing him. Instead, they pressed her to marry a man the community held in high esteem."

Jed's brow wrinkled in confusion. "What has this to do with the St. James account?"

"Don't you know, lad?" The manager seemed aghast. "The pair I speak of was Sarah Ann Benson and your grandfather. They were each other's true loves, and we pushed her into marrying the Reverend McClintock."

Jed thought about the initials on the locket in the portrait and those engraved on the casket. *Sarah Ann Benson . . . McClintock! SABM!* The realization staggered him and he had to sit.

"I'm sorry. I thought it would all make sense to you. I assumed you knew some of this."

"You have only added to my questions," Jed groaned. "What became of this Sarah?" he asked, though this was the one question to which he already knew the answer.

"No one knows for sure. They each married and carried on with their lives, dealing with the pain of their separation and betrayal. Then your grandfather returned home from Yorktown to a hero's welcome one day, and she disappeared the next. The governor ordered a fete to honor Jonathan Pearson for helping to save the republic, and Sarah begged my wife to make her a new blue dress for the occasion. My Dora tried to deny her request. Dora had previously made blue dresses for Sarah when your grandfather was courting her, and the thought of what Sarah intended was troubling." Mr. Pratt sighed deeply. "I can only guess what was going through her mind as Jonathan rode through town. The indentured, unacceptable schoolteacher whose proposal she was forced to deny not only became the wealthiest man in four counties, but he was a hero as well. The poor dear chased after his carriage like a loyal pup, humiliating her husband and drawing the ridicule of those who didn't know her story. Jonathan never even acknowledged her. He just . . . rode on. The next day she had poor Will, the jeweler, modify the locket Jonathan had given her when he'd asked for her hand, adding an *M*, presumably for McClintock, and then she disappeared. I nearly shed tears whenever I saw those little motherless children. Many in town felt we had played a part in destroying their mother."

Jed found a thread of hope in the distressing tale. "But my grandfather was a victim too, wasn't he? From what you've said, he committed no foul against the woman or to her family."

Pratt's eyes became pained. "No one's hands were clean. We entertained ourselves with our gossip while watching them torture one another for over twenty years. Their antics drove poor Sarah crazy years before that scene at the parade. As a result, her children were denied their mother long before she actually disappeared. As I said, we all destroyed that family."

Jed's momentary vindication vanished, and he felt sick to the bone. "And the account? Was that my grandfather's way of accepting responsibility for her . . . disappearance?"

Pratt shrugged. "I can't say. He asked that it be set aside to provide a nanny for the children and a housekeeper and cook."

"The children are long grown and the reverend is dead. Why was a codicil attached extending the agreement and diverting the funds to the church instead?"

Pratt stood and opened the door to his office, inviting Jed to leave. "You'll have to look elsewhere for those answers, Mr. Pearson. I've already told you far too much."

Jed felt numb when he left the bank, his greatest fears realized. Susannah Stansbury's hatred of his family was probably justified, and the obstacle that lay between Hannah and himself would be difficult to eliminate. He forced his mind to cease shuffling the impossible details and focused his attentions back on the immediate problems: Light-Horse Harry's situation and the location of the Snowden women.

Jed stopped by his city home to instruct Bartholomew to prepare for the women. It was late afternoon when he finally made it to the jail. No militia remained on guard, and the crowds had thinned out noticeably, though more city officials seemed to be gathering to the site.

He spent an hour pleading with them to accept bail for his friend, but they refused his five-hundred-dollar offer and denied him the right to even see the men they were now dubbing "Hanson's Mob." Jed noticed the turnkey pass outside the jail's door to speak to a Christian man offering meals for the incarcerated. The key keeper received the generous man's offer with obvious suspicion, and a few words passed between them before the patron nodded to the men in his wagon to bring the food to the jail door. An idea struck Jed. He attempted to meld in with the angels of mercy delivering the food, but the benefactor begged him off sharply.

"I sympathize with your desires to aid the captives, sir, but I have been watching that jail since morning and I have not seen a morsel of food or a pitcher of water enter the building all day. I warn you, if the jailor believes the gift of food had been offered for any purpose other than to relieve the suffering of the incarcerated, it might be turned away."

Jed reached into his pocket to display the five hundred dollars. "I would lower myself to bribing the turnkey for a chance to free my friend, sir. Take compassion on his situation and speak to the jailor for me, please."

"Your interest will spare but one man, sir. I'm sorry for your friend, but I cannot risk the welfare of the other twenty-two who were unable to escape before the militia routed them out."

While Jed understood the man's argument, such understanding did little to alleviate the heaviness of his heart. He mounted Tildie, and noticing the first streaks of orange breaking across the Baltimore harbor, he hurried along back toward Calvert Street and the Snowdens' house. As the dinner hour passed, the street rabble were again returning to Charles Street. A cold sweat gripped Jed as he noticed that few were coming empty-handed this night. Aside from the firearms that had been so customary over the past few days, many of them now came wielding knives, clubs, and even axes. His heart pounded as he thought how terrified Hannah and her sister would be as they watched from their windows and saw the bloodthirsty citizenry, and he cursed himself for being so derelict in their protection.

No longer caring about camouflaging himself, Jed was prepared to storm into the house and carry Hannah to safety. He would settle her in at his town house and then return for Harry. It was a good plan, and he slipped from Tildie's back, ready to approach the door when a series of observations struck him. No light shone from behind any of the windows, though twilight had set in firmly, and while cook smoke was still lingering atop the chimneys of other houses in the neighborhood, no wisp escaped the Snowdens' flue. Jed cursed himself again as he worried that the family had slipped away into the dangerous streets while he had been on his errands.

Riding Tildie, Jed scoured the neighborhood for signs of the Snowdens and Hannah. On the second pass of the house he saw a tiny light flickering through the curtains of the front window, like that of a single bedside candle, rising as if being carried up a staircase. He ran to the back of the house and noticed the faint glow through an upstairs window, and a second blush of light from the attic, indicating that the household was settling in for the night. Jed tethered his horse in the garden and prepared to head for the front of the house when the quiet was quickly shattered by the sounds of whispers beyond the hedge. "Shhh," said a voice. Jed crouched beside Tildie and watched as four well-dressed men in frock coats found a break in the foliage and crossed into the Snowdens' backyard.

"See?" one malevolent voice whispered. "I told you. This house is dark as pitch in back as well. No one is home here."

"I told you we should have brought our own guns along," the first voice complained.

"Then our wives would have known. Just find something here," said another.

"I think we can make some use of this chair," answered a third voice with a baleful laugh.

Jed saw one of the shadowy forms hoist an Adirondack chair high above his head and then hurl it to the ground with a loud smash.

Three of the four figures each grabbed a piece of the wrecked chair and tore it from the whole, then began thrusting the jagged wooden sections into the air like weapons, laughing menacingly.

"We'll give those traitors a lesson they'll not soon forget," one chortled.

Jed worried about the reaction of the women if they awakened to the sounds of men beneath their window. He reached for his pistol and considered challenging the four relatively unarmed men. Realizing that he might have to shoot to control them, he worried he would only incite additional anger among the inflamed populace already running wild in the streets. Opting for patience, Jed hoped the four would simply wear out their bravado and move along.

The fourth man in the group glowered at his associates and shoved the man who crushed the chair. "Slabs of wood? What sort of impression will that make? We are men of prominence and station in this community—veterans of the Great War. Knives and guns are what we need."

The men considered, then one snarled a reply. "Well, gentlemen, I believe this is where Captain Snowden lives. If the family is truly away, as it looks, then there should be no problem in 'borrowing' a few firearms."

"Roughing up some turncoats is one thing. Breaking into a man's house—an officer, no less—is quite another," argued one man. "What if we are caught? I have a reputation to uphold."

"The sheriff will ascribe it as the work of the riffraff running amuck in the streets. The Snowdens would never accuse their own neighbors," declared the angry man through gritted teeth. "Stand back," he warned as he swung a piece of wood at the kitchen window, sending glass flying into the room. He jabbed at the remaining sharp fragments littering the windowsill, continuing the unnerving sound of breaking glass. Jed knew he could wait no longer.

"That will be enough, gentlemen," he said in a commanding voice.

The four startled men turned abruptly in the direction of the voice and began scrambling to avoid being identified, though Jed thought he recognized the voices of two of them. If he was correct, one was an officer of the bank and another worked for the Baltimore

Sun, the newspaper whose editor had heightened the malevolent rhetoric against Hanson.

As three of the frock-coated thugs escaped through the shrubs, the leader of the group turned around and called to Jed, "There's no place in this community for British loyalists and traitors. If Captain Snowden was home, he would be with us, stringing up Hanson's crew."

"Captain Snowden is away fighting to uphold the Constitution of America that defends the freedom to express oneself—and the right to a free press as well. Whether he or I agree or disagree with Hanson is not the issue. They are entitled to protection under the law."

"Even traitors try to hide behind the very Constitution they attempt to undermine," one of the assailants sneered. "What are you doing here anyway, holed up in the captain's garden?"

"I'm a friend of the family," Jed stated firmly. "I'm protecting their house while they're away."

"Protecting it, eh?" The man pulled a cigar from his pocket and placed it in his mouth.

Jed watched warily as the man slowly pulled a match from another pocket and struck it against a button on his frock coat. He was excessively deliberate in his motion as he brought the match to meet the cigar, drawing long, exaggerated puffs until the end glowed brightly. He drew the cigar out of his mouth and held it in the air, each hand now in possession of a glowing object.

"Then protecting this house should be more important than apprehending four politically minded citizens." His right hand allowed the flaming match to slip into the dry grass near the box of kindling, where it immediately caught fire and began blazing. Simultaneously his left hand tossed the burning cigar into the dried grass at the base of the hedge. In the second required for Jed to react, the man slipped away, leaving two glowing patches of fire behind.

Jed immediately began stomping on the fiery patch by the base of the hedge. Out of the corner of his eye, he noticed a dried vine that ignited, transporting the fire along its length. As Jed fought to control that threat, the kindling box, with its highly combustible tinder and dried pine needles, erupted into a sudden blaze, spewing flaming embers that also landed in the dry autumn grass. He ran to the pump and drew water at a furious pace, but the fire moved more quickly than he could respond, and within a few seconds he realized he could not contain it. He looked up at the windows where the lamps had settled and cursed himself for missing the chance to move the women earlier. There was only one thing left to do, and this time he would not—could not—fail.

CHAPTER 33

The Snowden Home
Tuesday Night, July 28, 1812

Aside from George's visit to the market, Beatrice had wanted no sign that anyone was home in the Snowdens' house. She'd ordered the curtains drawn, a cold supper, lights out, and an early retiring to bed to maintain the ruse. After rechecking each bolt and latch on the doors, the servants had headed to the attic for bed, and Beatrice and Hannah had gone upstairs to share the master bedroom that over-looked the garden. They could thus avoid the street noise and its accompanying danger if another melee began this night. And though rest had eluded both women the previous evening, their now stress-induced fatigue worked better than a tonic to lull them quickly to sleep.

Somewhere in the fog of consciousness between sleep and awak-ening, Hannah began to hear voices . . . men's voices. Try as she might to dismiss them from her dreaming, she could not push the sounds from her mind. She'd turned absently to face Beatrice. As her semiconscious eyes fluttered open, she caught a momentary glimpse of a sight that stilled her racing heart and wrenched her into sudden alertness.

Beatrice lay as still as death, her face contorted with terror as she focused every faculty on the sounds from the yard. Hannah opened her mouth to utter a cry, but Beatrice's hand quickly clamped down over it and she shook her head rapidly, urging silence. A sudden crashing sound of wood made both women bolt upright. They clutched one another as the voices below grew more menacing and the threats of violence became audible. The room was fully dark when the women heard a sound like a tree branch moving against a window. As they'd forced their terrified minds to concentrate, they realized the sound was actually a light tapping, perhaps even scratching, on their bedroom door. They could scarcely breathe as they slipped from the bed to the floor.

"Miz Snowden! Miz Snowden!" repeated the shaky, whispered voice.

Relief washed over Beatrice's face. "It's George!" she gasped, nearly in tears as she crawled toward the door, keeping her head low as she passed by the window. She opened the door and found George and Martha huddled together, with Lydia, the young maid, close behind.

"Someone's in the yard!" George exclaimed. "I heard a crash. Whad ja want me ta do?"

Beatrice knew that despite the older man's noble intentions, he could do little to protect them. "Come in here, all of you." She pressed her finger to her lips. "Perhaps they'll leave soon."

At that moment the sound of crashing glass drew a collective gasp from the panicked group. They scurried into a corner, finding refuge in one another's closeness. Lydia began to cry, muffling her wails in Martha's prayer-bent shoulders. George and Beatrice likewise pleaded silently with the Almighty, while feelings of despair washed over Hannah.

Whatever was happening outside was changing rapidly. They now heard an argument—not loud, irate voices, but subtle indications of strong but opposing feelings on both sides. Then came the sound of rustling shrubs followed by low, menacing voices, and then an eerie silence.

A dozen scenarios raced through the captives' minds as they strained to hear even the slightest sound that would divulge the current location of the intruders. Instead, terror in another form appeared—curls of gray smoke began rising past the window, wafting into the room, and mingling with the darkness. Hannah now crawled to the window and saw the dried grass ablaze. It had reached the hedges and now raced along the perimeter of the property. Fiery debris, carried on the night air, had set new fires along the foundation of the house where sprawling ivy grew across the entire wall to the roofline. Some vines already blazed, sending flames up the viney track, igniting wooden windowsills and threatening the cedar-shingled roof.

"Beatrice, we must get out of here! The house is on fire!" Hannah felt along the wall until she found the door. She opened it and groaned at the smoky blackness accented by glowing spots of red and yellow. She couldn't tell whether the fire was showing through windows or if flames had already penetrated the walls of the house. Quickly closing the door behind her, declaring sharply, "There's smoke inside the house. The first floor may already be on fire!"

"We can't stay in here!" Beatrice shouted above Lydia's wailing. "And it's too far to jump down to the ground."

George stepped forward. "I think I kin jump from Miss Hannah's window over ta the front porch. From there I kin drop ta the ground and git help."

"What if you don't make it?" gasped Beatrice. "The fall must be at least twenty feet."

"I don't see no other choice, missy."

The little party followed George to the window in Hannah's room. Before they opened it, they could see flames leaping from the porch, cutting off that route of escape.

"If we can't go down and we can't go out the front, what options are left us?" Hannah asked frantically.

Again, George offered a suggestion. "The attic window is near a branch of the poplar tree. Not too good for climbin' but it might give us a way out."

As the foursome debated the new plan, Hannah slumped to the floor. Her heart began to race uncontrollably, rendering her powerless to draw a normal breath. She began clutching at her nightgown, clawing to free her throat from whatever denied her the air she craved. Then the old, familiar scenario overtook her. At first she resisted the hope the dream offered. It had been too deeply rejected, too long denied, for her to recall it clearly. But as she fought to still her fears, she felt the first blush of comfort soothe her heart and calm its rhythm. Her breathing began to slow and she felt awash with peace. Beatrice noticed the immediate change in her sister.

"What is it?"

"He'll come for us," Hannah replied in a breathy whisper.

"Who'll come for us?" Beatrice questioned impatiently, but Hannah's hopeful eyes calmed her and she answered her own question. "Andrew?"

"No," Hannah whispered as a strange revelation crossed her mind. "Jed. I understand now." She carefully rose from the floor, opened the door, and disappeared into the smoky darkness. "Jed?" she called out into the black abyss. "Jed!" she repeated, ignoring Beatrice's pleas for her to return to the room. Then, amid the sounds of crackling fire and exploding glass, came the expected answer.

"Hannah?"

She craned her neck to focus on the sound through the fiery crackling.

"Hannah!" he shouted from the first floor. "Hannah!"

"Jed?" she whispered in relief. "Jed?" Her voice became stronger. "We're up here!"

Jed was furiously working the pump and battling the first-floor fire to maintain an exit, and when he heard her reply, his heart nearly leapt from his chest. They had not exchanged a word since that dreadful meeting the previous year, and he wasn't certain how she would react to him once the immediate danger was past. But it was far from past, and as he called to her again, he knew what he had to do.

"Hurry, Hannah! Get everyone down the stairs to the landing as quickly as possible!"

"But Jed . . . I can't see you . . ."

"Trust me, Hannah, and hurry!" called the voice through the darkness.

"The fire! It's—"

Again, the voice called to her. "Please, Hannah. Trust me . . ."

Hannah called to the others and began making her way to the landing. The railing was on fire at the foot of the stairs and moving upwards toward the second floor. Terrified, she stalled on the second step.

"The fire's on the rail, Jed. Where are you? Can't you come for us?"

Jed closed his eyes and uttered a prayer to calm his voice. Mustering as much control as possible, he replied in a soft, assuring voice. "I can't come to you yet, Hannah, but follow my voice and trust me. You can make it, but you must hurry."

Hannah could not understand why he didn't come for her, but once again, placing her confidence in the rehearsed dream, she carried on past the spitting flames. With nearly every step she heard Jed reassuring her, encouraging her. At first he seemed so close she felt she could reach out to him. Then he sounded far off and muffled as if he were speaking through a fog. Trying to ignore her fears, Hannah remained tuned to his voice. Trusting in it, she headed down the stairs.

She noticed water puddled along the landing and saturating the rugs, and she peered left and right, looking for him. "Jed! We're here!" she cried. Then there was a splash of water before Jed appeared through the haze like an angel. He scooped her into his arms, holding her close to his soaked body. "Follow along quickly," he called to the others. Then, with one mighty kick, he sprang the lock and burst the door open. The porch was framed in fire but the floorboards had remained intact, and he sped across the span, leading the group to safety.

He checked for signs of fire on their clothing, and seeing none, he ran to the backyard, leading the group through the blaze to the moist, shaded grass that had acted as a barrier, protecting the carriage house. Framing Hannah's face with his hands, he whispered, "Good girl." Setting her down, he quickly harnessed the Snowdens' Morgan horses and urged the party into the coach. George took the reins and followed Jed and Tildie along the alley and down the street toward the Pearsons' home as the sound of the firehouse bells began to peal.

Little was said as the company made their way down Calvert Street. From time to time Jed and Hannah stole glances at one another, and Beatrice offered him a shy, apologetic smile of gratitude. Bartholomew and the maid stood on the Pearsons' porch watching the horse-drawn fire coach careening down Calvert Street toward the smoke-filled area from which the group had just come. Jed leapt from Tildie's saddle and handed the reins to the butler. "Are the rooms ready?" he asked breathlessly.

"Everything's jest as you requested."

After Jed helped the women from the carriage, he looked at Millie, his housemaid, and said, "Set some of Frannie's things out for the women, and please get George into some fresh clothes as well. And ask Cook to make some tea . . . and anything else they want, all right?"

"Yes, suh," she replied, and she and the other servants hurried off, leaving Jed alone with Hannah and Beatrice.

"Jed?" Hannah began in disbelief. "You sound as if you're leaving us. Surely you're not going back into town!"

"I must, Hannah. I can't explain it now," he responded softly. He could see the debris of lies and deceit that had littered their former perfect understanding. She still believed he had disregarded her once, and she would likely see his sudden departure as more of the same. He had no idea what toll the past year had taken on her feelings for him, or how that same year had affected her feelings for the lieutenant. All he knew was that he had but a few seconds to try to assure her that he would return, so he reached for her hand and spoke.

"You trusted me tonight, Hannah. Please trust me another hour."

Confusion remained in her eyes, but as she took his hand she slowly nodded her willingness to trust his word again.

Jed turned to Beatrice. "Mrs. Snowden, I am urgently needed elsewhere. May I have the use of your carriage?"

Beatrice met his gaze and their last, painful meeting passed through her mind. She turned to Hannah. "Dearest, the shock of the evening has left me surprisingly chilled. Could you ask the butler if I might have a wrap?"

Hannah stole a longing look at Jed, then acquiesced. "Of course." She seemed hesitant in exiting the room, as if she dared not let Jed leave her gaze, and as soon as she was gone, Beatrice spoke directly.

"Of course you may have my carriage, Mr. Pearson." She lowered her eyes humbly. "I owe you greatly, sir, and though I know I have no right to make any request of you, surely you must know the subject that wears on my mind tonight." She stepped closer and gently grasped his hands. When her eyes looked up into his, they were mournful and moist. "Please, Jed, if you must tell Hannah of Myrna's and my intrigue, please help her to also understand our intentions. Please leave us our sisterhood if you can."

Jed's throat tightened. He could deny neither the sincerity of her intentions nor her affections. With a hopeful smile he replied, "All debts are paid, madam. Let us begin anew this night." He began to climb into the driver's box of the carriage as Hannah reappeared with Bartholomew and a blanket.

"Jed?" Hannah implored. "There is nothing but trouble on the city's streets. What can be worth risking your life twice this night?"

"The very principles for which your dear sister's husband risks his own life, Hannah."

"But, Jed . . ." she pled.

"Hannah, this war with Great Britain is but forty-one days old. Our bloodlust threatens to destroy the very Constitution we say we are fighting to uphold. It is not the blood of the British they are spilling in Baltimore tonight. It is the blood of our neighbors and fellow citizens!"

Unsure where his loyalties lay, Beatrice said boldly, "You've used my husband to make your point, sir. May I ask which side you believe serves the nobler cause, Hanson and his men, or the masses?"

Time pressed upon Jed like an anvil, but he could not leave the women without a proper answer. "There is little nobility in the streets this night, madam. In truth, I wish there was another way but war. Like Hanson, I am not sure we are prepared for this fight, but as Great Britain insists on bringing it to us, I accept the fact that it is inevitable. So the answer is that I desire to serve the nobler cause itself rather than a side. I desire to serve freedom. Tonight I ride for freedom—and for friendship. Other than love and God, what two nobler causes exist?"

His eyes shifted to Hannah's, though he addressed himself to the butler.

"Bartholomew, treat them as if this were their home. Regard their word as mine." Jed's penetrating eyes remained fixed on Hannah. "I will be back," he promised emphatically, and then he was gone.

Beatrice urged her sister to come inside, but Hannah watched as the carriage disappeared into the dark night. Her dream had literally come to pass! It had not been merely a metaphor. He had come! His voice had led her to safety, and his arms had carried her there. She did not know how the dream would end—by whose side she would ultimately find herself—but she was no longer willing to have her future decided by fate. She would choose for herself, and she would begin this night.

CHAPTER 34

Baltimore City Jail
Tuesday Night, July 28, 1812

As Jed approached the city jail, he felt as if hell itself had risen from the earth's bowels to visit its wrath upon the city. Utter madness seemed to rule the night as crazed men ran amuck with crowbars and clubs while equal numbers ran away in disgust from the scene. Jed hid the carriage in the alley behind a shop and met one such witness on the street. He grabbed the man by the shoulder, alarming him to the point that he immediately raised his arms and begged for mercy.

"Friend, I mean you no harm," Jed reassured. "What insanity is happening here?"

Tears filled the man's eyes. "I'll never forget it! I swear, if I live to be one hundred I shall never clear it from my mind's eye!"

"What?" Jed asked as he tried to shake sense back into the man.

"I came to picket Hanson, to pledge my support for the war. But I never believed they would storm the jail. I heard the rumors, but I never thought they were planning murder!"

Jed's body went limp at the words. "Murder? How did they break into the jail?"

The man began backing away, fearful of Jed's sudden inquisition. "I can't say. A few slipped through when the doors were opened. Some say they sprung the doors with crowbars . . . some say the doors were opened so quickly someone must have slipped the key to the mob."

"Where was the mayor? Where was the militia?" Jed demanded.

"It was a fiasco, I tell you. The Fifth Regiment came out for a time. But once things settled down, General Stricker sent most of the soldiers home. He left just a skeleton force at the jail. They were no match for them devils that stormed the place."

"And what of Mayor Johnson? Did he abandon them as well?"

"Mayor Johnson and his colleagues made a stand on the front steps, but he was soon led away for his own safety. All I know is that what is going on there now is butchery!"

At the mention of the word, Jed sprang toward the crowd. He saw a few blood-smeared men laughing and jeering as if boasting over a good hunting kill, and it was all he could do not to throttle the barbarians. Instead, he crept near to listen to their filthy boasting to determine whether Harry Lee had survived the massacre.

"Mumma, tell me, what's easier, clubbing a steer or a Federalist?" a man asked the brawny owner of the neighborhood butcher shop.

"Can't say, but the steer is worth more. Leastwise you can eat it," the butcher laughed.

The smaller man sniggered maliciously. "Yep, they put up a good fight, I'll give 'em that. I didn't think any of 'em would make it past the steps alive, what with the gauntlet we had ready for them. And that old general must be near sixty and yet he's fighting like the devil himself . . ."

Jed's heart nearly skipped a beat.

". . . Yeah. Lingan's been slashed, stabbed, beaten, pounded—and he's still alive. The darned old rascal is the hardest dyin' of 'em all—thinkin' we would forgive him for sidin' with Hanson 'cause he fought in the Revolution."

"And what of that other so-called hero? That General Lee?"

Jed's blood boiled. It took all his efforts not to drive his fist into the face of the human scum before him while he waited for the answer.

"He's in that pile over there." The man pointed toward a spot where a crowd was gathered. "He's nearly dead. The boys is just arguin' over whether they've had enough yet or whether they should behead 'em, hang 'em, or dissect 'em," he laughed derisively.

Jed pushed past the pair, shoving his shoulder hard into the larger man. Mumma glared at him, but the fury in the younger man's face chilled even the conscienceless butcher, who quickly turned his attention elsewhere.

In vain, Jed tried to draw closer to the crowded spot where he believed Harry Lee lay. The crowd was eight men thick and wild with ferocity as another victim fell prey to its wrath. Jed struggled against the throng, trying with all his might to break through to save the unknown man whose eyes were being held open while hot candle grease was dropped into them. The pitiful man's screams and pleas for mercy actually enraged the crowd further. Jed turned his head in revulsion, and as he did, he caught sight of a familiar face in the crowd.

Lieutenant Robertson, dressed in his uniform, was hunched near the jail wall. Four rabid men were attempting to intimidate the officer, who dragged the limp form of a man in his arms. A flash of color told Jed it was a fellow soldier whose chance of rescue now rested in the fate of his beleaguered officer. Jed felt torn between two duties. He cast his eyes back in the direction of the screaming man, and he knew there was little hope of rendering him any assistance as long as the crowds remained so thick. Muttering a prayer for the crowd's victim, Jed headed in Robertson's direction.

Since the intended purpose of the mob's attack on Hanson was to support the call for war, few seemed willing to spill a soldier's blood. Nevertheless, Robertson and his wounded comrade were obviously in danger, and Jed deemed strategy a wiser tactic than force. He leaned in close behind the jeering man in the rear and warned, "More soldiers are coming!" Within seconds the message had been passed along to those closest to Robertson. After giving the officer a shove and a final threat for daring to rescue the traitors, the men left, sharing the news of the arriving troops as they went. Lieutenant Robertson's heart felt weak with relief upon hearing the news, and he turned around to see his deliverance firsthand. Only one face remained—Jed's.

"Pearson? What are you . . . ?" His voice was accusatory and his face went slack. "You started that rumor, didn't you? No more troops are coming." His disappointment was palpable.

"But you've got enough time to get away and *get* more troops!" Jed insisted.

"There's no one to get," Robertson barked. "General Stricker refuses to order the militia back out, and the fort deems this a civil matter. The corporal and I rode by to assess the situation when he was hit by a rock."

They argued as they dragged the soldier behind the jail and into the brush, then the lieutenant turned to Jed and asked, "What are you doing here? You're supposed to be . . ."

"They're fine. I've moved them somewhere safe while I see to a friend."

"A friend?"

"Harry Lee. We are hardly more than acquaintances, but I can't bear the thought that such a man would die here like this. But I hear I may already be too late."

"Perhaps not," remarked Robertson as he removed his military jacket and placed it over the soldier. "I heard some doctors speaking. They're pulling bodies from a pile of victims over there somewhere, presumably declaring them dead though they are barely, but yet alive." He pointed to the place where Jed had previously headed. "They can't be far."

The two made their way around the back of the jail and through the brush, nearing the spot from the opposite side. As a result of Jed's rumor, the crowd had thinned significantly.

The agonized cries of the man whose eyes had been burned by hot candle grease could be heard nearby. Jed and Robertson dragged his mutilated body into the brush, then knelt close to assess the extent of his injuries. One eyelid was burned badly, though its closing had protected the eye itself. The second eyelid had apparently been forced open, and that eye was bloody and mottled. Patches of blood and cuts in his clothes testified to the innumerable shallow stab wounds inflicted expressly with the intent of causing the man further pain and suffering.

"There are doctors close by. Lie still while we bring help," offered Robertson.

Again the two men crept forward. They could still see a dozen or so men kicking at bodies heaped near the jail. Off to their right they heard movement in the brush, and they froze. Craning their heads to listen over the sounds of jeering near the jail, they heard the rustling of brush and gentle voices offering words of comfort. They quietly drew near the spot where men in suits were tending to six or seven bloodied men. Jed spotted the back of a stout man who carefully dragged a body away from the spot, and he moved quickly to intercept him.

"Renfro!" he whispered excitedly, nearly frightening the young man to death.

Samuel Renfro dropped the man to the ground and clutched his chest in fear. "Jed! You nearly gave me a heart attack! I thought the mob had discovered us."

"Have you seen Harry Lee? Where are you taking these men?"

"I'm not sure if he's among this group. We'll know once we get them inside the jail."

"Into the jail? Why do that when we can help them escape?"

"Shh! Keep your voice down," Renfro warned as his eyes darted back and forth nervously. "The mob believes these men are dead. We must treat them thusly for now."

"These barbarians will not allow you to attend to the wounded?"

"No. But Dr. Hall has a plan. He's no respecter of Hanson's politics, but his humanity could not allow him to abide the thought that his fellow citizens were capable of such deeds as these. We were initially denied the privilege of providing medical assistance, but Dr. Hall convinced the leaders of the rabble to at least allow a few of us access to the dead to attend to legalities. We discovered, as Dr. Hall suspected, that most of the men, though just barely, were still alive. By this stratagem he secured possession of these 'bodies' until morning. He hopes that once they are declared dead, the citizens' hunger for revenge will ease and the men will leave. Then we can convey them safely away before this crowd follows through on their threats to hurl them into a mass grave or drop them into Jones' Falls. Or worse yet, to hack off their parts."

Lieutenant Robertson staggered near the pair. "I cannot believe that even men engaged in battle would sink so low as to inflict this type of horror on another."

Jed's eyes grew wider and he looked to Renfro's tearing eyes.

"It's true, Jed. Once you see these men up close you will not be able to believe what they have endured this night. Many of them forced themselves to feign death while they were stabbed, burnt, and mutilated. They uttered nary a sound for fear of death, though many now say death would have been a welcome release from their current agony."

The men moved silently, carrying the bodies into the jail. Each grasp of an arm or a leg, no matter how gentle, brought initial gasps from the mangled victims. Jed's hand quickly ran red with the mingled blood of the wounded. Once inside, most of the men were identified, and some, like Alexander Contee Hanson, were still lucid enough to reply. Dr. Hall administered drinks and opiates to these men to ease their suffering. The others, among whom General Henry Lee was not found, were too far past consciousness to identify themselves, which, Jed supposed, was a blessing in disguise.

The most battered of the group of unknowns suddenly moaned and reached a mangled hand toward Jed. Immediately he turned and knelt by the man's side, offering what words of comfort he could to the disfigured soul. His blood-soaked body was contorted and misaligned, but it was the injuries inflicted on his head and face that nearly broke Jed. Blood was caked in his graying hair from battery to his head and face, and some still oozed from the multiple stab wounds across his face. One eye had been gouged out, and deep puncture wounds near his other indicated that its removal had also been intended. A long, deep slash ran from the bridge of his nose across his cheek from an apparent attempt to sever the man's nose completely. All in all, the wounds rendered him nearly unrecognizable, as if that was the very purpose of the deed.

Jed blinked quickly and reached for a bucket of water and a cup. "Have a drink of water, sir," he whispered from trembling lips.

"Jed Pearson?" The voice was weak and weary.

"Yes, sir," muttered Jed in astonishment. "Do you know me?"

The man raised his bloody hand to tap against his chest. "It's me . . . Harry Lee," and then, with the wisp of a hopeful smile on his lips, Light-Horse Harry Lee slipped into unconsciousness.

Jed laid his face on the man's chest and cried, "Dear, brave, Harry. What have they done to you?"

It took a few seconds for the enormity of the situation to sink in, then Jed took action. He found Renfro and Robertson on the front steps of the jail with Dr. Hall, who was negotiating with the mob. On the ground to their left lay another pile of equally abused and mangled bodies, still receiving kicks and jabs from men determined to find a live one in the bunch. Dr. Hall was having limited success in convincing the crowd to retire to their homes when a new shout went up. A cart approached carrying a large man named Thomson, and the crowd immediately shifted maliciously in his direction. Though Thomson was hidden from Jed's view, the frenzied cry from the crowd as they menacingly regrouped told Jed that if he wasn't dead he soon would be.

He forced his attentions back to the task at hand and placed himself directly in front of Dr. Hall. "General Harry Lee is in there, and I'm taking him now."

Dr. Hall replied anxiously. "It's too soon. Wait until . . ."

"Until what?" Jed blasted back. "Until that mob tires of their latest prey and returns for these men? No! I have a carriage and I'm taking him, and hang anyone who tries to stop me!"

"All right! All right," the doctor conceded. "But at least ferry more than one man to safety."

Jed relaxed and nodded in agreement, directing the doctor into the jail to ready the patients. "Samuel, will you come with me? Harry needs immediate attention."

"Of course I will. Let me get my bag. In the meantime, you and the lieutenant check on these poor souls by the steps and see if there are any that can be saved."

A chill ran through Jed at the thought of the grisly task. "Let's attend to it," he groaned to Robertson. But as he went to take a step down, he felt a viselike grip hold him in his place.

"Pearson, you miserable dog," growled the lieutenant. "You said Hannah was safe!"

"She is," Jed spat back angrily.

"Is that so? Then how do you account for that?" Robertson pointed to the street where a large bay stood with a small female rider astride. It was Hannah astride Tildie.

Jed's stomach lurched. He grabbed the man's coat and jerked his face near his own. "I moved the entire household to my Calvert Street home. She must have followed me."

"You louse!" Robertson gritted his teeth in anger. "I trusted you!"

The young woman sat frozen in horrified wonder, unable to bear the brutal scene playing out before her yet unable to turn away. Mr. Thomson, the current prey of the crowd, had been dragged from the cart and tossed to the ground on legs so badly beaten they could not bear his weight. He sank to the ground, begging for mercy. Instead, the mobbers produced a bucket of tar and began slathering hot blackness across his stripped and beaten back, then pressed feathers against his tarred, scalded flesh. Next, as if reaching inward for the greatest inhumanity of which men are capable, someone lit a match, igniting the feathers. Thomson rolled on the ground, writhing in agony, attempting to grind out the fire, pleading for the men to grant him mercy and shoot him dead rather than submit him to further brutality.

Hannah's mind screamed for her to turn away, but she could not tear her eyes from the horrible scene. She wanted to believe she was witnessing barbarity far beyond the capability of decent men, to trust that these aggressors were twisted miscreants or devils unleashed from the subterranean realms of hell. But as she gaped at faces in the crowd, she began to recognize a few. There were wild-eyed men in the throng who had attended the Stansburys' barbecues, gentlemen who had even sat at their own dining table. Hannah shuddered at the undeniable realization of an awful truth: that the seeds of evil lay within even God's seemingly decent children. That knowledge killed a measure of innocence in her.

Jed saw the change in Hannah's countenance and lunged in her direction even as Robertson held him in place.

"Hannah!" he shouted as he struggled free of Robertson's grasp.

"Don't draw attention to her!" Robertson warned. "With the frenzy this crowd is in, who knows how they will react to her?" But Jed had broken loose and was already gone.

Bolting through the crowd with the lieutenant close behind, Jed punched and tossed men out of his way, setting off smaller squabbles in his wake. He passed Mumma the butcher, who instantly recognized him and readied his axe handle to deliver a mortal blow, but Jed would not be stopped. He ducked low and came up hard into the man's midsection, and although the club bit into his side and he heard a crack followed by a shooting pain, he tossed Mumma off his back, nearly dropping him on Robertson. Jed plowed on, using Mumma's club as a battering ram, tossing men right and left like sticks. Finally, when he was only feet away from Hannah, she saw him.

Obvious relief washed over her. Then Jed watched her face cloud with confusion as Lieutenant Robertson appeared behind him. In one moment, all the intrigue and subterfuge that had been employed in the name of "doing what was best for Hannah" had been undermined in the collision of her two separate worlds. Confusion now reflected in her eyes, and Jed wondered if she understood that two of the people she had trusted the most had deceived her.

Unable to fathom the ramifications the truth would bring, Jed forced himself to focus on what was still within his control. In one motion he hefted the startled lieutenant onto Tildie's back. Then, using the club, Jed cleared a wide swath through which the mare could move. Hannah looked over her shoulder as the crowd began to close in on Jed and she screamed. Before he was swallowed in the fury, he slapped Tildie on her hindquarters and she leapt forward, leaving her master alone in the swell.

Robertson soon became aware of Jed's plight, and he whispered in Hannah's ear, "Get inside the jail. There is safety there!" Then he slid off the horse and rushed back into the fray. Dr. Hall and Samuel watched the scene unfold from the jail steps. Armed with nothing more than his buggy whip, Samuel Renfro raised the lash high above his head and let it crack in the air while Dr. Hall shouted, "Enough!" It did little other than to momentarily jar the crowd. In that second, though, a small detachment of soldiers arrived in the company of the wounded corporal. The simultaneous effect sent some of the mob running, reducing the crowd by half. The mounted soldiers drove directly into the fray where Robertson and Jed fought for their lives, and the military threat persuaded the remaining ruffians to stand down.

The soldiers helped the two men into the brush, drawing the dispersing crowd's attention away from the events unfolding in and around the jail. Jed's head was bleeding and he was on his knees, doubled over, drawing short, rapid breaths. Lieutenant Robertson's face was battered and swollen. While neither man's injuries were mortal both knew that in the last few minutes Hannah had recognized their deception. They each cast glances at her as she stood in Samuel's compassionate care. Her anger was undeniable, and suddenly all their fears of losing her, all their stress from protecting her, and all their anger from fighting for her were unleashed.

"You swaggering idiot," snarled Robertson.

Jed rose painfully and jutted his face close to Robertson's. "Why did you follow me? Now she has seen us both together. Have you a second deception up your sleeve?"

"We would not be in this situation had you not failed to protect Hannah," Robertson sneered back as he placed his hands on Jed, accenting his words with a shove.

"She was safe when I left her!" Jed grabbed Robertson's lapels, and the two men began struggling in the brush, but Hannah's pain-filled rebuke brought them to their senses.

"What have I done to deserve being treated thusly?" she sputtered as she fought back angry tears. The men tried to offer explanations, but she shot them a scalding stare that silenced them. "I don't know what manner of selfish game you are playing, nor do I trust anything you have to say. My only concern is that Dr. Renfro has three wounded men loaded in the carriage, and the spectacle you two are creating threatens to endanger all of us. Tear each other apart if you desire, but kindly do it after we leave!" She shook her head in disappointment and quickly hurried away.

The disillusionment on Hannah's face and in her voice tore at Jed's heart. He leapt to his feet to follow after her, but Robertson grabbed his arm to hold him in his place. Jed spun on him and declared, "It's pointless to try stopping me. No amount of lies will conceal the truth now."

"And which truth are you referring to, Pearson? The truth of what brought us to this impasse, or the truth of what we did so she could survive it?"

"Only one thing matters now," Jed answered, "and I'll see to her."

Robertson glared at Jed. "And what will you tell her?"

"Whatever I must."

Robertson seethed. "And where will you go?"

"Once the general can travel safely, I'll see him to wherever he chooses."

"You know what I mean," growled Robertson. "Where will you take Hannah?"

"That will depend wholly on her."

Robertson's jaw tightened. "I'm tired of these secrets. Circumstance has granted you time to make your case to Hannah before you return her safely to Coolfont. Take it, but understand that I have leave scheduled for the twenty-first, at which time I plan to go to Coolfont myself and see whom she has chosen. If she'll still have me, I intend to set our wedding date at that time."

Jed had no ready reply. Robertson could afford to be generous. He knew that once Hannah was back at Coolfont, Jed would likely lose her forever. Still, there was no other solution. Jed had a small window of time to regain her trust, and that window was closing rapidly.

Samuel Renfro and Hannah were preparing to leave with General Lee and the two other wounded men assigned to their care. Two other carriages and a wagon were being readied to secretly convey the remaining "dead" away. Some were to be carried to the hospital, others to the homes of friends in the country, but all who had survived the ambush were being taken elsewhere. All but Mr. Thomson, whose fate was still unknown.

Renfro fidgeted over their arrangements. "I believe we should wait for Jed, Miss Stansbury. We'll need his help if we encounter any trouble."

"These men cannot wait on Jed Pearson's benevolence," Hannah stated forcefully. "Current circumstances prove one cannot rely on him or his *help*. I have greater trust in our own judgments."

Jed overheard Hannah's bitter rebuke as he approached the carriage. She had never lashed out at him before, and this first instance came when he was already emotionally spent. He looked at Samuel and pointed. "Get in the carriage with the injured. I'll take the reins." As he walked up to Hannah he strained to remain even tempered. "I know you're angry, and I know you're owed an explanation." Over and over he tried to organize his thoughts. "None of this . . . It wasn't supposed to . . . I was working things out!" he blurted in frustration.

"Oh . . . you've apparently worked them out just fine! You and Andrew appear together before me, offering me no explanation as to how or when you met. I can only assume that I am the common denominator between you, yet neither of you shared the news of your meeting with me. So, why did Andrew ask for my hand, Jed? Did you two flip a coin for me? And if so, who was considered the victor? He who won the toss or he who lost it?" Her voice waivered, but steeling herself, she came back with an even more bitter edge to her voice. "An hour ago I thought you were my hero . . . my protector, but now I see that you are my manipulator and deceiver!"

"What?" he returned incredulously. *"Your manipulator?"* He felt as if her words tangibly speared his heart, and his jaw became so taut he could scarcely form his words. "I have never sought to control you, Hannah! If anything, your liberty and freedom will have been my undoing! And as to my being a liar . . ." He was ready to disclose the true villains whose lies and deceptions now entangled the pair, and then he remembered Beatrice's teary-eyed plea. "Of all the hurts in this world, I would never have dreamed you could ever utter such things against me. Not you . . . Do you have any idea what I have *suffered* for you? I rushed into the city to *protect* you! I fought that fire to *save* you! Do you know what you've cost me by coming here tonight? If you had honored my singular request and remained at my home this evening, our situation would now be resolved!"

The sliver of mercy Jed's words had begun to elicit from Hannah closed shut again. "You dare blame me?" She drew a deep breath for her next tirade when Samuel stepped between the pair and scolded them both in low warning tones.

"Hush, you two! This is neither the time nor the place."

The red-faced pair looked at him and then glowered at one another as they moved to their places. Jed took his seat in the driver's box of the carriage and Hannah mounted Tildie, preferring the horse to the seat beside Jed. They rode along silently, through alleys and sparsely populated streets, scrutinizing every inch of the path until they neared Calvert Street.

Jed stopped the carriage in an alley two blocks from his house. As he climbed off the carriage, he urged everyone to silence, then scurried through the alleyways to scout out his home. Once assured that no one lay in wait for the group, Jed dropped Hannah off at the house.

He reached up for her waist to help her down, but she recoiled from his touch, leaving Jed unable to bear the standoff any longer. "I *will* give you an explanation, little one," he said earnestly in an attempt to break the silence, but the once familiar endearment fell flat.

Hannah slipped from the horse unassisted and gave him a long, cold stare. "I am not your little one anymore."

Without further word, Jed handed Tildie's reins to Bartholomew. Then he and Samuel drove the carriage to the hospital where Harry and his companions were to spend the night. Once situated in the hospital, Samuel tended to Harry's wounds and Jed kept a constant vigil, watching over the venerable gentlemen in case the mob came, grateful for an excuse to avoid Hannah until his mind was clear.

Sometime after midnight, John Thomson arrived at the hospital. He bemoaned the fact that after having been tarred and feathered, the barbarians demanded he sign an affidavit surrendering the names of everyone who had taken their stand with Hanson. In his excruciating state he had submitted to his captors. Once the document was secured, the mayor arrived and arranged for a cart to carry him to the hospital while, armed with the list of names, the mob began scouring the city for those of Hanson's crew who had escaped their judgment. Fearful that the mob would soon arrive, Jed and Samuel decided to convey Thomson and Harry Lee from the hospital as soon as possible and into Jed's home to spend the remainder of the night.

At first light Jed changed carriages and hitched up a fresh team. Neither of the women had risen yet, so he left a note promising to return for them in a few days, whereupon he would see them safely on to Coolfont. He wondered if they would still be there when he returned. Even so, he regretted how relieved he was to avoid another emotional exchange with Hannah. He was simply too weary for another attack on his battered soul until he was able to adequately defend his actions and express the feelings of his heart. As he prepared to set off, Hannah appeared on the stoop, bag in tow.

"What do you think you are doing?" Jed asked in utter astonishment.

"I'm coming along," she stated matter-of-factly.

"Absolutely not!" Jed barked back. "Do you have any idea what danger we are in?"

"You need me. Consider the spectacle you will raise. Why would a horseman like Jed Pearson drive a carriage out of town ferrying a medical student unless he was transporting wounded? Do you think your faces went unseen last night? Better they think you are carrying a woman home than to wonder what wounded man is hidden inside."

Renfro raised one eyebrow. "Her point is well taken, Jed."

"The men desire to go to York Town, Pennsylvania. Coolfont is in the opposite direction."

Hannah handed her bag to Renfro, who solicitously opened the carriage door. "Then I will travel on to York Town," she replied as she took the seat beside General Lee near the window.

Jed leapt from his seat. "What about Beatrice? How will it appear for a single woman to be traveling in the company of a league of single men?"

"I am just a traveler in a coach. Why would anyone find disrepute in that?" she argued.

"What about your *fiancé?*" Jed asked sarcastically. "Do you think the good lieutenant would agree to such an arrangement?"

Hannah leaned nearer the window and spoke in a measured voice. "I need answers, Jed. I can no longer move forward with my plans to marry Andrew until I get answers from you. I need to understand how you two met and why you didn't at least respond to my letter. Yesterday, you asked me to trust you." Her tone was still cold and indifferent. "I am trusting you to help me make peace with what has happened between us. You owe me this courtesy."

Jed could not deny her request, though believing that her intentions were clearly set on Andrew made him detest the plan all the more. The additional concern for Hannah's safety left him nearly beside himself with worry, scrutinizing every alley and turn, in search of possible dangers. The exit from Baltimore unnerved Jed, as if every eye was upon them as they passed, leaving him barely able to draw a full breath until they were well past the city and on the northern road. Renfro then joined him in the driver's box, craning his neck to watch for bushwhackers.

Ten miles out of the city, Renfro returned to the carriage to help Hannah tend to the wounded while Jed set an easy pace to spare Lee and Thomson further agony. The two days of travel were stressful and exhausting and all three rescuers collapsed from fatigue each night after Lee and Thomson were put to bed. On Saturday evening, the first of August, they finally arrived in the historic city of York Town,

Pennsylvania, the haven they had sought for Harry Lee. Jed successfully located the home of the hero's friends, who generously offered safety and board for the group. For their own safety, Renfro and Hannah were checked into an inn, while Jed maintained a vigil over the injured parties to protect against attackers who may have followed them. After a few days, the doctors treating Lee and Thomson assured Jed that their conditions were improving. Satisfied that he had done what he could for Harry Lee, Jed turned his attentions to returning to Maryland and settling things with Hannah. Then reports in the local newspaper brought him new alarm.

The "Baltimore Riot," as Hanson's stand was now called, was discussed in print and in every alehouse. Public sympathies outside Baltimore rested heavily with the editor, calling the violence a "horrid atrocity" and decrying "the brutal and murderous fury of the Mob" for attempting to destroy liberty of the press. While publishing some defensive statements from Baltimore authorities, the editorialists were quick to note that members of other local jurisdictions ascribed such terms as *partial, mutilated,* and *unjust* to their depositions.

Sobering reports of violence continued to pour from the beautiful harbor city. Small bands of anti-Federalists still plundered homes, seeking out the few of Hanson's crew who had eluded them. Hannah's words haunted Jed: *Do you think your faces went unseen last night?* He felt paralyzed with fear for Beatrice, Bartholomew, and the others, and his fears sped on to further worries of retribution and violence. What if they attacked the Willows? Or what if they discovered that he had headed north? What if they assumed he had carried their prey to Philadelphia, to Frannie?

He had no idea where to turn first. In a panic, he gathered Hannah and Renfro in the inn's dining room and laid out his concerns. Neither could deny the capabilities of the mob after what they had already witnessed.

"We should go upstairs and pack," Samuel said to Hannah.

"No," Jed stated firmly. "You'll be safer here. No one knows we've come to York Town, but they could be looking for me in Philadelphia. As soon as I'm sure Frannie is safe, I'll return for you and we'll make our way home."

"I don't think it's wise for you to travel alone, Jed," Samuel warned.

The strain showed in Jed's eyes, but he was immoveable on the matter. He withdrew several bills from his wallet and instructed Samuel, "Dash off two notes, one to Beatrice warning her to hurry on to Coolfont, and one to the Willows, offering the courier this bonus if he can deliver the notes in record time." With grave import he placed his hand on his friend's shoulder and continued, "I'll leave the carriage behind. See that Hannah makes it safely back to Coolfont if I become detained."

Samuel's expression indicated that he understood the implication. He nodded silently as Jed rose to leave.

Hannah fought the flood of emotions swirling inside her. She felt Samuel's hand clasp over hers, and when she looked at him she saw a knowing look on his face. Then he nodded in Jed's direction. Her trembling hand squeezed his as she hurried after Jed, whom she found standing by Tildie, fastening his pack. "How long will you be away?" she began.

His attention remained fixed on his task, though his shoulders slumped as soon as he heard her voice. "Three days . . . maybe four. If I'm not here by then, go on with Samuel."

Hannah felt her lips begin to quiver, but she tried to appear detached. "Why didn't you answer my letter? Why didn't you come to me instead of running to Andrew?"

Jed's head shot up and his face paled at her mention of his dealings with the lieutenant. Hannah noted the change and her heart nearly broke. "So, it's true. *You* were the one who went to *him*. You refused *me* the courtesy of a reply, yet you went to him? Why?"

He leaned his forehead against the saddle and groaned. "Please. Not now. Not like this."

She buried her pain and pressed on. "Why not, Jed? A year and a half has passed. Feelings change . . . I understand that we cannot calculate when or where love will come to us. Some matches are simply a better fit for us than others. I, of all people, understand that." She remembered back to the conversation she had overheard between Jed's friends in Botto's restaurant regarding Catherine, a mayor's daughter, a woman who could help Jed become a great man . . . even a governor one day. Hannah suddenly felt small and meaningless before him. Her hurt made her next words cross and bitter. "I cannot move forward confidently with Andrew until I know how I could have been so wrong regarding us—so, I'd simply like to know whether my affections were mere amusements to you." Hannah soon saw how deeply she had wounded the proud man.

"Mere amusements?" Jed faced her and moved from utter disappointment to anger, the irony of her accusations paining him anew. "I could ask you the same question. Why did you accept the lieutenant's proposal so quickly? It appears I was easily replaced!"

She had not expected him to pose a challenge to her own fidelity, but, refusing to give him the satisfaction of seeing her pain, she snapped, "You know, it's really quite unbecoming . . ."

"What?" he responded with equal sharpness.

"This latent chagrin of yours. It seems a tad insincere that you would care who now stands in a place you had already refused." She quickly turned and strode away, fighting her tears and wishing that she had done as he had requested and left the conversation for a later time.

Jed could not let it go, and he called out after her. "You said you were no longer my little one? Well, I am no longer your keeper. Go get your precious answers from your lieutenant." He leapt upon Tildie's back with such force that the startled mare reared and snorted. Hannah was nearing the door but his voice still chased after her. "I do want to offer you my congratulations, Miss Stansbury. You were right to choose a soldier. Your aim is far too accurate and your blows too deadly to waste on a simple farmer like me. No, one warrior deserves another." He could see Hannah mounting the inn's staircase, well beyond the reach of his voice, but nonetheless, he threw one final hurt in her direction. "I only hope you and your lieutenant enjoy drawing one another's blood as much as you've each enjoyed drawing mine." Then he sped away.

* * *

Upon reaching the City of Brotherly Love, Jed discovered that Frannie had already left, suddenly and without notice. Barely allowing Tildie time to rest, he turned her west, back to York Town for Hannah and Renfro. It was after midnight when Jed arrived at the inn, so he turned in, then dragged his weary body from the bed at first light.

He rapped on Samuel's door, awakened his sleeping friend, and bade him to ready himself quickly. Pausing outside of Hannah's door, he stalled, dreading the agony of seeing her again. His knocking produced no response, so he tried the door, which opened easily to a clean, tidy room. Rushing downstairs to check on her whereabouts, he found her staring into the cold fireplace with her trunks by her side.

Jed cleared his throat nervously to get her attention. Neither could bear the other's gaze, prompting them to cast their eyes away as soon as they met. "So you're packed? . . . Fine . . . You have a few minutes to eat if you choose to. Charge breakfast to my room for you and Samuel. I'll be hitching up the team," Jed said as he turned to leave.

"Thank you . . . but . . . I'm not hungry."

"Very well then." He was paradoxically both grateful and miserable that neither of them had the will to dredge it all up again.

"Jed? I'm sorry it became so unpleasant between us the other day." Hannah shook her head quickly as if she were trying to jar an image from her mind. "At times we've been so complementary to one another. But lately . . ."

He kept his back to her, replying, "We'll leave as soon as Samuel is ready." Then he walked out the door.

On the second day of their trip back to Maryland, the weather turned foul as the oppressive summer heat and humidity gave way to dangerous thunderstorms. Jed slogged on determinedly through the storm for two days, making only minimal progress in the clay muck. As the roads became flooded, passage was eventually stopped. The men threw off the canvas covering under which they had burrowed in the driver's box, and Jed jumped down to inform Hannah of their situation. He noticed that a window flap was loose, allowing rain to pour into the carriage. When he opened the carriage door, he found Hannah soaking wet and lying incoherently on the floor.

"Samuel! Hurry! Hannah's unconscious!" He cradled her limp body and felt her fevered cheeks. "She's burning up! Oh, dear God in heaven," he prayed, "please let her be all right."

Samuel checked her condition and spoke rapidly. "She was flushed last night but refused to admit she felt poorly. Such a drenching bodes ill for one already so compromised. She's barely eaten or slept since we left Baltimore, and her lungs are still weakened from the smoke of the house fire as well."

Jed shook his head. "She came along to protect us and find some peace, and look at what price she is paying. Please, Samuel. Help her!"

"The only shelter I've seen is that abandoned shanty just ahead. Let's get her in quickly."

Jed was frantic to get her warm. While Renfro attended to Hannah's health, Jed started a fire and caught rain in a kettle. Making use of the few cooking supplies he had, he set a pot of water on to boil and tossed in sassafras bark and peppermint leaves. Then he killed some pigeons that had taken up roost in the rafters, and with wild onions and root vegetables he found growing in an overgrown garden, he fashioned a stew that he spooned into her mouth little by little throughout the night. Dressed in the only dry frock she possessed, Hannah still remained cold to the touch and appeared almost blue-tinged. The horrifying image of his mother's frozen countenance haunted Jed, and he gathered the young woman in his arms and wrapped her like a child in a blanket, cradling her against him as he rocked her by the fire. Burying his face in her tangled hair, he sobbed, completely unashamed, as his friend huddled worriedly nearby. "Return to me, Hannah. Please, return to me."

* * *

By morning Hannah had stirred slightly, and Jed pressed Renfro so passionately for word that she was improving that the gentle man violated his conscience and said it was so. Throughout the day Jed continued spooning broth between her lips and holding her tirelessly. The scene became so pitiful that Samuel had to withdraw from the little hovel; however, by afternoon, he was able to give an honest report that her color was improving. Nonetheless, he cautioned Jed that her fever might rise again as night drew near.

His prognosis was correct. By sunset Hannah's cheeks were flushed, and by midnight she was sweat-soaked and shuddering with chills. Renfro applied alcohol compresses to her forehead and wrists and used what limited medicines were at his disposal. Jed read to her and prattled on incessantly in the hopes that the sound of his voice would keep her from succumbing to the call of whatever lay beyond the veil. By Thursday morning, her fever broke and she uttered her first lucid words in days. The two men were each nearly starved at that point, and Jed finally felt comfortable leaving the doctoring to Renfro while he took up his rifle and headed into the woods for game.

"Where's Jed?" Hannah asked upon awakening.

Renfro drew close and took her hand in his. "Thank heaven!" he beamed. "You're much improved. You had us both dreadfully worried, Miss Stansbury."

"But where's Jed?" she repeated, growing more alarmed. "He hasn't left me, has he?"

"Left you? Why, the man has neither slept nor eaten in nearly three days. He has been completely devoted to your every care. It's only because he feared I would die of starvation and be unable to treat you that he finally agreed to go hunting." Renfro laughed, drawing a relaxed smile from Hannah. "No. He would never leave you willingly. He loves you."

"But what *manner* of love does he feel for me?" She blushed as she asked the question and turned her head.

"May I speak freely?" Renfro asked as he stuffed tobacco into a pipe and lit it. "I once joked that my admiration of him rivals near reverential stature, and do you know why?"

Hannah's eyes grew wide with wonder and she shook her head in response.

"I have long held to a theory that the average person is the happiest of people. Their lives are simple, their paths straightforward. Their minds and time are not cluttered by grand choices and weighty responsibilities. Beside the simple needs of their family, they bear responsibility for no one but themselves. It was likely so for their ancestors and will likely be so for their heirs. So they are born into this world without great expectation and will exit the same, with few men debating the success or failure of their lives. It is the reverse for the great ones. They are born shackled by the expectations of family and community who debate their every choice and measure their life, day by day, 'til their last breath is drawn and beyond. Upon their shoulders rests not only the livelihood and fortune of their own family but the livelihoods and fortunes of hundreds, perhaps even thousands of others in their employ and circle of influence. In some cases, even freedom itself draws a restful breath upon the shoulders of such people. Jed is such a person. Yet he has no concept of his greatness, no understanding of the power he commands or of the influence he directs. He believes what respect others show him is rooted in their fear of his wealth, but it is the wealth of his character that awes us. And yet, for all these attributes he is the most troubled of souls." Renfro took a long draw on his pipe.

"I cannot, of myself, imagine," he went on, "what burdens one would bear, heading not only a family but an impressive empire of land and other assets at twenty-two years of age. I would imagine the person such a man is most likely to deem unworthy is more often than not himself."

Hannah pondered Renfro's words before responding. "If he'd only let me in, I could be a support and comfort to him. I wrote him a letter last spring." She blushed darkly. "I practically threw my affections at him. I begged him for a response, but he ignored me. I overheard your conversation that day in the café. I heard you discussing a woman named Catherine."

Renfro went pale at the memory of that day. "Ah, Catherine. Yes, she loved him, and he fancied her company for a short while, but he never cared for her, and he called it off abruptly. She then slandered him through two states, calling him a heartless man. In truth, she was right."

Hannah's face twisted at such a bitter accusation.

Renfro looked pointedly at her. "He no longer possessed one. Long ago he had surrendered it fully to you."

Tears welled up in Hannah's eyes. "But what am I to do? Wait decades until he finds his voice? And what if he never does? What am I to do?"

Renfro took her hand. "That I cannot say. I can assure you no man ever loved a woman more than he loves you. However, only you can decide if you can bear the tumult of being adored by one so troubled."

"And what is it that troubles him? Do you know?"

"I doubt even Jed clearly knows. The one observation I have made is that despite his self-proclaimed eschewing of social conventions and his intolerance of gossip, making his family name one of honor is imperative to him. Jed seems to be driven to right the wrongs of the Pearson past. I believe that is the prize he pursues most consciously, but there is another thing. It is the fear that grips most men at one time or another, but I do feel it strongly in Jed."

Hannah rose up on her elbow. "What is it?"

Renfro removed his pipe and shook his head with a disappointed smile. "One day you are going to be an amazing woman. But Jed is right in worrying that there is still much child left in you. When you are fully a woman, when you truly know Jed Pearson, you will not have to ask."

If any other man had censured her so, Hannah knew she would have become incensed, but somehow, when the advice drifted from Samuel Renfro's understanding lips, no ire was raised.

"How is it that you know so much about love at such a young age?" she asked.

"Ah," Renfro teased, shaking his glowing pipe at her. "You forget. I am one of the few men who have actually seen the human heart."

Hannah's face clouded momentarily. Then, as his meaning hit her, she chuckled loudly.

Jed entered the cabin with a canteen, two rabbits in tow, and a mile-wide smile. "Was that laughter I heard?" he questioned, dropping immediately to his knees at Hannah's side.

"Yes, it was," she teased softly as she stared at him.

"Skinning and gutting—now that is work more suited to a surgeon," Renfro chortled, taking the rabbits from Jed and exiting the log house, leaving the young pair alone.

Jed felt Hannah's eyes upon him as he poured water from the canteen into a glass. "I found a fresh spring running from a rock ledge," he murmured, gently raising the cup to her lips. She drank deeply while drops of cool water trickled along the sides of her parched mouth and down her chin. Jed swept his thumb along her jaw and over her lips, spreading the moisture across her fever-dried mouth. He felt his heart begin to pound and his breathing deepen from being so near her, and he worried that his eyes revealed too much. "And what made you so happy in my absence?" he asked as he pulled away slightly, avoiding her gaze.

"I was just counting my blessings."

"And for what are you so grateful that your thankfulness would turn into laughter?"

Hannah cupped his chin and drew his face nears hers. "For dreams . . ."

Jed attempted to resist her entreaty, but Hannah persisted, instead bringing her own face closer to his.

". . . and for time."

Jed hovered an inch from her mouth, longing to press his lips against hers but knowing that the object of his desire was promised to another. He began to pull away, but Hannah held him close and gazed into his eyes, finding the undeniable proof of the love Renfro had disclosed to her—the love that Jed had tried so hard to disguise.

"What are you hoping to find there, Hannah?" Jed asked in an anguished whisper.

"The truth . . ."

He lowered his eyes and his voice became husky. "The truth is . . . I've always loved you, Hannah. I know I have delayed too long in telling you, but there was a time when all I wanted was to disclose these truths to you . . ."

"And now?" she asked softly.

Jed sat back on the wooden floor and sighed deeply, forced to admit that Robertson had always been right. "Now the only truths that matter are those that will make your life sweetest."

Hannah fell back, surrendering to the fatigue. "And what are those, Jed?"

"First I must be sure that love alone is enough."

Hannah closed her eyes and smiled at the modest disclosure. "Decide quickly, Jed. Our time is growing short."

* * *

Jed stared at the pages of the little leather-bound notebook he carried in his breast pocket. It was Saturday, August fifteenth, and they had not yet left for Coolfont. Lieutenant Robertson would be waiting for Hannah on Friday, and if Jed failed to meet the appointed deadline, it would be one more thing her mother would charge against him. He told himself that the events of the past few weeks had numbed him to the opinions of others, but he knew in his heart that wasn't true. Perhaps it was for Frannie, but it was never so for him. And he was beginning to understand the history behind the sniggers that had quickly replaced the cordial smiles as his family passed by. For good or for ill, he was in a race against the devil himself, it seemed, to know the whole truth. Now his delay might sully Hannah's good name. He slapped the book against his thigh and groaned inwardly. Perhaps he would ruin her. Perhaps loving, even loving completely, was not enough. Perhaps one could not run from the past.

"A penny for your thoughts," Hannah's wispy voice offered.

Jed turned quickly to find her thin frame leaning against a tree a few feet from him. With unabashed longing he smiled at her. She was so lovely, even when wrapped in a dreary woolen blanket. He thought he noticed the same want reflected in her eyes, and he quickly sought to change the mood until his head was clearer. Raising his hands at the woods, he answered dryly, "A penny will do neither of us any good out here, I'm afraid."

Hannah would not be dissuaded. "Are you refusing my money or my company?"

"Does Samuel know you're up and about? He told me you needed another day's rest before we dare tire you with travel. I doubt he'd sanction a walk today."

Hannah lifted her arms in his direction. "You're right. Then carry me back."

Jed cocked his head and smiled knowingly. He lifted her easily and smiled as her arms instinctively wrapped around his neck. "You are the devil, Hannah Stansbury."

"I am saving my strength. It requires every ounce I possess to deal with you, you know." Jed didn't argue, and the mood shifted. "You've avoided speaking to me privately. Please just talk to me as you once did. At the very least, be my friend, Jed. Don't isolate me."

Jed touched his head to hers for a second, assessing the pain her request dredged up in his own heart. "Isolate you?" he said as he raised his head. He stared into the green of her eyes and she brushed a wisp of hair from her face. "Why haven't you told me about your dreams? I knew the fever brought nightmares on, but Samuel said you mentioned having being plagued by a recurring dream before the fire. If I was once your confidante, why didn't you speak of this to me?"

Hannah's face clouded and she brought her hand up to touch his face. "I need to. You need to know about them, but it's as you've said so frequently to me—the timing hasn't seemed right yet. Anyway, they are past now. Beatrice shored me up and got me through the terror. Bless sweet Beatrice . . . and Myrna. I would have shriveled up and died without them this year."

Jed's jaw tightened at the mention of the women. "So they've been good to you?"

"Oh, yes. We've suffered through dark days together, but now both are happily married and my parents are content. For the first time in my life I feel I am part of a truly happy family."

Jed's heart ached, both for her happiness and for what her simple statement boded for him.

"Beatrice kept me grounded. Now it is she who is beset with worries. She hasn't received word from Dudley in weeks, Jed, and she lives in mortal fear that word will arrive saying he's been mauled by Indians or shot dead by the British. It's hard to be a soldier's wife."

"Is it?" Jed's voice had an edge to it. "And yet you've promised yourself to an officer."

Hannah noted his tone. "Andrew has been very kind to me and my family," she replied defensively. "He comforted me *when I needed a friend.*"

She drove her point deep into his heart and it hit its mark, prompting Jed to retaliate snidely. "It's interesting to me, the way you and your family have rewarded this new friend so handsomely, while a lifetime of friendship yielded no such rewards to me. Had I noted the change in policy, perhaps I would have made my own desires more clear."

"Perhaps you should have!" Hannah tossed back.

Jed reeled. "If I had known your capricious heart was just as easily comforted by one man as another, I wouldn't have spent this past year castigating myself for my delay."

Hannah reared back in indignation, but as the words resonated in her head, she went limp and her face became sad. "Look at us," she moaned. "Each of us is spitting out horrid things without listening to ourselves or to one another. Why can't we just admit the truth?"

Jed pressed his fingers to her lips as he set her on the ground by the door of the cabin. His shoulders hung and he took a step away to break the spell he fell under in her presence. "Which truth is that, Hannah? That in six days the soldier you promised yourself to will be waiting for you at Coolfont, or the truth that he can give you everything you want? And what of the sadder truth that neither of us wants to admit—that you already *have* everything you want, Hannah. The happy family, the acceptable beau . . ."

"You have no idea what I want," she cried out. "And that has always been the problem with us. You left me thinking I was passed off to a more willing man like secondhand garb. Well, at least Andrew knows his own mind! You say you have loved me since we were children? Well, we are not children any longer, Jed. Instead of assuming what I want, perhaps it's time you asked yourself what it is *you* want."

Too many times in too few days he'd had his honor and his manhood challenged while he had held his tongue to the truth. Now pain and fury roiled in him, and he finally unleashed his tongue. "What I want? Did you really ask me that? After all we have shared, do you really not know?" An incredulous laugh escaped his taut mouth. "Miss Stansbury . . . I can assure you, we wouldn't be in this situation if what I want had mattered at all!"

"What?" Hannah asked as she grabbed his arm to hold him in place.

He spun around to face her and spat out his final words, regretting them even as they crossed his lips. "Ask that happy family of yours." And then he turned and marched away.

"Jed!" she demanded. "What are you implying?" She felt sick and slumped against the cabin wall as she wrestled with his words. "What of my family?"

Jed stormed on, catching Renfro by the arm as he headed for the horses. "I'm going to ride ahead and scout out the best road. Don't expect me back before nightfall."

Renfro looked in Hannah's pitiful direction. "Perhaps you should tell that to Hannah."

Jed ignored his friend. "Pack the carriage to make it as comfortable as possible for her. I plan to deliver her to Coolfont on the twenty-first."

Renfro winced questioningly. "She can't take six long days at a hard pace."

"Then we'll ride slowly and travel all night if we must. But be assured, we will be at Coolfont by Friday morning."

CHAPTER 35

Fort Detroit, Michigan Territory
Pre-dawn, Sunday Morning, August 16, 1812

Captains Dudley Snowden and Stephen Mack had to remind themselves that regardless of what might be transpiring in the muddled mind of General Hull, they were still military officers with duties to perform. They forced their sickened frames to walk erect as they surveyed the grisly scene that was Fort Detroit, assessing the integrity of the fort's defenses. Splintered chunks of wood and stone littered the ground from the constant British barrage that had begun battering the parapet the previous day, continuing well into the night. They passed by the root house that had been employed as a shelter of sorts when the accuracy of the British bombardment had become so precise that the buildings themselves no longer provided any real measure of safety. The fearful cries of women and the wails of children poured out of the earthen hole. Never before had either soldier seen or heard such a scene of lamentation and misery, as if the fallen city of Old Jerusalem had found its equal in Detroit. Upon hearing rumors of Tecumseh's approach, families from town had fled into the fort for safety. Now their cries mingled with those of soldiers' families mourning the loss of loved ones and fearing the attacks. The weeping of these innocents unnerved the officers far more than did the cannonballs and musket fire, and they nearly longed for the return of gunfire.

Mrs. Lydia Bacon, a stalwart young woman married to a quarter-master by the name of Josiah, stood near the root-house doorway alternately covering her ears and scribbling in a small book.

"Captains?" she called out, drawing the men's attention. "Have Colonels Cass and McArthur returned from their mission?"

Dudley looked cautiously at Mack, who replied, "I have not seen them as yet, ma'am."

"Is there no word from any of their party?" she asked, her hope diminished.

"I believe some of the riders made it back through the blockade. They are in with General Hull now." Dudley feared the next question as hope lit her eyes once more.

"Did they say if they were able to open up a supply line or send word of our situation?"

Dudley's expression answered the woman's question, and once again he watched the hope dim in her face. "You'd be safer inside, Mrs. Bacon."

She cast her eyes toward the heartrending scene playing out in the root house and spoke softly, "I feel safe nowhere, gentlemen."

"Can we be of any help to you, madam?" Captain Mack inquired kindly.

"I have concerns of a spiritual nature."

"I'm inclined to spiritual things, but I am not a minister, you understand," Mack explained.

"Then I should still like to hear your opinion on the matter." She drew a deep breath and began with quivering lips. "I am more concerned over the judgments of God than over the power of man, but I fear I have done something to deny two souls a place by His side—myself and a young physician who served here in the fort. He called for me when he was nigh unto death."

Dudley Snowden was impressed by the earnestness of the woman over a topic that increasingly concerned him as well.

"I squandered an opportunity to right a man on his journey to eternity. He appeared to feel perfectly confident of his acceptance with God on his own merits, though he acknowledged no Savior, saying that he needed none, believing his own righteousness was all sufficient. I failed to raise my testimony about the Savior. Do you believe we are both lost, sir?"

Both men felt the earnestness of her question, but while Captain Mack's face effused with the peace that came from a personal knowledge of God and godly things, Dudley had no such assurance, only questions of his own. He felt like an incomplete man, able to defend against physical threats but useless to lead or protect in a spiritual crisis. Feeling unqualified, he bowed to Mrs. Bacon before making his exit, leaving such matters to his more insightful friend.

After he left, Dudley couldn't get the woman's concern over faith and the hereafter out of his mind. Perhaps it was the presence of death and suffering all around him. He saw the bloodstained remains of the annihilated building where two officers had been cut down the previous day, before the very eyes of women making cylinders—bags to hold gunpowder—and scraping lint with which to pack the cannons. A twenty-four pounder exploded on the adjacent building, cutting the two men in half and amputating the legs of a third man as it passed through. He understood casualties were to be expected in wartime, but women and children were not expected to be a part of such horrors.

Crossing the debris-strewn parade ground, Dudley found a quiet corner near a fallen chunk of the parapet. A soldier's cap lay nearby, and Captain Snowden sadly recalled that a ball had cut a young man down at that very spot while he stood there on duty. Dudley pulled a small telescope from his pocket and strained to see by the dim light of the half moon. Although he couldn't make out any faces, he thought he saw movement in the rushes by the water's edge, likely members of Tecumseh's forces inching their way toward Fort Detroit's imperiled walls. Closing the glass, he slid down to the ground and pulled a few sheets of paper and a child's pencil from his coat pocket and began writing what he feared would be his last letter to Beatrice.

My darling Beatrice, he began. He closed his eyes and brought her sweet face to his mind. She would be worried by now, probably terrified by this long silence after so many solicitous letters following his departure from the capital. *What does a man write to his wife in his final moments?* He cast his eyes around the fort, searching for answers. He finally decided that less information about the war would be better, and he began sharing the contents of his heart. He wrote on and on, finding it surprisingly easy and cathartic to hold nothing back from the only woman he had ever loved: the one woman who had made him feel handsome and dashing, the one woman with whom he had dared to plan a life beyond the military.

He had filled both sides of three pages and had begun filling a fourth when he saw two boots appear silently before him.

"I thought I'd find you here." It was Captain Stephen Mack. He held up paper, quill, and ink, smiling back as he sat down. "Husbands' hearts beat alike . . ."

"Is there any news from General Hull's office?"

"None from him, but the word being scuttled about is that the British commander, a General Brock, has sent a letter demanding the immediate surrender of the fort. He made a complete mockery of the inflammatory proclamation General Hull sent July twelfth demanding the surrender of the whole of Canada." He laughed sarcastically. "Now look at us."

"'A war of extermination,'" mused Dudley sadly, recalling the words.

"Yes, sir. And Hull also claimed that no white man fighting by the side of an Indian would be taken prisoner. Instant destruction would be his lot. Now he fears he has set the pattern for our enemy to show us as little mercy as he promised them."

Dudley closed his eyes. "Neither is Tecumseh known for mercy. I see why Colonels Cass and McArthur attempted to depose General Hull. So what are our current orders?"

"To watch and wait," retorted Mack tiredly. "We could have blown that solitary British gunboat clear out of the water, but Hull would not give the order. Now that very boat has her guns pointed down our throats. And to think—after our complete superiority at Sandwich—that we would run tail and hide here because of rumored Indian advances. Then to then wait a week and watch anemically while the attack sets up at our very doorstep . . . well, it's so preposterous it's nearly laughable! We should be smarter than this! How could we be so poorly prepared—Our supply lines cut off, our food stores nearly depleted? The one thing we have—ammunition—we dole out against the enemy in dribbles and drabbles. Where is the threat of resistance in that, I ask you."

"Tensions and fears are running high," Dudley admitted, then asked gently, "Were you able to allay Mrs. Bacon's concerns?"

"At least somewhat. In times like these we all want to know where we stand with God."

"Indeed we do," muttered Dudley. "My heart breaks for the women and children."

"Yes, particularly the women," agreed Captain Mack. "The children take their cues from them, and they have borne this failure with courage until this last hour. Still, as much as I dread exposing the women and children to an Indian threat, neither can I stomach surrender. We have over two thousand men, most of whom are hungry to avenge the carnage wrought upon us the past twenty-four hours. I count twenty-eight cannons, and though battered, the fort walls are still strong. We can make a stand here. If we capitulate, there still will be no guarantees regarding anyone's treatment. Militarily, Britain gains a strategic fort, all our equipment, and control of the entire Michigan Territory. We cannot let this happen. If Hull does surrender and we survive this rout, there are many officers who have sworn to go straight to Washington City and see him court-martialed and shot."

"Did you know that Mrs. Bacon has been keeping a detailed diary? It may be a valuable asset if we are called to testify concerning the decisions that led us to this dilemma."

Mack shook his head again. "She's a good woman, that one. She also reminds me of my sister Lucy—strong, brave, fiercely devoted. Such women deserve better than this. They should not have to view such atrocities, nor should they have to tremble at home, praying for word from a husband, son, or brother who by rights should be celebrating a victory at Amherstburg this day."

Dudley nodded his agreement as he jotted his closing thoughts, folded and addressed the letter, and tucked it into his breast pocket. "I've never been a handsome man," he mused. "I'm too portly, too squat, and I can't dance or carry a tune. But my Beatrice always made me feel like a king. I only hope that, well—if the worst comes to pass—that some noble opponent will see to the mailing of this letter. I'd like her to know I was thinking of her 'til the last."

Stephen Mack held out his hand to his friend. "Let us make a pact. If one of us survives and the other does not, we will see to the other man's family. Agreed?"

A wash of peace rushed over Captain Dudley Snowden. "Agreed." He nodded soberly. "Yes, I can carry on knowing that."

The first light of dawn turned the eastern sky pink as the two men inched their heads over the parapet to survey the enemy's night-time advance. Nearly five hundred natives from Tecumseh's First Nation's alliance had crossed the Detroit River and now surrounded the fort, supported by seven hundred men from General Isaac Brock's British forces. An American lieutenant on lookout yelled down from his position.

"Indians are ransacking the town with no resistance. All the Detroit residents who didn't come into the fort have now either fled or are dead!"

The eerie whirl overhead sent the two captains to their knees for cover as the British bombardment resumed. Fiery balls of lead set fires where they landed, and the cries of agonized men signaled the success of the attackers' aim. When Dudley rose to gather his men to attempt a military response, he found Lydia Bacon standing nearby, watching the battle unfold.

"Miss Lydia, you must return to the root house!" Captain Snowden pled.

"I cannot, sir," she replied with resignation. "My feelings are wrought to such a high pitch, Captain, that I am devoid of further fear. My hair feels as if it is erect upon my head, and I cannot tear my eyes away from catching a glimpse of the bombshells and balls flying in all directions about me. I'm recording my observations in my diary, in case . . ."

"Please, Mrs. Bacon. The women need you, the children need you, and your husband wants you safe. Go back to the root house and offer them a measure of your courage. Please."

He offered her a small nudge toward the root house and she continued on. Dudley hurried to his detachment's location and had begun barking out orders when a nearly catatonic General Hull staggered onto the parade grounds in the company of his aides and senior officers.

"We must offer the British a response, sir!" one major demanded.

"Order the men to the guns!" shouted another, while the enlisted men's eyes darted nervously between their battle-ready commanders and their muddled general.

"I do not think it prudent to resist," wrangled Hull. "You've read their demands. They imply that they will not be able to control the actions of the Indians if we engage them."

"But we are nearly twice their number, sir, and our men are willing to fight!"

General Hull mumbled under his breath and waved his shaking hands in his officers' faces. "I've read the gory reports from survivors of Tecumseh's ferocity. You don't know!" he exclaimed with a trembling voice. "You cannot fathom the horror of which they are capable. I have a wife here, a family. Many of you do as well. What of them?" His voice rose into a whine.

More cannon fire exploded over the heads of the assemblage, and the general withered before his men's eyes.

"Wave the white flag!" he ordered as he cowered from the barrage. "Someone accept the terms of the surrender and wave the white flag."

One by one General Hull's majors declined the order. In defeat, he finally turned to his captains. "Captain Mack. I order you to accept General Brock's terms of surrender."

Captain Snowden watched as Captain Stephen Mack stepped forward, drew his sword from its scabbard, and broke it over his knee. "I will never submit to such a disgraceful compromise while the blood of an American continues to run through my veins!" he replied forcefully before launching the blade toward the lake.

While acerbic voices argued on, men continued to fall in bloody, moaning heaps as molten lead rained down upon them from every direction. At some point Dudley turned his head and saw the white flag of surrender waving over the parapet. Seconds later the British guns ceased their roar, and quiet ensued. The fort had fallen, the Americans having offered not a single shot in their own defense that day. General Brock sent an attaché to ascertain the meaning of the white flag, and when he was assured that General Hull was willing to accept every term of his proclamation of surrender, the noon hour was appointed as the time of capitulation.

Captain Dudley Snowden's anguished heart pounded as he was forced to march his men, alongside his comrades' troops, onto the parade grounds to deliver their arms to the enemy. Nearly choking with emotion, he offered his final salute to the American flag as she was lowered from her staff, her thirty-five-year watch over the young nation suddenly in peril. Despite his grief, he was fully aware of—indeed, enraged by—the irony unfolding before him. The very cannon taken from the British during the Revolutionary War was now lit and fired to commemorate the hoisting of the Union Jack in place of the Stars and Stripes. Then, as if to heap additional mockery upon their defeated—and cowardly—enemy, General Brock's regimental band merrily played the anthem "God Save the King."

To be sure, General Brock had secured a masterful prize of guns and ammunition, as well as a strategic vantage point. Additionally, his terms of capitulation included his promise to restrain the Indians in return for prisoners. Captains Mack and Snowden attempted to ascertain the fate of their men, but General Hull was unavailable. Following the surrender, he had immediately focused his attentions on his family's welfare and attended to personal business, leaving one of his aides to deliver the sobering news.

"Listen up!" the red-faced major bellowed between gritted teeth. "General Brock has the muster rolls. The volunteers and the Ohio and Michigan militia are to line up to my left. The regulars are to line up to my right. Step forward as your name is called."

Dudley looked to Mack, and understanding passed between the two men as Dudley silently withdrew the letter from his breast pocket and handed it to his friend. "It seems that you're a civilian again, Stephen. Please see that this reaches Beatrice."

"I'll get word to her as quickly as possible," Mack pledged with a broken voice.

Dudley smiled sadly and nodded his appreciation as a British soldier raised his gun to move the officer into formation with the other regulars.

"I'll watch over them until you return safely home!" Mack shouted to Dudley. Although another British soldier shoved Mack back and away from his friend, Mack raised his voice again and continued his pledge. "I shall count them as my own family until you return!"

The chasm between the two men grew wider as the British soldiers separated the militia from the regulars. "Where are they taking them?" Mack asked. "The regulars, I mean"

A young Brit smiled, taunting the fallen foe. Then, seeing the pain in the American's face, he softened and answered, "Quebec."

"Quebec?" Mack sputtered in shock. "That's almost seven hundred miles from here!"

The British soldier resumed his official stance. "General Brock plans to parade them through the cities along the way to boost British morale and humiliate your government."

Dumbstruck by the news, Captain Mack knew many prisoners would die on the march. The twelve hundred militia members were allowed to return to their homes after signing a pledge not to take up arms during the remainder of the conflict. The regulars, however—including General Hull himself—were remanded over to the British army as prisoners of war.

Mack lingered behind as the greatest torment of the surrender unfolded. He watched as the enlisted soldiers, Captain Dudley Snowden included, dug a large pit. Raw grief filled their faces as the Americans complied with the order to toss the bodies of their dead into the common grave for burial. Mack lingered as long as he could. Then, after the last man had been thrown into the earthen pit, an emotionally distraught Dudley Snowden glanced up, and the two friends sent silent messages across the parade grounds. As Mack raised a final hand in farewell, British soldiers forced him through the gate of Fort Detroit.

* * *

Stephen Mack hurried to his Detroit home, from which he conducted his business. There he found his housekeeper, Mrs. Trotwine, happy—like all the other settlers—to be free of the fort. She was already putting the place back in order after the ransacking it received from the Indians and British during the siege. Mack sent her to fetch the fastest courier available while he quickly dashed off a note to Beatrice Snowden. When the courier arrived, Mack handed him the two letters and an envelope of money. "I need these letters delivered to an address in Baltimore in record time. Spare no expense, hire horses and other riders as you see fit, but get this letter delivered and signed by Mrs. Snowden within a week. Upon your return, I'll reward you handsomely."

The boy was mounted and riding before Mrs. Trotwine had time to close the door.

"I need my bags packed, and have Dennis ready my carriage, please," Mack instructed.

"Are you heading home to Vermont?" the elderly woman asked.

"I think it wise for now. I fear the British will maliciously target the establishments of those of us who served in the militia. My presence puts you and the staff in jeopardy. I will leave the stores, the warehouse—everything—to the care of my managers, and ample cash to keep the wages paid and see everyone through. Tell everyone to manage as best they can, but don't place yourself in danger. I'll be in touch, and I'll return when I feel it safe to do so."

CHAPTER 36

London, England
Early August 1812

Edward Mitchell walked to a bench in Hyde Park, searching for a moment's solitude to wrestle with his thoughts, but his privacy was quickly interrupted by a frail female voice.

"Mr. Mitchell? Mr. Edward Mitchell?" the elegantly dressed woman asked timidly.

"Yes," he reluctantly admitted. "May I help you, madam?"

"May I join you, sir? I require a few minutes of your time."

Mitchell nodded and shifted left, inviting her to sit. She offered her lace-gloved hand and introduced herself. "My name is Felicity Ramsey. Stephen Ramsey is my husband."

Mitchell immediately felt the hair rise on his neck.

"So, my assumptions were right," she offered sadly. "Your association with my husband is no longer cordial, is it?"

His guard raised, Mitchell offered no reply as he waited for her to continue.

"My husband was once pleased to drop your name as a colleague. Lately, however, I've noticed that you two never speak or appear together. I've assumed that the same scurrilous dealings that have set my own nerves on edge have likely caused you to sever your partnership."

Mitchell stood to leave. "I'm afraid you are mistaken from the first assumption, madam."

Felicity Ramsey stood as well, placing her hand on his arm. "Please don't tell me that association with my husband has diminished your nerve or stolen your soul, Mr. Mitchell."

Mitchell turned his face from her as he sat back down. "Perhaps some of each, I'm afraid."

Mrs. Ramsey leaned close in earnestness. "I do not desire to know the nature of his current involvements, only to know if they may prove unflattering to my son or his good name."

"And what would you do if they were of such a nature?" Mitchell probed.

Her eyes bored into his. "I would try to persuade Arthur to leave the city with me, to flee far from here, where his father cannot involve him in his dealings or stain his reputation."

Mitchell turned to face her. "You would leave your home . . . your life . . . and defy your husband to shield your son from his father's influence?"

She looked at him with wonder in her eyes. "Of course. I'm sure you'd do the same if your son was similarly at risk. My Arthur is my life's work, Mr. Mitchell. When I leave this world, he will serve as the only lasting witness of my contribution to it. For him, for his good name, and for that legacy, I would sacrifice anything."

Mitchell wondered if his shame showed in his face. Did she know how very similarly he had risked his own sons' futures? He bent his head and sighed deeply. When he met her eyes, he could not deny her petition. "First, answer me one question. Has your husband ever spoken of a family in America named Pearson?"

"Are they relatives of Jonathan Pearson, his mother's childhood beau?"

"Pearson once courted Ramsey's mother?" gasped Mitchell.

"Oh, yes," Felicity Ramsey sighed. "As illogical as it is, Stephen scorns her for choosing his own father and belittles his father for winning her hand. In his flawed reasoning, he believes he was somehow cheated from his destiny. He's always been a driven man, Mr. Mitchell, but lately he's become a cruel one as well. Arthur refuses to accept that fact. As a man of God, he feels it is his duty to redeem his father, but I worry that such an effort will destroy him as well."

Mitchell rested his chin on his umbrella and momentarily closed his eyes. "You are a wise woman, Mrs. Ramsey. Instead of receiving counsel today, you have given it, and I thank you. In return I offer you this advice: get yourself and your son away from him, and do it now!"

* * *

Two weeks later, the post-theatre crowds poured from the Theatre Royal in Covent Gardens, bound for exclusive parties and eateries in the London area. The Right Honourable Mr. Edward Mitchell, MP, and his wife lingered in their box until the theater was nearly empty.

"Come, Edward," Deidre Mitchell encouraged. "You needn't hide from your colleagues." Tears glossed her eyes. "I know how hard this has been for you, but your brother David will do a fine enough job." She pulled his scarf tightly around his neck. "Your health is my only concern."

He took her hand and placed a kiss there. "I love you, Deidre," he whispered huskily.

Deidre Mitchell followed him down the stairs and to the lobby, where she saw Lord Whittington. Before Mitchell had a chance to divert her elsewhere, she had already waved to the earl and started in his direction.

"Lord Whittington," she said softly as she curtsied and smiled. "I couldn't leave London without first saying good-bye to you. I've always admired your leadership. I shall miss you greatly."

The earl cast a scornful glance at her husband. "You're leaving London?"

Mitchell feigned a coughing spell and excused himself as Mrs. Mitchell's eyes followed nervously. "My Edward is ill, my lord. We're moving to Scotland where the specialist lives."

"He's resigning his seat in Parliament? Was this a sudden illness?"

"Quite. It's a miracle really. He went to see the physician for a slight cough and this dreaded respiratory affliction was found. I guess I shouldn't be so surprised at the diagnosis. He's not been himself for such a long while."

The earl listened with veiled skepticism, weighing the news against his recent discoveries. Then he spied Mr. Ramsey heading in Mitchell's direction. When he saw him tap Mitchell on the back and pull the frightened man behind a curtain that led to the mezzanine, the earl excused himself to Mrs. Mitchell and hurried across the lobby floor to catch a portion of the exchange.

"Why are you following me, Ramsey?" Mitchell questioned anxiously. "Our association is ended!"

"Can't a friend offer a few words of consolation to an ailing associate?"

"Leave me alone! I have forfeited nearly everything to be rid of you. I have given the bulk of my money to charity, lied to my wife and family, and resigned my seat in Parliament to purge my soul. I am free, Ramsey, free! It is a feeling you will never know."

"Freedom is such an abstract concept, Mitchell, and you are still of great interest to me. I think there are many things from your recent past that certain people, including your dear wife and your brother, our newest Member of Parliament, would find interesting."

"What do you want from me?" Mitchell moaned as beads of sweat formed on his brow.

Ramsey sneered at the quivering man. "At this moment? Nothing. But I shall contact you."

Mitchell knew that if he had the means he would kill the adversary that threatened his peace. On this day, however, his only desire was to get away from the devil that stood before him. As he shoved past Ramsey and through the curtain, he came face-to-face with the Earl of Whittington.

"Mitchell, was your friend Ramsey offering his condolences on your recent diagnosis?"

Mitchell's eyes welled. "Is there nowhere I can go, nor a thing I can do to find peace?"

"You want peace? I want justice, a thing I cannot have unless you confess and testify!"

Fear shook Mitchell's frame. "I will say nothing as long as that devil walks the earth."

Lord Whittington's eyes burned into Mitchell's. "Is Ramsey still in there?" he snarled.

Mitchell nodded weakly and watched as the earl parted the curtain to search for Ramsey. His nervous eyes spotted his wife, who anxiously scanned the room for her missing husband. Trembling at the thought of her seeing him this way—and the questions that would follow—Mitchell slipped quickly behind a column and struggled to calm himself before rejoining her.

A handsome young man noticed her worried expression and offered his assistance. "Mrs. Mitchell? I'm Arthur Ramsey. We've met at St. Paul's. Is everything all right? May I be of help?"

She smiled warmly, recognizing the young man's face and name. "I seem to have lost my husband, sir. I wouldn't worry, except he was suffering from a coughing spell when he left."

"I'm sure he's fine, but I'll look for him if you like. Why don't you have a seat while I search?" He circled the lobby until he heard angry voices arguing from behind a curtain—one undoubtedly that of his father and the other, the voice of Lord Whittington. Arthur abandoned his search, his attention now drawn to the new drama.

"A communiqué is in my possession. Your name is mentioned in conjunction with a 'gift' you provided—a bloodthirsty mercenary named Duprée! We need to suppress the Americans, but in a way that will unite our people, not brutalize them!"

With a cocky tilt to his head, Ramsey replied snidely, "You think like a politician, sir. You have no idea what is required to win this war. I, on the other hand, am but a loyalist helping my country."

"You are no loyalist!" the earl spat. "You are playing both sides of this war! I know you profit heavily from illegal slavery, and I assume your 'help' to the military comes with pledges to divide the spoils of your plunder. You seek not for the welfare of England but for blood money!"

A long pause ensued before Ramsey snickered. "Prove it."

Arthur Ramsey burst through the curtain. "Father . . . is it true?" he asked in utter horror.

"Arthur!" Ramsey's face went slack with panic, and he turned to the earl. "You brought my son?" His voice became thready and pure hatred shot from his eyes. "It's a pack of lies, Arthur!" But he could not look at his son.

The earl pressed on, attempting to both break the man and free his son. "You bought Mitchell's vote, didn't you? What twisted tale did you concoct to cause a once-pious man to commit treachery against both his country and his own conscience?"

Ramsey sneered, "Shouldn't you ask your pious colleague?"

The earl stared menacingly at Ramsey. "You've done your job too well. He's terrified of you. The poor man feigned illness and resigned all that he cherished to get away from you."

"This is a witch hunt!" Ramsey shouted. "You're trying to disparage me before my son!"

"I wish upon all that is sacred that I could spare your good son from knowing what manner of man his father is. Tell me, Ramsey, how does a simple importer come to know an infamous mercenary like Duprée? And not only know him but command him, barter him for favors with an admiral in His Majesty's Navy?"

Seething at the earl, Ramsey suddenly despised his son for remaining and listening to the accusations. He responded to Lord Whittington through clenched teeth. "Your holier-than-thou consciences do not define the law! Neither do the people I associate with, nor their actions, need to fall in line with your definitions of morality. Principles come more easily to the well fed and the well bred, so don't presume to stand upon your altar of righteousness and preach to me about right and wrong. Poverty is wrong! Fear is wrong! Child labor is wrong! I have made my own rightness, and you cannot touch me with your laws!"

All remained quiet for a moment as Ramsey's anger echoed in the chamber. The Earl of Whittington looked from heaving father to shattered son and waited to assess the toll of the exchange. Arthur Ramsey's eyes dropped to the floor, and then he pulled his coat tighter around him.

"You're heart is so hardened, Father. I doubt anything can touch you anymore."

"Arthur . . ." Ramsey sputtered as he watched his son turn to leave.

"I defended you! I ignored the warnings and remained your loyal son and champion, but no more. You are not my father, sir. You may be the man who fathered me, but I can never be a son to a man who could do such things." He wiped a hand across his eyes, turned, and exited.

Ramsey thrust himself at the earl. "You took the one thing that mattered to me in this world, Whittington! You have a son of your own. You should have known where to draw the line, but the line is clearly drawn now. You place duty above all, above a man's relationship to his son? Then let it be . . . but I swear to you, you and your house will rue this day forever!"

* * *

Lord Whittington trembled as he parted the curtains and left Ramsey fuming in the dark. Suddenly, he wanted nothing but to get home to his son and tighten the watch on his home. As he exited the theater, he heard his name called from behind. It was Arthur Ramsey.

"Lord Whittington?" the young man began in a voice heavy with emotion.

"Arthur," the earl moaned as he went to him and wrapped his arm around him. "Please forgive me. I never should have involved you."

"No, sir. You are not at fault here. This confrontation has been a long time in coming. My own mother has tried to protect me, to help me see, but I rebuked her for disloyalty."

"Let me take you home, Arthur," the earl petitioned the distraught young man.

"I can't return there. Nothing but trouble waits there for me."

"But what of your mother? Surely you won't abandon her to face your father's wrath?"

"She's already gone, sir," Arthur explained with a sigh. "She begged me to join her, to flee from my father, but I refused. He doesn't know this, but she is in Ireland, hoping I will join her shortly."

"And so you must, son. I'll give you travel money and whatever else you need."

"I do need your help . . . a favor, actually. I've been thinking about it since I first heard the rumors. Perhaps I can protect my family's name and someday find a way to forgive my father."

"Anything, Arthur, anything. What favor do you seek?"

"A military post to the United States—to Maryland. Perhaps I can alert someone to this Duprée, or find some other way to serve my country by preventing barbarism to rule the war."

"Admiral Cochrane is already aware of Admiral Cockburn's military plans for the States. He likely knows about Duprée's *talents* as well. He will not rein his colleague in." The earl placed a tender hand on Arthur's shoulder. "Serve man by serving God, son."

"I believe I'll serve Him best by stopping Duprée."

"You're not a soldier. You're a man of peace. You're no match for Duprée."

"I can be a man of peace no longer! These past moments have stripped me of any sense of worthiness. I cannot feel God's Spirit in me. I need to do this, Lord Whittington. Please! Have you no contacts in the military that could use a man of letters and learning as a military attaché?"

Lord Whittington stared at the ground. "Perhaps your father was right, Arthur. Perhaps my vision of this war is unrealistic."

Arthur searched the earl's face. "What are you saying?"

The earl drew a heavy breath. "We need to conquer the States in order to reunite our people. I believe that. But I had hoped for a victory that also offered compassion to prevent these ceaseless conflicts from irrevocably tarnishing Britain's soul. Perhaps this is a statesman's folly."

Arthur straightened and stared at the earl. "Our cause is noble, and so must we be. Please, send me to America to serve the nobler cause."

Lord Whittington stared into Arthur's resolute eyes. "My heart condemns this plan, Arthur. It is only because I believe you will place yourself in harm's way if I do not intervene that I agree to this," he sighed. "My late wife's cousin is Major General Richard Ross. I have heard he will shortly be commanding the land forces in Maryland. He is a good and noble man. Come home with me, and I will make arrangements to assign you to his service in Maryland."

"Thank you, sir. Thank you."

The earl grabbed Arthur by his shoulders and stared into his face. "Do not make my part in this any more onerous. I deserve no gratitude for what I am about to help you do."

* * *

Two weeks later, Juan Arroyo Corvas stood at the helm of the *Ynez* as she sailed into Cadiz from a merchant trip. He gazed admiringly at a splendid, sleek, new vessel twice his old bucket's size, tied up in port this day. He admired her massive white sails—the largest of which featured a flying serpent painted in its middle—that were attached to broad, tall masts with gold rings painted every ten feet. A sculpture of a beautiful, dark-eyed woman with flowing black hair jutted out from the craft's bowsprit. The boat's lines were narrow and meant for speed, and ten guns appeared along each side, verifying the importance of her cargo. As he passed the stern he looked for her name, and the word made him shiver . . . *Ynez II.*

Juan knew he was being tempted the very same way his own father had been enticed into the creditor's debt. Before the lines were secured, Juan leapt to the dock and began scouring the port for the man with the ram's head umbrella who had previously served as the creditor's messenger. It took little time, as the man seemed not only willing to be found but glad to have been.

"Mr. Corvas," Ramsey greeted with a smile as he stood and stretched out his hand. "Today is a very good day for you, my friend."

Juan shrank from the offered hand and argued nervously, "I have a release! I have paid the debt and no longer owe the creditor."

Ramsey's smile broadened. "Of course . . . of course. My employer congratulates you on the way you have fulfilled the terms of your contract. That is why I am here. Because you have earned the creditor's respect, he has invited me to extend another offer to you." Ramsey waved his hand in the direction of the *Ynez II.* "She is beautiful, is she not?"

Juan began backing up while shaking his head and hands in refusal. "No, no, no!" he repeated. "I am clean and free! Tell him I don't want his ship!"

Ramsey stood in place and spread his hands conciliatorily. "The creditor knows you are a good man, a good God-fearing man. He respects that. His terms of repayment take that into account. He has other men to move his—shall we say—merchandise. The *Ynez II* is a transport vessel, made to move documents and important people, not bulky cargo. In short, Mr. Corvas, my creditor has hand-selected you to be the captain of his elegant, personal transport ship. Not only captain, but *owner.*"

The final word came out like a mysterious rush of north wind and it ominously chilled Juan. "No slaves? No illegal arms or goods? Just businessmen and documents?" Juan clarified.

"Yes," Ramsey assured him with a smile.

"And how long are the terms?"

Ramsey shifted his position and leaned upon his umbrella. "Let me explain that in addition to the privilege of commanding this fine ship, you and your crew would also receive a sizeable annual stipend. In short, your services would be exclusively dedicated to my employer's needs. He would need to know that you were always available to sail if and when he required it."

Juan felt the hair rise on the back of his neck. "For how long, sir?"

"You and your men would have the best of both worlds, Mr. Corvas. You could have a family and a life unlike that which you or your mother knew when you were small. You would be in port most of the year, except when called on to serve the creditor's needs. Imagine, sitting by the fire at night with your family in your beautiful home, watching your children grow, then sailing a beautiful ship on the open seas a few weeks a year rather than constantly battling the seas for fish or trade, hoping to scrape together a meager existence. Imagine the peace of knowing your wife does not have to scrub other men's laundry in order to keep food on the table as was your mother's lot. This could be your life, Mr. Corvas. What would you give for such a life?"

Juan's eyes were fixed ahead on a moment in time when he could see himself in such perfect circumstances. "And what is the length of the terms, sir?"

"Forever, Juan. For as long as you live."

Juan bit his lips and stared at that faraway moment in time. "No slaves?"

"No slaves," Ramsey repeated as he reeled Juan in.

"Only men and documents?"

"Exactly."

Juan ran a trembling hand across his mouth and breathed heavily. "All right. I'll sign."

Ramsey's eyes narrowed with pleasure as he pulled the document from his coat pocket and led Juan to a barrel that could serve as a desk.

Juan poised above the paper, quill in hand, and asked, "When do I begin?"

"Your terms begin today. As for your first voyage, the date is not yet set. Perhaps soon . . . perhaps not for a long time. But your readiness must begin today."

Juan nodded his understanding and signed his services over to the creditor.

CHAPTER 37

No words had passed between Jed and Hannah since their last bitter exchange. Jed's guilt was so great he couldn't bear the swollen eyes and trembling lips that met his own. He drove the team on for nearly two days straight, stopping only for necessities when Renfro called to him from the carriage. The pace had been gentle, designed to keep Hannah comfortable, but the slowness of it burdened Jed with excessive time to face his tortuous thoughts. With one sentence, he had destroyed Hannah's security, leaving her exactly where Beatrice and Robertson had predicted, trusting no one and utterly alone.

They had reached the small inn near Coolfont around midnight the previous evening. Jed had pounded on the door until the sleepy-eyed innkeeper arose and offered Hannah and Renfro his last two available rooms, as well as portions of bread and bowls of soup from the kettle hanging above a smoldering fire in the huge stone fireplace.

Jed had been offered a spot on a thick rug by the fire, but he had declined. "I prefer to be outside." *With the other dogs,* he thought. He examined the horses and found their legs swollen from overwork. He considered exchanging them for a new team, but realized they would arrive at Coolfont before noon. So he decided to press on for Hannah's home, then pasture his horses nearby to rest and graze for a few days. He was in no rush to get anywhere. The malaise of a year ago was returning like a fog. Jed was eager to let it engulf him.

Renfro exited the inn with a plate in his hands, offering it to Jed. Jed merely shrugged it off, refusing to accept any kindness for himself. Renfro scowled at him and tossed the plate angrily to the ground in the first show of temper Jed had ever witnessed from the man.

"Killing yourself will do nothing to amend the wrong you have caused her," spat Renfro. "Regardless of the provocation, you had no cause to wound her so and then storm away, abandoning her to mull over your accusations. Were you not the very person who pledged to protect her from hurt? Well, now you've given her cause to question *everyone's* intentions regarding her. I don't believe you could have been more cruel. I would not have thought it possible from you."

Jed's body became limp and useless, and he could barely lift his hands to attend to the horses. His feet felt like chunks of lead as he dragged himself around. Finally, he surrendered to the weight of his guilt, leaned against one of the exhausted geldings and answered his friend. "I would do anything . . . anything to make it up to her, but how can I restore the trust I undermined? I see no clear way through this." Jed looked into Samuel's now gentle face, seeking answers. The young physician-in-training stared back at him as if he were looking into the face of a stranger.

Six days of unshaven stubble hid the curves of Jed's mouth, replacing his affable smile with a stony grimace that seemed to draw his dark eyes downward as well. Worry lines crisscrossed his brow, and days devoid of ample sleep and food had left his face ashen and haggard. His dark wavy hair had been haphazardly finger-combed back, falling in thick clumps for want of washing, and his muddy pants and shirt had not been changed in a week. In short, he appeared to be a ruined man and by far the oldest-looking twenty-two-year-old Samuel Renfro had ever seen. From his professional and personal experience, the young doctor knew two lives hung in the balance that morning.

"Go to her," was all the advice he had to offer.

"What can I say? Why would she even listen?" Jed's voice fell off in a hopeless lapse.

"Whether she does or does not is not the point. You owe her answers. You dismissed her as if she were a petulant child. You may now reap what you sowed last week." Renfro tried to maintain disappointment in his friend, but his angry resolve melted in the face of Jed's sorrow-filled eyes. "But my guess is that the good you've sown with her over the long course of your friendship will earn her forgiveness."

"I have no delusions of salvaging any affection between us. I simply want to restore what I have taken from her."

"Then go to her."

* * *

Just as he had on that June morning more than two years ago, Jed stood watching Hannah from behind a tree, assessing her mood, watching the tilt of her head and the curve of her body as she sat on a bench in the garden. There was so little child left in her. Jed knew he had shut the door on the final, lingering moments of her adolescence. He had then walked away and left the lost woman to stagger alone like a new filly struggling to find her legs.

She was bent over a book, her Bible, he assumed—the same Bible she had read every morning on their journey, confirming to him that the spiritual hunger of her youth remained. He closed his eyes, praying that it would serve her well when he was gone from her life. Her black hair hung over her shoulder in a long, thick braid, and the skin of her neck already glistened from the morning heat. Her pink calico dress, one of only three she had packed for the three week trip, looked more mauve now, darkened by repeated washings in muddy streams throughout their journey. But even wearing the stained and rumpled dress, Hannah seemed nearly regal sitting there. Her eyes were closed, and Jed realized that she was not reading but praying. He drew back, desiring not to intrude. As his foot touched the ground, a twig snapped, bringing Hannah's attention to him in an immediate meeting of eyes.

"Hannah," he called out. "I . . . I didn't mean to frighten you."

She neither answered nor turned away. Jed stood frozen, unsure how to proceed. "We'll be at Coolfont by noon," he muttered with downcast eyes. Hannah's eyes never left his face. Her head was erect and like that of a deer, attuned to signs of danger, ever watchful and cautious. "I—I just wanted you to know that you'd be home soon."

The feeling of lead, of being stuck in his place, overtook him again. He pressed his hands against the tree to push himself away from the painful exchange, but honor held him there and he leaned his shoulder back into the tree trunk and called to her again. "I want you to know that I'm sorry . . . for what I said . . . sorry that I wasn't honest with you. I promised to answer your questions and I'm here to . . . to tell you anything you need to hear."

Hannah offered her silent acceptance with a dip of her chin and a tentative shift on the bench, making room for Jed to sit by her side. He approached slowly with a hanging head and fumbling hands, acutely aware now of his filthy, gaunt appearance. He sat on the furthest sliver of the bench facing forward, as was she, then drew a deep breath and closed his eyes, praying for the right words, the words to restore her happiness.

"I don't know where to begin," he stumbled with a nervous sigh. "I did get your letter, Hannah, but not until well after my father's death. It was in a box of . . . correspondence he had become too ill to attend to. I found it when I was putting his affairs in order, and by then . . ."

He saw her lips move but barely a sound could be heard. "They delivered it . . . they delivered it," she finally muttered as her crying head fell into her hands in relief.

"Yes, Hannah. Myrna and Beatrice delivered the letter to my father, but he was ill by then and preoccupied with other concerns so it never was forwarded on to me." He was surprised by the ease with which he withheld the full truth, but believing it likely that his hopes with Hannah were already lost, he was determined to at least protect her trust in her sisters.

"As soon as I read your letter, I sped to the Snowdens' home to respond, but by then . . ."

"I was already home at Coolfont . . ."

Jed sensed the understanding beginning to replace Hannah's doubts and mistrust. "Yes. You were already at Coolfont and engaged to Lieutenant Robertson."

Hannah's head lowered. A rush of air poured from her as she toyed with the pages of her Bible. Jed placed his hand over hers and squeezed it softly. "I went to meet him, Hannah, that very day. I found him to be a good man, a man completely in love with you, and . . . and . . ." he stammered as he struggled to know where to carry the tale to a conclusion that would assure her happiness. "And I remembered the talk we had the day we went on our last ride together, the day you first rode Druid. I asked you to wait to fall in love until I could judge for myself whether or not you had chosen the right man." A lump formed in Jed's throat, and he coughed hard to clear it before carrying on. "When I met your lieutenant I knew he cherished you. I knew he would make you his partner. I knew you had chosen the right man."

He quickly turned away and coughed. It had taken every ounce of resolve he possessed to choke out those final words. Now he waited to see if his verbal artifice had been sufficient to end her qualms and set her future clearly before her. He sat in silence away from her, parted by more than inches . . . by a door that he felt he had surely closed forever.

Hannah's tears fell upon the pages of the scriptures like salty rain. She wiped at the moistness there, staring at the darkened spots, unable to meet Jed's eyes. "Then what did you mean the other day? You spoke of your happiness. You said if it had mattered at all to my family, we wouldn't be in this situation. What did you mean by that?"

Those were the words for which Jed had neither rebuttal nor explanation. He thought back to the words of the silver-tongued Robertson, who seemed to have understood Jed's concerns better than he had understood them himself, and he drew his answer from them. "If I could have had my way, I would have never allowed you to grow up. I would have kept you my sweet little Hannah for as long as I could. Your family changed that, and I suppose I blame them for taking my best girl away from me."

He rose and extended his hand to her, huskily saying, "We should be going now." He felt her hand slip into his and stay there, motionless and waiting. Turning to see what prevented her from rising, he caught her staring at him with wonder, examining his face, determining the true account of his agonizing heartache. Mesmerized, he could not withdraw from her gaze.

Renfro's voice called across the yard to where the pair remained transfixed. He hesitated to deliver the news, but felt it of such urgency that he risked breaking the spell between the young pair. "A carriage is approaching, Jed. I believe the driver is Lieutenant Robertson!"

Jed's disappointment betrayed his earlier resolve, and Hannah saw it. She touched the burly stubble through which he had nearly hidden his deceit and said, "I have a question for you."

Jed's heart pounded at the realization that in a few seconds the girl he had loved his entire life would be swept away from him forever. The fear of it caused him to shiver. "What is it?" he asked, drawing her hands to his chest where his racing heart confirmed what she already knew.

"You told me you had loved me since we were children, but what manner of love do you feel? Tell me once and for all. Do you now love me, Jed? Not as a sister, not as a friend, but as a woman?"

Jed closed his eyes against the burning tears welling there. His mouth hung agape, struggling to draw enough air to keep his spinning head clear as he caressed her hands.

"Do you love me, Jed?" she asked again as she rose on her toes, nearly touching his face.

He couldn't bear the closeness of her, and he drew her against him and wrapped his arms around her, daring anyone to pull her from him. He bathed her face with kisses and moaned over and over in her ears, "Always and ever, my sweet Hannah . . . always and ever." Hannah melted against him. He savored the way she felt in his arms, finding himself awash in the essence of her. Cupping his hands behind her head, he drew her face close to his. "Am I now the one who is dreaming?" he whispered hungrily as he pressed his lips to hers. It seemed so right to be together that he forgot momentarily what had kept them apart. As the past returned again to haunt him, he looked into her smoldering eyes and breathlessly solicited her, "Do you love me in return?"

It was a woman who pressed her hands into the stubble of his beard and assured him, "Andrew received all that I had to give . . . mere remnants of a heart that has always been yours."

He pulled her to him again. "Oh, how I love you, Hannah!" His voice was raw with emotion. "But what of your mother? She loathes me and my family, and threatens to disown you if you choose me. Where do we go from here?"

Renfro's voice broke in. "Jed! The carriage is nearly here!"

Hannah clung tighter to Jed. "If we could only understand the reason for her feelings, Jed. Perhaps there is a way to win her approval."

Jed pulled himself away from her and crumpled onto the bench. "I cannot do it."

"What can't you do?" she uttered as her heart shattered again.

"I cannot put my wants ahead of your happiness." He slipped to his knees and grabbed his head. "I discovered the truth, Hannah—at least a portion of it—and it is uglier than I dared imagine. Your mother is justified in hating my family. My grandfather drove her mother away and sowed the seeds of her illness. Can't you see? Every misery you have endured began with my line. We are the cause of your mother's sickness and therefore the cause of your suffering."

"I don't understand," she murmured as she walked numbly to the bench and sat. Several minutes passed silently while she appeared frozen by Jed's confession. "You sound as if you believe it is hopeless," she whispered as she ran her fingers across lips that still burned from his kiss. Then she stood abruptly and faced him, tipping his chin toward her. "If I were to give myself completely to you, could you hear my words of affection over the chatter of our critics?"

Jed's troubled face softened. "You would sacrifice everything for me . . . for us?"

Hannah urged him to stand. "You asked if love alone is enough. If it is, we shall be fine."

His racing heart would barely allow him to draw enough air to speak. "It is for me . . . but I have nothing to lose and everything to gain. I cannot say if it will be enough for you." Feeling her entire body tremble, he added, "And until then I will not allow you to make such a sacrifice."

As he released her hands, the pain in her heart was almost physical, and she gasped.

"Jed!" Samuel warned again. "Our company is nearly here."

Jed's face contorted in agony. "I will find a way, but first, tell me you love me again."

She brushed the wetness from his cheeks and framed his face in her hands. "I knew you were coming to rescue me the night of the fire. I knew if I followed your voice, you would carry me to safety. I saw it in my dreams, Jed. Each terrifying night my mind rehearsed me through the fear, promising me safety if I followed your voice. All those dreams? They were of you."

Jed kissed her brow and whispered tenderly, "Even God believes you were meant to be mine."

She placed her hands against his pounding chest. "I love you. I always have, but there was more to the dream, Jed. I tried to ignore it, but I can't. I know that I am to be away from you now. There are things we each need to do apart. I think you know that too. In the meantime, trust that there is a plan. In time we'll understand it, but thank you, Jed. Thank you for loving me."

"What of your engagement to Robertson?" he asked carefully.

Hurt washed over Hannah's face at the mention of the good lieutenant. "He does not deserve to be treated callously. Will you trust me to speak with him in my own way and time?"

Jed nodded numbly, stunned by the reversal of events that had so quickly transpired. As he reached a hand up to touch her cheek, Renfro bellowed out a greeting to the lieutenant, hastily ending their time together. Hannah wiped her eyes, turned, and strode away in the direction of the carriage.

Andrew quickly leapt from the driver's box to reach her, but he stopped short, aware of the emotion that hung between Hannah and the disheveled Pearson. His face paled at once.

From the carriage, Beatrice saw it as well. She struggled to climb down and hurried to Hannah, drawing her sister to her, whispering questions of concern in her ear.

"I am fine," Hannah assured Beatrice and Andrew. "I fell sick with a fever, but Dr. Renfro and Jed saw to my care, and I am very well now."

"You look dreadful, Pearson," remarked the lieutenant tersely.

"I'm fatigued from pressing on to keep my promise." He stared down at his rival. "We have had much to attend to this morning, but I would have had her safely home by noon as agreed."

As the tension increased between the two men, Hannah looked to Beatrice, suddenly noticing the dark circles and lines around her sister's eyes. "Are you all right?" she inquired.

"There's been a change of plans, Hannah," Beatrice struggled to say. "The fort has fallen, and Dudley has been taken prisoner!" She fell against her youngest sister and began to sob.

"The militia was set free, but the regulars are being marched to Quebec," Andrew explained. "A militia captain, a Mr. Mack, sent word to me by courier. When he found the Snowdens' home half burned," he glared at Jed, "he brought word to Fort McHenry. Luckily, I knew that Beatrice had already fled Baltimore for her parents' home. I sent the message directly on and arrived at Coolfont earlier this morning."

Beatrice squeezed her sister's hands. "Hannah, I'm packing my things and heading to Vermont to meet up with Captain Mack. He will try to make arrangements for me to see Dudley. He offered to have us stay with his family in Tunbridge. Will you come with me?"

Hannah looked curiously at Beatrice. "Leave Baltimore?" Then, as the news struck her more deeply, she looked away, smiling knowingly at Jed. "Of course . . ." she whispered, as if suddenly blessed with enlightenment. "Of course, that's it." She turned back to Beatrice and asked quietly, "When do we leave? How long will we be away?"

Andrew's face appeared drawn and tense as he took her hand. "I don't think either of you should get your hopes up, Hannah. The British are not likely to release him from prison as long as this conflict continues. Dudley could be imprisoned in Canada for the duration. You may be away for some time, perhaps a year or longer." A question hung on his words.

Beatrice held Hannah close and whispered in her ear, "I know I am asking a great deal of you, to take you so far away for such a long while, but I would relish your company." She hung her head sheepishly and added, "I need you."

Hannah pulled away and attempted to share her new understanding with her sister. "Of course I'll go with you, Beatrice." Then more softly she added, "This is what I am to do."

There was nothing left to say, and to end the unbearably awkward moment, Hannah turned to hug Samuel Renfro. "Thank you, Samuel. You'll most likely be a practicing physician when I return," she gushed with tearful eyes. "Thank you for everything, my friend. I know you'll be a wonderful doctor."

The portly man engulfed her softly in his arms. His eyes were moist when he released her, and he hurried away to tend to her bags. Next she turned to Jed, dreading this moment. But as she glanced at him she was comforted to see understanding in his face as well.

"It's as you said," he whispered huskily. "There is a plan, and I'll try to understand my part in it." He clutched her to him and added, "I will find a way, Hannah," as he placed a soft kiss on her cheek. Leading her by the arm, he reluctantly set her hand in Lieutenant Robertson's, giving it one final squeeze before he withdrew.

As Hannah felt Jed's hand release its grip, she looked into Andrew's expectant eyes. She could see pain and worry there, and she realized what her departure would cost him as well. He closed his arms around her briefly, and images of the end of her dream came to mind. *Things are as they are to be.* Without looking back again, she climbed into the carriage, ready to leave the familiar behind on a leap of love and faith.

Jed could scarcely breathe as he watched the carriage depart. He had less than he'd once dreamed of, but more than he had expected, and the balance lay in making peace with the past.

* * *

A simultaneously wonderful and eerie feeling settled over Francis Pearson as her carriage driver turned up the lane. The plantation had never looked better. The fields bustled with activity, as everyone worked to assure a quality harvest. But something was awry, and Frannie finally pinpointed it. Guns! It seemed as though every man, woman, or child over the age of fourteen had a musket in their arms or four paces away. Suddenly, the words of Markus's letter, warning her to hurry home, hit her with renewed force.

She strode through the front door and went straightway into Jed's office to find a staff meeting of sorts in progress. Markus leapt to his feet when he saw her enter, beautifully attired in a rust-colored suit. He brushed his wild, reddish hair into place and his blue eyes beamed as he rushed to her, drawing her into his brawny arms in a warm embrace. "You're an elegant sight, Frannie," he gushed with his brogue. "I'm so glad you're here," he whispered, looking over his shoulders. "Isn't Jed with you?"

"No," she replied worriedly as she clung to the familiar arms of her friend. "So he's not here either?"

Bitty inched near and opened her arms wide to her surrogate daughter. "He sent a note to us from Philadelphia 'bout three weeks back. Least we know he made it safely to Philadelphia."

Frannie sighed and pondered the news. "It's as if he's fallen off the face of the earth."

"Not completely," Markus said reassuringly. "He sent word to Coolfont as well. It's a long story, but he has Hannah Stansbury in his care and intends to have her there today."

Frannie raised an eyebrow at the news. "It seems neither of us can escape our pasts."

Markus understood her double intent. "Things have been quiet between us and White Oak so far, but Bitty and Abel were just fillin' us in on some fencepost gossip they heard today."

Frannie turned to Bitty and her fears were confirmed. "Was it him, Bitty? Are we certain?"

Abel placed his giant hand on Bitty's shoulders for support as she replied, "It was him, all right. Sebastian Duprée is back." Bitty watched a familiar chill grip Frannie as each of the women dealt with old memories. "He slips on and off Stringham's property like a lil' moonbeam. He's never there long enough to get caught. He's been seen there two or three times since Priscilla's boy listened under the larder."

"Are we certain the boy heard correctly?" Frannie pointed toward the outdoors where she had seen the armed workers. "We can't go off half-cocked unless we're sure."

All the room's occupants stood stunned by Frannie's use of the irreverent colloquialism.

"What have you been learnin' in that new job of yours, missy?" Bitty huffed. "Your brother will tan your hide if he hears you speak like such."

"Forgive me," Frannie stated contritely as Markus turned to stifle a smile, "but my point is fair. Is there any other proof that the Stringhams and Duprée mean us harm?"

Markus turned to face her. "I know how hard this is for you to accept, Frannie, but what other explanation could there be? Look at the devastatin' alliance the British formed with the Indians!" His Irish tones underscored his anger. "Rumors have been circulatin' for some time that this cuss, General Cockburn, plans to do a similar thing here usin' the slaves. Duprée knows this area, the rivers, who lives where. He would be invaluable to a commander plannin' an attack by water. We know he's already hissed out threats against the Willows."

The confident young businesswoman suddenly seemed small and childlike. "And what of Frederick?" she asked as she nervously rubbed her hands over one another. "Certainly he's a weak man, but he's not an evil one. I can't believe he would agree to this."

Markus looked long and hard into her eyes, hoping she would accept the truth on her own. Finally he spoke, "Neither has he offered us any word of warnin', Frannie. We haven't spread the word of their treachery yet. We're waitin' for Jed's return, but you need to know that once we do, I expect everyone along the Patuxent to turn on White Oak with a vengeance."

Frannie brought her hand to her mouth as horrible images came to her mind. She turned and left the room soberly. Markus started after her, but Bitty placed a hand on his arm to stop him.

"She needs time, Markus. She loves loyal, that one. No matter what he's done to her, she can't accept he could do this."

Markus nodded, ending the conversation abruptly. He fell back into Jed's chair, wishing his friend would return and set his sister's thinking straight. The idea that such a woman should spare a moment's concern for the welfare of a traitorous weasel like Frederick Stringham gnawed at him, and he kicked at the desk in anger. Then he heard the sound of movement in the lane in front of the house and his heart soared in relief. Moving to the window, he expected to see Jed riding in but instead saw a rust-colored blur, racing across the Willows' lawn toward the road—on his own horse, no less. He ran a worried hand through his tousled hair and kicked the desk again.

Frannie had never ridden Markus's Morgan before, but a few moments into the ride, she and the horse understood one another. She urged the mount on toward the west fence line that separated the Willows and White Oak, and she saw the ancient oak coming into view—the tree under which she and Frederick had rendezvoused and made plans. Even as tears blurred her eyes, she did not falter. Instead, she urged the compact stallion toward the gate and over the obstacle, landing safely on White Oak property. Quickly running her arm across her eyes, she cursed herself for such a display. She no longer loved Frederick, not in the way she once did, but the betrayal by someone to whom she had once entrusted her heart unsettled her. She needed to know whether the man had finally succumbed to his father's influence, becoming truly wicked, or if he was—as she prayed he was—simply irretrievably weak.

Frannie spurred the horse across the fields until the manor house came into view. Then she saw it—the house Frederick had begun building for her. It now boasted curtains in the windows and flowers in the boxes, signs that it was another woman's home. Frannie was pleasantly surprised that the only feelings the scene stirred in her were those of relief.

After tying the horse to the smaller home's rail, she stormed across the porch. An aggravated Frederick threw open the door to challenge the intruder who dared interrupt his solitude. As he did so, pungent, amber-colored liquor sloshed from a glass held precariously in his hand onto his pants and shoes. He was rail thin, and his rumpled appearance and downtrodden face told her he had been drinking for some time, temporarily dousing the fire of her fury.

"Frannie!" he gushed as if a miraculous dream had come true. "I can't believe you're here!" He dropped his glass to the porch and threw his bony arms around her. She drew her head back in revulsion at the dank smell of his breath. Frederick stepped back, continuing to hold her at arm's length as his eyes scanned her hungrily from head to toe. "You can't know how long I've dreamed you would come to me."

His disloyalty to his wife made it easy for Frannie to recall the reason for her visit. She wrenched his hands from her and stepped back farther still. "I've come to ask you a question, Frederick."

The harsh tone in her voice brought him up short.

"Is it true you've been keeping company with Sebastian Duprée?"

Frederick became a spasm of motion. With fearful eyes darting left and right, he grabbed Frannie, yanked her inside, and threw the door shut as his body fell against the wood for added security. "Where did you hear that?" he gasped breathlessly.

"So it's true." Frederick's face reflected her immeasurable disappointment.

"It's not my fault!" he whimpered, his hands waving ineffectually to emphasize his point. "It's my father! I tried to talk him out of this madness, but he won't listen."

"I suppose it also wasn't your fault that my 'indiscretion' was the reason given for our engagement being cancelled and for my good name being sullied! I suppose you had no part in carrying tales all the way to Philadelphia to ensure that I would be tainted there as well!"

Frederick covered his face with his trembling hands and slid down the wooden door, landing in a heap on the floor and reminding Frannie of a broken Parisian marionette.

"You're right. I was weak. I allowed my father to manipulate me." He struggled to rise from the floor but then slumped down again. "Forgive me, Frannie. I made a terrible mistake. He was going to disown me and cut me completely from his will, but none of that matters to me anymore."

Though he sounded earnest, Frannie couldn't read his strange expression.

"It was always you—never Penny. I've only ever loved you, Francis, and now I see it all so clearly. I can save us both. Come away with me, and I can save us both!"

Frannie began slowly pacing in a circle. Frederick followed every step as he rambled on.

"I can't live here. I can't remain here after . . . not knowing . . ." he muttered as he noticed Frannie's efforts to reach the door. "Don't you see?" he pled, again attempting to stand. "Either way, I lose! I can remain here and lose my soul, or I can flee and lose White Oak." He grabbed Frannie's hands. "Help me, Frannie! In the name of love, come with me and help me save my soul!"

"There is another option, Frederick, one that will grant you both your wishes." Although Frederick's interest was piqued, his head shot sideways as he looked askance at her. "Report your father, Frederick, and turn Duprée in! Think how many lives you'll spare! You'll be a hero, and White Oak will revert to you."

Frederick's terrified retreat was so severe he nearly tripped Frannie to the ground, and his voice became dark and menacing. "You have no idea what you're asking. Never mind my father's retribution. You have no idea of what his colleague is capable. No prize—not even White Oak—is worth crossing Duprée."

Frannie was dumbfounded. "Stand up for something, Frederick! For once in your life, put someone else's needs ahead of your fears and do what is right!"

"I can do nothing," Frederick moaned. "Duprée is Cockburn's pet, a gift from some British investor who held control over Duprée's freedom. In exchange for his services in ensuring Cockburn's victory, the investor stands to make a fortune off this region. Duprée has been given carte blanche—a free hand. He may wreak whatever havoc he chooses, so long as his ends satisfy the admiral."

"All the more reason to stop him!" Frannie argued.

"No one can stop him!" Frederick shouted. "He has the support of the British behemoth. He's too valuable. He knows the tributaries too well, and his color allows him the stealth to move in whatever circle he desires. He can make alliances with white landowners and win the loyalty of slaves while remaining invisible to everyone else. It's already begun. Soon blood and terror will rain down upon this entire region."

Frannie slumped against the door. "And you have done nothing to warn your neighbors? You would have let Duprée destroy even the Willows without raising a single word of warning?"

Frederick placed his trembling hands on her shoulders, misery and shame burning in his eyes. "You still don't understand, Frannie. He doesn't intend to destroy the Willows, just the Willows' residents. You see, the Willows is his prize." He dropped his head and continued. "Duprée has been offered your plantation as payment for his services, and no one can stop him from claiming his reward. He hates your brother." Frederick shook his head. "That's partly my fault. Had I stood beside you that day and been the one to pursue Duprée, perhaps his anger would have been pointed in my direction instead of toward your people. In either case, the anger he harbors against everyone at your plantation is deadly."

Frannie felt numb. "Are we to be annihilated in our sleep?" she could hardly whisper the thought.

"Nothing can save your brother, Frannie. Duprée has vowed to hunt him down until he's dead, but I can save you." Breathless with emotion, he went on. "Father will disown me, but he won't allow Duprée to kill me if I flee. Come away with me! I can be strong with you by my side. I'll annul my marriage. Penelope will be glad to be rid of me. Please, let me at least protect you."

Frannie stared at him in revulsion. "I'd rather die with my family," she said angrily, having received the answer to her question. Throwing Frederick's inebriated grasp off her, she fled his home and rode away, leaving a destroyed man standing on his porch.

It was hours later when Frannie rode slowly up the Willows' lane and saw Jed astride Tildie. Samuel Renfro, Markus, and Jack were also mounted on horses. The siblings slipped from their horses and into one another's arms. "You've had us all worried sick," Jed said in Frannie's ear. "We were about to come for you! Where were you? At White Oak?"

Frannie nodded. "I was, but I've been riding for hours, trying to understand it all." She buried her face in the scruff of her brother's filthy shirt, sniffing loudly. "It's true, Jed. All of it. Frederick as much as admitted it to me."

"That's proof enough," grunted Markus as he mounted his Morgan and sped away.

"Where is he going?" Frannie questioned.

"Into town. He's going to spread the word about the Stringhams' alliance with Duprée."

Frannie sighed, leaning heavily into her brother. "At least the people won't be taken unawares. I suppose this means you'll be heading off with the militia soon."

Jed kissed her forehead. "I suppose so, but we still have a few hours to talk."

* * *

After supper the Willows' decision-makers and a few friends congregated on the porch as planning and strategy replaced fear with power. It was dusk when hoofbeats pounded toward the house.

"Timothy!" Jed hailed as the young lawyer quickly mounted the stairs.

Timothy Shepard smiled tentatively at Frannie. Noting her somber mood, he offered her only a bow and a warm smile before rushing to Jed. "So you're back," he declared happily.

"Just barely," Jed replied.

"No worse for wear, though. I heard how bad things became in Baltimore," Timothy remarked seriously. "How are General Lee and the Stansburys?"

"All safe in the care of friends and family," Jed answered heavily as he dropped into a chair, inviting Timothy to do the same. "I doubt Harry will ever be the same, though."

"Then you might draw some satisfaction from these." He reached into his breast pocket and withdrew three folded documents, handing them to Jed.

"What are these?"

"Affidavits. The assemblies of Prince George's and Montgomery Counties in Maryland and the town council of Georgetown have issued scathing, public indictments against the Baltimore leadership, and they have fully exonerated Hanson and his band."

"Meaning what?" Jed prodded skeptically.

Timothy shrugged his shoulders. "Legally? Perhaps little. Baltimore's mayor continues to express sympathy for the injured while standing foursquare behind his decisions, insisting that he and his associates were merely tending to the security of the Baltimore citizenry at large. However, they will ensure that no charges can be filed against the men who defended Hanson's place." He grew more thoughtful. "Georgetown held a memorial service for General Lingan. They procured a prominent local attorney, Francis Scott Key, to deliver the oration. It was splendid, Jed. He has such a way with words. You'd have been pleased by the way he honored Lingan."

"And what of the living? They've also been slandered. What of their reputations?"

"I believe they will be restored as well." Timothy pointed to the affidavits. "I believe these will ensure that all the old war heroes who were involved, General Lee included, will not have their names slandered as traitors. They may even become martyrs to the cause of liberty."

Sitting quietly, Jed reflected on the images that still haunted his sleep—images of men slaughtered for their opinions. Within a few moments another horseman rode up the lane, interrupting his reverie. Markus O'Malley rode his stallion right up to the front porch steps, pulled the beast to a halt, leapt to the ground, and stormed up the stairs. Jed stood abruptly, ready for anything and steeling himself for the worst.

"I take it things did not go well," he offered with a furrowed brow.

"To say the least," snapped Markus. "We were too late."

Frannie stepped forward, incredulous and frightened. "I don't understand."

Markus shot a look at Jed, and the young landowner closed his eyes and nodded sadly. "We'll discuss this later," he uttered under his breath, signaling the end of the discussion.

Frannie picked up on the efforts to exclude her. "I'll be hung first!" she exploded, shocking the men with her outburst. "What's this about, and don't try to buffalo me!"

Jed looked at Markus, struggling to deny the smile tugging at his lips.

"And don't patronize me either," she insisted, glaring at Markus.

Markus drew a deep breath, leaned in close to Frannie, and said softly, "Come inside where I can talk to you privately, all right?"

"There's nothing you can't say in front of this company, Markus, so out with it."

Markus shoved his hands deep into his pockets and gazed at the floor. "Stewart Stringham had already been to Calverton, fillin' the locals with ale and gossip. He told everyone that you were back in town, defendin' your story about being attacked by the Creole man. Only now he's makin' jest of it, sayin' that your newest ruse includes tales of how the man is now a British spy who's still pursuin' you."

Frannie gritted her teeth and closed her eyes in worry. "He must have seen me leave Frederick's." She groaned in regret. "Who knows what price Frederick paid for my visit."

Markus shrugged again. "I'm afraid I can guess. His father had evidently come into town to haul the doctor back to White Oak. He told everyone that Frederick was thrown off his horse yesterday and was just found today. He said both his legs were badly broken."

"That can't be true . . ." Frannie refuted weakly. "I just saw him. His legs were . . ." and then realization struck her. "Oh no!" she gasped aloud. "Do you think Duprée . . . ?"

"That would be my guess."

"What have I done?" she cried as she turned her face into Jed's chest.

"It wasn't your fault, Frannie," Jed whispered reassuringly. "I'm sure he was warned not to speak, yet to his credit, he confessed to you."

Markus piped back in. "I'm afraid this has just stirred up more gossip about you again."

She turned to face her brother. "And you expected this might happen?"

He pulled her close and tried to diminish the attack. "It seemed a possibility if you tried to challenge Frederick. A perversion of truth can be more effective than a lie."

"There's more," Markus continued as he stared at Jed. "They know about us armin' the slaves. They were furious about that. I expect we'll be hearin' from the sheriff on that account."

"So we're on our own?" Frannie asked flatly. "And those fools don't know to prepare?"

"It appears so," Jed sighed.

"What will we do?" Frannie calmly queried.

"We'll formulate a plan," Jed began. "Establish guard watches, and not just arm the men but make them crack-shots. If anyone asks, we'll simply say we're defending the crop from varmints. And we'll keep tracking Duprée."

"Egads," Frannie muttered under her breath.

"Egads?" Jed teased, trying to lighten the moment.

"It's slang, Jed. It means—"

"I know very well what it means, Francis. I'm just shocked to hear it coming from you."

She nudged him lovingly. "It's a new world, brother. Diverse people with diverse tongues pass through Philadelphia on their way west. Entrepreneurs loading wagons with goods to sell to the frontiersmen stop by Le Jardin daily. I can feel their frustration. I can even hear it in their speech. Americans aren't just weary of the British monarchy—they're ready to sever all ties to England, especially her social conformities and class structure. We're our own nation, Jed, but we won't really understand what that truly means until we allow the diversity of our people to create new customs, new traditions, even a new language, uniquely American."

"The challenge of freedom . . ." Samuel Renfro mused as he puffed on his pipe, speaking up for the first time since he'd arrived. "As we push westward to the frontier, the aesthetic will surrender to the practical. Knowing what to keep and what to abandon will be the challenge of this next generation."

"It worries me," Timothy interjected. "It worries religious and political leaders as well. They are debating the ramifications of a nation spread so far that its people are beyond their reach. They fear that anarchy could ensue. The Revivalists have begun whipping their congregations into conformity, but as Frannie has said, the hunger for freedom is strong." He paused. "It's what brought our forefathers here, but it's left some of their children reticent to follow either governments or religions tainted by the influence of any monarchy—American or British."

Renfro waved his pipe in Timothy's direction. "But our forefathers did follow a monarchy of sorts. They were guided by the soft voice of spiritual whisperings."

Timothy looked dubiously at his friend. "And what if a thousand men claim to receive a thousand different whisperings? Imagine the chaos!"

Renfro smiled knowingly. "Faith, brother. Have faith. Don't you think the Founding Fathers understood the risk?"

"What are you implying?" Frannie asked curiously of the young medical student, grateful for any diversion.

"That perhaps there is a future for this land that we have not yet foreseen."

"Hannah knew that," Jed remarked reverently. "She said there was a plan . . ."

"Isn't it exciting, Jed?" Frannie declared spiritedly. "Imagine the possibilities when we are finally free! It's a beautiful dream, don't you think?"

Jed recalled another promise about fulfilling dreams. "Yes, and it should begin here."

He immediately called for Jerome to gather everyone from the meadows and bring them to the house. During that flurry of activity, Jed went inside and returned with a bundle in his arms. He stood on the top step of the porch, with Frannie on one side and Markus on the other. Bitty, Jack, and Jerome stood beside Francis. Timothy and Samuel Renfro stood awkwardly off to the side, watching the unfolding scene as twenty dark faces stared up.

Jed looked into each face. He gazed into the wary eyes of Abel, who stood with his mother and his four children. He looked at Sooky and onto Royal and his wife, Mercy. They each were six-year residents of the farm, with Royal and Mercy now heading a family of six including a babe in arms. After coughing to steady his voice, Jed began. "There are those who want to break us—" He fought to keep his voice from faltering. "To destroy what we've built here. They would sift us, black and white, slave and freeman, as if we were little more than individual grains of wheat. But what they don't understand is that we are more than that on the Willows—much, much more. We're bound to one another, not owner to slave, but friend to friend, a family of sorts."

Abel's eyes were expectant as he glanced from Jed's somber face to Bitty's proud one and back.

"But friendship and family requires trust, and I am here tonight to extend that trust to you and to receive the same from you. You helped build this place. The day is not far off when each of you will be free men and women, and not just free, but landowners as well."

A hush went over the people, followed by the swell of cheering, praying, and singing voices. After a few minutes, they fell quiet enough for Jed to continue. He beamed as he went on, and Frannie wrapped her arm around him, never more proud. "The provisions are made. Jerome and Bitty can attest to them and explain how this is to be done over time." His voice became craggy and low. "I wish circumstances made it possible for me to grant emancipation to each of you tonight, but to do so in this political climate would place you and the Willows in peril now. So I ask you this. Stand by me. Help defend our home . . . your home. If you do, I promise that you will be landowners, free landowners, as will your children and your children's children."

A reverential hush came over the crowd as Jed finished speaking. Jerome moved within the slaves' ranks, assuring them that every word Jed spoke was true. Then they crushed in upon Jed with tears in their eyes, pledging their loyalty and faith to the young master who had promised them freedom. As if in a dream from which they did not wish to awaken, they moved wordlessly down to the meadows. Soon the sounds of fiddles and singing wafted up to the house. Bitty and all her kin had not yet moved, and Jed asked the small group to remain behind a little longer.

"It was a good thing you did here tonight, Jed," Bitty sighed, beaming at him with shining eyes.

"No, Bitty. It was the *right* thing. I wish I had done it sooner, but I do want to present the first set of freedom papers to those who have labored here the longest . . . to you and Jack."

The brother and sister stared at one another in disbelief as Jed laid the scrolls in their hands. Bitty stared at the paper until her hands began to shake. Jack, who couldn't read, had his sister speak the promises of the document aloud. They fell into a tight embrace, their tears flowing freely as Jed and Frannie stepped nearer.

"The two of you have served this farm for a combined total of seventy years. You are our family. I think that means you have earned these as well," Jed said, tearfully placing seven more scrolls in their hands.

They received the seven gifts of freedom as if each were gilded glass, then tenderly placed them into the hands of their family. Jerome and Sarah cried as they wrapped their arms around their grandchildren, who would each soon know a very different life than the one they had known. Abel's eyes met Jed's and locked there. No words were exchanged, but respect passed freely between two proud, strong, and now free men.

"You can hold onto them, or I can keep them for you. We'll keep the remainder in the safe in my office. Above all, this must remain a secret for now—a matter of trust between us. All right?" Jed warned gently.

Childlike, Bitty stared into Jed's face. "I think I'd just like to hold onto it, just so's I can read it whenever I want, if that's all right with you." Her voice trembled with emotion.

"Then that's what I want you to do, Bitty," Jed replied in a broken voice. Seeing her finally receive as a privilege the right that should always have been hers made him suddenly feel more like a thief than a savior. He hugged her and kissed her head, then he quietly withdrew, leaving Bitty and her family to celebrate the milestone with Frannie and the others.

Jed stole away to the fenceline overlooking the pastures to think, wondering if he was regarded by the slaves in the same manner he regarded the approaching British—as tyrants of liberty. The thought stung him more deeply than he would have dreamed possible. Born an American child, he had accepted liberty as his right, but what a gift freedom suddenly appeared to him. Lies and half truths had already invaded his world, carving up his freedom to be with the person he loved. Now Cockburn, Duprée, and the host of the British military behemoth were coming to show him how transitory freedom truly could be.

As Jed turned to see Frannie, Bitty, and the others standing on the Willows' porch, their forms silhouetted in the lamplight, a sudden fear gripped him. The fight was coming, of that he was sure. He did not know when, but he knew it would be bitter, and he knew the Willows' residents were directly in the line of fire.

Everyone he loved would be affected by the war. Hannah would soon be on her way north to Vermont, and perhaps on to Canada to see the British invaders firsthand. Every muscle in his body twitched as if already geared for battle. *Let them come.* He would not shrink. For Frannie, for Hannah, for Bitty and Jack, and for those without a voice, he would fight.

DARK SKY AT DAWN
HISTORICAL NOTES AND SOURCES

None of the Pearsons or Stringhams were real characters, nor was Lieutenant Robertson, Captain Dudley Snowden, Markus O'Malley, or the slaves. However, many of the characters were created using names from the author's Maryland genealogical research, and they reflect the people of their day. The only Stansbury that actually existed was Uncle Tobias, referred to in chapter 5, who was an actual general. Sebastian Duprée and the slave Jerome were likewise creations of the author, who used literary license in creating Jerome to represent the indiscriminate seizure of blacks for slavery, and Duprée to represent a composite of the men contracted by the British to terrorize the region.

The characters of Charles Kittamaqund and his father, Chief Four Eagles, were loosely based on the true story of a Piscataway family named Kittamaqund. The daughter, a princess of the Algonquin people, married a white man named Giles Brent and converted to Christianity. The author tied her fictional Piscataway characters to the Kittamaqunds to validate the scope of interactions between Whites and Indians in the area.

Lady Marine Thornton's account of King George III's upsetting display at court was described in an actual letter she wrote to her nephew, novelist E. M. Frostier.

The representation of the culture of the Guineas in the book was used to demonstrate the increasing presence of American-born free blacks in Philadelphia in 1812. Due to Pennsylvania's Gradual Abolition Law, slaveholders in the state eventually lost their slaves, and since importation of slaves into Pennsylvania ended in 1780, by 1812 the majority of free blacks present in the city had been born on U.S. soil.

The British characters are likewise fictional, although they too were written to represent the life and times of their settings and stations. The Shire of Whittington is likewise a fictional location created around our fictitious earl, Lord Whittington.

Obvious liberties were taken to interject fictional characters into historic settings and conversations, but care was taken to assure that all conversations occurring with historical characters were based on recorded positions, dialogues, or opinions attributed to them. For instance, many details regarding the new nation and the feelings of the characters about it came from correspondence written at the time. The following letter represents one such example which was especially meaningful in assisting to build the compassionate and patriotic sentiments Jed expresses about America. It is briefly referred to in the story. It is a quote by John Adams from a letter dated April 13, 1777. (See Jed and Frannie's tour of Philadelphia.)

> *I have spent an hour this morning in the Congregation of the dead. I took a walk into the "Potter's Field," a burying ground between the new stone prison and the hospital, and I never in my whole life was affected with so much melancholy. The graves of the soldiers, who have been buried, in this ground, from the hospital and bettering-house, during the course of last summer, fall and winter, dead of the small pox and camp diseases, are enough to make the heart of stone to melt away! The sexton told me that upwards of two thousand soldiers had been buried there, and by the appearance of the grave and trenches, it is most probable to me that he speaks within bounds. To what causes this plague is to be attributed, I don't know—disease had destroyed ten men for us where the sword of the enemy has killed one.*

Regarding the historical settings and documents described above, I feel it important to list such valuable resources for the reader, so he or she may be able to read such stirring accounts as well—many of which I was not able to incorporate directly into the novel due to length and story structure restraints. Therefore I am detailing a somewhat extensive list of resources below.

While I was researching the effect the War of 1812 had on the Patuxent River area, a park ranger directed me to two invaluable books, *Tidewater Time Capsule,* by Donald C. Shomette, published by Tidewater Publishers in 1995; and *The Burning of Washington,* by Anthony S. Pitch, published in 1998 by the Naval Institute Press. While Shomette's book details the archaeological hunt for the sunken Chesapeake flotilla of 1814, it also provides a beautifully documented history of the region's waterways and seamen. Pitch's book is an intricately detailed study, focusing primarily on the intense four-month period surrounding the burning of the nation's capital, including well-researched characterizations of the principal players. Both books are treasure troves of information.

The Patowmack Canal referred to in the book was among the dearest projects undertaken by George Washington. He believed that if the Potomac could be made navigable, and a trade route to the Ohio Valley established, that the government could "bind those people to us by a chain which never can be broken." The venture failed due to exorbitant costs incurred in attempting to tame the physical obstacles the Potomac presented. In 1828, the Patowmack Company turned over its assets to the newly formed Chesapeake and Ohio Canal Company. The remaining traces of the Patowmack Canal and the ruins of Mathildaville, the town designed to support the canal workers, are now protected by the Archeological Resources Protection Act of 1979.

The story of Jonathan Pearson's cunning scheme to hold a lottery in order to fund the building of a dock on his property is based on a historic account from Maryland history, found in Mr. Donald Shomette's above-mentioned book. Pieces of eight were the currency used. When this term is mentioned, it generally conjures images of pirates and buried treasure, but a piece of eight is actually a collo-quial name for a Spanish coin called a peso. These Spanish coins became widely circulated, and some were even minted, in North America during the colonial period. Because of the purity of their silver and their soft characteristics, they were often cut into halves or quarters to form smaller units of exchange, leading to the terms *two bits, four bits,* etc.

Though being a native Marylander weaned on Maryland and U.S. history, Mr. Pitch's account of the Baltimore riot was the first I recalled hearing. As soon as I read it, I knew that would be the climax of the book. Once enlightened about this painful event, I searched and located the transcripts of gruesome depositions from several of the survivors of the riot, recorded in Montgomery and Prince George's Counties in Maryland, and in Georgetown in Washington D.C. These are available at the "American Memory Project" of the Library of Congress at the following web address: http://memory.loc.gov.

Additional corroboration for descriptions of the riots, as well as further biographical information about Henry "Light-Horse Harry" Lee, was found in chapter 1 of Douglas Southall Freeman's Pulitzer Prize winning biography *R. E. Lee: A Biography*, published by Charles Scribner's Sons (New York and London, 1934) as well as on the website "The Robert E. Lee Boyhood Home—Virtual Museum," which can be found online at http://leeboyhoodhome.com.

Information on early nineteenth-century society, class distinctions, and life was drawn from a variety of sources including Richard Bushman's *The Refinement of America,* published in 1993 by First Vintage Books; and Heidi S. Swinton's, *American Prophet—The Story of Joseph Smith,* based on Lee Groberg's documentary.

Swinton's book also gave me important insights into the Smith family. However, the greatest of these came from Lucy Mack Smith's *The History of Joseph Smith by His Mother,* reprinted by Covenant Communications, Inc., in 2004. This book also provided the critical tie-in between the War of 1812 and the Smith family by providing tales of her brother Stephen Mack, who served in Fort Detroit during the war. Additionally, her inclusion of her sisters Lovisa and Lovina, and their visions and dreams, provided another perfect tie-in between the fictional characters and the historical figures.

The details on St. Paul's Cathedral came through a delightful resource (http://www.explore-stpauls.net), where one can take virtual tours of the cathedral. Likewise, the virtual tour of Fort McHenry (found at http://www.bcpl.net/~etowner/best.html) was helpful in keeping the particulars of the fort clear in my mind as I wrote.

Another virtual tour site (http://www.ushistory.org) allowed me to become familiar with the significant sites of historic Philadelphia before I toured them in person. More importantly, this site provided me with a tremendous living resource in the person of Mr. Edward Lawler Jr., the Independence Hall Association Historian, with whom I have corresponded. He has been a wonderful asset in helping me understand the times and the city itself. In addition to answering my innumerable questions, he guided me to http://www.ushistory.org/birch/index.htm, where *Birch's Views of Philadelphia in 1800,* a collection of paintings by the father-and-son team William Russell and Thomas Birch, are available. These views—along with those located through the University of Pennsylvania Library's digital image collection—give one a vivid glimpse into the Philadelphia of the early nineteenth century (http://imagesvr.library.upenn.edu/p/pennarchive/-index.html).

The most comprehensive resource I could find on Fort Detroit and the ensuing battle came from a GalaFilms website (http://www.galafilm.com/1812/e/intro/index.html) in connection with a documentary series they ran. Additional insight was available through encyclopedias and online sources and the U.S. History Resources Website, under the direction of Greg D. Feldmeth (http://home.earthlink.net/~gfeldmeth/chart.1812.html).

The journal entries of Miss Lydia Bacon, an actual person, provide a vivid glimpse into the emotional and military climate inside Fort Detroit during the attack. Her worries regarding the soul of the young, dying doctor are intimately recorded in her account, which can be found at http://clarke.cmich.edu/detroit/bacon1812.htm.

Other websites to which I referred include:

The Potawmac Canal
http://scienceviews.com/parks/patowmackcanal.html

Lexington Market
http://www.lexingtonmarket.com/History.html

Algonquian Words
http://www.native-languages.org/algonquin_words.htm

Parliament and British Nobility
http://www.chinet.com/~laura/html/titles12.html
http://www.parliament.uk/index.cfm
http://www.parliament.uk/works/locomp.cfm
http://www.parliament.uk/directories/house_of_lords_inform-ation_office/address.cfm

Haitian History
http://www.chinet.com/~laura/html/titles12.html

Slavery
http://eh.net/encyclopedia/article/wahl.slavery.us
http://www.questia.com/PM.qst?a=o&d=89175267
http://www.liverpoolmuseums.org.uk/maritime/trail/trail.asp
http://www.cincinnati.com/freetime/nurfc/J4_onaroadofsorrow.html

Slave Music
http://docsouth.unc.edu/church/allen/menu.html

Covent Gardens
http://www.coventgardenlife.com/info/history.htm

Maryland Medicine
http://www.medicalalumni.org/davidge/emedhist.html

Military Dress
http://www.jarnaginco.com/1812catframe.html
http://www.gentlemansemporium.com/store/coats.php

Weaponry
http://members.tripod.com/~war1812/weapons.html
http://en.wikipedia.org/wiki/Breech-loading

ABOUT THE AUTHOR

Laurie Lewis was born in a history-rich area neighboring Baltimore, Maryland, and has spent most of her life there. She and her husband raised their children in this area, and Laurie, a home-maker, used her free time to write novels and plays. Then, during a seven-year stint as a science-education facilitator in the Carroll County Public School System, Laurie honed her research skills, and as her children left home, she focused her energies on writing full time. She also became an avid traveler, constantly researching locales and their colorful people to flesh out her work. Laurie now spends her time bringing that research to life in family novels and historical fiction. Readers can write to her in care of Covenant Communications, P.O. Box 416, American Fork, UT 84003-0416, or e-mail her via Covenant at info@covenant-lds.com.